THE SIGN OF THE EAGLE

JESS STEVEN HUGHES

MILFORD HOUSE

an imprint of Sunbury Press, Inc.
Mechanicsburg, PA USA

MILFORD HOUSE

an imprint of Sunbury Press, Inc.
Mechanicsburg, PA USA

For information about special discounts for bulk purchases, please contact Sunbury Press Orders Dept. at (855) 338-8359 or orders@sunburypress.com.

To request one of our authors for speaking engagements or book signings, please contact Sunbury Press Publicity Dept. at publicity@sunburypress.com.

ISBN: 978-1-62006-036-0 (Trade Paperback)

FIRST MILFORD HOUSE PRESS EDITION: May 2018

Product of the United States of America
0 1 1 2 3 5 8 13 21 34 55

Set in Bookman Old Style
Designed by Lawrence Knorr
Cover by Lawrence Knorr
Cover art by Katrina Hughes Brennan

Continue the Enlightenment!

DEDICATION

To Patricia DeMars Pfeiffer: Mentor, friend, and fellow writer. Your honest critique and advice kept me writing at times when I was on the brink of despair. I will always be grateful.

DRAMATIS PERSONAE

Antonia – Vestal Virgin.
Helena Antonia – Sister of Titus and Macha's friend.
Titus Antonius – Military Tribune and Husband of Macha Carataca.
Titus Antonius the Younger – Son of Macha and Titus.
Pomponius Appius – Roman Officer.
M. Valerius Bassus – Roman Senator.
Macha Carataca – Celtic woman, protagonist, wife of Titus.
Clodia – Woman shopkeeper in Rome.
Crixus – Gallic horse trader.
Demetrios – Son of Nicanor.
Edain – Slave woman.
Rubellius Falco – Roman Tribune.
Jason - Horse groom from Thessaly.
Metrobius – House Steward.
Nicanor – Greek music teacher and slave.
Pollia – Aristocratic woman from Rome.
Cnidius Rufus – Friend of Titus.
Shafer – Moorish slave woman.
Titus Flavius Vespasianus (Vespasian) – Roman Emperor (historical character).
Viriatus – Spanish Slave.

CITIES AND GEOGRAPHICAL LOCATIONS

Italy

Ancient Name	Modern Name
Cremona	Cremona
Genua	Genoa
Luna	Luni
Mediolanum	Milan
Pisae	Pisa
Placentia	Piacenza
Dertona	Tortona

Other Locations

Ancient Name	Modern Name
Britannia	Britain
Dacia	Romania
Gaul	France
Germania	Germany
Hispania	Spain
Moguntiacum	Mainz, Germany
River Danubus	River Danube
River Rhenus	River Rhine

CHAPTER 1

Behold, the Traitor
Mediolanum - Late March, AD 71

"Mistress, armed cavalry are approaching the house!" The house steward's face was drawn and pale as he approached with the news. Macha leapt to her feet.

"Mother Goddess, it must be Titus," Macha said. "He's come with his whole command. I pray it's not another war. I'll meet him in the courtyard."

Metrobius bowed and raced away, his sandals clattering on the mosaic tiled pathway that cut through the garden. Quickly, Macha stood from the flower bed that she had been tending and brushed black soil from her long tunic and adjusted the wide-brimmed hat. She hurried to the sun-drenched courtyard as fast as her bulky clothing would allow. She arrived in time to see her husband, Titus, his uniform covered in dust, rein up on his sweaty mount. The jingling sounds of the metal pendants on the horse's breast collar died away. White foam dripped from the bay gelding's lathered mouth. Grabbing the two front pommels of the leather saddle, the tall tribune swung off his horse, and dropped to the ground.

Breathing deeply, he jerked off his helmet, pulling down the scarlet neckerchief that covered most of his face. He grabbed Macha roughly and kissed her before straightening and shaking the dust from his corselet tunic, and wiping his grimy hands on the side of his breeches.

"Titus, what's wrong?" Macha asked brushing the dirt from his forehead and his nose.

"I have to leave immediately. The Gauls north of here are in revolt—not more than fifty miles away."

She gasped. The province of Transpadana Gaul, including Mediolanum, had been under Roman rule for more than two hundred years. "But they're Roman citizens, I don't understand."

"It doesn't make any difference. We have to smash them. Now. Rome has seen enough civil war." It had been only two years since the last one had ended, nearly ruining the Empire.

Macha stared at the formation of mounted troops stringing down the road. "Your men aren't the only ones going, are they?"

"No, the rest of the legion is close behind," he answered, his voice terse. "Now, I must go."

"Sir!" a voice bellowed from behind.

Titus and Macha turned and watched as the rider approached at a canter. In the distance a large detachment of armed cavalrymen began moving north on the dusty road near the front of the house. "That's one of my squadron leaders," Titus said. He turned and gave Macha a brief embrace and turned to the cavalryman. "I'm coming, decurion!"

"Be careful," Macha whispered, desperately attempting to hold back the tears. She touched his muscular forearm.

"I'm always careful," he answered gruffly.

"No, you're not; you're reckless, but I can't stop you."

Titus winced and shook his head. This was an old argument they had time and again. Without another word, he turned and ran to his horse. Springing on the balls of his sandaled boots, he vaulted onto the gelding's back, and dropped into the saddle. He twisted about, covered his face, and waved to Macha.

Young Titus, their eight-year old son, ran through the courtyard and stopped at Macha's side as his father rode away. He tugged at Macha's skirt. "Is Papa going to war again?"

Macha sighed. "Yes, I'm afraid so."

"Will he die?"

"No! We will sacrifice to Mother Goddess Anu for his safe return." She took Young Titus' little hand in hers and returned to the house.

* * * * *

Macha sat in the garden at the rear of the small villa, strumming an old Brigantian love ballad on her Celtic harp. The soft mid-morning light filtered through the tall, overhanging cypress and poplar trees along the courtyard wall. Northern Italy and the city of Mediolanum, a short-ride from her villa, were experiencing an unusually mild spring; already roses and yellow poppies bloomed. Their sweet smell wafted on the cool alpine breeze flowing in from the north. What a contrast to the chilly, wet springs of her early childhood in Britannia, where, Macha recalled, she never felt warm. Although she preferred the mild spring weather of her adopted home, Italy, she still considered herself a Celt.

She smiled and thought of her good fortune. Once more Macha silently thanked Mother Goddess. Titus had returned home last night unharmed after spending two weeks in the field. The so-called rebellion was nothing more than a pocket of Gallic bandits who Titus' troops crushed in a skirmish near Lake Verbanus to the northwest. Duty required him to report to the garrison of Legion First Italica, outside of Mediolanum, this morning, but he promised to take the next five days off and would be back before noon.

Out of the corner of one eye Macha saw Metrobius, hurrying toward her. He glanced over his shoulder to the front entrance. Macha had given the household slaves strict orders not to disturb her during the music hour. She focused on the sundial, resting on a marble pedestal by a clump of violets; a half-hour still remained.

"What is it, Metrobius?" Macha asked. She palmed the strings of the little wooden harp and silenced the last melodious chord.

"I'm sorry to disturb you, Mistress," the slave said, "but the Tribune, Pomponius Appius, is waiting at the front door with an urgent message."

Macha's hand slipped, sending a squealing sound across the catgut strings. She inhaled deeply and set the instrument on the little stool next to her leg. "Did he say what his message concerned?" Macha asked.

The graying middle-age Greek shook his head. "No, my lady. He has orders to deliver it to no one but you."

"Very well. Bring him, but take your time."

Macha picked up the polished copper mirror on the table next to the harp. She did so out of pride rather than how she would appear to Appius. She noticed strands of her flaming hair had worked loose from the braid wrapped in a coil around the top of her head, in the Celtic fashion, and had fallen over her high cheekbones. An ebony pin kept the hair in place. She flicked it behind her ear. The silver antimony on the lids of her aqua-green eyes required no daubing. For a second she squeezed her pouting lips together and enlivened the fading elderberry juice applied earlier in the day. She returned the mirror to the table. Grabbing the blue woolen palla, laying on the bench by her, Macha wrapped the cloak about her shoulders. She shook out the hem of her bright green and orange stola, properly covering her ankles like any respectable Roman matron. Just to spite Appius, she wished she had been wearing a green tartan skirt like a *barbarian* Celtic woman.

Pomponius Appius entered the garden, and strode the long mosaic sidewalk towards Macha. This had something to do with Titus. Otherwise, Appius wouldn't be here without him. Where was he? It was almost noon.

Her son, young Titus, dressed in a long woolen tunic, emerged from behind a poplar tree. He stopped near a rosebush and peered in Appius' direction, and scratched his short, curly red hair. He frowned. "What's that ugly man doing here, Mama? He looks mean."

"Hush, Titus, and mind your manners," Macha said.

"Yes, Mama." Young Titus quietly backed behind the bush, but not before Macha caught him sticking out his tongue at Appius. She glared at her son, and sternly shook her head. He scampered out of sight.

Pomponius Appius wore the dusty scarlet tunic and knee-length woolen breeches of a cavalry officer. Tied across the silver cuirass, two limp purple sashes—symbol of his rank—covered his barrel chest. An iron helmet bearing wide cheek guards and topped by a red horsehair comb concealed his graying hair. The tribune stood little taller than the willowy Macha, who measured three fingers short of six feet.

The Roman halted in front of her, a few steps away, his sword slapping at his side.

"Welcome, Tribune Appius," Macha said, although she remained seated. His breath smelled of wine and garlic and his uniform of horse. As an accomplished rider, Macha usually enjoyed the musky odor, but on Appius it reeked.

"What brings you to my home?" she asked.

4

"I bring bad news, Lady Macha Carataca."

She flinched and caught her breath. "What is it? Has something happened to my husband?"

"He's been arrested for treason."

"Treason!"

"The charge is true, Lady Carataca." With a calloused hand, Appius grasped the hilt of his longsword, the Spatha, strapped at his side. A pale thin scar crawled up his forearm and disappeared behind his elbow.

"There must be a mistake," Macha said. Heat rushed to her face and her chest tightened. For a second she turned away from Appius, to calm herself. She said a quick prayer to Anu, Mother Goddess of hearth and home, to give her strength before facing him once more. What Appius said was impossible. Titus loved Rome. Only his love for her and their son was greater.

"He would never betray the Emperor," she said, her voice firm. "Titus has been loyal to Vespasian since he was proclaimed Emperor two years ago."

"He misled all of us, including you," Appius said.

Macha shot up from her seat and glared at the tribune. His accusations were outrageous. "What does that mean?"

"He conspired with others to overthrow the Emperor."

"Who are the conspirators?"

"I'm not at liberty to say to the wife of a traitor. They're still at large, but we'll find them."

"He hasn't been convicted yet. The others may be the real conspirators, not him. What is your proof?"

"That's not for me to divulge."

Macha clenched her teeth to hold her tongue. She wanted to demand that Appius take her this instant to see Titus, but that would be disastrous. It was in his power to arrest her on the flimsiest of excuses. Although she had never given up her Celtic roots, she had been raised as Roman since the age of seven, one year younger than her son. Celtic women in Britannia had more rights than their Roman sisters, including the making of laws and fighting in war. However, the Vestal Virgins were the only women who could make demands on anyone, including the Emperor.

"May I see my husband?" Macha asked in a voice as even as she could manage. "Where is he imprisoned—at the garrison?"

Appius twisted his scarred mouth into a mocking sneer. "No one can see him."

Macha narrowed her sea-green eyes. "That's outrageous! As the wife of a Roman officer, I have the right to visit my husband!"

"You can't and won't," he answered flatly. "You are a barbarian. I fought your kind in Britannia and Germania. You can't be trusted. For a few coppers you'd kill your own mothers."

"How dare you mock me and my kindred! For almost twenty years I have lived as a Roman—a better and more trustworthy one than you."

She knew why Appius hated her. Macha remembered Titus telling her Appius had been badly wounded as a young legionarie during the British campaigns and nearly died.

"Regardless of what you think of me, there is nothing you can do," Appius said, jolting Macha from her thoughts. "The wife of a man who has betrayed the Emperor isn't in a position to do anything except pray to the gods for mercy."

Macha walked away from Appius, her eyes following the line of poplar trees at the edge of the garden. She grasped the edge of her stola to rid her hands of perspiration. The Celtic torc, a golden collar encircling her neck, seemed suddenly tighter. The gold earrings, in the form of little swans, weighed as heavily as if they were anchors of a ship. She forced herself to turn and once more focus on Appius' haughty face.

"Why were you sent to break the news instead of Cnidius Rufus?" Macha asked. Her brother-in-law, Rufus, was a good man whom she respected. He was a tribune in the same legion with Appius and Titus and married to Titus's sister, Helena.

"General Valens wanted someone who wasn't related to a Gallic family to inform you."

She stepped closer to Appius feeling the full brunt of his sour breath. "Oh, is that because they're Celts like the Britons? Does he consider them barbarians, too?"

6

"No, only rebels and traitors—as they were during the civil war. I don't trust them either."

Macha huffed and shook her head. "You know my husband had nothing to do with that faction—he was born in Rome. His father was a Senator, appointed by the Emperor Claudius. Must I remind you Titus fought here in Italy against Vitellius, and was wounded twice at Cremona? No one was braver than he in that battle."

"Roman born or not, he's still a traitorous Gaul."

A shiver ran through her body. Macha could not believe what Appius was saying. If Titus were executed, what would she do? She and little Titus would have no place to go. She would lose everything. Titus's lands and fortune would be seized by the State.

Despite her marriage to a Roman citizen, Macha was still considered a barbarian, as Appius had been clear to point out. Titus's parents were dead. She had no news of her father since his disappearance from Italy eleven years earlier. She might return to Britannia, but all her known relatives were dead, and she couldn't be assured of what kind of welcome she would receive. For a few seconds, she listened to the peaceful gurgling of the water in the fountain and the droning of bees in the garden, and allowed the tranquil sounds to soothe her nerves as she considered how to deal with this perilous situation. What was Pomponius Appius' part in this travesty of justice?

She raised a hand palm upward in his direction. "What do you gain if my husband is found guilty and executed?" Macha asked.

"Nothing, I'm simply carrying out my duty."

"Do you think me naïve?" She dropped her hand. "If I recall, my husband obtained equal rank with you in less than ten years. Isn't it true you've been in the army twenty-five years?" Titus was a *Tribune Laticlavius*, senior tribune in the legion, and only twenty-nine years old.

"Aye, what of it?"

"Titus was due for promotion to second in command of the First Italian Legion. Didn't you covet the same position? Gods forbid you would conspire to have him accused of treason, simply for the sake of a promotion. Or is it because of your contempt for Gallo-Romans like Titus?"

"Watch your tongue, lady," Appius warned, his hand reached for the hilt of his spatha. "You, too, are placing yourself in danger."

"Being the wife of an accused traitor, am I not already?" She motioned for Metrobius, who still lingered at a discreet distance. "I see no point in continuing this conversation. If you have nothing more to add, please leave my house, at once."

Appius folded his arms across his burly chest, glared at her, but didn't move. "I'm not finished."

"You've said quite enough."

He curled his upper lip exposing yellowed teeth. "Your husband will be transported to Rome where he will be court-martialed in four weeks. The Emperor himself will hear the trial."

Macha nearly choked. Why Rome? It was so far away— three hundred miles! There must be something she could do for Titus before he was taken away, but what?

"Don't sound so gleeful, Tribune. He's not dead, yet." Macha took a deep breath. "Now, leave—this instant!"

Appius turned, brushed aside the house steward, and strode from the villa.

Young Titus peeked out from behind a bushy cypress tree. "Mama, why did that ugly man say awful things about Papa?"

"I don't know, son," Macha answered, too shaken to comment further.

"Now I know he's mean."

Macha sat down and unconsciously stroked her son's curly hair before he could move away. She hugged him while barely holding back her tears.

"Mama, you're hurting me," Titus said, startling Macha. He squirmed in her tight grip.

"I'm sorry, son." She gently released him.

"Can I go play?"

She nodded and Titus scurried away.

She remembered only two years before a raging civil war nearly destroyed the Roman Empire. Vespasian, commanding general in charge of quelling the revolt in

Judea, became the last of four emperors to take power in a period of a single year and had ruled ever since. His army defeated the forces of the gluttonous Emperor Vitellius at Cremona, clearing his way to the imperial throne. Titus's loyalty to the sixty-year-old ruler had been unquestioned. He had fought for Vespasian as a tribune in Legion Seventh Claudia, which had forced-marched more than eight hundred miles to aid the new Emperor.

Titus would never betray Vespasian, the first decent Emperor Rome had seen since the death of Caesar Augustus.

Macha inhaled deeply, opened her eyes and absorbed the garden's spring colors. She had to learn the details of the false charge against Titus.

But what if that meant traveling to Rome? She dreaded the thought. That would require at least seven days by fast horse, providing the rider changed mounts every twenty miles and stopped to rest for the night. The time was cut in half by ship if a traveler braved the treacherous storms and spring currents of Mare Tyrrhenum. If she went would it be enough time?

Macha had to see an old family friend and powerful ally, Senator Marcus Valerius Bassus. Surely he could obtain Titus's release.

If Appius believed her a helpless Roman matron or Celtic princess, he was badly mistaken. She was the daughter of Caratacus, the great British King. Like my father, she thought, I will deal with Rome in my own way.

CHAPTER 2

A Spoiled Cat

Exhausted from the afternoon ride on her favorite gelding, Macha dropped into the high-backed wicker chair in her bedchamber. She smelled of her lathered horse. As Edain, the short round-shouldered slave, wiped her face with a moist towel, Macha still fumed at the treatment she received at headquarters of Legion First Italica earlier in the day. The commander, General Lucius Valens, had refused to discuss the accusations against Titus and denied her request to visit him. She had cursed his name under her breath and fled his office.

With Titus' life at stake, Macha hated the idea of sitting idle, helpless to do anything. Rather than break crockery or snap at her twenty-year-old handmaiden, Macha had ridden out on Antaris, her dark bay. Cantering through the countryside on a good horse helped her to think. She prayed it would work today.

Instead of finding a solution, she had struggled with her misbehaving mount. A deer, bounding from the underbrush, spooked Antaris, and he nearly threw her from his back. He spun around and bucked. She wrapped her legs tightly against his sides. Each jolting buck threw her head back until it nearly struck the bay's rear haunches. Macha's grip had loosened, and she frantically edged her limbs forward until she braced her thighs against the saddle pommels. Thank Mother Goddess Anu she used a cavalry saddle. The double angular knobs gave her the leverage she needed to hold on until Antaris tired and quieted. Even four-legged creatures seem to conspire against her.

Edain, dressed in a beige chiton, used her stubby hands to unlace and pull off her mistress' riding sandals. Macha sighed. A slave entered the bedroom cubicle, informing Macha her bath was ready. Perhaps a relaxing soak in the copper tub and a rubdown afterwards would allow her to think with greater clarity.

"Are you still going to Mistress Helena's home for dinner tonight?" Edain asked as she pulled Macha's tunic over her head.

Macha bolted from her chair, nearly knocking the ruddy-complected slave off her feet. "Great Mother Goddess, I had forgotten all about it." She shook out her long hair, letting it fall behind her shoulders. "Food is the last thing on my mind. My only thoughts have been of my husband."

But that wasn't quite true. Macha worried about having to leave Young Titus, if she followed her husband to Rome. She had decided to leave him with her sister-in-law, Helena, who was a good-hearted woman. He would be well cared for, but she would still miss him terribly, and what would people think of her if she left her son behind? She prayed she wouldn't have to go.

Macha paused and exhaled. "I suppose I'd better attend. Helena will be disappointed if I don't."

Clothed only in her green and yellow plaid Celtic trousers, she stepped to the tall latticed cupboard and searched for an appropriate dinner gown. Cool evening air brushed her bare skin, and sent quill bumps down her naked chest and back. How could she dine out while Titus languished in the stockade? Dare she have an appetite so long as he was falsely imprisoned? But Helena Antonia was Titus's sister, and she and Macha were the best of friends. No doubt Helena was as shaken about her brother's ordeal as she. Consoling one another seemed to be the only alternative for Helena and Macha. Helena's husband, Cnidius Rufus, a fellow officer and friend of Titus, would lend her a sympathetic ear. Surely her brother-in-law, Rufus, couldn't believe Titus was guilty of treason. But what if he had betrayed Rome? She shook her head. Impossible.

Macha fingered a dozen brightly-colored stolas trying to decide what to wear. None of them were appealing. In her frame of mind they all seemed ugly. She didn't care what she wore, even one of her bright tartan gowns. No, on second thought, wearing a Celtic dress to the very Roman

11

household of Helena and Rufus would be inappropriate. She turned to Edain and studied her heart shaped face and small button eyes. "Come here and pick out something for me."

* * * * *

With the sun setting at her back, Macha arrived at the home of her brother-in-law, escorted by ten slaves. The house steward led Macha, Edain, and Nicanor, her Greek music teacher, past a gurgling fountain filled with tame eels, through the small courtyard of Helena's home to the dining area. A low, well-trimmed evergreen hedge and an array of painted statues lined the white graveled walkway. "What are you going to sing tonight?" Macha questioned Nicanor. She asked out of habit, because whenever Titus and she took him to a dinner party, he provided part of the entertainment. Tonight she only half heard his answer.

"A medley of Greek love songs and the Celtic ballads you taught me, Mistress," he replied. He carried a seven-stringed lyre wrapped in an ochre chamois cloth. The musician, slight and wiry, was in his early thirties. He had a clever face seasoned with humor, and Macha had observed that it was Greek slaves who truly kept the Empire running smoothly.

Macha barely listened as Nicanor recited the titles while they strolled along the trellis-covered pathway, their sandals slapping on the black and white tiled walkway. How could she think about music when her mind kept flooding with images of Titus' languishing in a rat-infested cell?

Nicanor viewed her quizzically. He probably guessed she wasn't paying attention. "I'm sorry, Nicanor. You know I appreciate your talents, but I have other matters on my mind tonight."

"I understand, Mistress. I'm very sorry about the Master's arrest. Forgive me for babbling like a fool."

"It's not your fault. You know I adore your singing and appreciate the time you've spent teaching me, tyrant though you are."

Nicanor bowed his head. "You are a good student."

"When this dreadful affair is over and Titus is free, we shall sing and rejoice together, Nicanor."

"I look forward to that day, Mistress," Nicanor grinned. His deep-set blue eyes glittered, and slightly yellowed teeth peered through the trimmed charcoal beard. "You have a wonderful talent—I would hate to see it lost forever because of this tragedy."

She took a deep breath and exhaled. "It isn't a tragedy, yet. I intend to see it doesn't become one."

Macha knew Nicanor had experienced great pain in his own life. He and his wife came to her house as slaves because he couldn't pay his debts. She died two years later. He still grieved for her, and sometimes it hindered his duties. Tears flowed from his eyes, usually, while giving Macha her lessons. Apologizing, he would say it was the memory of his wife flooding his mind. He could still see her suffering from the terrible wasting disease. She went from a plump healthy matron to a gaunt living skeleton in little more than a year just before her death. Nicanor's only consolation was his bright ten-year old son, Demetrios, left in his care. As a loving father, he did whatever he could to make up for the loss of his son's mother.

The strains of soft music drifted from a flute and lyre down the passageway. At the far end the sweet aroma of baked bread and glazed hams floated from the kitchen on the cool evening breeze. Macha's stomach churned. Despite the day's turmoil, she was hungry. A slave approached Nicanor and motioned him to a room set aside for the entertainers.

Macha entered the front of the *triclinium*, followed by Edain, who would act as her serving woman during dinner. Olive oil lamps hanging from tall bronze stands illuminated the dining area, casting a shadowy glow on the scarlet and yellow walls. At the far end three sloping couches had been arranged to form an open-ended square. Heavily padded with down cushions, the wooden benches were covered in bright orange linens falling to the tiled floor. On the wall above and behind the sofas were painted a quaint set of rules for dining behavior. They included admonishments against using coarse language and prohibitions against casting lustful glances at another man's wife.

The other guests had already arrived. Helena's childhood friend, Pollia, and her wealthy merchant husband, Julius Pedius, conversed with Macha's sister-in-law. Seeing Pollia was a surprise. She and her husband lived in Rome. What were they doing here?

They stood next to a wall painted with the image of a drunken Bacchus caressing a wood nymph. A slave came by and served the trio sweetmeats and wine on a gold tray. Suddenly the three burst into laughter. No doubt Helena had related an amusing piece of gossip, for which she was notorious.

In another corner of the room, Macha observed Rubellius Falco, a friend of Titus and known womanizer, reclining on a dining couch drinking a cup of wine. She rolled her eyes and walked away before he noticed her.

Macha spied a tall, balding gentleman, with his back to her, talking to Helena's husband Rufus. A broad, red stripe ran down the center and along the edge of his pure white toga, matching his dyed red boots. Both indicated he belonged to the nobility. It was Senator Bassus, her patron. Indeed, this was a stroke of luck. Macha had not expected to see him tonight. She needed to speak to him about Titus's arrest immediately. Bassus would know what to do.

After handing her cloak to Edain, Macha was about to approach Bassus, when her nose was touched by the scent of lavender and a soft hand tugged at her elbow. She swung about to see Helena. Her round face rouged with red nitre revealed a broad smile of slightly crooked but still white teeth. A blond wig covered her mousy hair, and a bright blue and red gown, decorated with silver butterflies, complimented her plump frame.

"Macha, I'm so glad you're here," Helena said. "With all that has happened today, Cnidius and I wondered if you would join us. I was about to send a slave to fetch you." Helena motioned for Pollia to join them.

"Helena, I hate to sound rude, but since he is here I must speak with Senator Bassus right away about Titus," Macha said.

"I think that's what Cnidius is talking to him about right now," Helena said in a lower voice. "Why don't you wait until you can speak to him in private? Besides, here's Pollia."

Helena turned to Pollia, "I was just about to tell Macha that you and your husband had traveled all the way from Rome on business. Something about inspecting his estates in the Po Valley?"

"Something like that," Pollia answered. "Personally, I find it tedious, but it was a good excuse to visit my good friends in Mediolanum." Sapphire encrusted gold earrings, surrounded by images of twisting snakes, swayed back and forth from her pale earlobes. Powdered chalk whitened her angular face. "The comforts I brought along made the journey bearable, and we stayed at the estates of friends along the way." Macha was aware Pollia never traveled anywhere without bringing most of her wardrobe and half of the household staff to cater to her every demand. Tonight she wore an indigo silk evening gown with a green mantle, a gold-trimmed sash cinched her slim waist.

"But Pedius and I would have understood," Pollia continued, "if you had cancelled your dinner." She glanced at Macha. For a second she primped and twisted back a couple of loose strands under the small gilded tiara. "This ordeal must be ghastly for both of you."

"As wife of an accused traitor, I'm surprised Helena allowed me in her house," Macha said.

Helena crinkled her pudgy nose. "None of us believe that nonsense. Isn't that right, Pollia?"

"Of course, darling. What a disgusting thought."

Helena continued in a lower voice. "But we can't say so openly. Remember, he's my brother and you're part of our family, too, Macha."

"You're under the roof of your husband, and a member of his family," Macha said. "It's not the same." A hush fell over the room. Macha turned about to see all guests staring at her. She glared back. "Well, it's true." The people resumed their conversations.

"My love for Titus as a sister hasn't changed anymore than yours as his wife," Helena said. "Surely the investigation will find him innocent."

"I trust you're right—so far I've heard nothing."

With a weak smile formed on her lips, Helena nodded. "In the meantime, come and join us. By the way, your evening wear is beautiful."

Macha forced a smile; she hadn't given much thought to what she had been wearing. Arrayed in a short-sleeve saffron stola made of fine linen, her dress was girdled beneath her bosom by an embroidered gold cloth band. Wrapped around her left wrist hung two narrow horse-headed bracelets fashioned in the Celtic manner. Sandals made of soft doeskin graced her feet.

"Yes, I saw something like your gown in the Subura last month," Pollia said.

For a split second Macha glared at Pollia before recovering herself. The idea of being compared to a prostitute infuriated her. In order to practice their trade legally in Rome, saffron was the only color the law allowed harlots to wear. Sometimes they also wore blond wigs. But this was Mediolanum. The edict did not apply to Northern Italy, and more importantly, she liked the yellow-orange color.

"Why Pollia," Macha said, "I never imagined you being caught on the same street with a professional woman."

"Usually, I'm not."

"Then what were you doing there?" Macha asked softly. "I'll loan you my gown if you need the practice."

"Don't bother, dear, I wouldn't want mine smelling of the fuller's shop."

Macha's face grew hot; the implication her dress reeked of urine made her seethe. Although Pollia made the first insulting remark, Macha had been foolish enough to continue with counter snipes. She must learn to think before she spoke. Many times, when she was a child, her mother, now dead for more than nine years, had chided her for thoughtless acts. "You should always think about your answers before replying; they have a habit of getting you in trouble," she would say.

"Ladies, please," Helena intervened. "This is no way to start the evening."

"You're right, Helena," Macha admitted. Difficult as it was, she had to acquiesce as gracefully as her headstrong pride would allow. She had already made a fool of herself. "Forgive me, Pollia?"

Pollia narrowed her eyes, and glanced to Helena who nodded. "Very well, Macha. We shouldn't let it ruin the evening." Pollia swung about and walked away.

As they stepped closer to the wall, Helena pulled Macha aside. "Macha, you shouldn't have been so rude. Why did you say those things?"

"The same reason the little slut implied I was wearing the gown of a whore. She's never liked me since I married Titus."

"Why not?"

"You mean you don't know? It's because your parents scorned Pollia's mother and father's request for a marriage agreement between her and Titus."

"That was ten years ago."

"She's never forgotten. Pollia may be married to one of Rome's wealthiest men, but she's used to having her way."

It wasn't as if Macha hadn't tried to befriend Pollia. Pollia had snubbed her from the moment her betrothal to Titus had been announced. Through Helena and other friends, she learned that Pollia regarded her as a barbarian. Pollia was from a family of the Equestrian Order and was a status climber. She only wanted to marry Titus because he was the son of a wealthy Senator and one day would be a Senator as well.

Strange, Macha had no say when she was betrothed to Titus. Although he was a little gruff and not afraid to speak his mind, she found herself not only liking Titus, but falling in love with him even before they were married. She was aware of his family's high position in the nobility, but it had never occurred to her to marry him strictly for his wealth. She had no doubt it was why her parents had arranged for the marriage. They never again wanted her to experience the wretched hardships they had endured when she was a child, especially, the cold hungry winters after the Romans had invaded Britannia.

Macha's thoughts snapped back when Senator Bassus turned in her direction. She must ask him now about the charges against Titus, not later. He had power and influence. If anyone could free her husband, it was Bassus.

CHAPTER 3

A Spy for Dinner

"Senator Bassus," Macha said in a delighted voice as she moved to his side. "This is a surprise. I was hoping to see you, but didn't expect your arrival until tomorrow." She acknowledged her brother-in-law, Cnidius Rufus, who stood next to the Senator.

"The survey of the Danubian garrisons went better than I expected," Bassus replied. "It's a pleasure to see you again. I'm sorry to hear about Titus. Rufus and I were just discussing it."

"Aye, the charge is unbelievable," the tall squared-face Rufus said. "But you must be aware, Macha, that this is the third plot made against the Emperor's life in as many years?"

Macha shook her head. "The third? I don't understand."

"Don't you remember?" Bassus said. "Two years ago, he exiled his close friend, Helvidius Priscus, the Praetor of Rome, for treason. Last year he did the same to that loud mouth Cynic Philosopher, Demetrius, who plotted to restore the Republic."

Now Macha remembered—she'd given little thought to the stories—just more palace intrigue. "Why weren't they executed?"

"Emperor Vespasian hates to execute anyone," Rufus, said. "He has been known to weep at the executions of common criminals."

For a split second Macha touched her face. "Even if Titus was guilty, and I know he isn't, then why is he threatened with execution?"

"The Emperor's mercy applies only to civilians, not the army," Bassus said. "He is a soldier's soldier, fair but stern. He won't hesitate to sentence a soldier to death if found guilty."

"Aye, it's true," Rufus said. "I witnessed the execution of five deserters three years ago when he was commanding the legions in Judea."

"But that's why I need your help, Senator—anything to free Titus of this terrible charge. I know he's innocent!" As soon as she had blurted the words Macha felt like a fool. Helena was right. She should have waited until she could have spoken to Bassus privately.

The Senator placed a finger to his lips. "Let's not speak any further on the matter, here. I'll pay you a visit in the morning and discuss the situation in greater detail. Then I shall begin my inquiries." Cnidius Rufus nodded in agreement.

"I'd be grateful." Relieved that Bassus had offered assistance, Macha was certain he would quickly clear up the affair and obtain her husband's freedom. As a Legate, he had the authority to override any legionary general's orders and investigate matters such as treason. Thank Mother Goddess Anu she would not have to go to Rome.

Rufus said in a lower voice, "Senator Bassus, if I can help you, please let me know. My brother-in-law did not betray the Emperor, I'm certain of it."

"You will hear from me tomorrow," Bassus replied.

As she approached the three, Helena said, "I hate to interrupt your little chat, but I want to introduce the Senator to Claudia, a most charming lady. After all, a widower like you can't share a dining couch alone."

Rufus chuckled, shook his head, and excused himself.

Helena whisked Bassus to the far end of the room and presented him to a handsome matron in her mid-forties.

Macha glanced about and observed Rubellius Falco gazing in her direction. He hadn't moved from his couch.

Returning to Macha, Helena saw her tersely nodding at the man. "Oh, do you know Rubellius Falco?"

"He's a friend of Titus," Macha answered coolly. Draping Falco's muscular frame, a wool toga trimmed in purple denoted his membership in the Equestrian Order.

"Since you're both alone, I thought you wouldn't mind sharing a couch with him."

Searching the area, Macha saw no space available at the other reclining seats. Each one contained enough space to comfortably hold three people. "It doesn't seem I have much of a choice."

Helena pursed her lips. "You're not fond of him, are you?"

"I loathe the insufferable boor. He thinks he's the gods' gift to Venus." Macha eyes returned to the rules of behavior on the wall. The admonishment about lustful glances reminded her of Falco. She remembered the tales related to her by Titus about Falco's amorous adventures. She knew some of the women involved because they were wives of Roman officers. She shivered.

Helena touched Macha's forearm. "I'm sorry, Macha. Perhaps you would rather dine with Senator Bassus. I know he's an old friend of yours. I'll see if he wouldn't mind changing places."

Reclining on the couch reserved for the head of the household and guest of honor, Bassus conversed with Claudia who relaxed on the adjacent couch, the same used by Pollia and Pedius.

Macha shook her head violently. "Don't you dare, Helena. That would embarrass Claudia, and she seems to be very charming."

A mischievous smile lit up Helena's face. "Isn't she? I think she would make him a wonderful wife."

Taking her time Macha walked to the corner where Falco reposed. At thirty, he was chief engineering officer of the First Legion. The gaze from his hickory eyes reminded Macha of a leopard about to pounce on its prey.

"Good evening, Macha Carataca," Rubellius Falco said. A wide grin crossed his olive face. "How are you this evening?"

"Well, I suppose, considering that my husband has been accused of treason," Macha answered. Falco's couch seated three. She was tempted to move to the far end, leaving the middle area between them empty. However, as a matter of courtesy, custom dictated she reclined next to him. She took her place, but stayed as far from Falco as the center cushions allowed. He reeked of strong wine, and the balsam scent escaping from his black wavy hair nearly gagged her.

"I'm sorry about Titus—we all are." He swilled a long drink of wine from a gold cup. "His fate seems to be in the hand of the gods."

"What do the gods have to do with it?" Macha attempted to nibble a honey cake taken from a silver-fluted plate, followed by a sip of a mild Albanian wine from a small silver goblet. Earlier she'd regained some of her appetite, but in Falco's company it fled.

"I only mean it appears there's little anyone can do for him. It's difficult to dispute confessions and documents listing conspirator's names."

Sucking in her breath, Macha nearly spilled her wine. She placed the cup on the table next to her couch. "You were there?"

"Of course, and it pained me to listen to Titus denying everything, and expounding his loyalty to the Emperor," Falco said. "The very man he sought to overthrow."

"Yes, confessions by torture and forged papers—I know all about those things from father and Senator Bassus and my own experiences." The memory of being imprisoned at the age of seven, in the filthy dungeon at Tullianum prison, when she was brought to Rome as a captive with her mother and father, was forever imbedded in her mind. She would never forget the stench, the darkness, the freezing cold, and above all else the boil-infested rats that stole her meager food. Those terrible conditions combined with the horrors of agonizing torture were enough to make anyone confess, lies though they may have been.

Falco glanced beyond the bridge of his long nose toward the Senator's direction. "I assure you we took every precaution to see nothing of that sort happened. Torture is reserved for slaves, not Roman officers and citizens."

Macha tried to regain her composure. She noticed the other six guests eating their food and conversing among themselves, oblivious to her and Falco. She took another sip of wine from the goblet poured from a blue glass decanter formed in the image of a side of grapes. "You said confessions. Who else confessed?"

"That's information I'm not at liberty to divulge."

She glared. "How many times must I hear the same answer? I'm told there are other conspirators. Are they

21

soldiers or civilians or both? There are many ambitious generals who have their eyes on the throne."

"Most perceptive, but I can't tell you."

"Then I am right. There are others. Titus is only a Tribune, a junior officer. He has nothing to gain from this, but what were you doing there?"

As if it were obvious, Falco held out his left hand, palm up. "To witness the questioning and report that it was conducted in the legal manner prescribed by the Laws of the Twelve Tables."

Macha wanted to laugh in his face. The edicts established to protect citizen's rights by the ancient institution were violated on a regular basis by the Imperial government. "Who uncovered the so-called conspiracy?"

"I'm not allowed to reveal the details, but the plot was real enough. Unfortunately, Titus, my best friend, was involved."

Macha laughed snidely. "Titus is your *best* friend? Surely, you are joking?"

"I wouldn't joke about something like that." Falco scrutinized the manicured nails on his left hand and turned to Macha.

"I don't believe for one minute he is guilty," Macha said. "The evidence obtained is fraudulent!"

"I assure you it is not."

Macha wasn't about to tell him that if anybody was willing to search for the truth, it was she. Macha had no doubt he would try to stop her efforts. She couldn't understand why everything was clouded in secrecy. There should have been nothing to hide if the conspiracy against the Emperor had been uncovered. Something was missing.

"Since you're involved with the investigation," Macha said her eyes studying Falco, "why did you come to this dinner? I'd think Helena wouldn't want you present."

"She invited me because I'm friend of both Titus and Rufus. In the meantime," Falco added, "we should enjoy the food and entertainment. Rufus has imported exotic dancers from Egypt."

* * * * *

Macha barely tasted her food. Titus's confinement and the real purpose of Falco's presence at Helena's dinner filled her mind. No doubt he was there as a spy, and Helena had no choice but to invite him. Macha must be cautious with her words around Falco. He was here to uncover any additional treasonous acts or conversations. Gods forbid if he linked Rufus to the conspiracy. Had he heard Rufus' offer to Bassus to assist in the investigation? She prayed he didn't. Then Helena would be in the same predicament as she.

Falco's closeness to her on the dining couch became more revolting with each passing minute. The more wine he drank, the more he reeked. It nearly overpowered the fragrant aroma of the dishes being served by Edain and Helena's slaves.

As Macha gazed across the couch towards Helena and Rufus, she caught Pollia glancing at Falco. She gave him a nearly imperceptible nod in the direction of the courtyard. No one but Macha seemed to notice. She wondered if it was only her imagination, but then Falco excused himself mumbling something about going to the privy. A minute later, Pollia did the same. Was something going on between those two? Perhaps, having an affair? Given Falco's reputation, she wouldn't be surprised. It was really none of her business. Still she was curious—nosy was more like it. From where did they know each other? Were they previously acquainted? She needed answers.

Macha excused herself and found Nicanor sitting alone on a padded bench in the nearby waiting room for entertainers. He was on his feet the moment she entered the room. "Is it time already?" Nicanor asked. "I didn't know it was so late."

"There's still time," Macha said. She glanced to the door and back to him. "Nicanor, I need your help. They might become suspicious if I stay away from the *triclinium* too long.

"May I ask, whom you are talking about?"

"Tribune Falco and Mistress Pollia."

"Does this have something to do with them?"

"Yes. I want you to quietly proceed to the courtyard. I believe that's where they went. Keep to the shadows, but see if you can spot those two together. Get as close as you can without being discovered and listen to what they are saying. If they sound like lovers, leave them be and return to the waiting room."

Nicanor nodded.

"But if it sounds more serious," Macha continued, "I don't know exactly what, stay as long as you dare right up until the moment before your recital begins. I want to know what is going on between those two."

"I'll do my best."

Macha eyed Nicanor's musical instrument. "Take your lyre along. If they see you, act as if you were returning from the privy."

"But if they discover me won't they think I am spying for you?"

"Tell them you were waiting for one of the serving women and were not aware of their presence until just a few seconds earlier. Offer your humble apology."

"What if they don't believe me?"

"Tell them I gave you permission to see Edain.

Nicanor raised a hand as if in protest.

She gave him a mischievous smirk. "You needn't look surprised; I know you two are lovers. You were waiting for her, and I'll confirm it."

Of course, Pollia and Falco might not believe her, but at the moment, she couldn't think of anything better.

A slight grin crossed Nicanor's lips.

"You'll wait until we return home before telling me what you've learned, if anything," Macha said. "When we leave here, you'll walk with Edain and the litter bearers as usual. Don't say a word to anyone about Pollia and Falco."

"I understand, Mistress." He bowed and hurried toward the courtyard.

* * * * *

Falco and Pollia hadn't returned to the triclinium until just before the beginning of Nicanor's recital. Falco resumed his place on the couch with Macha but made no indication he was aware that he and Pollia had been spied upon.

A few hours later, when the meal was finished and the performers had departed, the gathering began to break up. Quickly, Macha cleaned her hands and face with a damp towel.

As she rose to leave, Falco staggered to his feet and followed her to the doorway of the triclinium. "May I see you home, Lady Carataca?"

Macha gave him a withering look. "Why?" Did he know she sent Nicanor to spy on Pollia and him? Nonsense.

"It isn't wise for a woman to travel home unescorted," Falco answered. "Bandits abound the streets this time of night."

"My slaves provide sufficient protection, thank you."

Falco snorted. "Slaves are unreliable; they run at the slightest hint of danger."

"Mine are very loyal, and I carry a dagger," Macha said. She patted a fold in her mantle, wrapped about her head and shoulders, and braced herself against the cold night air. She straightened her back and unflinchingly stared at Falco. "Every British woman can use one as skillfully as a man. My father taught me well."

Bassus turned in Macha's direction and excused himself from Claudia. "Is everything all right, Macha?" He took a few steps in her direction.

"Yes, Senator Bassus, just fine."

"I was offering to escort Lady Macha home, Senator," Falco said.

"I told him I didn't need an escort," Macha answered.

Bassus viewed Falco with a look of disapproval. "I would be more than happy to provide one."

"Thank you, Senator, but I can manage."

"Very well, I shall see you tomorrow." He returned to Claudia's side.

"I have to pass by your home on the way to the legion camp, anyway," Falco said. "Would you mind if I accompanied you that far?"

"If you want, but don't think you can go any further."

"What else would I ask?"

Ignoring him, she thought, Anything you can get away with.

* * * * *

Macha, her ten slaves, and Falco arrived at the front of her home a short time later.

As a slave assisted Macha from her litter, she was alerted to Falco's approach on his gray roan. The squeaking noises from riding on a leather saddle and jangle of bronze ornaments hanging from the gelding's breastplates and straps echoed in the darkness. As Macha was about to turn and walk to the house, he reined up before her, dipped his head, and locked his watery eyes upon her.

"May I come in for a moment? Perhaps for a little conversation and wine before going home?" he asked.

The twin torch lights illuminating the tall mahogany doorway cast Falco's face in a ghostly light, and reminded Macha of a demon from a terrible nightmare.

"I beg your pardon," Macha said icily. "I warned you before not to get any ideas. I'm a married woman."

Falco grinned, his strong alcoholic breath hanging in the air like sweat. "But that was earlier; I thought you might change your mind."

"I haven't. It wouldn't be proper for me to invite you into my house, especially when my husband is imprisoned." She moved away.

"What happens when he's dead?"

Macha swung around and glared at Falco. "He won't die —he's innocent!"

"What if you're wrong? You'll need somebody to look after you and your son." Falco's eyes narrowed. "Remember, he'll forfeit all his property."

"What are you suggesting?"

"Nothing at this moment, dear lady, only facts. The widow of a traitor is no better than a beggar! Think about it. If you change your mind let me know." Falco turned his mount and rode into the darkness.

With the exception of Edain, Macha dismissed the slaves, who headed down the pathway for their quarters. As she and her hand-maiden turned to enter the house, Nicanor moved away from the litter bearers and hurried to her side.

"Mistress, may I speak to you, alone?" he asked.

CHAPTER 4

Romance in the Air

Macha turned to Edain. "Leave us. Go to my cubicle and prepare my bed."

The young woman bowed, glanced to Nicanor, and departed.

"What did you learn, Nicanor?" Macha asked, sensing her servant's reluctance as he kept his eyes on the moonlight before him. "Speak up, you have nothing to fear from me."

His voice croaked. "I am afraid my news is disappointing, Mistress."

"That's for me to decide," she answered softly. "Go on."

Nicanor raised his eyes meeting hers. "I went to the courtyard and stayed in the shadows along the portico's edge. As you suspected, I found Tribune Falco and Mistress Pollia huddled together. They kept their voices down, and I only caught pieces of their conversation."

As she started for the house, Macha motioned Nicanor to walk by her side along the gravel pathway leading to the front door. "Did they see you?"

"No, I'm certain they didn't—they seemed too involved to notice anything around them."

"What did you hear?" Macha leaned toward Nicanor as he lowered his voice.

"Tribune Falco said something about missing her and not wanting her to return to Rome."

"What else?"

"I think he said he loved her, because they hugged and kissed after that."

Macha stared down at the short Greek. Silently, she asked Mother Goddess Anu for guidance. This sounded no more than a romantic tryst. "Is that all?"

"That's all I saw," Nicanor answered.

"Did either say anything else?" Macha hid her disappointment as she continued her walk to the house. What had she expected Nicanor to discover?

"Falco said he was taking a huge risk being with her," Nicanor continued, "Mistress Pollia reassured him that they would not be discovered and kissed him again."

"What else?"

Nicanor looked away. "Mistress Pollia made a vulgar remark about you I would rather not mention. Forgive me."

"I wouldn't be surprised by anything Pollia said." Macha touched his narrow shoulder. She was right. Nicanor's tale was of no value.

"Is this information you can use?" Nicanor asked. He turned back to Macha.

"No. I believe Falco is being his womanizing self. This is something I would expect of him."

Macha dismissed Nicanor. As he disappeared down the shadowy pathway to the slave quarters, Macha wondered if he had heard more than what he was telling her. Could he be holding back information? If so, to what end? No, that wasn't like her music teacher. Nicanor would have told her everything. She frowned. Or would he?

As she was about to enter the house, the scent of horse sweat filled her nostrils. She spotted the shadow of an intruder lurking behind a tall potted plant near the front door. For a split second a tremor ran through her body and she wished she hadn't dismissed her litter bearers earlier. Knowing that would take too long, she checked the dagger in her stola's hidden pouch and summoned her courage.

"Whoever you are, come out this instant!"

Stepping out the darkness was Jason, the slender bow-legged Greek slave from Thessaly, a groom who lived in the stables.

"What are doing here at this late hour?" Macha questioned in a sharp voice, her fingers tightened on the dagger hilt.

For a few seconds Jason bowed his head before he spoke. "I won't lie to you Mistress; I was waiting to see Edain."

"You what?"

"I wanted to see her."

"How dare you sneak about my house without my permission?"

Jason swallowed and his dark eyes darted from side to side. "Oh please, Mistress, don't punish me, I did not mean any harm. I am a man who is in love with your handmaiden. I know now I have done a stupid thing; that's all."

In love with Edain? Does she know about this? Macha wandered. *Nicanor* and Edain are lovers. Wasn't that common knowledge within the household? Slaves always gossiped among themselves. He must know, but that wouldn't stop some men from making advances. She had just scorned the advances of Falco, now she had to protect Edain.

"Very well," Macha said. "You have never been a trouble maker, and you are a good groom. My trainer, Juba, thinks highly of you. However, you are to stay away from Edain, do you understand?"

Jason gasped. "But..." He paused as if he had changed his mind. "Yes, Mistress."

"If I ever see you around her, you shall be punished or worse. Now, leave me!"

The slave bowed and fled in the direction of stables beyond the villa.

Did Jason overhear the conversation between Nicanor and me? I doubt it, Macha thought. And what if the groom had? He would not have heard much. He had been standing by the house and she had dismissed Nicanor before they were within the groom's hearing. She did not think Jason had followed them earlier because she was certain he would have been spotted by someone in her entourage. Perhaps she was allowing her imagination to get the best of her. Jason was interested in Edain and nothing more.

Macha crossed the dimly lighted atrium and pulled her mantle tightly about her shoulders. For a split second, she searched the hallway shadows beyond the atrium leading to her bed cubicle. Had someone been employed as a spy within her own household? The spy would report not only Titus's every move, but Macha's as well, especially, to those betraying the Emperor.

29

She had learned from an early age not to trust household slaves. After her father, Caratacus, had been pardoned by the Emperor Claudius, his family had received apartments in the palace and the use of a number of slaves. She was only eight but remembered her father telling her mother he had discovered spies among the slaves. Macha learned most wealthy households contained informants either in the pay of a rival family, a political enemy, or the Emperor. A number of her friends had found them in their homes. They got rid of the men by sending them to the mines—a death sentence—and women to scrubbing the public baths and latrines for life.

But Macha had no proof there were any in her home. Nevertheless, she would give orders to Metrobius to keep a close eye on the movements of the household slaves. She prayed Metrobius wasn't the spy. Macha needed rest but she feared she would go sleepless after today's terrible events and revelations.

* * * * *

The following morning Macha received a message from Senator Bassus to meet him at the garrison of Legion First Italica outside of Mediolanum. He had made arrangements for her to visit Titus.

When Macha arrived, she found the Senator standing alone at the edge of the dusty parade field in front of the *Principia*, the legion headquarters. Bassus had been watching a *turma* of cavalry going through a series of drills in the morning heat, clouds of dust kicking up beneath their feet. He turned to greet Macha as the squadron of thirty horsemen finished their maneuvers and rode away.

His entourage of a dozen retainers, scarlet-cloaked Praetorian Guardsmen, which his rank entitled him, sat on horseback at a discreet distance. A groom held onto the reins of an unmounted gray Spanish Barb she recognized as Bassus's. She knew he was allowed a far larger escort of the Emperor's household troops, but he had said on several occasions, he found them an encumbrance, annoying, and limiting his mobility.

Bassus wore the uniform of a military legate. A gilded iron helmet topped by a red combed plume crowned his balding head. A gold cuirass with two purple sashes tied across the front covered his white pleated tunic. Scarlet knee-high sandled boots enclosed his feet. Compared to his clothing, Macha felt her cerulean stola and pale yellow mantle to be as plain and roughly made as a peasant woman's homespun shift and cowl.

After exchanging salutations, Macha told Bassus, as if in passing, about how Falco tried to impose himself on her once they had arrived at her home.

"He has good taste, but he must stay away from you," Bassus said.

Macha frowned. "That's not all. Nicanor heard a conversation between Pollia and Falco earlier in the evening." She gave Bassus the details.

"Sounds like he wants Pollia's money as well as her," Bassus said. "His appetite for women is insatiable."

"It's disgusting."

"What does this have to do with your husband?"

She shrugged. "Not a thing, I suppose. I'm too nosy for my own good."

"I know you don't like Pollia, but whatever it is between those two, it's none of your concern."

She turned from Bassus and peered across the dusty parade field toward the stables at the distant whinnying of a horse, and wished she was riding one, far away from here. Instead she said a silent prayer asking for strength and forgiveness.

"I'm going to pay General Valens a visit and get to the bottom of this outrage. Now it's time to see your husband."

CHAPTER 5

Imprisonment

Macha wrapped the mantle tightly around her head and shoulders and pulled the expensive Indian cotton stola closer to her body as she followed the turnkey down the stockade's dimly lighted passageway to Titus' cell. A draft from the outside enveloped her like an icy wind sweeping off the Alps.

Because of her harrowing experience as a child of seven in Rome's Tullianum Prison, Macha was no stranger to the stockade. She shuddered as the memories flooded her mind. After waging guerrilla warfare against Rome, her father's treacherous cousin, Cartimandua, Queen of the Brigantes, had betrayed Caratacus to the Romans. He had been captured, along with her mother and herself. The family languished in the filthy dungeon, surviving on watered-down gruel and moldy bread for two weeks before being paraded through the streets of Rome in lice infested rags to appear before the Emperor Claudius. Even now she could feel the awful pests crawling on her body and the pangs of starvation within the walls of her stomach. Thank Mother Goddess her father's compelling speech convinced the old ruler to grant him pardon. Afterward Macha's family lived honorably for many years in Antium, south of Rome.

The memories faded as the stubby one-eyed turnkey stopped before a narrow entrance, and Macha peered over his shoulder as he unlocked and opened the cell's creaking iron door. A rat scurried into the shadowy corner of the dingy graffiti-ridden wall and disappeared. Although she despised the loathsome creatures, her experience in Tullianum had taught her not to fear them. She remembered screaming, throwing her shoes, and a drinking bowl at a huge mottled rat when it tried to steal her crust of bread one day. The earthen bowl shattered on the rodent's back, and the animal fled squealing.

The turnkey nodded. Macha entered, and the door slammed shut behind her. Titus huddled on the low cot with a rough woolen blanket wrapped about his muscled shoulders. A few thin rays of light filtered through the high narrow window and an open grate in the door. Titus looked up as she entered. Because of the cell's poor lighting, a second or two passed before he recognized his wife. Throwing off the blanket, he leaped to his feet.

Macha and Titus rushed into one another's embrace, his stubble face grazing her soft rouged cheeks. She ignored the stale smell of his unwashed hair and tunic. They were together—that was all that mattered.

Seconds later Titus pulled away from Macha's grip. She looked about and noticed fresh straw covered the stone floor. The smell permeating the cell reminded her of a well-kept stable—more acceptable for a horse than a human. She saw a footstool, a small plain wooden table, and a drinking bowl near one edge.

As he tilted his head to meet her eyes, he pressed his lips into a thin line and scowled.

"Macha, why are you here?"

"I'm your wife remember? I had to see you."

"You must not!" he snapped. "Your son's life is in danger and so is yours."

Stunned by his remarks, she couldn't understand his hostility. What threat could there be to the lives of her and Young Titus? "But darling, I'm here to help, so is Senator Bassus."

Titus grabbed her hands, giving them a gentle squeeze. "Sorry, I'm gruff. It's not your fault. Maybe the Senator can get me out of this pest hole."

"I know he will."

He grimly nodded. "When he does, I'll find the real traitors." For a moment he let go of her hands. "Why were you allowed in here? I was told I could not have visitors."

"Senator Bassus ordered General Valens to let me see you. Mother Goddess, this is no place for a Roman officer—you don't deserve it."

"I'm all right. I've been in worse conditions in the field."

"You're talking to me, remember?" Macha chided. "And I have eyes."

She studied Titus' haggard features, the angular scar that crossed the bridge of his large straight nose, his crumpled scarlet tunic, and blue knee-length breeches. His thick brown hair, growing low over his forehead, was combed back over his ears. But the glint remained in his deep blue eyes.

Titus shrugged. "I'm not concerned with how I look—getting out of here is all that matters. Once I'm free, I'll start inquiries right away." One of Titus' duties as an officer was to investigate murders involving soldiers of the legion that occurred in the garrison or in Mediolanum.

"This is a conspiracy, not murder."

He shook his head. "The same principles apply, and the Emperor's life is at stake. Suspect everyone, gather evidence, and by process of elimination find the real culprits. Trouble is, a conspiracy may involve many. Solving a murder is easier."

"At least you'll be free to try. But you must be released first."

"Aye, that's true, but I'm confident the Senator will get me out of here. When I was first imprisoned, I was angry and wanted to kill everyone, but that isn't the answer. A thorough investigation is the only way."

"And you shall, darling."

Without saying another word, Titus led Macha to his cot. They sank onto the straw mattress, leaning back against the cold wall. A shiver shot up Macha's spine when Titus placed his arm around her shoulder and drew her to him. She shook it off and pulled away.

"Wait," Macha said. She wanted to be close to him but not in this stockade. She first needed Titus to answer questions about his arrest.

"I still want to know who made up this ridiculous charge?" she asked. "Where did it come from?"

"I have no idea," he answered as he shook his head. "General Valens' interrogators said I'm accused of plotting against Vespasian's life. The charge is a lie. He's the first decent Emperor to rule Rome since Octavius Augustus."

"Why would anyone accuse you of treason?" Macha wrapped her slender arms around her body and leaned back against the wall.

He eased his hold. "Once I've explained everything, you must leave. I don't care if the Senator's here, you are in danger."

She relented and slowly he pulled her forward. "No one will harm me, darling."

"Don't be so sure." Titus removed his hand from around her middle and took her hands in his and kissed them. A slight tremor flowed up her arms, her pulse quickened. "Valen's men questioned me about your role in the plot, too. I told them over and over you played no part in it."

"Why do they suspect me?" Macha asked. She didn't think she had given anyone a reason to believe she was part of a treasonous plot.

Exhaling, Titus released Macha's hands. He bent his head and closed his eyes. A minute passed before he opened them. "Remember the bracelet I bought you three months ago?"

"The silver one encrusted with lapis lazuli?"

"The same. After I left the street of the silversmiths, I was approached by a couple of wealthy merchants whom I had conducted business with in the past. They were displeased with the new taxes imposed upon businesses by the Emperor Vespasian."

"Everyone knows the civil war wrecked the Empire's economy, and the treasury is empty. What did they expect?"

A grimace crossed Titus' broad face as he shook his head. "That's the point. They were outraged because the increase in taxes ate up much of the huge profits they and others made during the great crisis. So, they made me a proposition. The bastards wanted me to conspire with them and others in overthrowing the Emperor."

Macha gasped. "Titus, why didn't you tell me?"

He placed a hand on her delicate shoulder and leaned closer. He twisted his mouth. "I couldn't tell anyone!"

"Why did they want you?"

He snorted. "Since my parents were Gallic, the damned fools believed I would be sympathetic to their proposition

35

and to the lost Gallic cause of two years ago. They intended to stir up the Gauls again."

"You mean that nest of outlaws you smashed?"

"That was a coincidence. No, much bigger, the whole province and more. They said other Roman officers were involved including a general, but refused to say whom."

"That could be half the commanders in the army."

Titus bent his head and whispered, "All of them, Macha. There's not one who wouldn't try for the Imperial purple if they had the backing of the army."

Appalled by the startling revelation, Macha trembled. Both she and Titus knew that north of the Po River, Italy and Mediolanum had been Gallic territory for centuries before Roman occupation. Despite being under Roman control for more than two hundred years, they were well aware that old festering animosities still raged against Rome.

"But that's madness. The Empire would plunge into another civil war, and this time might not recover." Macha balled her fists, fingernails gouging her palms.

"I agree," Titus said, "but there's more." For a second he eyed the cell door. Titus went on to describe how he had been inwardly outraged when the traders made the proposal, but in order to obtain incriminating evidence, Macha's husband had to pretend to fall in with their plans until he discovered the conspirators' names. One of the merchants told him a secret list had been written and a copy hidden. He didn't know where.

"I wasn't going to get involved without confiding in someone of higher authority," Titus continued. "Unfortunately, I told Julius Aquela, the Camp Commander and second-in-command."

Macha's hand shot to her mouth. "The one who died in the hunting accident six weeks ago."

"I should have suspected it sooner. His death wasn't an accident. Someone discovered he was my confidant."

"What about the list?"

"I was arrested before I could learn where it was hidden. I gave the interrogators the names of the merchants and told them about the unnamed officers involved. The Gauls vanished before Pomponius Appius could apprehend them. They probably took the list with them. As for the officers, Appius said I was lying. I'm not—I'm being used. The interrogators said General Valens' informants had been watching me for about two months. They saw me in the company of the Gauls."

"Why didn't they arrest you before you went after the bandits?"

"I don't know, they wouldn't say. Once Senator Bassus gets my release, that's one of the first things I'll learn."

"Officers within the legion must be part of the plot," Macha said. "Don't you think Appius might be involved? He hates you. I remember you once said he complained that Vespasian didn't recognize him for his bravery in the civil war."

Titus shook his head. "That isn't proof. There were many who fought bravely with honor who didn't get recognition. But I'll confront him when I'm out."

"Wouldn't it make sense? Maybe he was offered a command of the legion if he betrayed you and the Emperor."

"That's speculation, but tell the Senator and see what he thinks."

"The Senator will help you, I'm sure," Macha said.

He grunted.

"Senator Bassus will straighten out the situation. He's upstairs speaking with General Valens right now. But I'm not idly sitting by while they try to kill you."

Titus frowned. "This is too dangerous for a woman to deal with. Leave it to Bassus and me."

Macha bristled. Silently she asked the Mother Goddess to give her patience. "Don't you think I'm capable of taking care of myself? Or is it because I'm female and you consider this a man's duty?"

Taking Macha's soft hands, Titus intertwined them through his fingers hardened by ten years riding cavalry mounts, weapons training, and war.

"You have many talents, Macha," Titus replied evenly, "but I'll not see you harmed. Think of our son—he needs you."

"And I need you. I won't see you executed," Macha argued. "Even with Senator Bassus' assistance, I'm afraid not enough will be done to free you. I must try. I can go places with him I couldn't go alone."

"You're bound to run afoul of our enemies."

"Don't worry, I'll be protected." Macha looked into Titus's eyes. They seemed to say what she felt. A tingling sensation filled her, and spread through her limbs, leaving her breathless. She pulled herself away.

"No, darling, I can't"

"Why not?" Titus unwound his fingers from hers and gripped her shoulders.

"It's not right, not in this awful place. I can't think about that while you are in here. My mind is fixed on setting you free. I'm sorry, my love, but until you are, nothing else matters." Macha pulled away, turned, and called for the turnkey. She refused to look back at Titus lest he see her tears.

CHAPTER 6

Courtyard Revelations

Macha sat brooding on an oakwood bench in the hallway near the entrance to General Valens's office at the Principia when Senator Bassus stepped outside.

His footfalls grew heavier with each approaching step. His face appeared somber when he found her. "Macha, I have bad news."

She sprang to her feet nearly losing the palla wrapped around her shoulders. "Couldn't you do anything for Titus?"

"Your husband's situation is impossible." Slowly Bassus shook his head as he halted before Macha. "Personally, I'm not convinced by General Valens so-called evidence, but under military law, it is enough to hold Titus for a court-martial on charges of treason and conspiracy."

Astonished, Macha hardly breathed. She swallowed, heat rushing across her cheeks.

"Treason? How can that be? He's innocent!"

"I'll explain on the way out," Bassus answered.

Macha and Bassus walked in silence through the long crosshall adjacent to General Valens's office. The drafty building opened onto a dusty courtyard where the legion commander addressed the troops from a raised tribunal during muster. They trekked by the entrance of the Legionary chapel, passing two muscular, six-foot legionaries posted in front of the entrance, bordered by a wrought iron gate. Dazed, she barely registered the life-like images of Mars, Minerva, and the lucky twins, Castor and Pollux, adorning the three inside walls. A tall bronze statue of Emperor Vespasian stood on a pedestal, wearing a general's uniform, arms outstretched before the legion standards. They were dominated by a proud golden eagle, Rome's symbol of power, mounted on a hardwood pole, its wings outstretched, gripping a thunderbolt in its talons. A

39

trap door, set in the wooden floor near the base of the statue, led to the basement. Macha remembered Titus had said the legion bank and payroll were stored there, locked in an iron bound wooden chest.

Bassus spoke in a low voice when no one was within hearing. "One of General Valens informers found Titus in company of two Gauls known to be displeased with the Emperor's new taxes."

Macha paused as they turned into the courtyard surrounded by a pillared veranda. A dozen official bulletins plastered the nearest wall. "Titus was trying to get proof to present to General Valens. I don't understand why the General trusts informers. They're the rubbish of the earth. They'll lie about anything for money or revenge."

"Informers are a scummy lot," Bassus agreed, "but unfortunately, General Valens believed them. The information they possessed was enough to incriminate Titus."

She leaned toward Bassus as they continued to walk. "What information? The merchants fled Mediolanum."

"They didn't take their slaves. General Valens's interrogators questioned them as the law prescribes."

A chill shot through Macha's body, as she understood what he meant. "I know it's lawful, but torture is a horrible way to extract a confession. Wouldn't you say anything to prevent your legs from being ripped from your sockets, or worse?"

They approached the courtyard entrance. A bored sentry snapped to attention upon Bassus's approach and saluted.

Bassus acknowledged the guard, then answered Macha's question, "I know what you're saying. But two of them confessed to overhearing that Titus was the leader of the conspiracy."

Macha suddenly stopped. Equal to Bassus' height, she twisted around and studied his sunburnt face. A fading battle scar sliced across his broad forehead. "You know they're lying. Did they confess about any written documents?"

"Yes, but that was a false-truth they believed, and none have been recovered."

"What about the unnamed officers? Isn't General Valens going to investigate that accusation?"

"The slaves said nothing about officers." He snorted. "General Valens believes Titus made it up to save his own skin."

"And on the word of two poor tortured slaves my husband is held to answer for treason. That's outrageous!" She slapped the side of her leg so hard it stung.

The Senator shook his head as they continued to walk. "I will carry on my own investigation independent of General Valens, but for now Titus will remain in custody. When it comes to charges of treason, even with my authority I can't get Titus released. I'm sorry, Macha."

Furious, she bolted ahead of Bassus. She didn't place much faith in his *independent* investigation. So far he had failed to win her husband's release. Bassus had been a family friend for many years, but now Macha felt betrayed. As far as she was concerned, he had only made a half-hearted attempt to free Titus.

Macha bitterly recalled how her father, Caratacus, had spared Bassus life. He was a young centurion, during the early days of the Roman invasion of Britannia, and his cohort had marched into a trap set by the king and his army. They were surrounded and destroyed, leaving a blood smeared Bassus the sole survivor. Encircled by a pile of dead Roman legionaries and Celtic warriors, Bassus stood in a defensive crouch defiantly brandishing his bloodied short sword expecting to be slain at any moment. Instead, Caratacus allowed him to live because he admired his courage. He sent Bassus back to Roman headquarters with a warning that if Rome failed to withdraw its forces from Britannia, he would destroy them all.

Rome did stay and Caratacus was defeated. But Bassus never forgot Caratacus's clemency and befriended her father after his capture and pardon by the Emperor Claudius. Now, it seemed to Macha, that Bassus no longer valued his friendship for her family, as if Titus's life no longer mattered. She was alone, and it would be up to her to find a way to exonerate her husband. But...could it be her husband was guilty? She shook her head. No! It isn't possible, not Titus. He is too loyal. She put the idea out of her mind.

Bassus followed Macha at a brisk pace. The day was growing warmer and a trickle of sweat rolled down the side of Macha's neck. Outside the courtyard, they found the carriage waiting on the cobbled stone street next to the buttressed and walled granary.

"Didn't you speak to Titus's friends—his fellow officers?" Macha asked when Bassus caught up. "Didn't you speak to my brother-in-law?"

"I did. Rufus protested Titus's innocence to General Valens, and was rebuffed. The General had threatened to detain him for questioning, to see if he was involved with the conspiracy."

"That's terrible. He's one officer I'm sure had no part of it."

"I agree," Bassus said. He brushed aside the slave footman and assisted Macha into the white canopied wagon drawn by two matching bay horses. She collapsed upon the cushioned seat.

"When I learned about this," Bassus continued, "I warned Valens I would relieve him of his post as legion commander if he further abused his power. He knows I have the right as Legate and representative of the Emperor. It was then he revealed his evidence against Titus."

"Oh, Mother Goddess!" Macha turned away attempting to hold back the welling tears. This wasn't the time to lose her composure. She couldn't. She took a deep breath and wiped the moisture from her eyes with a jasmine scented handkerchief.

"What is Falco's and Appius's involvement?" Macha asked in a voice little more than a whisper. "Falco said he was at Titus's interrogation, and Appius brought me the news."

"Falco told you the truth. He acted as a witness verifying the interrogation was conducted legally. Appius had nothing to do with the arrest or questioning. General Valens deemed it appropriate you should be informed by a senior officer."

Macha told Bassus that Appius was sent because General Valens didn't want someone, such as her brother-in-law, who was related to a Gaul, to bring her the message. "His personal contempt for foreigners was all too obvious," Macha added.

Bassus stepped back from the wagon's side, looking up at Macha. "That's not the proper way to handle a case. Titus's family origins shouldn't have anything to with the investigation."

Macha agreed. "Falco has more than just an interest in *justice*. He seems only too eager for my husband's death."

He narrowed his chestnut eyes. "What are you talking about?"

She reminded Bassus of Falco's avowed intentions towards her after he had escorted her home the night before.

"I don't care if he is having an affair with Pollia, that's her problem," Bassus said. "But that womanizer must stay away from you, even if I have to order him."

A frown erupted across Macha's bowed lips. "No, Senator, not yet. I don't want him to know that I told you. But gods forbid, if Titus were executed, the state would confiscate everything—I would be left with nothing. Falco thinks I would eagerly fly to his arms for security; he's badly mistaken."

"That won't happen." Bassus shook his balding head. "As your patron, I won't allow him to touch you. Despite your protest, if he comes near you, I will transfer him to a garrison on the Lower Danubus River, the outer reaches of the Empire. In the meantime, although you may not understand Titus's confinement, don't go near the stockade."

Macha's eyes flared with sudden anger. "I understand his confinement better than you will ever know! His cell is smaller than the one I spent time in as a child in Tullianum Prison. I may be freer than I was at seven, but I'm still confined to a woman's place in this Roman world. I've never tasted the freedoms enjoyed by my Celtic sisters in Britannia—but I will!"

43

CHAPTER 7

Death at the Stables

As she returned from the garrison on this unusually hot day, choking clouds of dust, churned by the carriage bouncing along the country road, permeated Macha's clothing and skin. She needed a relaxing bath to cool both her body and her anger. Even though Bassus didn't seem convinced by General Valens's evidence, Titus still remained imprisoned. She was certain the allegations were fabricated

Assisted from the carriage at the front of her house, Macha passed through the entryway into the atrium. She told a slave sweeping the mosaic floor to fetch Edain.

No sooner had the slave departed than the light sound of children's clattering footsteps echoed beyond the far end of the atrium. Seconds later young Titus rushed in with Nicanor's son, Demetrios, trailing behind him.

"Mama! Mama! Nicanor's dead!"

Tears stained Demetrios' pale face. The ten-year-old sniffled and wiped them away with a grubby hand. When he noticed Macha watching, he lowered his head.

Shocked, Macha stood still for a moment, unable to speak. Macha grabbed Titus by his scarred little hands so hard he winced. "Is this one of your games?" She asked, looking him in the eye. "Death is serious."

"No, Mama, it's true—Demetrios told me." Nicanor's son lingered a few paces distant, fidgeting with his homespun tunic. He snuffled and then wiped the tears running down his narrow face. He was a little bigger than Titus, and brighter than most boys his age, almost as articulate as an adult.

"Where is your father's body?"

"In the stables, Mistress," the boy answered in a quivering voice, averting Macha's eyes.

Oh, the poor little boy, she thought. He must be in shock. He lost his mother two years ago, and now his father. Still it was strange. Nicanor seldom went to the stables. "Do you know how he died?" Macha asked.

Demetrios gulped loudly, sniffled again and wiped his nose on the sleeve of his tunic. "They...they beat his head with clubs—a lot."

Spiny bumps like a back bone rose on her arms. Why would anyone kill Nicanor? Was this somehow related to Titus' arrest? She wheeled, taking a step in the direction of the barn, but stopped. She couldn't rush to the barn without obtaining some details. It was her duty as mistress of the house to learn the truth no matter how much Nicanor's death pained her. She still couldn't believe it was true, that this gentle good man was murdered. He had never harmed a soul.

Not wanting to frighten or alarm the boys, Macha steeled herself to remain cool. She stooped, softly placing both hands on Demetrios' little shoulders.

"Who told you he was beaten to death?"

The muscles in his face tightened. A few seconds later he blinked back the tears and wiped his face on his sleeve. He bit his lip and shook his head. "I...I watched it. I wanted to stop them, but I was afraid."

"You poor boy." Macha gave Demetrios a tight hug. His hair and clothing smelled of moldy straw. She wanted to hold him until all his pain vanished. Mother Goddess, she hated having to ask him questions in his time of grief.

"Did you tell anyone else about this?" she asked.

He croaked. "No, Mistress. My papa said I could only trust you."

"But you could trust me," Titus interjected.

"I'm sure he does, son," Macha said. "But this is very serious. I'm the one who must ask the questions." Macha sighed. Demetrios may be right, she thought. Who, in the household, could he trust?

"Who did this to your father?" Macha asked softly, releasing Demetrios and stepping back half a pace.

He shook his head. "I don't know. They were two real big men."

"Did you ever see them before?"

"No," he answered, nearly choking on the word.

"Where did they go?" Macha's eyes scanned the area around the atrium.

"They ran for the gully behind the stables."

"Where did they leave your father?"

"In Apollo's stall," Demetrios answered.

Macha understood. Apollo, her half-trained, half-wild stallion would take the blame for Nicanor's death. Only Macha, Titus, and the trainer, Juba, could enter the stall without risking injury. Others he bit and kicked, only because he was cornered and couldn't escape.

"Did these men carry your father into Apollo's stall?"

He snuffled. "No. They...they lifted him over...over the stall door and threw him in." Again Demetrios wiped the tears flowing down his cheeks. "I heard them say they wanted to make it look like he was trampled to death."

"Does anyone else know?"

"I don't think so," Demetrios, replied. "No...nobody was there. I...I ran and told Titus right away. I knew he would tell you." Although fidgeting, and stepping from one foot to the other, Macha's son smiled at the compliment. He remained silent, as Macha had taught him not to interrupt when she was speaking.

"When did this happen?" Macha asked.

Demetrios stammered. "I...I don't know. I didn't think about time—I was too scared."

"Would you say less than a half hour ago?"

He thought for a few seconds. "I think so."

The assassins must be long gone. Macha stood and again her eyes searched the reception room. No one lurked about. Still, that didn't guarantee their conversation hadn't been overheard. She faced Nicanor's son.

If what Demetrios said was true, Macha thought, she didn't want anyone to know that he had witnessed his father's death. Someone might think he could identify the assassins, or, gods forbid her son would have knowledge as well. She couldn't alarm the boys anymore than necessary, but had to get answers quickly.

Macha turned to Titus. "I am going to the stables. You and Demetrios are to stay in my bed cubicle until I return.

46

Neither of you is to say a word about this to anybody, do you understand?"

Young Titus paled as he glanced towards Demetrios' tear-stained face. The slave boy quickly nodded, followed by her son.

Upon leaving the boys, Macha found Edain. She explained they were staying in her bed-cubicle for the time being and instructed her slave to make sure they didn't leave. Apparently Edain hadn't heard Nicanor had been killed. Knowing she would be devastated, Macha didn't tell her she was on her way to investigate his death.

*   *   *   *   *

Macha hurried toward the stables at the far end of the villa. Beyond the barn a gully deep enough to hide anyone's movement ran a short sprint from the building. The ditch drained into a tree-lined stream, a tributary of the River Addua, at the bottom of a long sloping hill. A light breeze swept up the ravine, swirling around the outbuilding and softly rustling the bushes along one side. The mortared structure with a red tiled roof housed Macha and Titus' best horses. Eight stalls, four on each side, bordered a hard pack earthen walkway. Overhead rested the hayloft. A storage area for tack and other equipment stood at the far wall. Close by, within a corral, birds flitted and chirped on the dusty ground, pecking seeds trapped in a drying pile of horse dung. As Macha hurried past, one of the mares nickered. Perhaps Metrobius or Juba would know something, but where were they?

She shook her head and wiped the sweat from her face with her silk handkerchief as she speculated on the assassins escape route. No doubt they used the concealment of the gully to flee after the murder. Macha guessed they headed for the river and used its shelter to complete their escape. They might still be in the area, but it was too dangerous for her and her slaves and Juba to search for them. Others could be waiting for the assassins' return.

Macha touched the outline of her dagger hidden within the folds of her dress as she placed her sweat-stained handkerchief back within one. Despite her training with the weapon, she didn't feel confident enough to challenge

any murderer on her own, let alone two or more. Juba
hadn't wielded a javelin since retiring from the army five
years ago as an auxiliary cavalry sergeant with the *Alae*.
She considered the dark Numidian too valuable a trainer to
risk his life. She would send a messenger to the garrison,
and request a detachment of troops to hunt them down.

As Macha approached the barn, Metrobius dashed
outside to meet her. "Something terrible has happened,
Mistress. Apollo has killed Nicanor!"

Brushing him aside, Macha rushed into the barn and
halted at the stall entrance. Milling nearby in the
breezeway stood Juba and the slave groom, Jason.

Juba and Jason, both covered in dust and smelling of
horse, approached her. She waved them over to where
Metrobius hovered just inside the stable entrance.

She glanced inside beyond the open top of the stall's
split doors. Nicanor's crumpled body lay on the straw-
covered floor next to the iron-grated drainage pit. Buzzing
green flies circled and landed on the corpse's glazed eyes
and waxy skin. Macha pinched her nose from the reeking
odor of ruptured intestines mixed with the smell of urine
and feces. Dark blood oozed from his mouth, and more
covered his head and back. Pushing her fist against her
teeth, she turned away.

Macha spied Apollo in a stall at the far end of the barn
where he was peacefully munching on a clump of hay and
swatting flies with his thick tail. He stopped, his mouth
full, and turned. Catching sight of Macha, he swallowed his
food and nickered. Juba must have moved him there after
Nicanor's body had been discovered, she thought. But
horses don't rip tunics or intentionally kill people on their
own. She steeled herself and asked the Mother Goddess to
give her courage. There was no time to weep—too many
questions.

"What was Nicanor doing here?" she asked Metrobius,
who had silently moved to the entrance. "He never visits
the stables, and he certainly wouldn't enter Apollo's stall."

For a split second Metrobius hesitated. "I don't know,
Mistress. He hadn't been seen in the house since early this
morning. I assumed he was giving a music lesson
elsewhere."

Macha turned to her tall wiry trainer, Juba, sweat running down the side of his ebony face. Beside him hovered Jason, stepping from one foot to the other, on his bandy legs.

"Juba, where were you two?"

"At the ring breaking a new horse, my lady," Juba replied in heavily accented Latin. He nodded his dark close-curled head to the bow-legged groom. "I ordered Jason to assist me."

How convenient, she thought. "How long were you at the ring?"

"About two hours," Juba replied.

More than enough time for the assassins to enter and leave the stables without being noticed, she thought. "Who found Nicanor?"

"I did," Juba answered. "I heard a commotion in the barn. I knew by the snorting it was Apollo. He was kicking the sides of the stall. That's when I went in and saw the body. Apollo wanted out. The smell of blood was driving him mad. I moved him to another stall before he hurt himself."

He motioned to the same pen Macha had already observed. "I ran to the house and told Metrobius," Juba continued.

"It's true, Mistress," the thin Greek steward said. "After seeing the body, I was returning to the house when your carriage arrived at the barn. I knew you would want to know immediately."

She nodded. The wagon was always taken to the barn when she returned from a ride. "Didn't anyone see him enter the stables?"

"No, Mistress, not that I know of. Everyone was working. It's impossible to see the barn from inside the courtyard."

Metrobius was right. A storage shed, a bake house, the workshops, and slave quarters lined the courtyard's inside wall. Still, the question lingered in Macha's mind. She wondered if he might have been lured from the house. How did the killers get Nicanor outside to the stable without anyone seeing them? How and by whom? More importantly, why?

"Take Apollo out of the stall," Macha ordered. "I will check his hooves for blood. If he did this, you'll geld him."

"But he's worth a fortune, Lady Macha," Juba protested.

"Not at the cost of Nicanor's life. He may have been a slave, but I prized him far more than any horse. I'm taking a closer look at his body," Macha said. She didn't believe the horse was at fault, but duty demanded she take control of the situation. If Titus were here, he would know where to search. He was a veteran of many battles and seen his share of death.

It had been Titus' duty at the garrison to investigate murders, in which legionaries were suspected, whether they were committed in camp or in Mediolanum. Macha remembered him saying he treated everyone as a possible suspect. By conducting interviews, searching crime scenes and collecting evidence, he narrowed down the number of persons who might be involved. Macha didn't know what she would find and prayed her stomach wouldn't heave. She entered the stall.

Covering her nose with a stained handkerchief, Macha stooped and pulled up Nicanor's shredded tunic. For a split second she turned her head away. She looked back. A piece of bone jutted through Nicanor's skin and a trickle of drying blood coated the side of his rib cage.

Macha willed herself not to vomit as she stepped from the stall. No wonder Demetrios was so upset, the poor child. She approached Juba at the far end of the stable, where he stood holding the horse by a halter.

"Pull up Apollo's legs, one at a time," she ordered. She didn't know exactly why, but something in the back of her mind said she must examine the horse's hooves. No more than a few strands of straw and dirt from the stable floor were caught in the sole and frog of Apollo's rear hooves.

"Show me the left front, Juba," Macha ordered.

Standing to one side, the sinewy brown trainer reached down and squeezed the lower tendon forcing the horse to raise its forefoot. Among the matted straw lodged in the hoof Macha spotted a long black splinter. She looked about. It didn't match the sides of the stall. They were constructed of graying oak timbers. She pulled the sliver from the stallion's hoof for a closer examination, along with a couple of white threads resembling the color of Nicanor's tunic. With Juba and Jason peering in her direction, Macha palmed the sliver and placed it in the fold of her stola. She would think later where Apollo might have picked up the black splinter.

Difficult as it was, Macha re-entered the stall and studied Nicanor's body again. She noticed scrapes on his gaunt cheeks. Near the bottom of the adjacent stucco wall were a couple of bloodstains. Caking dark blood matted the side of Nicanor's skull. Gray slime dribbled from the same area. Embedded between the thick strands of his curly black hair her eye caught five black splinters she missed before. They had to have been there before the stallion kicked him in the head. Earlier that morning Apollo had been turned out to pasture between the nearby gully and stream at the bottom of the hill. There wasn't anything in the field containing wood splinters. The nearest trees were elm and sycamores lining the banks of the stream. As was the custom, his hooves were cleaned before returning to the barn.

Then she remembered Demetrios saying he had witnessed the murderers beating Nicanor with black clubs. Her slave was slightly built, and if the two assassins were as big as Demetrios described, they could have easily have lifted him over the split door and tossed him into the stall. No doubt Apollo kicked Nicanor but only because he smelled blood and panicked. Her slave was already dead.

"I've changed my mind, Juba," Macha said. "Don't geld Apollo—just turn him out."

"Yes, Lady, thank you," a relieved Juba answered.

Macha ordered Metrobius to fetch slaves from the household to carry Nicanor back and prepare him for burial.

When the servants had removed Nicanor's body, Macha took Metrobius aside. "Summon all the slaves to the library; I'm going to question them."

For the length of a heartbeat, Metrobius' face tightened. Another second passed before he cleared his throat. "May I ask the reason, Mistress?"

"I don't believe Nicanor's death was accidental."

51

"But Apollo kicked him—the wounds."

"I'm not convinced all the injuries were caused by Apollo. Now, do as I say."

Metrobius bowed and left the barn.

Macha was taking a chance by letting her suspicions be known. She was almost certain this was the work of a household spy, but why? Did Nicanor have knowledge regarding Titus' arrest that could exonerate him? No, he couldn't have, Macha thought. Remote as the possibility might be, she had to learn if anyone saw the assassins enter or leave the property. Her household would find out soon enough when she requested assistance from the garrison to hunt for the killers.

Although it was her right, she wouldn't see her slaves tortured even if they all denied knowledge of the murder. She didn't want the death of another innocent person on her hands. Too many had been wrongfully accused by poor slaves giving the first name called to mind to escape the horrible pain of the rack and white hot irons.

Before she interviewed the slaves, she must return to the boys and see if Demetrios could give her any further details on his father's murder.

CHAPTER 8

The Young Witness

By the middle of the afternoon, after Macha finished examining Nicanor's body and had him removed in preparation for burial, she returned to the bed cubicle. She hadn't anticipated being away so long and speculated whether the boys would still be there. And if not, where? Macha's heart quickened, the pulse roaring in her ears. If one of them says a word to the other slaves about what Demetrios saw, their lives could be in danger. There must be a spy among them. She shook her head. But I must get a grip on myself. I'm allowing my imagination to run wild.

She entered her room finding Titus and Demetrios seated on the tiled floor at the foot of the bed, playing *latrunculi*. She said a silent prayer to Mother Goddess Anu in thanks for the boys' safety. They jumped to their feet and her son ran to her.

"Mama, I beat Demetrios—the first time! Look at the board!" He pointed excitedly to the square cedar board. Most of the thirty-two pegs were holed at his end of the slate.

Macha stooped and gave him a big hug. "Good for you. Perhaps one day you'll be as good as Demetrios."

Demetrios met her eyes, and Macha understood. He had allowed Titus to win, and she had no doubt he had only reluctantly joined in the game, his mind on his father's death. He appeared calmer, not as shaken as he was earlier. Perhaps numbness had set in as sometimes occurs after the initial shock of witnessing a death wears off.

"I'm pleased that you stayed in the room," Macha said. "I'm sorry I took so long."

"Well, I got tired of waiting, so I said to Demetrios," Titus's little eyes brightened, "'let's play games.'"

"That's good," Macha said.

"But Demetrios wouldn't play. I told him if he didn't play *little outlaws* with me," he motioned to the pegged board, "I'd leave the room."

"Titus, you didn't," she said, ashamed.

"It worked didn't it?" His rosy-face beamed. "He said he didn't want to get in trouble because he couldn't stay in the room without me."

Macha shook her head, scarlet strands flicking alongside her face. "Don't you ever threaten him again over a game. He's a good boy."

"Is it true, Mama? Demetrios said slaves get in trouble if they don't do what they're told."

"Yes, they're punished."

"He said he couldn't disobey you."

"Demetrios is very obedient and wise for his age."

The young Greek slave stood silently, dried tearstains still smeared his long pale face.

"So am I." Titus's expression was both sulky and defensive, and she knew he was unnerved despite his behavior.

Macha summoned a smile. "Of course you are—most of the time."

Sitting in the chair by her dressing stand, Macha removed the mantle from her shoulders and draped it over the table's end. She motioned to Demetrios to sit on the stool next to her. Titus bounced onto Macha's bed and sat at the foot, his freckled legs dangling over the side.

Bending her head, Macha studied Demetrios' dark puffy eyes. The smell of hay and horse oozed from his slight frame. She lightly touched his bony shoulder. "This may be very hard for you, Demetrios, but I want you to tell me everything you can remember about your father's death. Can you do that?"

Demetrios bowed his head. Bangs the color of a dark bay horse drooped down his forehead touching his thin eyebrows. "I...I went to the stables about noon to feed a pony I like. When I was ready to leave, I heard footsteps outside the barn. I heard voices, and they sounded mad, like they were fighting."

The young slave stopped for a moment and took a deep breath. Then he related, "I peeked through the barn's open door and saw strangers walking toward it. They were wrestling with someone held between them, and at first I couldn't see who it was.

"I...I don't understand," he croaked. "How they could have gotten that far without being seen. Usually, there are other workers around the compound. I was afraid they would see me, and so I ran up a ladder just inside the barn door and hid in the hayloft."

Demetrios paused, his intelligent eyes searching beyond the bed cubicle.

Macha nodded. "It's all right Demetrios, you are safe with us. Please continue."

He swallowed before he went on, "The men drew closer, and I heard a familiar voice. I peeked over the edge and saw Father held by two men. Father groaned and there was blood running down the side of his face. He started to say something, and the tall one, he had a big jaw, hit him across the mouth." The young slave grimaced, his body shaking, he wept.

Macha reached out and pulled Demetrios to her lap and quietly held him. "You don't have to say another word, Demetrios. I am so sorry."

"But...but I have to," he stammered as he pulled away from her. He sniffed and rubbed his face on his dirty sleeve. "Someone has to find them—Father was a good man."

"And we will," Macha answered. "What did they hit him with?"

Demetrios wiped the tears from his face. "They pulled out big black sticks and beat him all over. I was really scared because they were killing Father, but if I yelled they'd kill me, too."

"Why didn't you run for help?" Macha inquired. "There is an opening at the back of the loft and a ladder to escape."

Demetrios shook his head. "I...I don't know. I was afraid they'd see me, and I couldn't move. My hands and feet wouldn't let me. I should have, shouldn't I?"

Macha sighed. The poor boy had been terrified, and now he was experiencing pangs of guilt. "Go on, Demetrios."

"I saw one of them take a torn sheet," he rasped. "A scroll I think, from father's tunic."

What scroll? Her mind raced ahead. What would Nicanor be doing with a scroll? Did it contain a list of conspirators or was it nothing at all? Is that why they killed him? Mother Goddess, don't tell me he was involved with the plot? My loyal Nicanor? It can't be!

"Can you tell me more about this scroll, Demetrios?" Macha asked.

"Only that it's torn and made of parchment—the kind I've written my lessons on."

"Then what happened?"

Demetrios face tightened and he snuffled. "They threw father's body into the stall with Apollo, and they walked away like nothing happened. But Apollo reared and...and I thought he would trample Father, but he didn't. It was like he knew he was dead. He just lunged back and forth, and kicked at the sides of the stall."

Again, he wept, and Macha stroked his straight black hair.

After another minute, he looked at Macha and struggled on. "I was too scared to move for a long time. But when they were gone I got brave enough to leave. I found Titus and told him."

"That's right," Titus said. "I did the right thing, didn't I, Mama?"

"Yes, you did," Macha answered quietly. "You are a good son."

Young Titus smiled and vigorously nodded.

"Now I must ask Demetrios some more questions, so I need you to be still for a while. Can you do that?"

"Yes, Mama."

"Good." She turned back to Demetrios. "You said the taller of the two was scarred and big jawed," Macha said. "Do you remember anything else about him or the other one?"

"They wore homespun tunics and breeches," Demetrios answered. "I think they were Gauls. The other man was pale, and had a pushed-in nose. They looked like gladiators—like the ones I've seen marching from their school to the arena for the games. That's all I remember. I was so scared, and I kept thinking about my father."

"Why didn't you tell Metrobius?"

"I don't like him, and father didn't either. And I was afraid he wouldn't believe me. You do, don't you?"

Demetrios breathed louder and faster. He appeared to be seeking an answer from Macha. She knew he wasn't lying.

"I know you're telling the truth, Demetrios," Macha assured him. She gave the boy a warm hug and noticed a couple little strands of straw in his hair. "You did a brave thing hiding and remaining quiet. There was nothing you could have done for your father. I know he would be proud of you for telling me. I'll see that he's cared for. You'll be cared for, too, Demetrios. You'll always have a place in this house, I promise."

"Why did they kill my father, Mistress? He wouldn't hurt anybody?"

"I don't know why, but I intend to find out." Macha believed she knew but couldn't tell the boy.

Shadows from the afternoon sun crept through the open bedroom doorway, crossing the room which darkened with each passing minute. It was time to round up the other slaves and question them at once, but Macha was exhausted—mentally drained. She would feel better if she stopped now for the evening meal and interviewed them after she finished eating.

Macha dismissed Demetrios, reminding him it was time for supper. She warned him again, before sending him to the slave quarters, not to tell anyone he had seen his father murdered.

"Can I go with Demetrios, Mama?" Young Titus asked.

"No, you stay here. You'll have to wash up for supper in a few minutes."

"Oh, Mama, can't I be with him? He's so sad."

"I know, but you can see him after we eat."

He jutted out his lower lip.

"Here, come to me," Macha said. A hesitant grin flashed across Titus' face. He jumped off the bed and leaped onto her lap, nearly knocking the wind out of her. She recovered and embraced him.

"You can sit with me for a few minutes if you promise to be quiet. I have to think about some things."

"Yes, Mama, I promise."

As she stroked young Titus' curly red hair, Macha's thoughts returned to Nicanor's death. If the murderers were Gauls as Demetrios described, than finding them could be a nearly impossible task. Half the population of the province, including Mediolanum, were Gauls. The city had been founded by their ancestors four hundred years earlier.

What about the scroll? Where did Nicanor get the parchment, and was it important? Did it list the conspirators or nothing? The assassins would not have murdered Nicanor unless there was something substantial about the list, perhaps incriminating evidence. Right now, that was all speculation. She had nothing to go on. The list, if that's what he saw, would further substantiate this fact. But the roll had vanished. The arrest of her husband had distracted the authorities from the real conspirators. Once he was executed, the security around Emperor Vespasian would loosen enough to more easily assassinate him. What puzzled Macha was how they expected to reach the Emperor without help from his household troops, the Praetorian Guard, or others he trusted.

It all seemed too complex for Macha, her suspicions pure speculation. For a moment she doubted her ideas made any sense. She had to convince Bassus to investigate further. He knew the intrigues of the palace all too well and believed anything was possible.

"I'm glad I didn't have to go to the stables," young Titus said, snapping Macha out of her thoughts. "I'm afraid of going there."

"I understand, darling," Macha answered, as she brushed back the hair drooping over her son's forehead. "One of these days you'll have to get over your fear."

The year before, she remembered, a feral cat had attacked Titus in one of the horse's stalls. He had found and attempted to pet her litter of newborn kittens nesting in a recess behind the manger. Instantly, the cat pounced on his hands, and bit once savagely and clawed his fingers and thumbs. One thumb required three stitches to close

58

the deep wound. The nail split and never grew back. He had not returned to the stables since the incident.

Macha smiled at her son. "It's time for you to clean up." He scampered from the room.

As soon as Titus left, Macha summoned Metrobius.

"My lady, the slaves are waiting in library."

"And by now they must be hungry like me," Macha said. "I had not realized how late it had grown. Reassemble them after the evening meal is finished."

A sense of relief seemed to cross his ferret face. "Yes, Mistress."

"But again, you are to say nothing as to the reason. Do you understand?"

"Yes, my lady."

After supper, Macha interviewed the slaves one at a time in the library. They all swore they hadn't seen any strangers on the grounds. She wasn't satisfied with their answers--something was missing, but she didn't know what. When she finished, Macha sent a message asking Senator Bassus to question them the following day. As a veteran soldier of many campaigns, he had interrogated hundreds of prisoners-of-war and short of torture would be far more *persuasive* than she.

* * * * *

The next morning came too early for Macha. Gradually, her eyes adjusted to the dawning light creeping through the latticed mahogany door. The growing sunlight illuminated the pastoral paintings etched into the upper half of the bed cubicle's walls and caught her attention. Softened by the copper tone of the wall's lower sections, the bucolic settings seemed out of place after yesterday's dreadful events.

Macha felt Titus' side of the bed, cold and empty. When he wasn't on campaign, she was used to snuggling next to him in the early morning hours, and now he was gone. Stiffly, she climbed out of the covers. Feeling empty inside, she shook out of the clinging woolen nightshift and drank tepid water from a silver cup embossed with a crown of daisies. She missed him more than she believed possible.

Macha looked up as Edain entered the room. She wore a beige chiton and carried a bronze pan of warm water and a blue woolen towel for Macha's morning ablutions. Dark rings surrounded the eyes of Edain's usually pleasant face, now glum. The slave lit the charcoal-filled iron brazier, resting on three fawn-shaped legs, and rearranged Macha's combs, ivory hairpins, and bronze mirror on a table at the foot of the bed.

"You couldn't sleep either, Edain?"

She shook her head. "No, Mistress, I kept thinking about Nicanor." She placed the pan and towel on the dressing table near the bed.

"Tragic."

Cupping her face in her hands, Edain burst into tears.

Macha motioned for the young woman to sit next to her. She placed an arm about her shoulder.

"I'm sorry Edain. I should have realized what a terrible loss this must be for you."

Edain barely nodded as she attempted to dry her tear-stained face. Macha handed her a cloth for her nose. For a moment the room lapsed into silence as Macha pondered Edain's grief.

"You two were lovers, weren't you?"

"Yes, Mistress," Edain sniffled. "He wanted to marry me, but slaves are forbidden the right. Now it doesn't matter."

"But it does. You'll have his memories, and what's more important—he was a good man. I'll miss him, too."

Edain eyes darted to the cubicle entrance. "Mistress," she whispered, "I couldn't say anything before." She took a small crumpled piece of parchment from inside her waistband, and handed it to Macha. "I thought you might know what the writing said."

With trembling fingers, Macha unfolded the tattered-edged document. "Where did you find this?"

"When I was preparing Nicanor's body for burial, Mistress. I removed his clothing and found it tucked in a secret pocket inside his tunic."

"I don't recognize this handwriting," Macha said as she scanned the text. "It's in Greek." It must be part of the scroll Demetrios had seen, she thought. What was Nicanor doing with the scroll? Why didn't he tell me? Was he involved with the plotters after all? I can't believe it! Why did the assassins kill him? Did he know too much? Did they think he might be arrested and tortured to reveal the conspirators?

A jolt shot through Macha's body. On one corner was a crudely drawn picture of an eagle holding a wreath crown in its talons. Not only did the eagle represent the power of Rome but also the legions, without whose support no Emperor could rule. Macha recalled passing the legion chapel with Bassus and seeing the eagle proudly displayed by Legion 1st Italica. Somebody from the legion must be involved in the plot against the Emperor, but whom? The wreath had to symbolize the Emperor Vespasian. What else could it mean? There were dozens of officers in the 1st Legion. But officers from other legions might be involved and perhaps, gods forbid, the Praetorian Guard, which had been loyal to him. Why had the picture of the eagle been drawn? Was it supposed to be the symbol of the conspirators and their intentions against the Emperor? The possibilities were endless.

She scanned the names. They were abbreviated, and she didn't recognize any of them. Some type of code denoted their meaning. One name was underlined and another circled. A third name was lined out. A fourth name or word contained only the first two letters, the Greek equivalent of the Latin VE. Were the names related to the plot? Perhaps the one crossed out belonged to someone who backed out of the conspiracy. But the VE could mean anything.

"Edain, what do you know about this?" Macha asked. She pointed to the list.

The slave gulped and pressed her lips together. "I just found it on him. I can't read." She looked about.

"Don't be afraid to tell me the truth," Macha said in a quiet voice. "I believe there is more to this than you are telling me."

"That's all I know, Mistress."

"Edain," Macha said in a firmer voice, "you have never lied to me before. This is not the time to start. Do you like being my hand-maiden?"

She nodded. "Yes, Mistress, very much."

"Have I not always treated you well?"

"You are very kind."

Macha narrowed her green eyes. "Then why do you hesitate in telling me the truth?"

Edain kneeled before Macha and bowed her head. Her ruddy face tightened, as if holding back further tears. Her lips pressed into a thin line. She shook her head. "Forgive me, Mistress, I'm afraid," she answered a few seconds later.

"Look at me, Edain."

The slave raised her head, her eyes darting from side to side.

"What are you afraid of?" Macha asked.

Edain stammered. "The ones who k...killed Nicanor will kill me."

"Why?"

"Because if they learn that I found the parchment and gave it to you, they will think I know what's in it."

"Do they know who you are, and do you know what's in the parchment?"

"They don't know me, and I can't read. Nicanor wouldn't tell me."

"Why didn't he tell you?"

Edain glanced to the bed-cubicle opening and back to Macha. "Because he stole the list."

The breath caught in Macha's throat. She rasped. "What! Where did he steal it and from whom?"

"He wouldn't tell me." She shook her head. "He said it was too dangerous for me to know. I could be arrested and tortured, if I wasn't killed first."

"What was he going to do with this information?"

"I don't know, I swear it. I wish he had brought it to you. He would still be alive."

"So do I, Edain. I hope that's what he had meant to do. His information might have vindicated my husband. I do hope Nicanor was not a spy."

"Oh, no, Mistress, I'm sure he wasn't. He respected you too much, and so do I."

"I believe you." Or did she? Had Nicanor meant to give the names to her? If so, why did he wait so long? Had he stolen the parchment while she was visiting Titus at the stockade? Was he part of the plot but changed his mind? I just cannot see him betraying Titus and the Emperor,

Macha thought. Whatever the truth, Macha would have to solve the mystery of the parchment herself and see if she could clear Titus. To do otherwise meant losing everything she held dear and unthinkable bondage to Falco.

"I don't know if this had anything to do with Nicanor's death," Edain said, jolting Macha from her thoughts, "but I saw Metrobius leave early yesterday morning, riding in the direction of town. I thought he was going on weekly business as usual, but he returned about an hour before Nicanor was killed. Maybe he had nothing to do with his death, but now, I'm not sure. I've never trusted Metrobius and neither did Nicanor."

Macha told Edain to stand. "What about Jason?"

Edain frowned, the nostrils of her button nose flaring. "Jason is nothing. He hated Nicanor. Metrobius warned Jason to stay away, but he keeps looking for the chance to see me."

Macha got to her feet, shook out her night shift, and stepped to the dressing table. She splashed the luke-warm water on her face, toweled off and dropped the cloth by the bowl. She turned to Edain, who had not moved, and studied her tear-stained face. "You know I ordered him to stay away from you after we returned from Helena's the other night."

"Yes, Mistress. Now that Nicanor is gone, I hope he will continue to obey you."

"He will, if he is wise."

Edain nodded.

"Do you think Jason would betray my husband?"

"I don't think so. He isn't clever enough. I think he is only interested in gaining his freedom so he can be a horse trainer."

Macha pointed to the long work tunic hanging in the latticed cupboard used for storing clothes. "Bring it to me, Edain," she said. She took off her shift and Edain assisted her in pulling on the tunic. She sat before the table and motioned to the slave to comb her hair. As Edain pulled the whale-bone comb through her thick tresses she asked, "What about Metrobius?"

63

"I don't know, Mistress. All I know is Nicanor didn't trust him. I can't say exactly why, but I don't trust him either."

She winced slightly as her hand-maiden gently combed out the tangles. Was Metrobius or Nicanor the spy Macha had suspected to be among the household slaves? Mother Goddess, what a terrible thought. Metrobius had been her trusted steward for years, and Nicanor an extremely loyal servant and loving father. She prayed Edain was wrong about her house steward and that she was in error about Nicanor's part in the plot.

What shall I do next?

CHAPTER 9

A Matter of Torture

Late in the morning, the day after the murder, Macha passed through the hallway on the way to the study. A slave hurried towards her and announced the arrival of Senator Bassus. Macha paused. So soon? Was something amiss? Nevertheless, any news would be better than none.

"Send him in; I'll wait for him here. Macha stopped in front of the pink marbled *impluvium*, the small pool in the center of the atrium.

"Thank gods you're here, Senator Bassus," Macha said, as he approached her. "I couldn't say it in the message I sent you, but I may have information proving Titus's innocence." They turned and strolled across the reception area toward the study. Slaves hurried about their morning duties, cleaning and dusting, their chattering dropping to whispers as Macha and Bassus passed.

"Is this related to Nicanor's death?" He asked.

"It is."

The Senator removed his helmet and rubbed the red line across his forehead. The clattering on the mosaic floor of his red hobnailed boots echoed down the corridor.

"For your sake, the information better be good—the outlook for your husband is very grim," Bassus said. "The day after tomorrow he'll be escorted to Genua, where he'll set sail for Ostia and Rome."

A sudden chill ran through Macha's body. For a moment she crossed her arms and braced her shoulders. She had thought it would be at least five days before Titus was moved. "Great Mother Goddess, then what I've learned is more important than ever, but I can't tell you out here. You never know who's listening."

In the library Macha and Bassus sat on stools built with crossed bronze legs. She peered at the tall senator

65

across an ornately carved table, its wood encrusted with coral from the coast of Gaul.

"Nicanor's death was no accident—he was murdered," Macha said.

Bassus leaned forward, placed an elbow on the table, and rested his chin on his thumb and forefingers. For a few seconds he studied Macha. "Where did you receive that news?"

Why is the Senator looking at me like that? Macha puzzled. Does he think I'm lying? She told Bassus about what Demetrios had seen.

"Are you positive the boy is telling the truth?" Bassus inquired. "We don't know what was in the scroll, if anything."

"I'm certain he is being truthful. But the scroll must be related to the conspirators. Why else would anyone murder Nicanor? He must have known it was related to Titus' arrest."

"Yes, and it may have shown that Titus was involved."

"I refuse to believe that."

"Your belief is not enough." Bassus dropped his hand to his knee, and straightened in his chair. "You know children sometimes get facts mixed up, or allow their imaginations to get in the way of the truth."

"Demetrios is a bright boy, and not one given to fantasies. Watching his own father being clubbed to death was no figment of his imagination. Nicanor's tunic wasn't torn by a trampling horse." Macha didn't tell Bassus about the fragment of parchment with the names. For now, something told her to withhold that information. How do I know the Senator is not involved, she thought. This is madness, I'm allowing my imagination to play tricks with my mind.

"But that isn't all," she continued, "This may have been coincidental, but my slave, Edain, saw Metrobius leave early yesterday morning and return about an hour before Nicanor's murder. She and Nicanor never trusted him." Macha also informed Bassus about Jason lurking in the shadows of her house after returning from Helena's home.

66

Bassus exhaled. "That certainly puts a different twist on the matter. I will question Edain, Metrobius, and Jason, thoroughly, as well as the rest of your slaves."

"Please promise me one thing," Macha said.

"If I can. What is it?"

Macha clasped her slender hands together on the desk.

"Demetrios mustn't be involved in the investigation. I don't want the child subjected to the horrors of the rack or hot irons—he'd never survive. You must find evidence another way."

"I make no promises, but I'll do what I can. Bring the slaves here, one at a time. I'll question them now, alone."

* * * * *

When Bassus finished his investigation, he sent for Macha.

She returned to the library and took her place behind the desk. "Did you have any luck?" she asked.

"I have placed Metrobius under arrest. My retainers are taking him to the stockade as we speak."

"Metrobius? Is he one of the conspirators?"

"That remains to be seen, but after questioning your slave woman, Edain, and the groom, I called your steward back for further questioning. His answers were too evasive, enough to have him held for further questioning. Although I didn't mention the scroll, I got the distinct impression he may know why Nicanor had it. I can't say more than that right now. I may be wrong."

"Then you don't believe Jason had anything to do with the murder?"

"No. He wasn't anywhere near the scene. When I asked him about the other night when you arrived home, he swore he had been waiting for hours to see your slave, Edain. He's a bit of a rake but not a traitor. He admitted to stalking nearly everyone of your slave women."

Macha shivered and considered selling Jason. "I find it hard to believe Metrobius would have plotted against my husband. He has been my steward for years."

"That may be why he is involved. Does he not have access to nearly every part of the house and farm?" Bassus motioned with both hands as if it were obvious.

"Yes, but—"

"All the more reason to question him further."

"But he'll be tortured." She shook her head, frowning.

Bassus narrowed his large deep-set eyes and seemed to stare right through Macha. "We've been through this before. I regret that I must use my powers as Legate. Although Metrobius is your property, the treason laws allow the State to confiscate slaves who may have knowledge of crimes against the Emperor and question them by torture."

"Must you? I know he left yesterday without telling me where he was going, but is that enough to place him on the rack?"

"It is and we will."

Speechless, gripping her hands tighter than before, Macha drew back in her chair. Even if Metrobius had betrayed her family, she found the idea of torture too revolting for words. It was as if Bassus had betrayed her, even if what he did was legal under Roman law. The Senator had been her family's oldest and dearest friend since she and her parents arrived in Rome in chains twenty years before. A chill made the downy hair on her arms stand on end. Her hands perspired. She unlocked her fingers and, unladylike, wiped them on her green stola.

"Will Demetrios suffer the same fate? You did not mention that he was arrested."

"No, he can stay here with you—I have no need to torture any child. Metrobius will be enough. He knows more than he told us."

Macha sighed. Thank Mother Goddess, Demetrios was safe for the time being.

"I don't enjoy extracting a confession by torture, Macha," Bassus continued. "But the Emperor's life is at stake, and so is your husband's. I'm duty bound to learn the truth, whatever the source. Unfortunately, because Metrobius is a slave, his testimony is only valid when given under extreme duress."

"But what if he truly doesn't know anything?"

"Then he will be released."

"Yes, and you and your sadist rack-masters will send back a broken and crippled man. And we still won't know if the scroll the assassins killed him for was of any importance." Macha realized the fragment found by Edain may be a part of that original document. If so, may prove to be invaluable.

"Pray it does not come to that. However, I will do anything to protect the Emperor. Believe me, I take no pleasure in this task."

Macha sat mute, weighing the situation, thinking she had little choice in the matter. At least little Demetrios has been spared, she thought. I must trust Bassus no matter what reservations I have. He is the only one who has the power to gain Titus's release.

"Do what you must," she said. "I only pray he tells you the *real* truth."

* * * * *

Macha went into the courtyard with Bassus and stayed until he rode away with his Praetorian Guard retainers. Dust churned from the hooves of their departing mounts leaving a choking cloud in the noonday heat. Young Titus raced to his mother as she stepped from the covered walkway bordering the quad. His red hair fell over his forehead and half hid the streak of dirt beneath.

"I saw the soldiers take away Metrobius, Mama. Why did they do that?"

"He's going to be questioned about the death of Demetrios' father."

"But you were going to keep it a secret."

"No one except Senator Bassus knows what Demetrios saw. As long as you and Demetrios don't tell anyone else, it will remain a secret, do you understand?"

"Yes, Mama, but what about Metrobius?"

"The Senator has other ways of questioning Metrobius without telling him Demetrios saw anything."

"Good, I'm glad it's Metrobius—I don't like him!"

"Titus!"

He darted down the corridor and into the house.

Macha wasn't ready to return. She viewed the empty, silent courtyard. It was siesta time, stifling heat sucking the life out of all activity. Even the noisy birds nesting in the poplar trees by one corner were hushed. She leaned against a narrow fluted pillar, the hard marble edges pushing into her back, and pondered the events surrounding Nicanor's murder.

She recalled how Pollia and her husband, Julius Pedius, had arrived in Mediolanum about a week before Titus' arrest. He had been inspecting his estates in the Po Valley. But it seemed strange they were returning to Rome right after her husband's incarceration. Did Pollia have anything to do with Titus' arrest or involvement? Doubtful. She and her husband seemed too wealthy to dabble in imperial intrigue. Macha had heard Pedius had the ear of the Emperor. Pedius said he was selling a portion of his lands to cover recent financial losses. Pollia said the trip was a good excuse to visit her dear friends in Mediolanum. Perhaps it was except for the hostility Pollia had shown Macha.

As far as Macha was concerned, that didn't explain who assassinated Nicanor, or where the murderers were hiding. Even if arrested, their confessions would probably reveal little. At best all she could get for proving the slave's murder was a monetary settlement to replace his loss. Not only had the truth about the conspiracy been harder to prove but far more dangerous than she had expected. The truth lay somewhere deep within the tangled ball of lies.

* * * * *

The following morning Macha received a message to expect Senator Bassus for an official visit later in the day. The courier provided no further details. His call was too soon after Metrobius's arrest, and she was certain it concerned her steward.

In the meantime, Macha went to the library, a simply furnished office, where she conducted all planning for the household's daily activities. As husband, Titus was head of the family, but it was she who kept the villa running like a well-greased chariot wheel.

She summoned Zeno, the assistant steward.

The young slender Greek arrived, bowed and stood quietly waiting for Macha to speak.

"I don't know how long Metrobius will be gone," Macha said, "but in the meantime, you are now in charge of overseeing all slaves of my household."

"Thank you, Mistress, I shall do my best," he answered in a soft voice. "It is regrettable about Metrobius. I hope he returns; I have learned much from him."

Macha nodded. She stood and came around the front of her desk. "Come with me, I'm going to make the rounds."

They strolled outdoors and headed for the kitchen, part of the outbuilding complex, the *villa rustica*. Macha consulted with the chef about the daily menu, made some minor changes, and inspected the kitchen for cleanliness. Satisfied, she and Zeno departed and went to the spinning room next to the sheep pen.

Waiting outside, three slave women arrived just ahead of Macha and the steward to spend the day spinning wool. The oldest of the women had brought a large basket of raw wool from the storage area. Macha took out a set of keys, hanging from a leather thong, from a pocket inside her long work tunic, and unlocked the door. Inside, she took a portable scale from a table in the corner and weighed the fleece. She told Zeno to write down the amount on his wax tablet. That evening she would return to make sure the spun yarn matched the original weight.

From the spinning room, Macha and Zeno hiked to the granary and food storage rooms at the far end of the compound where another slave waited. Unlocking the door, the three entered and Macha inspected the large goat-skin sack from which wheat had been withdrawn the day before. She checked the amount listed in her scrolled ledger against the amount ground into flour the day before, and ordered Zeno to place the bag on a hanging scale. The weight still matched the amount withdrawn. Recent problems with slave thievery had forced her to double-check all withdrawals of wheat and other supplies.

As Macha and Zeno left the granary, a slave hurried forward and announced that Senator Bassus had arrived. Macha told the slave she would see the Senator right away. It was an hour before noon.

Macha entered the library and found Bassus waiting for her. She took a seat.

"I have grave news, Macha," Bassus said, as he sat across the desk from her. He avoided her piercing emerald eyes.

71

"Don't tell me Metrobius was killed under torture!"

"Nothing of the sort happened."

Macha slumped in her chair, relieved for a second.

"Unfortunately," he resumed, "Metrobius died sometime last night from food poisoning."

"Food poisoning?" Exhaling, Macha leaned over the desk and slapped her palms on the hardened surface. "Great Mother Goddess, how could that be possible? Are you sure that caused his death?"

"Absolutely, I regret to say." Bassus eyes met hers and appeared full of sorrow. "He ate the same food as the other prisoners in the guardhouse—legionaries being punished. A couple of them also died, and another is near death."

"Oh, no, poor Metrobius." Putting her hand to her face, Macha quietly began to weep. First Nicanor, and now her steward. She wondered whether this was an accident or something more sinister? His death seemed so senseless. Bassus patiently sat in silence.

She had to bring herself under control. This was neither the time nor the place to grieve. Pulling out a silk cloth from the fold in her stola, she wiped her eyes. She knew the tears had smeared the silver antimony eye shadow, turning her face into a frightful mess, but it didn't matter.

"I'm sorry, Senator Bassus," Macha said.

"I understand," he answered. "He was a faithful servant."

Was he? "Where did the food come from?" Macha asked.

"The mess hall—it's the same eaten by the troops."

"Did anyone else but the prisoners die?" Not Titus, she prayed. Surely, Senator Bassus would have told me first.

"No."

Relieved, she asked, "Don't you think it's odd that no one in the mess hall suffered the same symptoms?"

"Not especially," Bassus replied. "The prisoners wait until after the troops eat before they're fed. They get what's left over. Perhaps the food spoiled before they ate. You know how common food poisoning is."

"Then why didn't my husband die?"

"Important prisoners, politicians, and officers like Titus receive their meals from the officer's mess. The rations are of better quality, and they're fed at the same time as the officers."

True, death by food poisoning was all too common. Macha recalled the year before when five members of a family she knew in Mediolanum died at the same time within a few hours after taking the evening meal. But she wasn't convinced the food killed Metrobius. Somebody deliberately wanted him out of the way. Did he, in fact, have any connection with the conspirators? Did Nicanor and Metrobius know? If so, someone went out of the way to murder both of them. For good measure it was made to appear as accident with other prisoners dying in the process. Perhaps her husband had been meant to be murdered as well. Perhaps whoever did this had not known he would have been fed separately and at a different time. Thank goodness for that. She speculated the conspirators feared Metrobius would confess under torture and that was why he was poisoned.

So far no one knew what little Demetrios had witnessed, and Macha was hopeful no one would discover the truth. If that happened, his life would be in grave danger, and perhaps even the life of her son.

She had no proof and only a fragmented parchment with a few names and the picture of an eagle, and five black splinters removed from Apollo's hoof and Nicanor's skull. They were meaningless without corroborating proof. But she had to tell Bassus, even if it meant her remarks were considered the rantings of a hysterical woman—something men were all too ready to believe.

"Senator Bassus, I have something to show you." She pulled from within her stola the fragment of parchment and handed to him.

CHAPTER 10

A Revelation?

Bassus scanned the document, his face expressionless, except for a split second when he flinched.

"I wonder if these names are in the scroll taken from Nicanor?" Macha said. She explained that Edain discovered the torn parchment, hidden in Nicanor's clothing while preparing the body for burial. But where did he get them and from whom?

Frowning, Bassus said, "Your slave could have obtained these names anywhere."

Macha's heart sunk. "What about the picture of the eagle—symbol of the legions?"

"There are thirty legions—it could be any of them." He crinkled his bushy eye-brows together as he studied Macha.

"But the First Italica is the only one based in Italy. Wouldn't that be the most likely?" she asked.

"Perhaps, but the symbol of the eagle in itself is not enough proof. Remember, it's also the symbol of Rome's power. More investigation is required to confirm that, one way or another."

"But without the backing of the legions, no emperor has power. Perhaps this will convince you," Macha said. She pulled out of the fold in her stola a couple of black splinters she had found on Nicanor's body. She held back the rest. Something told her she might need them later. "Do you remember the black clubs Demetrios said were used by the assassins to kill his father? I found these splinters on his skull." She handed them to the Senator.

Bassus carefully examined the pieces and touched the ends, nicking a finger tip. He looked back at Macha. "This wood is very hard. It's either ebony or walnut. A club made of this is expensive. To leave these splinters behind, I'm surprised the assailants did not literally smash in your slave's head."

"It was horrible enough."

"The chance of finding the weapon or weapons matching these splinters is remote, but it's enough to warrant further investigation. I was planning to return to Rome; now, I will leave sooner than later. My suspicions tell me that's where I'll find the answers."

"Then I'm going to Rome, too," Macha said. "I'll not stay here."

"No, you cannot go."

"But you'll need my help."

Bassus narrowed his eyes. "I could place you under house arrest."

"You wouldn't!" Macha couldn't believe her ears. "What kind of man are you? How can deny me passage when my husband could die!" Did Bassus know more than he was telling?

The Senator frowned. For a moment he seemed to ponder Macha's words before arriving at a decision. He snorted. "Knowing you as I do, you would escape and follow anyway and get killed in the process."

"Honestly, do you really believe that would happen?" Macha shuddered.

"Indeed. Whoever is behind this plot will attempt to keep you from interfering, even if you stayed here. The only way I can protect you is take you with me to Genua. From there we'll take ship for Ostia and barge up the Tiber to Rome," Bassus said. "Word would get out soon enough that you've gone to Rome, but under my protection you'll be safe."

Her fingers touched her cheek. "What about my son and Demetrios? Won't they be in danger?"

"Take them to your sister-in-law, Helena. They'll be in no danger there."

"Thank you, Senator Bassus," Macha answered with a sigh of relief.

"However," Bassus growled. He squared his aging but still powerful shoulders and motioned with a big leathery hand. "You will leave the investigation to me. Rome is too dangerous for a woman to make inquiries on her own. If you interfere, I will be forced to place you under arrest for your own safety. Is that understood?"

"I promise I won't do anything rash." She knew she was lying. The Senator sounded just like her husband.

"See that you don't," Bassus said.

"In the meantime, once you place your son with Helena, I'll see that roving cavalry patrols are assigned to the area around their home," Bassus said.

"I'm afraid someone will be suspicious about keeping Demetrios at Helena's home and not mine."

"It's doubtful anyone will pay attention to the moving of a slave child."

"Unless someone knows he witnessed his father's murder. I can't take the chance of leaving him at my house while I'm in Rome."

"Do what you think is necessary, but be ready to leave at dawn on the day after tomorrow," Bassus ordered.

* * * * *

The following day, about noon, Macha was returning to her villa in a canopied wagon from Helena's home. Earlier, that morning, she had taken Young Titus and little Demetrios there.

As she sat in the rear cushioned seat, Macha reflected on the tearful departure. How can I leave my son, she thought, even Demetrios, for who knows how long? She wiped her tear-stained face with a lavender-scented cloth as she slumped on her seat barely holding the padded iron arm rest, hardly noticing the choking dust swirling up from the bumpy road.

Macha wiped her face again as she remembered telling the boys, late yesterday, that she was going on a long journey to Rome and they would be staying with Aunt Helena and Uncle Cnidius. Young Titus wept as the clung and begged her to stay. Even Demetrios, who stood nearby began to cry, seemingly terrified she was about to depart. She nearly gave in, the thought of leaving the children in possible danger was unbearable.

Macha had steeled herself and calmly explained that Papa was in trouble and she had to travel to Rome to help him. Young Titus wanted to help, but Macha said only she and Senator Bassus could go. He and Demetrios would be well cared for by his aunt and uncle. For the moment, Macha's reassurances seemed to ease their concerns. But the weeping started again once she had dropped them off at Helena's home and was about to depart.

In agony, Macha didn't want to leave but couldn't let the children see her own suffering. Promising that she would return with Papa as soon as possible, she left them standing at the front door with Helena, and held back the tears until she was on the road heading home. She knew a number of Roman matrons who took extensive journeys and left their little ones at home in the care of nurse maids. She never thought that was the right thing to do. Children belonged with their mothers. Macha had prayed to Mother Goddess Anu she made the right decision and would never have to go through such an ordeal with Young Titus again.

Helena and Cnidius Rufus had reassured her that the children would be safe and extra security precautions would be taken at their home. Her sister-and brother-in-law knew about the deaths of Metrobius and Nicanor, but Macha informed the two about what Demetrios had witnessed and swore them to secrecy.

As Macha's carriage jolted along the dusty driveway leading to her villa, she glanced out the open side and spotted a cloud of dust churning in front of her home. As the wagon drew closer, she saw what appeared to be a *Turma* of thirty armed cavalryman lingering by the entry to the main courtyard, along with Senator Bassus' dozen scarlet- cloaked mounted Praetorian Guardsmen. She noticed nearly as many spare horses and six pack mules herded by a number of grooms. What are they doing here? They look as if they are going on campaign!

At the head of the chained mail spatha-wielding troopers was the arrogant Pomponius Appius. Lately, her thoughts had been so much on Nicanor, his murder, and possible part in the plot, she had forgotten about Appius. She could not help but think he was involved. And now, he was to ride with them. Why?

Macha ordered her driver to pull up beside the tribune. "What is the meaning of this intrusion, Tribune Appius?" Macha demanded. "Why are you here?"

"Ask the Senator yourself," the craggy face Roman snarled. "He's inside."

Macha hurried into the Atrium where she found Bassus, in full uniform, handing a wax tablet to a slave. He turned, and upon seeing her, exhaled as if in relief.

"What is wrong, Senator Bassus? Why the soldiers?"

"Thank Jove you've returned," Bassus answered. "I was about to leave without you after finishing this note." He nodded to the wax tablet. "Titus left with an armed escort for Genua last night."

She jolted. "Last night? Why didn't you send me word immediately?"

"I only learned about it at mid-morning. I sent messengers here and to your sister-in-law. Obviously, they missed you. Valens took it upon himself, without informing me, to send your husband earlier than planned."

"How could he?"

"It's called abuse of authority, and I relieved him of his command. Had I more time, I would have court-martialed him. Now, that will have to wait until after I am finished in Rome."

"Do you think General Valens will just sit back and not interfere any further?"

"For his sake, he better not. I have my suspicions about his part in this matter, but not enough proof to place him under arrest. Have you finished packing?" Bassus glanced in the direction of the hallway that lead to Macha's bed cubicle.

"Almost."

"You have fifteen minutes to gather up your things. Take only what is absolutely necessary for the journey. You'll be traveling by horse, not carriage. We have no time to waste if we are going to reach Titus before he sails from Genua."

CHAPTER II

A Little Horse Sense is Required

Prior to leaving, Macha changed from her cumbersome stola and gown to a tartan tunic and padded breeches. Running half-way up her calves and tied in front with leather thongs, a pair of cow-hide booted sandals over light woolen socks protected her feet.

Edain trekked behind Macha along the mosaic tiled hallway to the outer yard. The slave carried Macha's leather satchel stuffed with changes of clothing, including three dresses, small silver boxes containing red ocher and silver antimony for her face and eyes. Titus kept an army issue bag handy for use on short trips. Once in Rome Macha could purchase additional clothing and borrow from the wardrobe kept for guests staying at Senator Bassus' home.

As she quickly packed, Macha found herself already missing the children. She was also uncomfortable about Bassus' interrogation of the slaves two days before. Despite their denials, she didn't believe they all told the truth. Although Metrobius was taken into custody, she had no doubt his death by food poisoning was murder. Did he know who murdered Nicanor and more importantly, why? Someone within the garrison must have known why Metrobius was arrested and arranged for his so-called food poisoning. The question was, who? She hated leaving with that question unanswered.

Because Edain and Nicanor had been lovers, Macha ruled out the young woman's involvement. She suspected nearly everyone else in the household. Edain couldn't read, but knew the parchment Nicanor had stolen might be important and had intended to give it to Macha. Or did he?

Macha motioned for Edain to stop. She scanned both directions of the hallway—empty.

"Edain," Macha said in a low voice, "I can trust no one in the household but you. I need your help."

The slave froze, her pursed mouth slightly parted as she cleared her throat. "Anything, Mistress—I'm honored."

"As long as I'm away, you're to keep your eyes open for any suspicious activity around the household. The same holds if you see strangers on or near our lands."

"Yes, Mistress. What shall I do if I see anything?"

"Seek out Lady Helena—you can trust her. She'll send word to me in Rome."

"May I say something, Mistress?"

Something about Edain's tone alerted Macha. "Of course."

"Forgive me, if you think I'm wrong, but Jason hated Metrobius and Nicanor." Edain bowed her head, the close-set eyes looking blankly at the ground. "I don't think he cares that both of them are dead."

Speechless, Macha stared at Edain. Did Jason play any part in either Nicanor's murder or that of Metrobius' death at the stockade? He was only a horse groom and stable slave. Edain had informed her earlier that Jason's only ambition was to be a freedman and a horse trainer. Under the circumstances she thought it strange Metrobius had been arrested and not Jason. Was he that good of a liar? Perhaps, he was.

"Are you saying Jason was involved with Nicanor's and Metrobius' deaths?"

Edain pulled the long flaxen hair away from her face. "Oh, no, Mistress, I have no proof but more than once I heard him say Nicanor was your favorite and Metrobius was the best of stewards."

"I treat everyone fairly."

"Of course, Mistress, but Jason has never liked them. Metrobius was always chasing him away from the house."

"As I have ordered him to do. What was he doing here this time?"

"He was looking for me."

Macha groaned. "Again, when I had forbidden him to see you?"

"He found me after Metrobius was arrested. He wants me for his woman. Now, that Nicanor and Metrobius are dead, he will be even more aggressive."

"That will stop. If I had more time, I would personally lock up Jason, but I don't. I will give instructions to Zeno, the new steward, to confine him to the isolation cellar for the next three days. There he will live only on bread crusts and water."

It was Macha's right to beat or kill her slaves, but she abhorred those practices as much as she did torture. She found punishing slaves by isolation, confining them to the deep and cold chamber below the slave quarters just as effective. They were stripped of all clothing and forced to sit and sleep on the dirt floor in total darkness. When released, they would stagger outside shivering, hungry and thirsty, and blinded by the light, falling to the ground begging forgiveness. Fortunately, Macha seldom had to resort to this form of discipline.

Edain shook her head. "Oh, please, Mistress, I'm afraid Jason will only make things worse when he is released and you are gone."

"No, Edain, he won't bother you, I promise."

"But, Mistress?"

"Edain," Macha said in a low but firm voice, "that is enough."

"Yes, Mistress, forgive me."

She nodded. "I will give orders to Zeno with instructions also to Juba, that once Jason is released, if he comes near the house again, he will be sold."

"I don't want to cause trouble, Mistress. Was I right in telling you about Jason?"

Her slender fingers touched Edain's rough hand and withdrew them. "You did no wrong, Edain. Unfortunately, I have to leave, but I will remember what you said to me. Don't forget to see Mistress Helena if you see anything suspicious."

Macha found Edain's accusations about Jason more upsetting than she realized. A stable slave involved in the killing of two of her most indispensable servants sounded too absurd to believe. Edain sounded like a grieving lover ready to accuse anyone of her loved one's murder. Petty

81

jealousies were all too common among slaves. Yet, she could not afford to brush off this possibility without someone at least keeping a watch for her.

She stopped and called to a passing slave to find, Zeno, and send him to her at once. Because of Metrobius' death, he was now her permanent house steward.

Within a minute, Zeno of Corinth arrived. Macha took the wax tablet and stylus he was carrying and quickly wrote a note to Helena. She explained Edain's suspicions and asked her to keep in contact with her hand maiden and a watch on her household. After Macha finished, she instructed Zeno to immediately confine Jason and deliver the message himself to Helena. At this point she entered the courtyard.

* * * * *

Macha caused a stir among the troopers when she appeared in the yard, trailed by Edain. Casually standing by their horses, the soldiers muttered among themselves, making no effort to hide their contempt.

"A woman wearing breeches is barbaric. It's not befitting a lady," Pomponius Appius remarked. He and Bassus stepped from the shaded entrance leading to the stables.

Bassus said nothing and knowingly grinned.

She expected this reaction by the troopers, especially to her heritage. Most Roman men preferred women to be helpless and submissive. No doubt they looked forward to seeing her bitten or tossed from her horse as she climbed into the saddle.

"You consider me a barbarian anyway, Tribune Pomponius Appius," Macha said. "What difference does my clothing make? Your troops wear trousers—are they barbarian?"

Macha had learned from her husband that each legion was assigned three hundred soldiers to its cavalry detachment who served as scouts and couriers. Unlike the *Alae*, foreign cavalry cohorts recruited from the provinces, these were Roman citizens.

She sniffed. Her people, the Celts, were better horse riders than the Romans.

The men glared at Macha and grumbled in low voices. Contrasting with the dull blue woolen breeches and red tunics worn by the horse soldiers, Macha was arrayed in a riot of vivid blue, green, and yellow plaids. Her scarlet hair added to the collage of colors.

"That's enough!" Bassus barked to the troopers. "You shall give Lady Macha Carataca the respect entitled to the wife of a Roman Officer." Instant silence fell over the turma and Bassus' Praetorian Escort.

Dust churned on a mild breeze, and the earthy smell of horse sweat and leather permeated Macha's delicate nostrils. For a few seconds she studied the horses ridden by the troopers. They were African and Spanish Barbs. The little horses, barely fifteen hands tall, traveled sixty to seventy miles a day on poor forage. Macha thanked the gods they were traveling in Italy. At least the detachment would stop at way stations to water and feed on decent fodder. Of course, the way stations would not have enough food and replacement mounts for an attachment this large. It was necessary to bring along the extra feed and horses to change off periodically so they wouldn't wear down.

"Did you bring a horse for me?" Macha asked Bassus. Her Arabs possessed the speed, but not the stamina of the Barbs.

"Over here," Pomponius Appius said. He nodded in the direction of the spare horses. "I found one especially for you, my lady."

His sarcastic tone alerted Macha. She glanced to Edain whose hand flew to her mouth.

Upon Appius' signal a trooper led a bright chestnut mare forward. A white blaze ran down the middle of her nose. For a cavalry mount, the confirmation of her body was better than average. The shoulders, limbs, and hind quarters were well-proportioned. Like most army horses, she didn't wear shoes. Fortunately, the hooves were well-trimmed and not split. The animal stood a good chance of surviving the trip to Genua without turning lame.

As Macha approached the mount, the mare flattened her ears, swung her head and lunged forward attempting to nip Macha. Instinctively, Macha stepped back to one side, barely avoiding the animal's big teeth. Turning to the horse she shouted, "Quit!" and smacked the animal across the soft muzzle of the nose with the palm of her hand.

Wide-eyed, the mare jolted backward, churning dust and clattering the metal pendants hanging from her leather breast collar. The trooper grabbed the reins behind the animal's mouth and after a brief struggle managed to settle her down.

The men hooted and bantered among themselves. "Feisty wench for a lady, isn't she?" one soldier said.

"No fear of horses in her," Macha heard another say. "Nor men either, I'll wager—must be Epona's sister." Macha smiled to herself. Being identified with the horse goddess, Epona, even in a jocular manner, was an honor.

Moving closer to the mount, Macha stared into its liquid brown eyes. "You need to learn manners, mare," she said evenly. She knew how to deal with cantankerous horses, and in her experience, mares were far worse than geldings.

"Is this your idea of a joke, Tribune Appius?" Bassus growled.

Appius took off his iron helmet and wiped the perspiration from his weather-beaten face. "No sir, I had no idea she was a biter. Maybe she's in heat—the horse I mean," he quickly added. He placed his helmet back on his head and glanced away from Bassus, his face crimson.

Bassus flicked his eyes to the spares and back to Appius, giving him a withering look. "Get her another mount."

"No, Senator, I'll keep her," Macha insisted. "So long as we're on the road, I'll make it my purpose to teach this beast to behave."

Macha faced the square-jawed soldier restraining the mount. "What's this mare's name, trooper?"

"Artemis, my lady," he replied.

She nodded. "Give me the reins." The animal certainly hadn't acted like the Greek goddess of motherhood and children. Macha snatched the leather reins from the soldier. Holding them tightly in one hand, she drew closer to Artemis and quietly stroked the coarse hair on her bony nose. The mare made no move to flee.

"Artemis, you and I shall become good friends, won't we —whether you like it or not."

A few seconds later Macha stepped away and confronted Appius. "As for you, Tribune, make no mistake about me, I'm an accomplished rider—and no, I'm not in heat either." She glared at the cavalrymen and then laughed, breaking the tension as they joined in.

Holding the reins Macha, grabbed the front pommels of the saddle, and pulled herself onto the mare. Her long legs dangled freely down each side of the horse. Edain handed Macha the goatskin pack and said a tearful good-bye.

Macha turned to Bassus, now mounted on his dark bay gelding. "I'm ready to ride, Senator."

CHAPTER 12

The Road to Genua

Escorted by Tribune Pomponius Appius, a turma of thirty cavalrymen and a dozen Praetorian Guardsmen, Macha and Senator Bassus departed the villa in a clatter of hooves, squeaking leather, and jangling pendants. Heading south, they streamed down the country road to the *Via Amelia,* churning up a cloud of hot choking dust.

"Why do we need such a heavy escort for the trip to Genua, Senator?" Macha asked. "I know you usually don't like large numbers."

"Your life may be in danger, Macha," Bassus answered.

She nodded. "I admit, I knew I might be. The question is, how much?"

Holding his reins in one hand, he wiped the sweat running down the side of his weathered face. He twisted about on his saddle and studied Macha with a look as if to say, *Can't you guess?* "Two of your slaves have been killed and word will spread soon enough that you are riding with me to the coast. There may be an attempt on your life. That's why I brought along extra troops."

Despite the afternoon heat, a chill raced through Macha's body. Until now, she had refused to believe she was in any danger. Her son and young Demetrios had been her concern. Now, she realized her insistence and interference into the investigation and prosecution of her husband, had marked her for death. Bassus words must be taken seriously.

"Why is Tribune Appius in charge of the squadron?" Macha asked. "He hates Titus and me."

"Despite what you think of Appius, he is a good commander and a fierce fighter. He'll guard you with his life."

Macha found this difficult to believe. "Is that the only reason he is in command? I know from Titus that a decurion usually leads the turma."

"Under normal circumstances that's correct, but Tribune Appius is coming along for reasons that at this time I can't divulge."

She shook her head and brushed back the loose scarlet strands of hair from her face. Macha wasn't satisfied with his answer but knew it was useless to question him further.

The afternoon sun crested over Mediolanum and began its slow descent in the west. Macha and Bassus and the cavalry escort wouldn't stop the first day until reaching Placentia, fifty miles distant. They didn't expect to arrive until after midnight.

Riding along the rut-filled lane, Macha noticed for the first time in many days, the blooming of spring. Her nose filled with the fragrance of the bright white cherry blossoms from the orchards they passed. On the opposite side of the road, pink and white blossoms draped the bare branches on a row of apricot trees. Bees buzzed and hovered among the limbs and petals. Golden orioles chirped and gray naped jackdaws crowed as they flitted and glided from one tree to the next, and she felt a stirring of hope for her own cause.

The entourage turned onto the dirt horse trail bordering the basalt covered Via Amelia. They encountered a steady stream of traffic, mostly supply wagons, ox carts, and peasants on foot heading north for Mediolanum behind them.

A large estate sprawled across both sides of the highway. Its huge vineyard stretched from the road and wound its way around a sheltered hillside in the distance. Macha spied the first tiny leaves and buds which had sprouted on the barren but skillfully-pruned branches. Propped up by wooden stakes and crosspieces tied together with willow shoots, the grapes wouldn't be ready for harvest until autumn. A small army of slaves, stripped to the waist, labored in the fields. Their sweaty muscles glistened in the hot mid-morning sunlight. Noisily they cleared debris washed down by the spring rains from the trenches between the endless rows of vines with spades and iron mattocks. A stern overseer, dressed in a dusty blue tunic and gripping a long vine cane with one hand, shouted a continual string of orders.

In the distance, on the Po River Plain, the first young shoots of wheat had burst through the loamy soil, painting the vast landscape a bright green.

Macha glanced to Bassus' perspiring face. The tall Roman peered straight ahead, oblivious to the dust kicked up by the horse's hooves. He hadn't always been a Senator. Years ago he had told her and Titus how he gained his title as Roman Senator. He wasn't born to a wealthy family. He was raised the son of a prosperous blacksmith in Placentia. Built on the southern bank of the River Po, it was one of the wealthiest small cities in the province of Cispadana Gaul. At the age of eighteen, Bassus joined the army, and in less than five years was promoted to the rank of centurion.

When Bassus campaigned in Britannia against her father, Caratacus, he caught the attention of Gaius Flavius Porcius. Famous for his knowledge on British affairs, the Roman Senator had lived in Britannia for many years. On several occasions Bassus accompanied the corpulent Roman when he negotiated with various British tribal chieftains.

As the years passed, their friendship grew. Porcius considered Bassus the son he never sired. Unknown to Bassus, before the Emperor Nero forced Porcius to take his life, the old Senator secretly adopted him. Upon his death, Bassus learned he had been named Porcius heir. The old man had left him his entire fortune and his title of Senator.

Although he had legally assumed his adopted father's name, Gaius Flavius Porcius, Bassus insisted on being called by his birth name. He never forgot his earlier life in Placentia. He seldom traveled with the entourage of slaves, freedmen, and junior officers to which his rank entitled him. He found them annoying and having them following in his trail cumbersome. At heart he was still a foot soldier.

* * * * *

Jolting Macha from her thoughts, Artemis bolted ahead of the escort, and galloped down the path alongside the highway. Automatically, Macha sat her lithe body straight down in the saddle. Once and for all, she was determined to break the mare. Gripping the sides of the mount with her long legs, she kept the reins low, just above the saddle pommels. Pulling firmly back on them, she reined the horse to a sudden halt. Violently, the mare attempted to shake loose her tight grip, but Macha held firm. During the next ten minutes, Macha forced Artemis to turn in tight circles, first to the left and then to the right. When the mare resisted, Macha jerked the reins in the opposite directions, keeping a firm grip with the legs, but kicked the obnoxious nag's sides when necessary.

Artemis began to relax, her struggle against Macha flagging with each passing minute. Macha rode in wider circles to ensure the mare had calmed sufficiently enough before rejoining the troop.

"If you ever try that foolishness again, mare," Macha said a few minutes later, "I'll see you harnessed to a grist mill grinding corn for the rest of your life."

Artemis snorted as if she understood the warning. The mare's jolting trot smoothed to a fluid pace, pleasing Macha. No one would have guessed by her willowy, almost delicate appearance, she was a strong rider. Years of experience, exercising her mounts, had developed lightly muscled, yet deceptively strong shoulders, arms, and legs.

A hot and sweaty Macha returned to the entourage, waiting near a shaded clump of poplars. They had halted when she began to discipline Artemis. She had been aware they were watching and probably hoped the animal would make a fool of her. Bassus waved her over to his side.

"A most impressive drill, Macha," He said. "You made believers out of the troops."

"I don't need to impress anyone," Macha answered. "Getting to Genua before Titus sails is all I want."

Appius and the troopers shook their heads. A couple of the men raised their hands in mock salute to her and grinned. "You ride like a trooper, your ladyship," a squadron sergeant said.

Macha nodded her appreciation. Now perhaps she would be accepted for her ability, despite being a woman.

Bassus turned to Appius. "Are you convinced this woman knows how to ride, tribune?"

"Yes, sir," Appius replied. His scar-lined jaw tightened, and he hesitated for a moment pondering his next words. "I never said she couldn't."

Macha shot a scathing glance to Appius. "If I have to train an ill-mannered horse along the way, then I will. I won't be delayed."

Appius glowered at Macha but held his tongue.

"Move out the troops," Bassus commanded.

Although certain Pomponius Appius deliberately set her up with a recalcitrant mare, Macha couldn't accuse him without proof. That would mark her as a hysterical female who had no business riding a horse. Men! Why did women have to put up with them?

"All right, move out!" Bassus barked. "No more halts until we reach Placentia."

CHAPTER 13

A Missed Opportunity?

After spending the night at the small villa Bassus maintained in Placentia, Macha, the Senator and Appius' escort of troopers, left at dawn the next morning. For the first few miles they paralleled the murky swift running River Po, still running high from the melting spring snow in the Apennines. Unaccustomed to traveling on so little sleep, Macha rode in a stupor for the first hour as they journeyed along the *Via Postumia*.

The road veered away from the river, cutting a straight line through the vast plain to the west. She was familiar with the road between Placentia and Genua having traveled the route into Mediolanum when Titus was transferred to Legion First Italica.

Gradually, Macha came fully awake. Spring was her favorite time of the year and she admired the farms dotting the landscape. Most included market gardens newly planted in carrots and beans, lettuce and radishes. Beyond were fields of alfalfa and recently planted wheat. She wished she were at home working in her own garden. Unlike so many Roman matrons, she wasn't afraid of soiling her hands.

Gardening reminded Macha of her son. Often he would play nearby as she toiled and offer to help. She smiled at the thought. It's been only one day since I left my son and Demetrios, she thought. I know Helena will take good care of them, but please Mother Goddess, watch over them. For a moment, she put a hand to her chest and bowed her head. Praying they will be all right eased the hurt in her heart.

Raising her head, Macha looked about. On her left ran the distant Apennines, shadowing her and the band of troopers since leaving Placentia. Every hour they drew nearer to the craggy limestone mountains. By early afternoon, they approached the foothills. Macha watched herds of sheep grazing on lush spring grass in the sheltered meadows and tiny valleys between the fingered outcroppings reaching down to the river plain.

A gusty wind spun down from the mountains. The further they traveled, the cooler and harder it blew, whistling in Macha's ears. Holding her mantle snugly with one hand, and the reins with the other, she hunkered down in her saddle. Macha pulled the woolen cowl over her head, but the pelting dust and grit still stung her cheeks and forehead. She squinted, barely seeing the road ahead of her.

"How much further to Dertona?" Macha shouted to Bassus.

"Three miles from that mile post," he answered. He motioned to the granite stone standing by the side of the road showing the distance to Genua—sixty-one miles.

"Thank gods, it's no further. This wind is freezing—it might even snow. I had forgotten how cold these mountains are in the spring."

* * * * *

Amid a passing flurry of snow, they arrived in Dertona, where the wind abated, turning its onslaught westward over the mountains. Snuggled at the foot of the snow-capped Apennines, the ancient Roman colony was little more than a village bordering the southern edge of the Po Valley.

Bassus used his authority as Legate to commandeer the Inn of Hercules, a state run guest house, for the entourage's use. There was a state inn built every fifteen miles along the Empire's vast highway system, contracted out to private business owners.

From the innkeeper, Macha and Bassus discovered Titus and his escort had ridden through about three hours before, stopping briefly for dinner. They disregarded the proprietor's warnings about the approaching night's freezing chill, and hazards in the mountains after dark. The troops wouldn't halt until they reached Libarna, a way station far up in the mountains.

Macha, Bassus and the pot-belly innkeeper stood beneath the porticoed entrance of the hostel facing a wide

92

courtyard. Bassus had given the order to the troopers to dismount and lead their horses to the stable behind the building.

"We must go on," Macha insisted. "We can't stop now."

"No, we're staying here tonight," Bassus replied. "You're exhausted, and so are the men."

"But Senator, we've nearly caught them."

"Didn't you hear what the innkeeper said? The troops are heading right into a storm. No, I'll hear no more."

Bassus turned to the innkeeper. "Show us our rooms. Afterwards, we go to supper."

Macha opened the splintered door to inspect her room. She was too annoyed with Bassus to pay attention to the cubicle. She didn't understand why they stopped for the night when they were so close to overtaking her husband, but once Bassus gave an order he wouldn't bend.

Holding a smoky, olive oil lamp in one hand, Macha set her travel bag on the dirty stone floor. The place reeked of stale urine and other foul odors she couldn't identify. She glanced about her lodging in the shadowy light. By the looks of the place, rules of cleanliness set by the state weren't strictly enforced. She was used to seeing graffiti on tiny bedroom walls, but the writing in this one caught her attention. Crudely scrawled in charcoal were the caustic words of an earlier dissatisfied guest. *Innkeeper, I deliberately pissed on your bed. Want to know why? There was no chamber pot!*

Searching the room, she immediately found a smelly earthenware chamber pot in a dark corner. To her relief, it was empty. She checked the straw-filled bed mat atop a wooden pallet. Although dusty, there was no smell of urine. Instead, she found the usual bedbugs crawling in and out of the cracks where the straw poked through the goat skin mat. She flicked them off and squashed them under her booted sandals. Many years ago she had gotten over her squeamishness of these filthy vermin.

Bassus knocked and entered. He looked around and scowled. "This is an outrage! You deserve better than this, Macha. I'll throw the innkeeper out of his room and give it to you."

Macha shook her head. "You'll do no such thing, Senator. I've slept in worse places than this, including Tullianum Prison. So long as I have a chamber pot and my traveling bag, I'll be fine."

She sighed. "And since you've forbidden me to ride after my husband now, we might as well go to supper."

The Senator and Macha entered the *taverna* next to the inn. She scanned the place to see if it were as dirty as her room. It was not. At the front was a long masonry counter with an oven. Large earthenware jars embedded into the bar contained hot food, including an aromatic goat stew spiced with leaves of rosemary and thyme. A spacious room filled with small round tables and backless stools passed for a dining area. Tolerable frescos covered the walls, scenes depicting eating and drinking. Strings of hams, sausages, dried garlic, and other edibles dangled from the ceiling. A smoky brazier sat on an iron tripod, and ten olive oil lamps provided light. The noisy room was packed with her escort of troopers and Praetorians drinking wine and playing knuckle bones and little outlaws. Pomponius Appius sat in one corner table surrounded by the squadron's decurion and sergeants, eating and chatting.

Macha learned from the tavern keeper the wine and food were good and prices reasonable. He boasted his place was frequented by only honest tradesmen and travelers. He didn't allow brawls, and Macha believed him. He was a burly fellow with hands almost as big as one of his hams.

She sat quietly eating the tangy goat stew and drinking the acidic local wine. At least the tavern keeper hadn't lied about the food. Occasionally she made small talk with Bassus. She couldn't get the thought out of her mind that Titus was so close. She wanted to reach her husband, even if it meant riding into the teeth of a storm. Macha frowned and shook her head. The thought of having to stay in the filthy inn infuriated her.

"I don't see why we have to spend the night here," Macha said. "Despite your order we must go on." She set her wine cup on the dining room table and got up.

"No, Macha, we're staying," Bassus said.

"But I must. You can stay if you wish, but I'm going on." She rose from the table.

"Don't be a fool. These mountains are full of bandits and worse," Bassus bluntly advised. "Under no circumstances will I permit you to leave tonight."

"You wouldn't dare stop me," she said folding her arms.

A hush fell over the room. Pomponius Appius and the soldiers eyed Macha and Bassus.

"I certainly will," Bassus answered in a hardened voice. He nodded to Appius. "Even if it means tying you up and placing a guard outside the room."

Macha sat back down at the splintery bench in a sullen silence. She realized she had made a fool of herself. Bassus was right, but she had been afraid to admit it--she wanted to be with her husband so much it had clouded her judgment. To pursue Titus and his escort on a narrow and dangerous mountain road, in the middle of a storm, would be suicidal. Yet, she wondered if Bassus had been holding back his troops. Was he involved in the conspiracy after all? At this point she was too tired to follow through with her thoughts.

Briefly the Senator touched her shoulder. "This has been a long and exhausting day for all of us," he added in a consoling manner. "Our chances of catching them tomorrow are excellent. We've gained most of the lost ground."

"It's not enough," she answered, staring at the door.

The Senator drank the last of his wine from an earthen cup and set it down on the scarred wood table. "True, but even when Titus arrives in Genua, he'll have to wait for the incoming tide before sailing. The weather is another factor. It's too unpredictable this early in the spring. A storm could blow through at anytime delaying the voyage."

"Or catch them at sea, and sink the ship!" Macha retorted. "Why are they going by ship anyway?"

"You know full well the reason. Despite the unpredictable weather, it's swifter than by road. We all need rest, Macha. We'll leave before dawn tomorrow."

* * * * *

Near dusk, the next day, the entourage arrived at the outskirts of Genua hemmed in on three sides by the

95

Apennines. As they descended the road from the foothills to the city, Macha scanned the Gulf of Liguria just beyond the ancient Etruscan seaport. Large swells rose and dipped along its wine-dark surface. Cool air swirled about her face as she recalled the last time she had visited Genua during a balmy July.

But Macha had no time for memories. Praying Titus hadn't sailed, she rode at a canter straight for the docks, with the escort hurrying to keep pace. As they approached the harbor, a sea breeze carrying the stench of floating garbage, the reeking smell of dead fish engulfed her nostrils. Long shadows spread like tentacles from the ships and warehouses over the dock. The sun hovered above the distant rim of the sea, a dark red orb, ready to disappear over the edge.

Scattering the busy dock workers along the quay, the horse soldiers rode by a dozen stubby merchantmen moored bow to stern before halting in front of the wharf master's weathered little office. Busy slaves neatly stacked dozens of bales of flax and as many crates of pottery beyond one end of the building.

Macha and Bassus dismounted and encountered the short leather-faced master who had stepped from his quarters on hearing the clattering hooves.

For a few seconds the wharf master scanned Macha's wind burnt face and dusty tartan tunic and breeches. Then he apparently spied Bassus. "Afternoon, general, not often we get high Imperial officials here. What can I do for you?"

Bassus nodded to Macha.

"I'm looking for Tribune Titus Antonius," she said. "He's with a detachment of soldiers who are planning on sailing from here to Ostia. Have you seen them?"

The bandy-legged official viewed her with contempt.

"Answer her," Bassus ordered. "She's a Roman lady, and wife of Tribune Antonius."

"Oh, aye, my lady," the master said. "You just missed them. Their ship left port not more than a quarter of an hour ago. But I'd say they're mad. There's a storm brewin' to the north that's apt to catch them." He pointed to the tell-tale dark clouds. "You can still see the vessel, if you look closely." He nodded towards the gulf.

Macha remounted her horse and raced to the end of the dock. Leaning in her saddle, she strained her eyes in the direction of the fading black-purple light at the sea's distant edge. Just as she spotted the silhouette of the squatty merchantman, it disappeared below the horizon. Her eyes clouded with tears. The ship had sailed away with her heart and happiness.

Why hadn't she insisted on leaving last night? Macha twisted about in her saddle and saw Bassus watching her. A puzzled expression crossed his face. She gave him a look so foul that even the Furies would cringe.

CHAPTER 14

It Rains in Genua

Titus' vessel vanished over the horizon as if falling off the edge of the world. Macha suppressed the panic welling within her. To stop the shaking that started in her arms and rushed through her entire body, she gripped Artemis's side with her legs and grabbed the protruding front saddle pommels. We barely missed him, she thought to herself. This is Bassus' fault! Mother Goddess Anu forgive me, but if I had a javelin to hurl, I would kill him!

Oblivious to the icy wind sweeping in from the sea, Macha quietly wept, then wiped tears from her large aqua eyes, and brushed back the hair swirling around her face. She must suppress her anger and find another means of traveling to Rome. Frustration rankled—she still had to rely on Bassus for help.

She turned her horse away from the pier's edge and rode back to the wharf master's office. The bandy-legged official watched her approach where he stood near Bassus, who was still mounted. "We shall need a ship sailing for Ostia," she said.

"Not in this weather you won't," the wharf master answered. "No captain worth his salt sets sail in the middle of a storm. You'll have to wait 'til tomorrow, when it passes —if it does—or the day after."

Macha clinched her fists, but knew it was useless to argue. The iron-black clouds racing across the sky, the foaming sea swells, and the billowing wind stinging her face like nettles said he was right. Even Father Neptune thwarted her efforts to see her husband again. She prayed to the Mother Goddess that Titus's ship stayed ahead of the storm.

During the night, the gale pounded the coast. Rain sheeted, obscuring the shoreline and sea, splashing high on Genua's cobbled streets and quay, forcing everyone inside. Drips and gurgles from the tile-roofed buildings and drains echoed loudly throughout the city.

By the following morning, the harsh weather had abated, but not enough for Bassus and Macha to find a ship's master willing to venture out of Genua's protective harbor.

"It'll be at least another day before the weather's good enough to sail anywhere," one scaly old sea captain said. He stood with Macha and the Senator beneath a sheltering arch at the entrance of a brick warehouse. Exhaling, he surveyed his moored ship as its wide oaken beam slammed violently against the stone quay, the cracking sound echoing along the shoreline. "I've prayed to old Neptune and asked him not to smash my ship into a pile of splinters—she's all I've got."

Macha understood the old master's reasons. Sailing in these tumultuous waters meant disaster, no consolation to her. The weather worked against her by taking Titus further away. She thought about riding down the coast on horseback, but would risk catching the lung sickness as long as the cold rain continued unabated. And she could do nothing for Titus if she fell ill, or worse, died.

After speaking to several other ship masters, Macha and Bassus returned to the villa of their host, Cassius Pius, Prefect of Genua, where they had found lodging outside the city gates. Surrounded by a sprawling vineyard, the home sat at the foot of a sheltered hillside, ideal for growing grapes and producing fine wine. Pius had taken his leave earlier that morning to inspect the harbor's docks and warehouses for storm damage.

Genua was famous for its exports of expensive finished wooden tables, cattle and sheep, hides, and honey. The Prefect had explained, before his departure, that part of his responsibilities included making certain nothing hindered the operation of the city's port. Any damage by the storm had to be repaired immediately. "The economic life of Genua depends on it," Pius said. "To stay in the Emperor's favor, it's my duty to see the treasury receives its share of the tariffs."

Macha smirked. Rumors abounded that Cassius Pius was as corrupt as a week-old dead mullet. His words were for Bassus's sake; the prefect knew the Senator had the Emperor's ear.

Later, after they bathed and changed clothes, Macha and Bassus met in the *triclinium* where they quietly reclined on couches near the brazier and sipped warm Calda. Macha wore a silk blue and silver gown perfumed with jasmine. The attending slave had whispered the Prefect was a notorious womanizer, and the dress had belonged to a former mistress. All the same, Macha was appreciative of the smooth luxuriant garment after several days wearing the same sweaty tartans.

"I've spent most of the morning thinking about leaving —we could be delayed for days," Macha said. "As soon as the rain stops, I shall ride south along the coast road on my own. Every minute I stay here means less chance of freeing Titus."

"I forbid it," Bassus said. "You have no business riding the *Via Aurelia Scauri* by yourself."

Macha's eyes smoldered, barely keeping her temper under control. With slow deliberation, she set her bronze cup on the ebony table. "You forbid it?" she asked coolly. "Roman men—always forbidding women. No one shall deny me my husband's life."

She leaned closer to Bassus and peered into his narrowed chestnut eyes. "We have been through this before. By what authority do you command me?"

"In the name of the Emperor, and as Imperial Legate escorting you on official business to Genua," he answered sternly, facing down her glare.

"Your authority ended when my husband sailed away." She knew by custom and because the rest were dead or missing, the only living relative who had power over her was Titus.

"The road is very dangerous, and no respectable Roman woman travels alone," Bassus advised.

"I won't stand by and become a disgraced widow." He kept his eyes on her.

Turning away from Bassus, Macha focused on the black and white mosaic floor. The soft thump of rain drops drummed on the portico sidewalk outside as she considered his words. Bassus was right. In her rush to reach Genua, she had neglected to bring along Juba as her retainer. How could she have been so foolish? She never dreamed of going beyond the seaport by herself. What made her think she could do anything to free Titus without help? Macha didn't know, but she had to try. Despite acting impulsively, she was determined to attempt the journey. If she arrived safely, she would buy passage on a ship at either Luna or Pisae, south of Genua, and sail to Ostia. Two days of hard riding lay ahead of her along the rocky coast to the former, and an additional day across some of Italy's worst marshlands to reach the latter. If the storm followed her, she would still be out of luck. But she refused to sit and wait for better weather conditions.

"I know you mean well, Senator Bassus," Macha said. She raised her head and returned his gaze. "But I must chance it."

"Decent innkeepers won't receive you at night without proper escort, Macha. At the least they'll consider you a trollop, or, observing your clothing, a barbarian. And I wouldn't advise stopping at less reputable inns."

"I should say not!" Macha said. She would be subjected to outrages worse than customers wanting to buy her favors. Macha breathed deeply and blindly looked about. It was only at that moment the reality of such a foolish attempt struck her. Riding down the coast by myself is not only irresponsible but extremely dangerous, she thought. Even a man would not travel by himself. I should have thought through this whole matter first. If Bassus' decision to forbid my traveling alone is final, then I will abide by it, but I must at least try another approach first. It might be the only way of getting him to act.

"If you're so concerned about my well-being," Macha said, "why don't you provide me with an escort? Be honest. I've known you too long, you won't let me ride by myself."

Bassus stood. For a moment he slowly paced around the *triclinium*, viewing with disinterest the cheap imitations of the busts of Hermes and the Emperor Vespasian. The noise from his hobnail sandaled boots echoed off the tile floor. Finishing his Calda in one gulp, he wiped his mouth on the sleeve of his borrowed scarlet and white dining tunic. He cleared his throat and returned to the couch.

"No, you're right. I could prevent you easily enough, Macha, but I won't because I'm riding with you. It appears I shall arrive in Rome sooner than expected—the Emperor will be pleased."

"I knew you would help," Macha answered, relieved that Bassus had acquiesced. She dreaded the prospect of going alone, but only now admitted how much the journey frightened her. She shuddered. "Are you the only one going with me?"

"No, I'll take along my Praetorian escort, but I have to send the regular troopers back to Mediolanum. The Legion needs every last man. I didn't say anything before, but the legions of the Rhenus garrisons and the First Italica have been placed on alert."

"What on earth for?"

Knowing Macha was familiar with military affairs, Bassus explained, "Headquarters received news that another Gallic uprising is imminent."

"You need an army for another group of bandits? Titus easily smashed the last bunch."

"No outlaws this time. Spies uncovered a genuine threat to the Empire. The Emperor is dispatching as least one, perhaps two Praetorian Cohorts from Rome to reinforce Legion First Italica. He's sending additional cohorts from legions on the Danubus as well. He expects the outbreak to erupt in Northern Italy, in Transpadana Gaul."

Great Mother Goddess, Mediolanum, their home would be threatened once again. Macha immediately thought about the safety of Young Titus, Demetrios, and her sister-in-law, Helena. As far as she knew, the Italian Gauls had never attacked the city or rampaged through the Po Valley. But if the right leader emerged they might. Am I doing the right thing by going to Rome, she thought, or should I return home to be with my son? Why did this have to happen now?

"The chances of Mediolanum being attacked are minimal," Bassus said, interrupting Macha's thoughts. "It's heavily fortified, and has enough food and water to outlast any siege. Most likely, if there is revolt, it will break out further north or in the countryside."

"In the area where Titus crushed the bandits?" She recalled her husband's unit found the brigands about forty miles north of Mediolanum.

"Further north."

Relieved that Mediolanum and her home were in no immediate danger, Macha was determined to ride south. "Then I must go to Rome, and do what I can," Macha explained. "Titus is one of the legion's best commanders. They'll need him if there is a rebellion." As much as Macha would hate to see her husband leave again, he would never forgive himself if he didn't take his place at the head of his troops in time of crisis. It would also allow her to return home to her son.

"Most of the day is gone—the rain makes it too treacherous for riding in the darkness," Bassus said. "Be patient a little longer—we'll leave early tomorrow morning."

CHAPTER 15

Thieves, Deserters, and Slackards

Shortly before dawn, at the inn commandeered for the troops' lodgings, Bassus informed Pomponius Appius of his plan to escort Macha. Her patron found the tribune mustering troops in the courtyard as well as the Praetorians for roll call. A steady drizzle soaked the muddy ground as the shivering men stood next to their rain drenched mounts. The animals' wet coats glistened, and the dank smell of leather waterlogged saddles and bridles pierced Macha's nose. Despite wrapping themselves in woolen sagum cloaks, the men were nearly as soaked as their horses.

Dressed in her freshly washed tartan tunic and breeches, Macha bundled herself in a green woolen cloak covered by a protective oiled cloth. She wore fox-skinned gloves, good for controlling the reins of her mare, but worthless in eliminating the chill of rain. She hovered a few paces away from the formation, rain splashing on her sandaled boots, soaking through her protective woolen socks.

"Along with you," Bassus explained to Appius, "my Praetorians will escort Lady Macha and me south. Notify the decurion commander that he and his squadron are to return to Mediolanum."

Macha gasped, surprised by Bassus' choice. Although Appius had been civil to her on the journey to Genua, she still despised him.

Appius' weather-beaten face tightened, and for a split second he scrutinized Macha with his speckled yellow-brown eyes. His stare sliced through her like a sword.

"Is that necessary, sir?" Appius questioned. Raindrops rolled down the front of his helmet into his eyes and along the bridge of his beaked nose. "Now that Tribune Titus is gone, I'm in command of First Italica's cavalry, and the First Infantry Cohort."

"You know why you are journeying with us, Tribune Appius," Bassus snapped. "The senior centurion will take command until the rightful commander returns."

Through tightened lips Appius gritted, "Yes, sir." He stepped to his mount.

"Since you seem to think I'm in danger," Macha said to Bassus, "are you sure your men will be enough escort?"

"It'll be sufficient against any ragtag group of bandits fool enough to attack us. Chances are slight since the Praetorians are marching north on the same road. They'll sweep any robbers out of the way."

She understood the *Via Flaminia* over the Apennines in Central Italy to the *Via Aemilia* and Mediolanum was a quicker route. "Why are they moving up the coast?"

"Right now, the mountain passes are snow-blocked," Bassus answered. "The *Via Aurelia Scauri* to Genua, and through the Po Valley, is the only clear highway."

* * * * *

Macha and her escort rode south along the coast over a paved road of soft volcanic stone. Initially the Apennines, rising steeply out of the flatlands behind Genua, shadowed their journey. Soon the mountain range curved away to the east, leaving a desolate line of rocky foothills and cliffs overlooking the sea. Small farmsteads dotted the way where free peasants continued to eke out a living. Macha wondered how much longer they would work their meager lands. In the Po Valley they had been evicted by the great landowners, and replaced by slaves.

By noon on the second day, the little entourage entered the wide dreary plain north of Luna. Through the distant haze the mountains of Carrara, famous for its white marble, hovered above the town. The rain had stopped, and a warming sun pierced the fleecy domed clouds. Macha peered skyward, watching the billowing wind push the rising thunderheads out to sea. The change of weather raised her spirits and that of the Praetorians.

"If the weather continues to improve," Macha said while riding beside Bassus, "we can charter a ship from Luna."

Bassus agreed. "With all the marble transported down from the mountains, Luna's harbor will be clogged with ships eager to sail."

"While we're seeking a boat, we'll spare time to buy food and wine," Macha said. They would purchase Luna cheese, famous throughout Italy for its quality and taste, and their equally prized wine. Their early morning breakfast of salty porridge, stale bread, and watery wine in the village of Bodetia left a sour taste in her mouth. Still hungry, only her pleading persuaded Bassus from having the innkeeper flogged for serving such dreadful fare.

The little group trotted down a ravine on a wide graveled road between two rolling hills speared with poplars and pines, and fields of early spring wildflowers— blue, orange, and yellow.

As Macha's stomach rumbled at the prospect of Luna's cheese, cries erupted from behind the trees and bushes on both sides of the highway. At least three dozen bandits on foot and horseback rushed from hiding and charged the outnumbered band of fifteen. Bassus, Pomponius Appius, and the troops formed a defensive ring around Macha. For a moment she froze as the fierce struggle erupted. Metal slammed against metal as the sword-wielding bandits clashed with the soldiers. Macha wanted to flee but dared not, leaving her too vulnerable to attack. The cries and groans of soldiers and bandits echoed around her, along with the clattering of hooves, the banging of weapons and shields, and splattering blood.

Dodging the jabbing thrusts of the soldiers' lances, one outlaw managed to slip through. He grabbed Macha's ankle and attempted to yank her off Artemis. Trained for battle, the mare instantly turned its body, pulling Macha's leg out of the bandit's filthy hand. The horse bit the cutthroat's cheek. He howled as he cupped his bloody face in his hand. His outcry snapped Macha out of her panic. She spun the mount around; the heavy weight of the animal's body slammed the bandit to the rocky ground, and trampled him underfoot. She glanced to the side. Bassus and the troopers still battled fiercely. She pulled a dagger from her waistband.

"Stay in the middle!" Bassus shouted. Frantically, the Praetorians struggled to maintain a protective circle. They were too few, the highwaymen quickly hacked apart five defending soldiers. Appius, Bassus, and the others retaliated slaying a dozen outlaws with their jabbing spears, trampling horses, and slashing longswords.

Macha screamed when another brigand rode toward her with a drawn sword. Pomponius Appius whirled about, intercepted him, and decapitated him with his longsword—spatha. Blood sprayed from the stump of the victim's head, splashing Macha and Appius as the body toppled off its mount.

She had no time to thank him when another bandit on foot grabbed her leg. Without thinking, she drove her dagger through his beard-covered throat and twisted it violently until she heard a bone snap. For a split second his pocked-face froze in disbelief. Blood gurgled and bubbled from his mouth. He slumped to the ground. The smell of his loose bowels and urine gagged Macha—she had never killed anyone before.

A loud clatter of hooves echoed in the distance, and Macha turned to see a huge swirl of dust rolling along the road. Breaking through the dirty cloud, scarlet cloaked horsemen of the Praetorian Guard galloped in their direction.

"Soldiers!" One of the bandits shouted. "Run!"

Vainly attempting to flee, the outlaws scattered. The cavalry, followed by double-timing chain-mailed infantry, charged ahead as the Emperor's troops fanned both sides of the highway killing all those fleeing.

Bassus spurred his mount ahead and shouted to the centurion in charge, "Take them alive!"

A short time later, the guardsmen dragged the three survivors near an outcrop of boulders. After being manacled, the prisoners were brought to the road where the cohort had regrouped. Part of the Guard stood shield-to-shield in a defensive perimeter along both sides of the highway.

"Looks to be one of these three pieces of scum is a deserter," a tall burly centurion said. He motioned to one of the prisoners, perhaps in his late twenties. "Found him carrying a spatha and wearing army sandals." He handed the cavalry longsword to one of his men.

"Interrogate him first," Bassus ordered as he dismounted his horse and approached the bandits.

Macha noticed the ragged leather and hob-nailed *caligae* on the scarred-face brigand's feet. Two toes were missing from his left foot. Her gaze shifted to his right hand, and she spied six fingers.

The centurion saluted Bassus and identified himself as Sextus Humanius, commander of the Fifth Praetorian Cohort. He explained the Emperor Vespasian had dispatched his unit from Rome to Mediolanum to reinforce the First Italic Legion. "I knew there was trouble ahead when one of my scouts signaled that his detail spotted bandits attacking horsemen."

"But couldn't this one have stolen or bought the shoes and weapon?" Macha asked. She motioned to the prisoner.

The centurion eyed Macha suspiciously.

"It's all right, Centurion Humanius," Bassus said. "She's Lady Macha Carataca, wife of Tribune Titus Antonius of the First Legion."

"I can answer the lady's question," Pomponius Appius interjected. "I know this sniveling maggot. His name is Sergius Faunus, a deserter from the First Legion's cavalry detachment." Appius grabbed the prisoner's tunic and ripped it to the waist. Tattooed on his right shoulder was a blue eagle with spreading wings grasping the letter I in its claws. The eagle again, Macha thought.

Appius spun the bandit around and pointed to the long white scars across his back. "Flogged about a year ago—I forget what for—then he disappeared. He's from the First Italica Legion all right. A man with six fingers on one hand and missing toes isn't something I forget."

Appius grabbed the man's sixth finger, and with a slash of his dagger snipped it off. He hurled the bloody appendage into a nearby bush.

Faunus screamed and fell to his knees, grasping the wrist of his wounded hand.

Macha gasped, appalled by Appius' barbaric act.

"First time I ever got to heal a poor deformed cripple and make him normal—like the mad Jew, Cristus," Appius said. "When I was in Judea, I heard tales he hopped around the countryside raising the dead. Then *he* was crucified."

"Tribune Appius," Bassus interrupted harshly, "before you conduct another religious miracle, please consider the presence of the lady."

Macha nodded her appreciation to the Senator.

"Is the Tribune telling the truth, deserter?" Centurion Sextus Humanius grabbed the bleeding deserter by the throat and began squeezing. "Answer him!"

"Y...yes, sir," the prisoner choked.

By this time Macha had dismounted Artemis and stood near Bassus as the questioning proceeded.

Sextus Humanius threw him to the ground. "My Lord Bassus and Tribune Pomponius Appius have a few questions for you. If you don't tell the truth, my interrogator will perform another miracle for our amusement." He flicked his eyes to the cohort torturer. The *quaestionarius* leaned against a boulder, protecting the fire from the wind; he had started heating his irons. One instrument of truth had turned a bright cherry red.

"I'll tell him anything he wants to know," the prisoner blubbered.

"Only the truth," Bassus advised. "Is your name Sergius Faunus?"

"Yes, that's me." Appius kicked him as a reminder, and he added, "My lord."

"Who sent you to kill us?" Appius questioned.

"Don't know his name, sir—he wouldn't say. Said he followed you from Mediolanum." Faunus added that the size of Bassus' contingent made attack impossible. When he learned only a small retinue was escorting Macha south, he recruited Faunus and other bandits with a promise of a large reward if they successfully killed Macha and the troopers.

"Why did he want our deaths?" Bassus asked.

"He didn't say, my lord, and we didn't ask. He had gold —it didn't matter why—we took it."

"How did he recruit you and the others so quickly?" Bassus inquired. "We left Genua only two days ago."

"Easy," Sergius Faunus answered. "Thieves and honest men out of work will do anything for the right price."

Appius kicked him and corrected, "Thieves, *deserters,* and slackards you mean!"

"Slaves took all the honest jobs. You can find hungry free men anywhere, and he did." The prisoner explained they had followed Macha's band from Genua. "I knew if the storm cleared you'd stop at Luna—couldn't chance you'd ride to Pisae."

He explained that when Macha's group had spent the night at the village of Bodetia, twenty miles north of Luna, Faunus and his men rode ahead to set their trap.

"Describe the man who recruited you," Appius ordered.

"He's got a deep nasty scar down the middle of his face," Faunus answered. "Cuts across the forehead and through a blinded eye. It splits the bridge of his nose and rips right through his lips and chin—ugly sight to see."

"That sounds like Horse Arse," Centurion Sextus Humanius said.

"You know him?" Macha asked.

"Aye, Lady Carataca, he's a horse trader. He has a contract to supply the way stations with replacement mounts in this part of Italy. They say he killed a man in a tavern after laughter woke him from a drunk. Seems some lout placed a horse-apple on the table by his 'horse arse' face. No sense of humor, that one."

"Do you know his real name?" Macha persisted.

"I don't know, but you could learn easy enough in Rome."

Macha wouldn't have to wait. By the culprit's description, she believed she knew him. "I would like to question the prisoner."

The centurion turned to Bassus who nodded.

"Go ahead, Lady Carataca." Humanius turned to the deserter and glared a warning.

"Did you see the horse this man was riding?" Macha queried.

"Aye," Faunus replied.

"Describe it."

"It's a black Libyan Barb. It had white stocking feet and a white diamond on its forehead."

"I know the man," Macha said. "His name is Crixus."

Bassus raised an eyebrow. "When did you associate with the likes of him?"

"He's a Gallic freedman. I wouldn't have described him as Horse Arse, but his face does remind me of a cleaved melon."

"Are you certain?"

"Positive. I didn't know he held the franchise for providing horses, but I've dealt with him before. He's a cheat. A couple of times he tried selling me sick horses. Thought because I was a woman he could rob me."

"Who is his patron?" Bassus asked.

"As far as I know, his own," Macha replied.

The centurion proceeded to question the other two prisoners. They added little to what Faunus had told Bassus and Macha.

After Humanius finished the interrogation, Sergius Faunus asked, "Are you going to take me to Mediolanum for court-martial?"

Pomponius Appius flicked his eyebrow in the direction of a distant stand of trees.

A look of horror crossed the deserter's face. "What are you going to do?"

"You'll see." Sextus Humanius motioned to a squad of ten infantrymen standing nearby and nodded to the prisoners. "Take these pieces of slime far enough from the road, so as not give an odorous offense to passersbys." They dragged the screaming prisoners away to behead them.

Moments after the outlaws had been executed, Macha remembered that she too, had killed a man. Guilt, disgust, and pain enveloped her. She had slain the thug in self defense and her horse had trampled another to death. If she hadn't killed him, he certainly would have butchered her, after doing gods knew what.

Macha had been trained since she was a child to use a dagger in self-defense. She was the wife of a soldier and knew of their hardships and dangers. Titus had told her many soldiers, after fighting in their first battle and slaying the enemy, felt what she was now experiencing. It was nothing for which to be ashamed. Then why did she feel the way she did? Suddenly nauseous, she couldn't hold it back. Macha ran behind a nearby poplar and vomited. Afterwards, in the shade of the trees, she slumped to the weed-covered ground and wept.

* * * * *

"Crixus must be arrested as soon as we reach Rome," Macha said to Bassus as they approached the outskirts of Luna. "He must be involved with the plot. Why else would he pay the bandits to attack us?"

"I will start an investigation once we arrive in Rome," Bassus answered. They followed behind a dusty convoy of eight teams of oxen-drawn wagons filled with blocks of white marble, heading for the docks.

"By himself," Macha said, "Crixus is too lowly of a man to have hatched this conspiracy by himself. Don't you think?"

"*If* he is involved. But you're right. A plot to succeed against Vespasian would require a person or persons in high positions. If Crixus does confess, the political ramifications might be such that everything must be in place before we make any arrests. All those involved in the conspiracy must be seized and imprisoned at the same time."

"How many people do you think are involved?"

"I don't know, but we shall arrest Horse Arse and put his feet to the fire."

CHAPTER 16

Welcome to Rome

About dawn, after a four-day voyage from Luna, Macha, with Bassus and Appius, arrived in Ostia, Rome's seaport at the mouth of the River Tiber. Leaning against the merchantman's oaken rail, Macha viewed the noisy activity along the wharf as the ship docked. An army of clerks, money changers, and port officials shouted and haggled with sea captains and merchants about the stacked goods sprawled about the dock and porticoed warehouses. Moored bow first, the squat hulled vessels lined the concrete and granite quay. Stripped to the waist in dirty tunics, a churning river of sweating slaves and freedmen, unloaded cargo arriving from all parts of the Empire. Shipmasters and warehouse foremen shouted and snarled orders to the hapless laborers. Toting sacks of grain and large amphorae of wine and oil, the workers trudged with their burdens to the awaiting barges for transportation upstream on the Tiber. Others unloaded their cargo into carts and wagons traveling the Ostian Way to Rome.

Raucous seagulls circled and dived for scraps and garbage dumped from anchored vessels into the harbor's filthy waters, seething with offal, dead fish, and rotten food. The rank odors assaulted Macha's slightly turned-up nose like a volley of flying arrows. One small aggressive flock alighted on the quay near a fishing boat unloading a fresh catch of mullet—a delicacy for Rome's nobility. Several slaves using clubs vainly attempted to chase away the thieving birds from this expensive catch.

Macha had changed from her sweat-stained tartans to a green linen stola trimmed in yellow. The dress was one of three she hastily packed for the journey. A woolen blue palla draped her shoulders and head, covering the long twisted braid flowing down her back. Two plain golden bracelets encircled each wrist and small looped gold

113

earrings, encrusted with tiny rubies, hung from her pierced ear lobes.

She had managed to take a quick bath in Luna, but desperately needed another. Four days was too long without a decent wash. Fresh water stored aboard ship was for cooking and drinking, not for the luxury of bathing. Wishing she had fresh water, Macha scrubbed off the stink and perspiration with a bucket of salt water in the captain's tiny cabin. Although cleaner, the salt left a crusty film on her body.

To make matters worse, she suffered from three days of seasickness, and the foul taste of vomit still lingered in her mouth. Aggravating her misery, a day into her sickness she developed painful cramps in the lower abdomen. She prayed to Mother Goddess Anu her monthly cycle wouldn't start until she arrived at Bassus' house in Rome. There she could bathe again and suffer in comfort.

At the sound of heavy footsteps behind her, Macha turned about. Beak-nosed Pomponius Appius, dressed in a clean uniform, with a shined cuirass and helmet, swaggered to her side. A foul odor emanated from the Tribune's body. She didn't know if he had bathed while they were in Luna but was certain he had not rinsed himself off during the voyage. She slipped back along the railing a couple of paces.

"Lady Carataca," he said, "I know I've treated you roughly, and offended you and your husband's name."

"Quite true, Tribune Appius," she answered coolly, "you've made your contempt abundantly clear for both of us."

For a second his face tightened. "Unfortunately, yes. But after the attack and confession by the deserter, I could be wrong. The way you held your ground and slew that highwayman showed more bal-uh, spirit, than most men would boast."

"I know you have misjudged us, but still I'm grateful you saved my life."

"All in the line of duty," he said gruffly, "I'm not completely convinced Titus is innocent, but too many events have occurred that don't make sense. Faunus' confession is one of them. The closeness of your two slave's deaths is another." Pausing, Appius gazed upward, he searched the hazy blue sky beyond the port. A couple of silent minutes elapsed before he turned back to Macha.

"Providing the deserter wasn't lying and this horse trader isn't either, maybe your husband isn't a traitor."

"I appreciate your considering the possibility, Tribune Appius," Macha said. "Titus had no part in this terrible situation. He's a loyal Roman."

Appius exhaled, readjusted his helmet, and tugged at the purple sash strung across his silver cuirass. "Your stubbornness was another reason for my doubts. Most women would have thrown up their hands in defeat or fallen at the feet of the Emperor, begging for mercy. You're no sniveler."

"It's considered an admission of the husband's guilt. That's why I refuse to do it. If it will free Titus, I may yet kiss Vespasian's feet."

Appius grinned. "I'm assisting Senator Bassus in his inquiries. It's my intention to find and arrest Crixus, better known as Horse Arse. With a face like his, he won't be too difficult to catch."

"If he's in Rome."

Was this a ruse? Macha questioned herself. Does Appius believe Titus is innocent or is he attempting to throw me off his scent? Perhaps he saved my life, during the attack on the coast road, because Bassus was close by. I must remain cautious about his true intentions.

* * * * *

Within the hour after arriving in Ostia, Macha, Bassus, Pomponius Appius, and the Senator's Praetorian retainers transferred to a shallow draft naval bireme for the seventeen mile journey up the River Tiber to Rome. The Legate's banners fluttered as the ship glided past large villas and flourishing truck gardens on the Campanian Plain. In the distance, snaking among the gentle ridges, the gray-brown Aqueduct of Appius carried drinking water from the distant Alban Hills to Rome. Built upon solemn stone arches, the flume stretched to the horizon and melted into the golden haze of the Italian sky.

Standing near the stern, Macha turned and caught a glimpse of Tribune Appius as he conversed with Senator

Bassus and the ship's captain a few paces away. She smirked as she thought, Appius is a common name. I'm sure he is no relation to the great family who built the aqueduct more than three-hundred-fifty years ago.

By late afternoon the ship approached Rome, and Macha saw an ugly sight that was all too familiar. A brown haze hung over the area like a blanket, the result of smoke blending from dozens of huge rubbish heaps that circled and continually burned day and night outside the city gates. The vessel glided toward the Emporium, the Capitol's huge grain dock. Beyond the port, overlooking the rest of the city stood the majestic Temple of Jupiter on Capitoline Hill. Jutting past the temple, the Palace of Augustus pierced the smoky skyline on top of Palatine Hill. Macha found the activity along the river front as noisy and hectic as in Ostia. The hortator, who pounded a slow rhythmic cadence on his drum, to which the ship's oarsmen rowed, bellowed a command. The sailors drew in the ship's double bank of oars as other crewmen tied hawsers to the granite quay alongside dozens of barges.

Moments later, as Macha, Bassus and the rest of the retinue began to disembark, Vasili, the Senator's chief steward and freedman, met them at the dock. Behind the gaunt stoop-shouldered Greek, hovered an entourage of servants and a litter carried by six muscular slaves clad in copper colored tunics. When they had arrived in Ostia, Bassus sent a fast courier on ahead to notify his household and the Emperor of their impending arrival.

As Macha followed Bassus and Appius down the gangway, Appius muttered, "What? No emissary from the Emperor to greet us?"

"Emperor Vespasian knows how I hate to be greeted by perfumed senatorial officials," Bassus replied as they stepped onto the wharf. "In this he and I are of like minds. He is a man of simple tastes and an old soldier at heart. He loathes formality."

"Greetings, Lord Bassus," the Greek freedman said with a slight bow. Turning to Macha he added, "And to you, Lady Carataca."

"And you, Vasili, what news from the Emperor?" the Senator inquired.

"His messenger said you are to report to the Emperor tomorrow morning."

"Very good, I look forward to seeing him once again."

Bassus motioned to Macha to ride in the adjoining litter as he and Pomponius Appius mounted awaiting horses at the head of the party. While she was being assisted into the awaiting palanquin, one of Bassus' household slaves approached her.

"Why Shafer, I didn't know you were here," Macha said.

The elegant Moorish woman bowed as she stepped to Macha's side. Physically strong, the tall ebony servant had once been an acrobat and despite being nearly thirty, still possessed a quick and nimble body. "I stayed with the other slaves behind Vasili as is my place, Mistress," Shafer answered. "He said I am to be your personal slave while you are here in Rome."

"You are more of a friend than a slave." Macha had known Shafer since she arrived in Bassus household eight years before.

Shafer smiled. "Thank you, Mistress." She had a reputation for being resourceful and trustworthy.

Macha looked away from Shafer as the group passed through the entrance in the ancient Servian Wall and entered the city. Even after many visits to Rome, Macha still shook her head in awe as she scanned the city's teeming crowds. Neither the villages of her childhood memories in Britannia, nor later as an adult in cities such as Mediolanum, did she remember people living in such cramped and squalid conditions. The retinue proceeded up a dismal narrow lane, surrounded by dark and ugly multistoried *insulae*, their thin sagging walls propped up by numerous support beams jutting into the street. Scattered among the wooden apartments were busy shops and drab industrial buildings. There was barely enough room to carry a litter through the crowded lane. Hordes of people jostled and darted around shop wares, blocking the street and sidewalks. Somewhere in the distance a cry of "Stop thief!" drifted unanswered.

Macha noticed the countless aliens as they mingled with sharp-eyed Latins, who gestured incessantly as they bartered in open shops lining the streets. Everyone shouted to make a point. A hawk-nosed Arab in white robes argued vehemently about the price of Myrrh with a wizened gray-haired woman. Behind him, a glowering, red-bearded Dacian, dressed in a black wool tunic and trousers, pushed his way through the crowd.

She shook her head. Nothing had changed since her last visit to Rome two years before. The city was noisy and dirty, but very much alive, something she enjoyed.

Piled nearby on a sidewalk and in the street, rested sacks and crates full of vegetables, fish, poultry, and sausages from a cookshop. A foul smelling stream, reeking of rotting food and other filth, ran down the center of the lane. Macha pulled a handkerchief from within her stola and placed it to her nose and mouth.

Dusty sweaty workmen stood or lounged, eating a late lunch and drinking wine. As a young slave guarded the smoking braziers, nearby, cooking chicken and peas, the laborers chatted with the proprietor. He continued to clean and chop a dozen fish, tossing the guts into the center of the street to join the rest of the garbage.

"Mistress, Look out!" Shafer shouted. "To your left!"

Jolted from her thoughts, Macha turned. For a split second she stared at a gaunt young man, dressed in a ragged tunic, who barreled between the litter bearers, leaped into the sedan, and landed on his knees next to her legs. His left eye was stitched closed with a white scar running from above the eye from right to left down the cheek. Terrified, Macha's body turned rigid. Mother Goddess, he's going to kill me!

He snatched a small dagger from his tunic waist band. The sight of the weapon instantly brought Macha to her senses. She rolled to right as he slashed his weapon and barely missed her side. Slipping off the edge of the palanquin, Macha nearly fell to the street, but was caught by Shafer just before she struck the cobbled surface.

The bandit turned and fled before the bearers and Bassus' retainers could respond. He melted into the teeming crowd and disappeared.

Bassus rushed to her side, the crowd scattering out of the way of his horse's stomping hooves. "Are you all right, Macha?"

"Yes, Senator," Macha answered. Shaken, she gasped several times before continuing. "He gave me a terrible fright!"

"Thank Castor and Pollux he missed. I'll send my men to search the area immediately."

She quickly described the assassin and added that the upper right part of his mouth was sunken, a possible indication of missing teeth. Bassus dispatched ten of his twelve Praetorians, lead by Appius, to scour the surrounding area. Two soldiers stayed behind to protect her.

"You won't find him in this crowd, Senator," Macha said. "He's disappeared by now."

"Nonetheless, we will keep searching. I won't let this pass without a concerted effort."

"If it hadn't been for Shafer's warning, I would be dead." Shafer bowed.

It was obvious someone didn't want her in Rome, Macha thought. This was the second attempt on her life in less than a week. No doubt the news had spread, by the time she had arrived in Luna; the first assassination attempt had failed. A fast rider must have been dispatched to the conspirators in Rome who had planned another attack on her life. Again, she wondered if they were listed among the names or initials on her partial fragment hidden in the small travel bag she brought with her.

Macha looked about and shuddered at the thought of this latest attempt on her life. "Why did only one assassin try to kill me, Senator?"

"Easier to mingle with the crowd and quickly sneak through the escort," he answered.

"But what if he is captured?"

"He'll be interrogated. But as we know from the first attempt on your life, the assassin probably won't know who hired him. If he is arrested he'll be useless."

"Perhaps when Horse Arse is found we will learn who this was as well."

"We must find him first."

CHAPTER 17

The Praetorian Camp

After a near sleepless night, at Bassus's house, Macha left her bed cubicle. Still upset by the attempt on her life the day before, she wasn't afraid to confide her thoughts to Shafer who came to escort her.

"Don't be afraid, Mistress," Shafer said. "The Master has arranged for a heavy escort this morning. You will be well protected on your journey to the Praetorian Barracks."

"Thank you, Shafer. Mother Goddess, I do look forward to seeing my husband. It has been too long, and I miss him so much." She shook her head. It seemed impossible to subdue the ache in her heart at the mention of his name. "Now that he has been accused of treason, I need to see him more than ever."

"I'm so sorry about your husband, Mistress," Shafer said. "The word in the Master's household is that he is an honorable man."

"He is, but I must prove it." More than ten days had passed since she had seen Titus, but it seemed a lifetime since he had been in her arms. Although she was suffering through her monthly cycle, and could ignore the pains, she couldn't ignore the strong feelings for her husband.

Dwelling on yesterday's events, Macha barely noticed the court's exquisite beauty as they passed through the atrium. Carved from green Spartan marble, four elegant columns upheld the roof around the wide impluvium. Bronze dolphins and ornamented sea horses shot great jets of water into the moon-colored marble fountain beneath the light well. The soft gurgling echoed throughout the spacious reception room. Elaborate frescoes, broken by heavy olivine and saffron drapes, framing the bedchamber-cubicle entries, covered the walls.

Macha debated telling Titus about the attempts on her life. She wanted to be honest with him, but for certain he would forbid her to get involved in the investigation. Whatever his reaction might be, she would still search for the truth. But where to start? Shafer would assist her with any inquiries. Perhaps Macha could begin by contacting her good friend, Antonia, one of Rome's Vestal Virgins who had influence and power. Responsible for the sacred flame and hearth of Rome, the Vestals maintained the Temple of Vesta, keeping a constant vigil on the eternal fire Romans believed that so long as it burned, Rome would survive. The Vestal Virgins were accountable only to the Emperor.

Macha must make it a point to see her today or tomorrow at the latest. She checked the dagger hidden in her stola once again before being helped into the litter.

Escorted by a retinue of slaves and a dozen heavily armed bodyguards, Macha left Bassus' palatial house on Aventine Hill. They departed through black iron gates set in the high white-washed wall at the front of the two-storied mansion and descended Aventine Hill enroute to *Castra Praetoria.* Built outside the east city wall, the Praetorian camp sat along *Vicus Patricus* Street, an imposing monolith.

* * * * *

Nearly an hour later, Macha's entourage entered the central gateway of the Praetorian Camp, passing through a massive wall built of brick and concrete and crowned with battlements. The fortress reminded her of her husband's base outside of Mediolanum, but on a much smaller scale. Fine marble statues adorned the vast fortress entryway. Inside, a mass of office buildings and a small temple dedicated to Mars and the deified Emperors, Augustus and Claudius, rose in the center. The side walls of the enclosure were extended on the inside by enormous vaulting arches and dozens of barracks housing the members of the Guard. In the open area adjacent to the parade ground fountains gurgled and played. The sun sent a flying glory of light from the burnished armor of a cohort standing at attention during an inspection by its commanding tribune and centurions.

121

The size of the fortress intimidated Macha. A person could be swallowed up within its towering walls and never be seen again. Would this happen to Titus?

As she drew closer to the visitor's courtyard, her body tightened. Upon being assisted out of the litter, Shafer peered at her quizzically. "Are you all right, Mistress? Your face is so white."

"I'm all right, Shafer, really," Macha lied. "I'm just eager to see my husband." This was true. "Wait here for me." She went into Praetorian headquarters.

Minutes later, Macha was escorted to Titus' room by a burly guardsman who slammed the door behind her and waited outside. Sparsely furnished with one cot, a plain wooden table, and backless chair, Titus's room was no different from the other junior officers'. At least it was clean. Facing the courtyard, the cubicle's windows framing the upper part of the brown stone wall allowed ample sunlight.

Titus bolted up from the straw cot. Macha ran to him and wrapped her arms about his neck. His firm hands grabbed Macha's shoulders and pulled her to his chest. He slowly kissed her soft lips, smooth cheek, and then they tightly embraced.

"Macha, by the gods, you're here! I knew you would come." He added in a hoarse voice, "But the wait seemed like ages."

Faint nausea roiled in Macha's stomach followed by a weakening in the limbs, but it quickly passed. She drew back and studied Titus' broad face before a gasp escaped her lips. "What happened to you? You're so pale and gaunt."

"I could say the same for you."

"I've been seasick—I'm better now."

"The surgeon thinks I had a bout with food poisoning," Titus said, "but can't be sure. At least I'm still alive."

"Barely, by your looks." Macha thought about Metrobius' death by the same means. Could someone have attempted to murder Titus? Was it the same person? She warned Titus to be careful of what he ate and told him of Metrobius' death.

As if reading her thoughts, Titus exhaled and touched Macha's soft cheek with his rough hand. "Thanks for the warning. I've been careful about what I ate."

Macha felt the warmth of his body through his tunic as she leaned against him. After being away from him for so long, it seemed a miracle of the gods they were together once again, even if for a little while.

Quietly, they moved to the cot and sat side by side. Titus placed an arm around Macha's back, his hand coming to rest on her shoulder. A pleasurable shudder raced down her spine.

Titus looked into her eyes. "Has Senator Bassus found a way to get me out of here?"

"No, not yet." She sighed.

"Damn!"

Macha winced. His grip tightened on her shoulder.

"I can't stay here caged like a lion. I must be freed so I can search for the *real* traitors." Titus loosened his grasp. "Sorry," he added.

"Senator Bassus is doing everything he can to release you. He left his home earlier this morning to see the Emperor."

Titus exhaled. "Good. Vespasian will listen to him. I'll get out of here, yet."

They lapsed into silence for a moment before Macha told her husband of the hazardous journey from Genua to Luna. She described the bandit attack at which time Titus grew alarmed. Macha calmed him by explaining her group was rescued by the Praetorians and the confession by the deserter, Sergius Faunus, revealed that Crixus, known as Horse Arse, had planned the ambush. She also relayed the attempt on her life upon arriving in Rome.

For a split second Titus' hand tightened about her upper arm. "Thank Castor and Pollax you survived," he said. "You took a great risk coming to Rome."

Macha shivered when she thought of the attacks.

"You're shaking, Macha," Titus said. "This has affected you more than you want to admit."

Macha sighed. "You're right, my love, but I had to. Your life is too important to me and little Titus."

"Not at the risk of losing yours." He drew her closer, but she pushed away. Macha turned and took his hand into hers and softly kissed it.

"Don't be foolish, my love. If I hadn't, we would have never known about Crixus' involvement. But now he must be found and placed under arrest. Then we can learn who the plotters are."

"If he knows and confesses. No doubt those involved are among the nobility and command officers of the army."

Macha released Titus's hand. "Surely the Emperor will listen, especially, if Crixus is arrested and confesses."

"Only if documentary evidence accompanies the confession. Anything else Vespasian regards as innuendoes and lies, especially, if the statements are made by a freedman of Crixus' questionable background. "

The only documentation Macha knew about were the parchment fragments she received from Edain. That wouldn't be enough. There must be more information written down somewhere.

"But what about confessions by slaves?" She asked.

"He regards them with the same suspicion. People will say anything under torture. Besides, if members of the Senate or influential merchants are involved, then we are dealing with wealth and power and the influence it carries."

Something sank in Macha's stomach. Softly stroking Titus' hand, she thought the fates are against Titus. There has to be something I can do for him, she thought, but what? I didn't journey to Rome with all the dangers to give up without a fight.

"I know money buys power, but that much?" Macha asked. She gestured broadly with both hands.

"The Empire is desperate for revenue and needs their financial support. The treasury is nearly empty. Vespasian is doing all he can to stabilize the economy and fill the treasury legally."

"Can't he raise the taxes? As distasteful as that sounds, this is a time of great need."

"He can collect only so much, and unlike his predecessors, he refuses to fleece the people," Titus said. "He's depending on many of the wealthier merchants and nobility to contribute generously by making high bids on

Imperial contracts and monopolies. He has to tread lightly until the coffers are filled."

"But what if the evidence reveals involvement by the aristocracy?" Macha asked. "Surely he'll do something."

"Vespasian will, but the evidence must be ironclad."

It appeared to Macha that no one had attempted to find such information. She resolved to search for it on her own. No one else would.

A loud rapping on the cell door jolted Macha and Titus.

"Time's up!" bellowed the turnkey.

They glanced to the door and looked at one another again.

"I'll return soon, I promise," Macha said.

Titus took her slim hands into his and softly kissed them. "I know."

Macha pulled away, stood, squared her shoulders, and fled from his room, determined to do everything in her power to get Titus' release.

CHAPTER 18

Old Friends

In the Praetorian visitor's courtyard Macha sat on a hardwood bench waiting for Bassus. If it weren't for Titus' perilous situation, it would be a wonderful day to play the harp, like at home. She admired the yellow crown daisies, purple iris, and red spring roses being cultivated by barracks slaves. Swirling on a light breeze, their fragrances drifted through the garden.

But the beauty around her couldn't overcome Macha's disappointment. No doubt influential enemies had the Emperor's ear, and no documentary evidence implicating the conspirators had surfaced. Unless she found a way to obtain his release, Titus would languish in confinement until his court-martial. She prayed that Crixus' arrest was forthcoming, his confession possibly the key to Titus' freedom. But she couldn't rely on that. She had to find someone trustworthy to shed light on the conspiracy and had to uncover the answers to the fragmented list found on poor Nicanor's body. To whom did the names belong? What about the name crossed out and the one underlined? And the letters, VE, what did they mean? Did the drawing of the eagle have any significance?

"How is Titus?" Bassus asked, jolting Macha from her thoughts. She turned and found him standing to one side of her bench dressed in his white and purpled-trimmed senatorial toga.

"As well as can be expected," she answered. Macha stood and strolled with her patron to the courtyard exit, at the edge of the parade field where her entourage and litter waited. "Did you see the Emperor?" she asked a moment later.

"Yes, I informed him about General Valens overstepping his authority by sending Titus to Rome behind my back while I was still making inquiries."

126

Macha turned to the Senator. "What was his reaction?"

"He was very displeased and agreed Valens should be sacked."

As Bassus and Macha stepped along the brick pathway approaching her retinue, they halted. A ragged formation of new Praetorian recruits, carrying oval shields and wooden practice swords, marched past, led by a snarling drill centurion.

"Did you tell him about the attacks here and on the coast?" Macha asked loudly, trying to be heard above the clattering of the formation and profanities of the centurion.

"I gave him a full report," Bassus answered. "He told me to continue with my investigation. However, he was surprised you came to Rome."

She sighed. "I want to be with my husband, isn't that enough?"

"That's what I said to the Emperor, but, I know that isn't enough for *you*."

The troops passed and Macha and Bassus continued across the dusty courtyard, both of them coughing to clear their throats of the dust.

"That reminds me," Bassus said afterwards. "I'm seeing Titus in a few minutes. Perhaps he can add something to this whole affair."

Macha shook her head. "I doubt if he can. I told him all about it."

"I'll speak to him anyway." Bassus paused, looked about and brought his balding head closer to Macha. "I had an interesting conversation with an old army friend while waiting for you."

"What about?"

"A woman."

She narrowed her eyes. "What woman?"

Bassus explained he had met Furius Crasippes, an old centurion and crony from his days in the army. Years before, the crusty soldier transferred from the army to the Praetorian Guard. Now he was chief turnkey and described to Bassus his life as a jailer.

"The duty is easy," Furius had related. "For a price, I give the rich ladies access to their husbands or anyone else for that matter. Now, take this Titus fellow, one woman

127

paid me one hundred *denarii* just to let her know who visited him."

The last remark had aroused Bassus' curiosity. "Really, what else did she want?"

The craggy old centurion roared. "It's what I got from her. When I said he was expecting a visit from his wife today, she gave me a gold ring right off her hand."

Bassus frowned. "When was she here?"

"This morning."

"What's her name?"

"Fausta. I doubt if she gave me her true name."

"Describe her."

Furius did. She wore a veil and kept her head covered with a mantle. She walked with a hobble, but Furius believed it was faked.

Bassus had instructed the old war horse to keep him apprised of any further questions and activities by Fausta.

"She doesn't fit the description of anyone I know," Macha said, once he finished his story. "Obviously, it's a disguise, but whoever the person is, she won't be paying any more visits to Castra Praetoria."

Bassus agreed.

As far as Macha was concerned the woman had more than a passing interest in Titus' well being—or lack of it. Why else would she want to know about his visitors? Who was the woman? The ring was proof of wealth and influence. Macha had no doubts spies were watching her every movement.

* * * * *

Five minutes later Macha's heavily guarded retinue left the Praetorian Barracks. Shafer walked alongside Macha's litter as the entourage pushed its way through a crowded shop-lined street. The sedan lurched to a stop when a squad of ten Praetorians bullied its way ahead of them. Macha immediately recognized a vegetable and flower shop she had frequented on earlier trips to Rome, little more than a cubicle in the wall. Her eyes focused on Silvia, the nine-year-old daughter of the shopkeeper, Lepidus, and his wife, Clodia. She watched them carefully but quickly fashion laurel wreaths. Sitting behind the wooden counter, mother and daughter framed the green aromatic leaves with willow twigs and covered them with spring roses and tiny sweet-smelling lilies. No doubt they were for a dinner party scheduled that evening.

"I know this place, Shafer," Macha said to the servant who stood alongside the sedan. "It has been at least two years since I was last here. I must see if Clodia and little Silvia remember me."

Macha ordered the slaves to set down her litter, and she stepped onto the uneven cobblestone sidewalk. Given the circumstances of yesterday's attempt on her life, she motioned Shafer to follow. Macha told Viriatus, the big Spaniard and head of her armed escort of slaves carrying truncheons, to stay outside but to keep a close watch on anyone entering or leaving the shop.

Approaching the stall, through the din of the mob, Macha saw Silvia speaking to her mother.

Clodia said something to her daughter, kissed her on the cheek and motioned her back to work. With a slight turn of the head, her sunken eyes focused on Macha.

Macha waved a greeting.

Clodia responded, "*Ave*! Greetings, Lady Carataca, I have fresh roses today—a special price for you alone!" Once glowing in matronly plumpness, Clodia had wasted to a gaunt shell. Sallowed skin hung in loose folds from her arms and cheeks. What once were fleshy fingers now reminded Macha of chicken claws. If so, she wondered if the woman suffered from the throat disease as her own mother had. She wouldn't live another six months.

"Why, thank you, I would love some flowers," Macha answered. She loved flowers as much as her music and horses. In their beauty and fragrance perhaps she would find solace.

"Only the best for you, Lady Carataca!" Clodia's voice rasped. She glanced toward Shafer, and apparently recognizing the ebony woman as a slave, crinkled her nose in contempt. Leaning to one side, Clodia snorted, and spat a glob of blood towards the trash-filled gutter, adding another course to the buzzing flies' banquet. Then she wrapped a dozen yellow roses in a big lily pad and handed it to Macha.

Macha held the flowers close to her face, closed her eyes and inhaled the soothing fragrance. The muscles throughout her willowy body relaxed as she took in the flowers' wonderful smell. She opened her eyes as Clodia watched approvingly.

"These are lovely, Clodia. I won't forget this." Macha gave her two copper *asses*.

"Lady, this is too much, I said I had a special price for you."

"Never mind, Clodia, these flowers are special."

"Bless you, lady."

She said farewell and returned to the sedan. As her litter moved down the lane, she thought about poor Clodia and her condition. She wanted to do something for the family, but at the moment could not think of anything.

Macha's entourage entered the crowded Forum, built in the valley between the Capitoline and Palatine Hills. The great porticoed temples of Saturn, Castor and Pollux surrounded the huge plaza along with castellated government buildings—the Basilica of Julius Caesar, the Senate, and the tablinum housing the Imperial archives. About midway across the statue-clustered busy square, she caught sight of the white and gold-plated chariot belonging to her friend Antonia, a Vestal Virgin, moving through the mob. The timing could not have been better, as she had intended to visit her.

Because Vestals were expected to remain aloof in public, Macha didn't know if Antonia would respond when she waved and called her name, but Antonia raised her hand, and ordered her female driver and escorting slaves to stop. She motioned her servants, husky African and German women clothed in long white tunics, to clear a path for Macha to approach her carriage. Bassus had made Antonia's acquaintance at the Emperor's court, and had introduced her to Macha three years earlier and they had become good friends.

Antonia greeted her in a soft but confident voice as she stepped from the car. "What a pleasant surprise. I didn't know you were in Rome."

"I arrived yesterday afternoon," Macha answered with a slight bow of the head, a courtesy rendered to all Vestals in public.

Antonia motioned with her small hand. "Step closer, Macha, please. For goodness sakes, I'm no holy relic to be gazed upon at a distance. I'm your friend, remember?"

Macha caught herself blushing as she stopped a couple of feet before the priestess, as required. At thirty-five Antonia's finely-sculptured face revealed few signs of aging. She must have visited the Emperor, Macha thought. Her hairstyle and clothing were too formal for a simple jaunt through the city streets. Antonia wore dark brown hair in six plaits. As prescribed for the Vestals, she turned them up over six pads of artificial hair kept in place by bands with leather strips hanging down on either side of her slender shoulders. A long white robe of the finest linen draped her short frame and she wore leather sandals dyed white.

Her position as a Vestal Virgin never stopped men from casting furtive looks at Antonia. On more than one occasion, Macha noticed men, including Bassus, gazing upon her with more than reverent glances.

Antonia peered about, faced Macha and lowered her voice, "I heard news at court that Titus has been arrested for treason."

"The charges are lies. I've traveled to Rome to prove it."

"Can you? The charges are very serious."

Macha hesitated. "Can I speak in confidence, Antonia?"

"By all means." She nodded to her escort to move back a few steps.

"I must prove Titus' innocence—I just visited him at the Praetorian Camp. I'm certain the key is in Rome."

"If I can help, you have only to ask."

Macha stepped back speechless, grateful and excited her friend would use her status and power in aiding her. "Perhaps you can use your influence with the Emperor." The Vestals had access to him anytime day or night.

Antonia crinkled her pale forehead, accentuating the fine lines at the corner of her amber eyes. "I'll do what I can, Macha, but the Emperor Vespasian is one to keep his own counsel. In the meantime, I shall sacrifice to Fortuna and Minerva on your husband's behalf."

"I appreciate any help you can give us," Macha said.

"It's a pity I didn't see you earlier, I left the palace no more than a few minutes ago."

"Did you see Senator Bassus?"

For a split second Antonia stiffened. "Yes, he left the Emperor's private apartments as I arrived. We exchanged greetings before he was drawn aside by a couple of self-important senators."

Macha found Antonia's reaction to the mention of Bassus' name curious but for the time being allowed it to pass. Perhaps she was reading too much into Antonia's facial expression and body movements.

After further small talk, Macha and Antonia went their separate ways. Macha prayed Antonia would use her influence with the Emperor to obtain Titus' release right away. Then a thought occurred to her. The list found on Nicanor's body included the letters, VE. Could these be the first two letters of the word Vestal? Did the conspirators have something to do with the Vestal Virgins? Then again, there were many words that began with VE. She must give further thought to this notion.

* * * * *

Upon returning to Bassus' home, Macha was met at the door by the stooped house steward, Vasili. "Lady Carataca," he said, "there is a courier from Mediolanum waiting to see you. He's in the atrium."

Alarmed, Macha brushed by the old servant. There could be no reason to receive a message from the north unless something was wrong.

The dusty soldier stood when Macha slipped into the sun-filled reception room. "Lady Carataca, I have been instructed to inform you that your son, Titus, has been kidnapped!"

CHAPTER 19

Anguish and Determination

A courier stood before her, his clothes smelling of horse sweat. Macha suppressed the panic sweeping through her, sank into a curved wicker chair by the atrium wall and wiped sweaty fingers across her forehead. "Little Titus! No!"

"It is so, lady," the haggard young courier, wearing the uniform of a tribune replied. "I have ridden all the way from Mediolanum to inform you."

For a couple of minutes Macha said nothing, taking several deep breaths. Gods, this couldn't be happening! Not her son! Her throat thickened, her mouth dry. In a rasping voice she asked a passing slave to fetch a cup of water and one for the young officer.

"What happened?" she asked over a lump in her throat.

"He was snatched from the courtyard of Tribune Cnidius Rufus' house."

Mother Goddess! At her brother-in-law's estate, in the care of his wife Helena. "How?"

"The kidnappers struck just before sunset." The courier rested his hand on the hilt of his sword. "Tribune Rufus was spending the night at the legion garrison, on duty as officer-of-the watch. Once word came, we hurried to his home with a squadron of cavalry and found Lady Helena frantic." He took a deep breath, exhaled, and shook his head.

"Please, go on," Macha said barely above a whisper.

"Lady Helena said she had spent the afternoon indoors supervising dinner preparations while your son played outside in the courtyard with his cousins. She was expecting guests for the evening meal and gave instructions to the house steward to leave the courtyard gate open. The slaves had been working in the quad when one of them heard hoof beats. He spotted a dozen riders to the south emerging from the forest and told the overseer and other slaves. They watched the horsemen gallop toward the villa in a cloud of dust, ford the river, and cross the field next to Tribune Rufus and Lady Helena's villa."

Macha knew the villa's location all too well. Situated on a knoll about a mile north of Mediolanum's city gates, their home sat between a small tributary of the River Po and a thick stand of woods.

Macha's slave returned with a silver tray holding an earthen pitcher and two blue glass cups. He handed each a cup.

"Drink up," Macha said, "You must be very thirsty." Macha shut her eyes and sipped, allowing the water to cool her mouth and soothe her parched throat. After she dismissed the young slave, Macha said in a clearer voice, "Please continue."

The tribune set his cup on the short legged wooden table in front of Macha. "The overseer thought the riders were cavalry, because they rode in columns of two. The slaves were used to Tribune Rufus riding home with a detail of cavalry when patrolling the highway and paid little attention."

"The fools!"

"True, but the lengthening shadows of dusk deceived the workers. It wasn't until the riders neared the villa they saw the horsemen's homespun tunics and shabby cloaks. They were a mean looking bunch who reined up in the courtyard—all scarred faces and missing teeth. Before the slaves could sound the alarm, the brigands corralled them."

"My son?"

"I'm coming to that, Lady Carataca. Their leader was a broken-nosed, big-jawed brute. He saw your boy playing at one end of the yard with the Greek slave boy."

"Demetrios?"

"Aye, boys were unaware at first of what the commotion was all about. When your son ran, the leader rode him down, snatched, and placed him in front of his saddle. The slaves say Young Titus screamed for you, Lady."

"Oh, my poor son!"

134

"The leader yelled to one of his men to kill the slave boy. A big red headed Gaul caught and slew the boy with his sword."

"Mother Goddess! Poor Demetrios."

"None of the slaves understood why he was slain and they were not."

She knew why but kept the reason to herself. "Go on," she said.

"The leader signaled to his men, and they galloped out of the compound. Darkness made it impossible to follow them."

"But the slaves must have told someone after they fled."

"They immediately ran to Lady Helena. She sent her steward on horseback to Tribune Rufus. The First Italica Legion dispatched cavalry units to search the area around Mediolanum. But by then the outlaws had vanished."

"Exactly when did they kidnap my son and kill Demetrios?" Macha asked, leaning forward.

"Three days after you left Mediolanum."

Macha dropped the cup she still held in her hand, shattering it on the tiled floor. Her son had been taken seven days ago, seven days of captivity and terror before she ever knew he was gone. And Demetrios. Someone must have known he had been a witness to his father's murder. She swallowed and took a deep breath as she struggled to keep her emotions under control. Gods knew how her son was being treated. Was he still alive? It was all her fault for chasing her husband to Rome. But she had to search for the truth. Why would anyone kidnap or harm an innocent child? Ransom was the answer. Demetrios had no value as a slave; his killing eliminated the only eye-witness to Nicanor's death. However, the life of young Titus, son of a nobleman and Roman officer, would be worth a hefty sum of gold—enough to force her to keep her mouth shut and from interfering in her husband's case.

Interrupting Macha's thoughts, a slave hurried into the atrium to clean the floor of the cup's fragments. Following closely behind, another slave poured a cup of water and left it on the small table by her chair. She and the courier remained silent until the slaves departed.

135

"Somebody knew we survived the attack outside of Luna," Macha said as if thinking out loud.

The youthful tribune gazed at her quizzically. "Begging your pardon, Lady?"

"No matter," she said as calmly as she could. "How much effort has been spent on finding my son?"

"Tribune Rufus is leading the investigation. Because you placed your son in his and Lady Helena's care, he feels personally responsible."

"Has there been a demand for ransom?"

"Not by the time I was dispatched to you, Lady."

Macha attempted to collect her thoughts. A demand for gold could have arrived after the courier departed.

For a moment neither said anything.

"I thank you, tribune. What is your name?"

"Cornelius Tacitus, madam."

"Tacitus, you have a great gift for detail, but you must be hungry," she said. "Go to the kitchen and have a decent meal—you deserve it."

"Thank you, Lady. We'll do everything in our power to find your son."

"I pray he still lives."

"So do we all."

Tacitus saluted and followed a slave to the kitchen.

Her hand shaking, Macha took a sip of water from the new cup. She thought about her son and Demetrios. It had been swift, violently executed murder, and abduction, well-planned and expensive. Whoever planned her son's kidnapping and Demetrios murder had studied her family's daily activities. No gang of thugs was going to risk their necks snatching a noble's son without being handsomely rewarded. Or have reason to kill a child of nobility who could bring a rich reward, as long as the possibility of a ransom remained. She must believe that. But Demetrios deserved a better fate than death!

The riders had scattered to the Aeolian winds, carrying her son, gods knew which direction. If they expected Macha to choose between the lives of her husband or son, or to react hysterically, they were grievously mistaken. She was determined to see both her husband and son remained alive, and would settle for no less than death to anyone who did harm to them, and she would seek vengeance for Demetrios.

It made chilling sense. The conspirators expected her to sit and remain idle like a helpless matron. Macha couldn't afford to jeopardize her son's life, but she refused to be intimidated by thugs and watch her husband and her son die. Still she must move cautiously.

She made no attempt to stop her hands shaking, as she placed the cup on the table, nor contain the tears welling in her eyes. She cupped her face in her hands and wept.

* * * * *

The following morning, Bassus' gatekeeper found a sealed parchment addressed to Lady Carataca slipped beneath the iron grate at the house entrance. Vasili, the house steward, approached and gave Macha the scroll as she sat in the brisk air of the sunlit garden, strumming the lyre to soothe her nerves. She laid it aside and suspecting what the message contained, broke the wax seal and unrolled the letter with a sense of dread.

Your son will be released after your husband has been executed. If you insist on sticking your nose where it does not belong, the boy will die.

Her chest tightened. For a second she couldn't breathe. Should she send the threatening letter to the Emperor? Quickly she discarded the notion, fearing he might suspect her contriving the letter for her own purposes. Forcing herself to inhale deeply and slowly, she slumped against the padded backrest of the bench.

The marble fountain bubbled noisily. A fine mist filtering through the early morning sunbeams evaporated into a small rainbow. Macha could too easily imagine little Titus' fear of not knowing what would happen next. "Please Mother Goddess Anu, keep my son safe," she prayed out loud.

Pangs of doubt, guilt and a sense of hopelessness assailed Macha. What should she do next? Had she been too proud in assuming more responsibilities than expected of a woman? Perhaps the investigation did belong in the hands of men after all. She tried to imagine what her husband would do in her place.

Macha couldn't tell him about the kidnapping yet. She could picture his rage upon hearing the news of his son being abducted by a pack of filthy bandits. He would swear vengeance to kill them all. Titus' imprisonment would become unbearable, because he could not participate in the search for the abductors. But she must tell him and soon.

She wondered how Bassus or her father would have dealt with the situation. Then again, she never understood how men thought. Gods knew they weren't practical or sensible as women. But so far she had accomplished little in freeing Titus. Everything she touched turned to disaster. Macha placed the letter inside her girdled sash.

* * * * *

The night before, Macha had told Bassus about the kidnapping of her son and early the next morning informed him after receiving the threatening message. Later that afternoon, she was about to leave for the Praetorian Barracks when she received a message to meet him in his library. The Senator assured her he would order the new acting legionary commander, who replaced General Valens, to assign extra troops in the search for the kidnappers and have his spies scour Mediolanum for any news regarding the threatening letter.

Dressed in a light green stola, girdled at the waist with a yellow and blue-trimmed sash, Macha arrived minutes ahead of Bassus. The afternoon sun streamed through the side window facing the garden and reflected off the leather canisters of scrolls and books lining the shelves from floor to ceiling. A new bronze bust of the Emperor Vespasian rested on a marble pedestal in one corner. Another corner contained the bejowled statue of Bassus' adopted father, the late Gaius Flavius Porcius.

She heard Bassus' heavy footsteps echoing along the tiled corridor outside. He greeted her in a pure-white woolen senatorial toga with purple stripes. Bassus took a seat opposite Macha and said his informants had discovered Crixus' hiding place. "He's right here in the Aventine District."

Unconsciously, Macha gripped the side of her chair with her fingers. "Do you mean he's been hiding under our noses the whole time?"

"A grain of sand hides best on the beach. Rome is ideal for the likes of him," Bassus responded. His deep-set eyes peered at Macha across a cedar table inlaid with ivory. "Apparently, he didn't know about the botched attack on the coast or the one here in the city."

Macha caught her breath and shook her head. "That's difficult to believe. Whomever Crixus is working for must know."

"Whatever the reason, he's buried himself in the Aventine slums."

"Maybe he was involved in my son's kidnapping or knows who is."

"That's another reason for his arrest. I want to find your son before he's harmed."

"When are you arresting Crixus?"

The sound of approaching footsteps echoed from the hallway. Bassus shot a fore-finger to his lips as they turned and watched a slave pass by. "This evening," Bassus said after the slave had departed. "The Aventine is like a clogged sewer. From time to time we unplug it. I'm leading a detachment of troops from the Watch—it's all been arranged. Surprise is our best weapon."

"Are they from the barracks on *Vicus Piscinae* Road?"

"Yes, the Fourth Cohort."

She recalled Titus mentioning they were assigned to the precinct station next to the *Porta Rudusculana* Gate, and patrolled Rome's Twelfth and Thirteenth Districts, including Aventine Hill. Six other cohorts of the *Vigiles*, the Watch, protected the rest of the city.

"Strange," Macha mused, "Crixus must know you live here."

"Rich and poor live together in the Aventine, cheek by jowl," Bassus said. "To his kind, it makes no difference."

Macha and Bassus knew hundreds of places existed in the Aventine where Crixus could disappear, including the labyrinth of caves beneath the Circus Maximus. The great race track and stadium sprawled beyond the foot of the Aventine's north side.

"Fortunately," Bassus continued, "my spies greased the right palms with enough denarii to buy the needed information. Thirty pieces of silver opens nearly any mouth."

Macha looked past Bassus to the library door and noticed the shadows creeping down the hallway. It was nearly evening. An idea crossed her mind. "When you go to arrest Crixus, I want to be along."

"Why?" Bassus jerked back in shock.

"My husband may be executed for a crime he didn't commit. I have the right to be with you when Crixus is arrested."

"No, Macha," Bassus said. His steely eyes glared at her from a weathered middle-aged face. "You're staying home. I won't have time to keep an eye on you."

His answer surprised Macha. She didn't expect a direct refusal. "Must I remind you about the attack near Luna and here in Rome?" Macha said as she locked eyes with him. "If you recall, I defended myself well enough on the coast and escaped death here. I insist on going—I must!"

Bassus scowled. "You must?" He shook his head. "You're staying here. Remember, Pomponius Appius saved you from another cutthroat. And had not the Praetorians arrived, we would have all been murdered. You were plain lucky here in Rome."

"But on the coast I defended myself like a man," she persisted.

"That's not enough. I've never doubted your courage—you fought bravely. But you were very fortunate. You're not a skilled fighter. We don't know if Crixus is alone or hiding with other ruthless characters."

"I assume you're taking reinforcements—I wouldn't be alone."

"Naturally. They'll arrest Crixus and anyone found with him. What good can you do there?"

For a moment Macha hesitated. She peered into Bassus' eyes and sensed he was determined to refuse her request. She turned away and scanned the room attempting to think of an answer that would change his mind. Macha couldn't tell Bassus the true reason, yet. Although she had shown the parchment to Bassus and the scrap with the eagle, she still carried the fragments in a leather bag in a fold of her stola. Perhaps Crixus would know the meaning of the names and initials, VE and that of the eagle. He might confirm if VE was associated with the Vestal Virgins or if the eagle was from Legion First Italica.

· "I want to question him about my son's kidnapping," Macha said a moment later. That much was the truth.

"The interrogator will extract everything. And what he'll do to Crixus no lady should witness."

"There you go again about women," Macha chided. "I've seen my share of bloodshed. I killed a man, and my horse trampled another. I watched Pomponius Appius cut off Sergius Faunus's finger, feed it to dogs, and then execute him and the other prisoners. Then I was nearly murdered here in Rome. I wouldn't call any of that an outing at the theater of Pompey."

"Yes, you've been involved in all those things. But that's not a valid reason for going, Macha."

"I need to see if this is the same Crixus. If it hadn't been for me, you would never have known his true identity."

"There is only one Horse Arse," Bassus advised. "We would have learned soon enough."

Macha was about to protest, but Bassus raised his hand. "There will be no further argument, you're staying here and that's final."

Macha turned and stormed from the room. She must find a means of being present when Bassus' men seized Crixus.

CHAPTER 20

Encounters on a Roman Evening

Macha was well aware Rome was a dangerous place when enshrouded in darkness. Lamplight escaping from stalls of all-night cookshops and taverns, and torches posted in wall niches lining alleys leading to the city's better brothels did little more than allow a victim to see which shadow picked his pockets. Besides hardened teamsters driving produce and goods wagons, by law allowed to make deliveries only after dark, few people ventured forth without an escort or the company of friends. Robbers, footpads, and gangs of toughs roamed the streets searching for hapless victims to rob, rape, beat, and test the sharpness of their iron blades. Gods help the lone woman, including prostitutes, working the streets.

From earlier conversations with Bassus, Macha understood the Vigiles, Rome's police force, were spread too thin to patrol every street and alley. Besides peacekeeping duties, they doubled as firefighters. Along with swords and wooden batons, they carried rope ladders and buckets lined with pitch tar, and javelin-prods for pushing down burning timbers. The populace nicknamed them bucketmen.

Macha would depend on her own resources if she were to follow Bassus and the detail of watchmen secretively. How dare he forbid her just because she was a woman? She must take an escort, Shafer, the only one she could trust. Although most of Bassus' slaves had belonged to his household for years, usually one discontented slave could be bribed to report the house activities to an outsider. Immediately, Macha's horse groom, Jason, came to mind. Macha wondered if he had not been a spy in her home after all. Then again, what about poor Nicanor and the list he stole? She would give it more thought later.

That evening, disguised as licensed prostitutes in saffron gowns and dark woolen mantels, the prescribed clothing of the trade, Macha and Shafer followed Bassus, Pomponius Appius, and the bucketmen. Because Titus was born in Rome, he and Macha often visited the city when he was on furlough from the army. She knew her way around most of the city, especially, the Aventine District, where Bassus resided. Staying at a safe distance, the women began their trek along *Vicus Piscinae* Road as the troops left the precinct station near the old Servian Wall. The women had bundled themselves against the evening chill. Macha carried a thin dagger hidden in a cleft, sewn inside her dress. Slaves were forbidden to carry weapons, but Shafer was no fool. Macha believed it wiser not to ask her questions. A full moon slowly climbed into a clear eastern sky filled with an infinite number of stars.

As they followed the troops, through the dark, dingy, trash-filled lanes of the Aventine, Macha recognized the area. "Clodia and Lepidus live nearby," she whispered.

"But this place is terrible at night, Mistress Carataca," Shafer said. "Thugs roam here—we must be careful. They raped one of the master's stable boys last month. He most nearly died."

"We'll keep to the shadows," Macha assured her. "We can't afford to be spotted by Bassus."

The women trailed the detachment as it turned onto Ursus Street, one of the Aventine's wider lanes. Between the glow from the bucketmen's lanterns and the moonlight, Macha and Shafer managed to watch them from a discreet distance. An occasional freight wagon rumbled by and momentarily blocked their passage.

A distant voice cried, "Robbers! Help!" Typical night sounds in Rome.

She and Shafer had to carefully tread the city streets. The women had walked about a half block when they heard the shatter of an amphora bottle followed by a cat's yowl nearby. A chill ran up Macha's back. She gave Shafer a knowing glance, and they ran. Too late. Five young toughs sprang from a black side alley. Quickly they surrounded and grabbed Macha and Shafer by their arms, forcing them to halt. The grip by Macha's assailant dug painfully into her flesh, but she didn't dare scream because she and Shafer could be murdered before the watchmen rushed to their rescue.

"Look at what we've got here," one of the older thugs said. Big in chest and arms, he appeared to be the leader. The smell of his rotting gums and the sour wine on his breath struck Macha's face like a blow. She turned her head away.

"We got us barbarian whores, Balbus," the one holding Macha said to the leader. "At least they're pretty, not the usual snakes we catch."

"Gods, they're tall," a broken nose youth of about fourteen remarked.

"But I've got a *mentula* to satisfy them," a pimply faced character roared. He pointed to the bulge between the legs of his dirty tunic.

"Looking for business?" Balbus asked, his thin ragged beard and face matching his tunic. "We'll give you a little."

"For free!" the tall thug of about fifteen who held Shafer sneered.

Because these boys, pretending to be men, had mistaken them for street walkers, Macha realized that might work to their advantage. She sent a warning glance to Shafer in the moonlight.

"Easy," Macha said calmly to Balbus. She could barely speak, the word catching in her throat. It was all she could do to keep control, fight the urge to panic, to flee. She had her knife, but in these close quarters she couldn't pull it out before it would be grabbed and used against her.

To buy time, she said, "Why should handsome lads like you," nearly choking on the words, "use force when we'll give it willingly? We're professionals—you'll enjoy it more."

"I'll enjoy it anyway," Balbus said, "whether you're alive or dead."

"Don't be in such a rush. Fannia and I will give you the best time of your lives," Macha advised in an enticing voice. "But we can only please you one at a time."

That brought a roar from the group. "They'll pay us by the time we're through," Balbus said to the gang. "What's your name?" he asked Macha.

"Rectina," she answered demurely. "Maybe you've heard of my pleasures?"

"I bet I know where you like it most," Balbus said.

Macha smiled. "If you release us, we promise you pleasure you won't forget. But we can't be at our best when you're hurting our arms."

Balbus considered it. "Let loose, they're not going nowhere. Besides, it's been too long since a woman willingly polished my knob—the tall one looks like she could suck both balls right through my rod."

Even in the dark, Macha could see Shafer flush with anger.

They released the women. "Just give us a few seconds to get ready," Macha said, winking. "After all, you don't want any disease." She turned for a moment, but the toughs continued watching her. "Look," she said, "I'm not going anywhere, but even a whore needs a little privacy. Can't you turn your heads just for a few seconds?"

They did.

Her eyes darted to the alley across Ursus Street. "I know just the place where we can lie together," Macha said to Balbus a few heart beats later. She saw a wagon noisily driving down the lane towards them. The driver wouldn't get involved. She gave Shafer an almost imperceptible nod to edge her way out into the street. Suddenly, Macha stomped Balbus' feet and elbowed him in the stomach.

Shafer kicked the fifteen-year-old in the groin. As he howled, doubling over and dropping to the ground, she kicked Balbus twice in the same place. He dropped like a sack of wheat from a tall-masted galley. Taken by surprise, the other three toughs stood in shock at the sight of the dagger now in Macha's hand. It gave the women a few seconds, long enough to make their escape. They darted across the way, barely ahead of the rumbling vegetable wagon pulled by a team of four horses.

The rig blocked the thugs from chasing them for a few precious seconds, and Macha and Shafer raced down the trash-filled alley, oblivious to the garbage and dung sliming beneath their feet.

Minutes later they nearly ran into a wall blocking the way. From its direction drifted a fetid stench. Macha heard the curses and clattering footsteps of the pursuing gang drawing nearer with each passing second.

"Why are we stopping, Mistress?" Shafer asked in a fearful voice. "We must climb over the fence before they catch us."

"Follow me, Shafer!" Macha said hurriedly. "I know this place. We're next to the *insula* where Clodia and Lepidus the shopkeeper live. Directly on the other side is a great dung cart."

A dung trader kept his wagon parked outside the apartment in the alley every evening, and drove it away early in the morning to collect offal around the city.

"There's a bench where people step up so they can dump their slop buckets over the wall," Macha said. They stopped at the base of the fence.

"We're not going to jump into that awful mess, are we?" Shafer asked in an indignant voice.

Macha shook her head. "No, just as we climb over the fence, there is a roof to the side. It's part of the stable next door. It's next to the wagon, but you can't see it until you're on top. At night it's impossible to see unless you know where to look. Help me up and follow behind—I'll show you."

They climbed the low wall and scooted onto the roof. Seconds later the gang flung themselves over the wall, into the filth-ridden foul-smelling barrels. Cries of surprise and obscenities erupted.

Macha and Shafer laughed as they scampered across the roof and down the steps on the other side of the apartment. "It looks like the spirit of the chase drained right out of them," Macha said.

"I know the one I kicked between the legs had his drained," Shafer said. "I doubt the Aeolian winds could suck his swollen balls through the city gates."

Reeking of garbage, but otherwise safe, Macha and Shafer found another way to Ursus Street. As they rounded the corner, at the intersection with Serpent Lane, they spotted Bassus and Pomponius Appius at the head of forty watchmen. The two turned to head in the opposite direction, but it was too late.

"Stop right there!" Bassus ordered.

CHAPTER 21

Honest Horse Traitors are Hard to Find

Bassus glowered at Macha and Shafer where they lurked in the shadows ten paces away. He stood at the head of the watchmen with Pomponius Appius. Light from the smoky lanterns, carried by the bucketmen, cast a dingy pall on the uniforms of Bassus and the troops.

Macha and Shafer glanced at one another. A cool breeze streamed up the hill from the River Tiber, bringing the stench of floating sewage and the fetid smell of the wharfside cattle market. In the distance, two drunks bawled a slurring ditty, followed seconds later by the shatter of a wine jug and a string of obscenities.

Bassus nodded to a couple of troopers and back to the women. Wriggling a forefinger he said, "Come here, you two."

There was no escape this time. "We don't need an escort," Macha said. She became aware of the reeking smell rising from her and Shafer's clothing and the filth oozing from her sandals and between her toes. She nearly gagged, but suppressed the feeling. She and Shafer approached Bassus.

"What in the name of Mars are you doing here?" Bassus inquired in a voice tinged with menace. "I ordered you to stay home."

"I did for a while," Macha admitted. "I'm sorry, but I had to follow. I take responsibility for bringing Shafer. Don't punish her, and don't send us back, not now." This wasn't the time to mention their harrowing escape.

Bassus crinkled his nose. "You smell like you've waded through every garbage heap in Rome. Explain why you followed us."

"I'm not going to lie—I wanted to see Crixus arrested. He may not have my son, but he might know where he is hidden."

147

Crixus, also known as Horse Arse, was only a freedman. But Macha suspected the plot against her husband, and the kidnapping of her son, came from the highest levels in Rome. Most likely young Titus was being kept somewhere more secretive and safer than a dingy apartment among Rome's poor.

"And in doing so, you could have gotten yourselves killed," Bassus answered, snapping Macha out of her thoughts. "You know how dangerous Rome is after dark."

"I thought we would be safer dressing as prostitutes." Now she knew how wrong she had been.

The bucketmen viewed the women and murmured among themselves. "What in Mars are two whores doing here?" one watchman muttered.

"To service us, what else?" another sneered.

"At ease!" Appius growled. "Keep your mouths shut! This is a lady and her slave."

Bassus struggled to maintain a sober face. "Very clever, Macha, sometimes you amaze me. Consider yourself fortunate not to have been accosted tonight."

"We managed," Macha answered truthfully.

The Senator grunted. "No doubt your son's kidnappers know you are in Rome and asking for my help in finding young Titus."

"But they wouldn't know you are about to arrest Crixus, or that I was present when it occurred."

"If he's in there." Bassus motioned to a sagging tenement down the shadow-filled street.

"Shafer and I can wait outside while your men arrest Crixus."

"Only because I have no men to spare escorting you home. But you *will* stay out of the way."

"I promise we will."

Minutes later the bucketmen arrested Crixus, dragging him from the dingy apartment bound in leather straps. Macha recognized him in the flickering lamplight as soon as the troops wrestled him from the apartment. His face matched the description given by the deserter, Faunus, after the attack outside of Luna. A long deep scar split the middle of his face from forehead to chin. Short of killing him, an axe couldn't have done more damage to his face.

Gods knew how he had survived such dreadful wounds or where he had received them. No wonder he was also known as Horse Arse.

Bassus followed the prisoner. He shook his head when he met Macha's eyes.

"My son wasn't with Crixus?" She asked.

"No, I'm sorry."

Macha turned away, dropped her head, and held a cupped hand to her face. She knew the chances of finding young Titus with the horse trader were slim, and his arrest confirmed her disappointment. She prayed Bassus' interrogation would reveal where her son was hidden.

The women tagged along as the Watch transported him by wagon to Lautumiae Prison for interrogation. Surrounded by the troops, the wagon holding Crixus bounced along the tufa stone *Vicus Jugarius* Road. The noise from the wagon's wheels and the tramping bucketmen echoed down the street, off the sagging tenement walls.

The detail turned out of the dreary shadows of the narrow lane and entered the Forum. Ebbing light from the watchmen's lanterns silhouetted dozens of statues dotting the plaza. In the surrounding gloom towered the colonnaded courthouse, Basilica Julia, the Temple of Saturn, and other public buildings. Latumiae Prison waited on the far side of the square.

As the party trudged up the slight incline past the Rostra, the prison emerged out of the purple darkness. The austerity of the grim-faced edifice seemed out of place among the elaborately designed buildings surrounding the Forum. Entering the prison's cramped reception room, the group headed down the murky narrow corridor leading to the cells and torture chamber below. The door from the outer room slammed behind the women, the sound echoing down the passage way as Macha and Shafer followed Bassus and Appius into the bowels of the prison. A couple of torch bearing Watchmen led the way as two guards followed behind with Crixus between them.

The smell of excrement and urine seeped from behind the solid iron doors of the cells, through narrow slots at the bottom where food was shoved to the prisoners. In the dim light outside one door Macha noticed a chipped bowl, crawling with vermin.

The troops led Crixus to the torture chamber, a shadowy fetid room in the lowest level of the sprawling lock up. Because this was Macha's first visit to the jail, Bassus explained it was used at one time as a barracks for prisoners taken in Rome's many wars. Now only common felons and high-grade misdemeanor offenders awaiting trial were incarcerated within its rough hewn stone walls. Occasionally inmates lingered in the filth-ridden rat-infested cells for more than a year. In some instances, for years at a time, prisoners were forgotten, accidentally or otherwise.

Smoky torches burning in iron casemates along the stone walls and two braziers resting on bronze tripods near the interrogation wheel provided the chamber's only light. The acrid fumes stung Macha's throat, causing her to sneeze and sniff. Others, including Bassus, fared no better as they snorted and cleared their throats. She scanned the room hoping to find a pitcher of water. All she saw was a splintered wooden tub filled with scum-covered water and iron prods. She covered her mouth and nose with a silk handkerchief. She may have dressed as a prostitute, but that wasn't going to stop her from carrying one bit of luxury. Shafer followed suit with a piece of homespun cloth she pulled from inside her long tunic.

Macha spotted a rack in one corner of the dungeon. A stone hearth containing hot irons and red coals rested at the other end. Nearby, dressed in a heavy black tunic and a dirty leather apron, a stubby interrogator with broad shoulders and a fat belly waited.

Bassus sat at a wooden plank table in front of a high double-sided wooden wheel. Macha and Shafer huddled behind him in the darkness of the hot stuffy room, dreading what was about to take place. The watchmen shoved Crixus to the front of Bassus' table. Crixus reeked of filth and horse sweat. Unconsciously Macha pressed her silk handkerchief closer to her nose again.

"I swear I've done nothing wrong," Crixus protested.

"We'll see if you'll change your story once the Quaestionarius gives your feet a love tap," Pomponius

Appius said. A head taller than Crixus, he stared at the shorter man, his eyes brightening. "But the irons aren't warm enough...yet."

Two bucketmen grabbed the prisoner's arms and dragged him to the upright wheel. It reminded Macha of a waterwheel. No doubt plans for Crixus provided for something far more dreadful than grinding wheat.

Stepping out of the shadows, the tall, horse-faced assistant torturer ripped off Crixus' tunic, leaving him clothed only in a dirty loincloth. Both interrogators untied his hands from behind his back and spun him around, facing Macha and the rest. The two men spotted Macha and Shafer. For a moment they stared as if puzzled by their presence. Women were not allowed in the torture chamber. Bassus gave them a sharp nod to continue.

As they pulled Crixus' arms above and behind his balding head, he shouted, "No!" and attempted to wrench himself free. The torturers yanked his arms tighter eliciting from him a scream that echoed through the chamber. They shackled his wrists with clattering iron chains to the wooden cross slats connecting both sides of the wheel's frame. Quickly, they clasped his ankles in leather restraints and iron buckles anchored to the stone floor at the wheel's base.

Crixus groaned. "But I tell you I'm innocent."

"Maybe you'll change your story once the irons have turned hot enough to blister and char a little, but not so white hot as to cauterize the wounds," Pomponius Appius grinned.

Bassus motioned to the torturers to begin. Gripping the spokes on both sides of the wheel, they began turning until Crixus' body was extended tautly, standing him on his tiptoes. He grimaced and closed his eyes. Sweat poured down both sides of his face as if anticipating the forthcoming agony. Macha doubted if she could bear to watch, yet she couldn't turn away.

The Senator leaned forward, resting his elbows on the table, and clasped his hands together under his chin. He glared at Crixus. "What part did you play in the attack on Lady Carataca, Pomponius Appius, and myself on the road to Luna?"

"Don't know what you're talking about, Lord Bassus," Crixus replied. "I'm a horse trader, not an outlaw. I demand to confront my accusers."

Appius approached Horse Arse and a sadistic grin crossed his thin lips. "That would be difficult, considering they're now in the bellies of wolves or festering as their droppings." He pulled a dagger from his scabbard and shot it to the base of Crixus throat. Barely pricking his skin, it sent a trickle of blood flowing down the side of his neck.

"Merciful gods, don't kill me."

"Answer truthfully," Bassus cautioned. "You are a freedman. Who is your former master?"

"I'm my own master!"

"Liar! Your manumission is recorded in the Imperial archives."

Crixus swallowed hard and his face reddened. He licked dry lips and rolled his eyes from side to side. Somewhere down a distant corridor an anguished scream of terror echoed. Blood from his wound coursed down the side of his body, dripping onto the stained stone floor.

"Let's not waste any more time with him," Bassus advised. Pomponius Appius agreed.

"Interrogator, ready at my command," Bassus ordered.

"Yes, my lord."

"Wait!" Crixus cried. "The merchant Julius Pedius and his wife Pollia freed me."

"What!" Macha caught herself whispering. The revelation jolted her. She had no inkling that Crixus had been their slave. We're they part of the plot?

"What do they know about your criminal activities?" Bassus questioned.

"Nothing," Horse Arse croaked. "I haven't seen them in five years."

Bassus glared. "Why? They are your patron. As a client you have obligations to them."

"Hah! Once when I needed help, those rich bastards would not give me so much as a copper *as*, the Empire's smallest coin." Crixus shook his head. "I went my own way."

"Who hired you to kill Lady Carataca and my troop on the coast road to Luna?" Bassus inquired.

"I don't know what you're talking about."

Appius slapped his face. "Liar!"

Crixus head snapped backwards. He groaned as his skull thudded against the wheel slats behind his head. Blood flowed down the side of his neck from the slight cut inflicted earlier by Appius' knife and onto his narrow shoulder. "I'm no bandit, I swear."

With a flick of an eyebrow Bassus motioned the interrogator toward Crixus.

The chief torturer pulled a long glowing iron poker from the burning coals. Slowly, to heighten the fear and accompanying pain, he crept to the wheel. Although Macha stood behind Bassus, she felt the heat radiating from the prod.

At the sight of the hot iron, Macha and Shafer braced one another. Shafer's fingers dug deeply into Macha's arms, sending a twinge of pain.

"Forgive me for touching you, Lady, but this is so horrible," Shafer whispered. She lessened her grip.

"It frightens me, too." Macha held Shafer closer, and it seemed to comfort them both.

As the torturer was about to lay an iron on Crixus feet, he cried, "Stop! I'll tell you everything! I can't stand pain!"

The torturer paused. "I'll spare your feet." He nodded to his assistant, and dropped the iron in the nearby brazier. The Quaestionarii with practiced professionalism grabbed the spokes on both sides of the great wheel, and ever so slowly started stretching Crixus' body. His face contorted as he bared his brown teeth attempting to contain a scream. But as his limbs were pulled tighter a loud groan escaped his lips. He twisted from side to side, fighting against the iron chains. Bound so tightly, the rubbing motion soon cut his wrists, and blood flowed down his dirty arms.

Macha heard bones popping from sockets, and shuddered. Shafer's fingernails dug into her arms, and they held one another tighter.

Crixus screamed.

"Stop the wheel," Bassus ordered. The interrogators complied. "Now, are you ready to tell the truth, Crixus?"

"There's nothing to tell."

Bassus nodded to the rackmasters.

Again they turned the wheel. Crixus let out a gut-wrenching howl. He vomited and fainted.

Shafer trembled and turned away, tears running down the side of her smooth sepia face.

"It's all right, Shafer, we won't stay much longer," Macha whispered. She struggled to overcome her own shaking and the roiling sickness in her stomach.

"Revive him," Bassus ordered. "I want answers, not a dead man on my hands."

The torturers loosened the tension, allowing Crixus to slump on the floor face down. They threw a bucket filled with scummy water on his prostrate body.

Macha turned in disgust, shocked by the barbaric methods used on Crixus. As she did, she noted most of the men present instinctively clutched and checked their limbs. She understood why. Crixus was a loathsome creature, but there had to be another way of extracting the truth. No doubt Horse Arse would confess to anything after his ordeal, but she hoped it would be the truth and not more lies. Then again, she dared not protest or she and Shafer would be removed from the chamber, none too gently, she suspected.

Shafer wiped the tears from her face. "I'm sorry, Mistress," she whispered.

Macha hugged her. "There is no need to apologize, Shafer," she whispered in reply. "This place is enough to make the strongest weep."

"But you didn't."

"No, but I will later, you'll see."

Minutes passed before Horse Arse regained consciousness. His sweaty face glistened. He groaned. "Crixus, can you hear me?" Bassus asked quietly.

"Aye," he rasped still lying on the floor.

"Are you ready to confess?"

Crixus turned his face to one side. "Yes, have mercy."

"Depending on what you tell me, I may offer you immunity, and spare you from a broken limb."

"Anything, but...but no more wheel!"

Bassus pointed a forefinger at Crixus. "Providing you tell us the truth and we can verify the information."

"Whatever...you...want to know." He groaned once again before continuing, "My face was nearly chopped in half. I can't...take any more pain."

"Can you stand on your own?"

"I...think so."

"Get up."

Crixus moaned as he staggered to his feet. Bassus ordered his ripped tunic returned to him.

"Come over here and sit."

Crixus shuffled a few steps along the gritty stone floor, and stiffly sat on the backless stool across from the Senator. He slumped forward propping his elbows on his thighs and bowing his head.

Bassus motioned to the torturer. "Get him a towel."

The interrogator brought a dirty cloth and handed it to Horse Arse. He wiped the blood from his neck and torso before dropping it to the floor.

Bassus leaned forward. "Now, I want answers—the truth."

"Aye," Horse Arse rasped.

"Who hired you to recruit and kill Lady Carataca and me?"

"I...I don't know his name," he whimpered. He weakly raised his arm and dropped to the table. "Please, don't hurt me. He wouldn't tell me, but he wore a merchants rich clothes. Like me, he was a Gaul."

Macha nearly choked. It has to be one of the Gallic traders that had approached Titus to lure him into the plot against the Emperor's life, she thought.

"What did he say to you?" Bassus questioned.

"He...he was a go between for someone else," Horse Arse answered in a hoarse voice. "He said he would pay well for your deaths, especially, the Lady Carataca."

Macha inhaled deeply, shuddering at this revelation. It confirmed what she had suspected all along. That's why the young assassin had attempted to kill her upon her arrival in Rome.

"Did he say why he wanted our deaths?" Bassus inquired.

"No, only that he wanted you dead," Crixus replied. "I was interested in the money."

155

"Why did you return to Rome?"

Horse Arse gulped. "Because...because the attempt on your lives failed. I was of afraid..."

"Of what?"

"I would be blamed for the foul-up and killed by those who hired me. That's why I came back. It's easy to lose yourself in this city."

Bassus grinned. "But we found you."

Crixus hung his head. "Aye, you did."

"Are you willing to spy for us?" Bassus asked.

"Aye," Crixus whined. He cast his eyes upon the table. "Whatever you want. I'll even kill for you."

"Spying is enough—it's that or crucifixion."

Horse Arse grimaced and looked away. "I said, aye! Just...don't hurt me anymore."

"You are to listen," Bassus instructed, "at the river docks, the forum, and especially, at the baths for any and all stories and rumors regarding the conspiracy against the Emperor. I want names of those who might be involved."

Macha soon realized the true incentive for him to confess. Bassus offered to extend Horse Arse's current contract to supply horses, to the way stations of Northern Italy for an additional three years. The Senator told him that his debts would be forgiven if the information led to the arrest of the conspirators.

"However," Bassus emphasized, "the names you give me must be of persons truly involved. Only after we have arrested and they have been convicted will you be awarded the contract. Do you understand?"

"Aye."

The Senator turned to one of the torturers. "Bring him wine."

Horse Arse nodded his thanks and greedily drank the vinegary-wine given to him, spilling it from the side of his mouth and down his neck. He admitted involvement with the assassination attempt on Macha and Bassus on the road to Luna and also in Rome. "My mistake was...was recruiting my idiot brother-in-law...for the attack."

"Sergius Faunus never mentioned he was related to you," Bassus commented.

"No, he's the worst liar I've...I've ever known." Horse Arse took a deep breath and paused as if gathering his thoughts. "He lies...even when the truth is to his advantage."

Just like you, Macha wanted to say.

"What is the name of the assassin who tried to kill Lady Carataca here in Rome?" Bassus asked.

"S...Silius Rufus, but he's dead."

Bassus raised his eyebrows. "How convenient. When and where?"

"I swear it's true." Crixus turned in the direction of the wheel.

"Go on."

"Heard he got caught picking the pocket of...of some ex-gladiator." He gulped. "Killed him on the spot. Happened early yesterday morning...on the wharf. Anybody there will tell you."

"What's the ex-gladiator's name?"

Horse Arse shook his head. "Don't know for sure, Pug something or other. Never heard of him."

"What happened to the body?"

"Heard the wharf men threw it into the river. Ask them —they'll tell you. Don't know if it's still out there."

"I will, but it's one less criminal to deal with," Bassus said. "In the meantime, I need to learn more about the ex-gladiator. He may have been involved in the kidnapping of Lady Carataca's son."

Macha nodded. Yes, I want the same thing, she thought. Perhaps he can lead us to the real traitors. She stepped out of the darkness and approached Crixus. "Do you remember me?"

"Lady Carataca," he gasped. He nearly dropped the cup of wine. "About the horse I sold you, I didn't—"

"I'm not here to accuse you of cheating me, though you are a thief." Macha pulled out the scrap of parchment with the letters VE and the three names she didn't recognize, and the piece containing the image of the eagle. She dangled the segment in front of Crixus' eyes. "What do you know about these?"

"Begging your pardon, Lady?" His mind seemed dulled by pain and wine.

"Read it. Who are they, and what do the two letters mean?"

"I...don't read Greek. What does it say?"

Macha translated the names and letters into Latin.

"I've...I've never heard of them," Crixus answered. "VE makes no sense."

"The eagle?"

"A picture? I don't know what you're talking about."

"This is not the time to lie, Crixus," Macha said.

"But I swear...I don't know anything about a picture or names."

The torturer stepped to the table, shoving his red hot iron prod within a finger's width of Crixus' dirty feet. The horse trader shoved himself away from the prod and groaned. "I'm telling the truth!"

Bassus held up his hand, and motioned the torturer to back away.

"He might be telling the truth, Macha. Why did you show him the document?"

"I had to learn for myself if Crixus knew its meaning." Macha handed Bassus her copy of the list and the picture.

Bassus placed the scrap with the image of the eagle on the table and for a second he scrutinized the names. "I didn't tell you before, but now that you've shown these to Crixus, the name of the one crossed off the list is interesting."

"Why?" Macha asked.

Bassus tapped the parchment with his hand. "He was a member of the Equestrian order. He died at sea in an accident about two-three weeks ago off Messalia."

How coincidental, Macha thought. Julius Aquelia, the camp commander, died several weeks before Titus's arrest in a hunting accident. He knew her husband had no part in the conspiracy against the Emperor.

"Maybe this one knew too much or changed his mind about joining the conspiracy," Macha said.

"If he was involved at all," Bassus reminded Macha. "We still don't know for sure. All we have are the notes of a dead slave."

"And the other two names?" Macha asked.

"Both are powerful merchants who are very influential in the palace," Bassus replied.

Macha's mouth tightened. She stepped back and whispered to Bassus, "No doubt these merchants are involved in the conspiracy, and one of them is the thug that Crixus hired to kill us. I'm positive the letters play a part and so does the eagle."

Bassus motioned to the parchment. "The letters could mean anything, and nothing—the same for the picture."

"Maybe, but something tells me they hold a major key, and it's here in Rome. It's probably right in front of us, screaming to be heard."

"If so, it's falling upon deaf ears."

Macha turned to Crixus. "Do you mind?" she said to Bassus. "I have only a couple more questions to ask him."

"Go ahead."

She shot a forefinger in Crixus' direction. "Why did you kidnap my son?"

"I swear I had no part of it," Crixus whined. "Gods, it's true I hired assassins to kill you and Lord Bassus, but... but I don't kidnap or kill children."

"Why wouldn't you?"

Crixus winced and slowly moved a shaky hand to his bony chest. "I've a score of nephews and nieces. They're a bunch of...of little brats, but I like them. I...I swear I don't know anything about it. If this ex-gladiator like you say had something to do with it, then I'll scour Rome myself 'til I've found him. I swear it!"

Macha turned to Bassus. "Please, Senator, we must conduct a search of the city for my son—at once!"

"I agree." Bassus nodded to Pomponius Appius. "Send a message to the Commander of the Watch. He is to organize a search of Rome for the son of Titus Antonius."

"Yes, sir."

Macha continued her questioning of Crixus. "Why did you return to Rome?"

"Had business," he answered. "I rode ahead of you and caught a ship. I believed you dead."

"Didn't you encounter the Praetorians on the way?" Bassus inquired.

159

Crixus groaned as he attempted to straighten his back. "I saw them riding in the distance and hid. I didn't want to meet nobody I ever sold a horse to. They might accuse me of thievery—me, an honest horse trader!"

Macha stepped away from Crixus, not believing a word he said. Again the letters VE churned in her mind. Great Mother Goddess! It was so obvious, but she had been as blind as a beggar. She might be wrong, but VE could provide the clue she was seeking. Tomorrow she would visit Antonia at the house of the Vestal Virgins.

CHAPTER 22

The Sacred Order of Vesta

The following morning Macha sat peacefully in the garden with Shafer. At the far end a slave splashed water from a bucket on a row of budding lilies. Nearby, clippers snapped as another worker trimmed a box shrub.

Macha closed her eyes and tilted her head, welcoming the warmth of the spring sun on her tired face. Although Shafer and she had returned home exhausted after witnessing Crixus' interrogation and had taken a bath, Macha slept poorly. She relived last night's horrors in the torture chamber.

When she managed to push the awful scenes from her mind, thoughts of young Titus's kidnapping flooded her head. She agonized over his possible treatment, and prayed the thugs hadn't injured him. Perhaps she should have stayed in Mediolanum. But she refused to languish there doing nothing so long as Titus was imprisoned. At her urging, Bassus sent a message to the Commander of the Watch to begin a search for her son. But the city was so big, nearly one-million souls, and there were so many places where her son could be hidden. Hundreds of caves honeycombed the hills on which the Imperial capital was built—an ideal place to hide. She prayed Mother Goddess the bucket men would be successful.

Those thoughts had rolled through her mind a dozen times since awakening. Would they never stop? She needed to calm herself and keep the ugly images under control if she were to help Titus and Bassus. What more could she do? Bassus' intercession allowed her to question Crixus in the torture chamber. To her knowledge, no woman had been allowed that right before. She considered herself fortunate the Senator had not sent her back to his house, escorted by a detail from the Watch.

The garrison of Mediolanum was searching for her son, but he could be any place in Italy, including Rome. Gods forbid if the kidnappers carried him to Gaul or worse, Germania, and sold him as a slave to the barbarians, but Macha doubted they were that stupid. She prayed he would be ransomed instead.

Would the abductors be bold enough to bring him to the city? Macha tossed aside the idea as being absurd. Still she had to consider the possibility he was closer to Rome than Mediolanum.

Shafer rose to her feet. "Mistress, Lord Bassus is here."

Immediately, Macha cleared her mind and rubbed her eyes. She glanced to the garden's entrance and spied Bassus approaching at a brisk pace, his face pinched and eyes narrowed. He wore a Legate's uniform and a scarlet-plumed helmet.

Shafer bowed. Macha started to rise, but Bassus motioned her to remain seated. He halted before her marble bench and removed his helmet.

"I have received orders from Vespasian to sail to Misenum," Bassus said. He looked down at Macha, frowning.

Macha sat straighter, her senses now fully alert. "My gods, Titus is to be court-martialed in ten days. Will you return in time?"

"I'll make it a point to be here, but even if I sail from Ostia this afternoon, the earliest I can return is five days."

Situated on the Bay of Naples, Macha knew Misenum was the home of Rome's western fleet. If he departed, how could she make inquiries on her husband's behalf without the Senator's assistance? "Exactly why is the Emperor sending you?" She asked.

"I'm to inspect the fleet's ledgers." Bassus shifted his helmet from one hand to the other. "Some discrepancies have surfaced. There's evidence that Admiral Apollinaris siphoned money from the seamen's burial fund for his personal use. Vespasian ordered me to take immediate action if the charges are true."

"But shouldn't the audit be conducted by one of Vespasian's Greek accountants?"

"I'm taking one along. Because I'm a Legate, the Emperor says the authority to deal with the situation rests solely with me." Bassus shook his head. "The accusations against Admiral Apollinaris are rubbish. He's one of the most honorable men I know and wealthy in his own right."

"It wouldn't be the first time an honest man has succumbed to greed."

Bassus nodded. "Unfortunately, you're right. Vespasian's Greek treasury secretary, Phidias, advised the Emperor of the allegations." He snorted. "He thinks the only man capable of resolving the problem is me."

The Legate paced back and forth on the gravel path before Macha's bench. "Something doesn't smell right about this, Macha. The Emperor didn't have to wait for my return from the Danubus to deal with this matter. Someone wants me out of Rome."

"Aren't there other officials the Emperor could send to Misenum?" Macha asked.

He paused and glanced to Shafer and the garden slaves before returning his gaze to Macha. "Vespasian dispatched me, and I can't argue with the Emperor's commands. Unfortunately, I am the logical choice. I have the authority to solve the matter of embezzlement if that's the situation. Once I've arrived and conducted a preliminary investigation, I can delegate overseeing the audit to someone else."

"If Admiral Apollinaris is honorable as you say, then this journey is a ruse," Macha said.

He exhaled. "I'll learn soon enough."

"Still, your leaving is very sudden. What am I to do while you are away? What if I learn something important that pertains to Titus' case?"

"Contact Tribune Appius—he has been informed of the events and will make inquiries on my behalf."

"Is there no one else?"

"Macha, you can trust him. He knows more than you think and does have reservations about Titus' guilt."

"So, he once said."

"It's true," Bassus answered.

* * * * *

Later, after Bassus departed for Ostia, Macha and Shafer, escorted by slave guards, went to visit Antonia, in the house of the Vestal Virgins, astride the eastern edge of the Forum. To Macha's surprise, the female gatekeeper said the priestess wasn't seeing anyone, and didn't know when Antonia would receive visitors again.

Puzzled by Antonia's sudden change of heart, Macha and Shafer turned away. Yesterday, Antonia had been friendly and willing to help.

Riding in a litter as her entourage crossed the noisy Forum, Macha paid little attention to the spirited haggling between customers and shopkeepers at the portable vending stands surrounding the public square or the many smells wafting through the area on a light breeze. She kept mulling Antonia's refusal to see her.

As the wife of an accused traitor, Macha realized she had placed Antonia in a precarious position by speaking to her in public at the Forum. No doubt the Chief Vestal, Licinia, had received word about the conversation. As *Virgo Maxima*, she had the authority to prohibit Antonia from further contact with Macha. Somehow she had to find a way of relaying a message to Antonia. Conceivably, if she informed her friend about young Titus' kidnapping, the priestess might change her mind about speaking to Macha. Antonia had been the most accessible of all Vestal Virgins.

Macha expressed her concern to Shafer, who walked alongside her sedan.

"Maybe there is a way, Mistress," Shafer said.

"Right now, I'm open to all suggestions," Macha answered. They skirted the Basilica Julia and turned onto shop-lined Jugarian Way.

Shafer drew closer to the litter and Macha bent her head. "I know a house slave at the Vestal home," Shafer said in a voice almost drowned by the noisy passersby's crowding the street. "She owes me a favor."

"That's wonderful. Can she be trusted to deliver a secret message to Sister Antonia?"

"I think she can."

"We must chance it."

"But we should wait until early tomorrow morning, when she goes shopping for the kitchen staff," Shafer suggested. "If you allow me, Lady Carataca, I'll leave at dawn and find her."

"You have my permission."

Before returning to Bassus' home, Macha and her escort stopped at the busy flower and produce shop of Clodia and Lepidus. The fragrance and possession of newly cut flowers had been one of Macha's few comforts in alleviating her anguish over the kidnapping of her son and imprisonment of Titus.

Trestle tables containing baskets of fresh and weathered fruit and yellowing vegetables were displayed beneath the canopy on the crowded sidewalk. Macha spied the flower woman passing by the entryway as she headed for the stall's interior. Again, Clodia's gaunt appearance shocked Macha. Her long homespun tunic hung from her thin shoulders, and she spat dark thick blood into an old rag she kept inside the fold of her blue and yellow apron.

Assisted by the litter bearers, Macha stepped out of the chair and entered the vendor's stall. She scanned the array of roses, daisies, and other sweet smelling flowers, as Clodia greeted her. Shafer browsed at the far end of the room while Macha's slave guards, lead by the big Spaniard, Viriatus, stood outside around the shop's perimeter and kept a suspicious eye on the jostling crowd.

Clodia gossiped about the neighborhood while Macha listened and smiled. When the woman mentioned the commotion the night before outside their flat, Macha turned to her from a display of lilies. Shafer stopped and peered across a tray of cabbages, her almond eyes focused on Macha. Even Viriatus swung about from his position on the sidewalk outside and appeared to be listening.

"Those awful thugs chased two women," Clodia said. "Prostitutes they looked by their clothing, but they were smart and they stayed to the roof. Those sons-of-slime, pardon my language, Lady, jumped the fence and landed in the slop barrels of Patronius' dung cart," she added with a crooked smile. "Served them right for running after those poor wenches. Kept slipping and sliding they did. Must have taken them a quarter hour to climb out. A stinking lot they were—covered head to foot in filth. Even the daughters of Venus don't deserve rape and murder. Like us, they're only tryin' to survive."

Neither Macha nor Shafer said a word.

After Macha purchased a bouquet of Persian roses, Clodia wrapped them in lily pads tied up with flaxen twine. "Could you do me a favor, Lady Carataca?" she asked while tying the last knot.

"If I can, certainly."

Clodia snatched a clump of orange poppies from another bundle to fatten the ones she had tied, then handed Macha the flowers. She wiped her scaly hands on her threadbare apron. With practiced aim she turned her head and spat blood out the open partition into the alley.

"I know you're a kind woman," Clodia said. "It isn't for me I ask—it's for my daughter, Silvia." She searched about and saw her husband, Lepidus, haggling with a customer at the other end of the shop. She lowered her voice. "This isn't easy to say, but I'm dying."

Clodia shook off Macha's protest. "No, it's true, and nothing can be done. Isn't it obvious?"

There was an uneasy silence. Macha wanted to say a few comforting words, but concluded denial would only insult Clodia.

"Can you sponsor Silvia as an initiate into the sacred order of Vesta?" Clodia asked. "It would bring honor to our home and some peace to my husband when I'm gone."

"I'm flattered by your request, Clodia, but right now there aren't any vacancies."

"Rumors say Priestess Antonia is retiring soon," Clodia persisted. "It's not too early to make your wishes known. We are poor people, Lady Carataca. Our little girl's only chance of being chosen is through someone of your rank and influence."

"But I'm the wife of an accused traitor, Clodia. What influence I once had may be gone."

Clodia paled and coughed several times in quick succession, spitting blood onto the hard packed dirt-floor. Clodia stumbled, but Macha steadied her and led her to a stool in one corner. Clodia sat there, catching her breath.

"I'm sorry, Lady," Clodia rasped. "I didn't mean to carry on like this but sometimes I can't help it."

"You don't need to explain."

"I'm frightened for my family, especially for Silvia," Clodia related. "She's a bright girl and has a knack for business. But she's too young, and I want something better for her. If I hadn't seen her born between my own legs I'd swear me and the old man couldn't produce such a gem. She's...special. Everyone knows it."

"I understand," Macha answered. "She's intelligent and has a magnetic personality."

Macha recalled how Silvia smiled sincerely at prospective customers when selling flowers. She complimented men and women alike on some aspect about their appearance or speech. So much did she charm and impress her patrons, they found the nine-year-old irresistible and bought anything she offered. She also had an eye for displaying produce to its best advantage, attracting more buyers. Indeed, the girl was worthy of admission to the Sacred Order. The Vestals needed a woman with a sense of business, sacred duties notwithstanding.

At the same time Macha couldn't help but think Clodia was appealing to her sympathetic nature. She understood the woman was desperate and knew Macha was her best, her only hope, to keep her daughter from a life of drudgery and squalor.

Clodia pulled Macha out of her thoughts. "Lady, your husband is known to be a loyal Roman officer. My husband and I believe he's innocent. We believe in him and you. That's why we still want you to sponsor our girl."

"All right, Clodia, I will," Macha said.

"Bless you, Lady Macha. May Mother Vesta praise you." Clodia's face gained some of its original coloring, and her voice cleared. A smile rippled across her gaunt face, revealing gaps in her yellow teeth.

"There is one important question I want answered," Macha said, almost in a whisper. She pulled the thin green mantle, she was wearing over her stola, tightly about her chest.

"Yes, anything." Clodia seemed unable to stop smiling, and forced another bundle of flowers into Macha's hands.

Amused by what seemed to be a miraculous recovery, Macha asked, "Does Silvia want to be a Vestal Virgin?"

"Oh, yes, very much. I think Silvia understands what's involved. When other women are getting married and having children, she'll be giving thirty years of her life to the House of Vesta."

The Sacred Order contained no more than ten members at one time, and competition for a coveted opening was fierce. Although children from poorer families had been selected before, the wealth and power of the rich usually prevailed. But there were few girls among the nobility who possessed little Silvia's qualities and fewer as deserving as she.

"Don't worry, Clodia," Macha said touching the flower woman's rough hands. "Silvia is a unique girl. I shall do everything in my power to see that she is admitted to the order. The Priestess Antonia is my friend. I'll seek her help —she'll recognize what your daughter has to offer."

Clodia's eyes moistened. "Thank you, Lady Carataca. I pray that my wish will come true before I die."

"It will," Macha assured her, "and you will live a long time."

Macha hoped she would be right on both counts. Highly regarded by the Emperors, the Vestal Virgins possessed special powers of dispensation. The Vestals had been known to pardon common criminals condemned to die. They sat in a special box in the arena next to the Emperor, accountable to no one but him. As keepers of Rome's sacred flame and hearth, they kept important documents such as wills and other papers in a securely-locked vault within the temple confines.

Macha realized something else was within their powers. Their vault was the perfect place to hide a death list.

CHAPTER 23

Anguished and Urgent Meetings

The next morning Shafer found the Vestal slave and had her deliver Macha's message to Antonia.

Upon returning home and discovering Macha in the library, Shafer said, "She says I'm to meet her this afternoon in the Forum of Julius Caesar for her mistress' reply."

"Pray that Priestess Antonia has one," Macha said, without much conviction. "In the meantime, I shall visit my husband."

Macha, escorted by her entourage and Shafer, journeyed from Bassus' home on Aventine Hill to see Titus. The Praetorian Barracks, built outside of Rome's west wall, loomed ahead of them. Knowing how Titus would respond to the news of their son's kidnapping, she had dreaded this moment. For two days she had postponed this trip. But her husband had a right to know.

The jailer slammed the door to Titus' cell behind Macha. Titus jumped from the backless stool and started toward her with open arms. Appalled by his haggard appearance, she gasped, took a step backwards, then shot up an arm in front of her, palm outward.

Titus halted. His dark ringed eyes widened as if surprised. "What's wrong?'

"Darling, you look awful, what have they done to you?" His stubble face seemed more pale and gaunt than when she last saw him three days ago, his hair dirty and matted. A rumpled tunic hung like a limp rag from his broad shoulders.

"Nothing has changed since you were last here," he answered.

She put her hand to her mouth. "But you're so pale."

"You would be too, if you were caged like me." Titus looked beyond Macha's deceptively delicate shoulder to the

169

cell door before bringing his eyes back to her. "Please, Macha," he asked in a soft voice, "Let me hold you. It's been too long."

Macha had missed him so much, all the empty days and lonely nights without him. Just his presence without even saying a word was company enough. His appearance didn't matter. She ran into his arms and tight embrace. His rough whiskers against her soft face felt like small jagged rocks and his clothing reeked of sweat—it made no difference to her. They were together again, even if for only a short time.

After lingering for a few minutes, reluctantly, she pulled away. "Darling, there are matters we must discuss."

In Titus' cramped room, they sat across from one another at the small table, Macha on the cot and he on the lone stool, their hands entwined on the table. She looked into his piercing blue eyes and choked out the words, "Our son has been kidnapped."

Titus head snapped back as if punched in the face. A guttural sound escaped as he jerked his hands away from Macha. "What!" he rasped. "Kidnapped!" He bolted from his stool.

Macha winced and turned away as if slapped.

"By the thundering gods," he roared, "it's bad enough I may lose my life, but not my son!" His eyes widened and he balled his big fists. "What harm can he do?"

"Cnidius Rufus is searching for him," Macha said attempting to calm her own emotions. "I'm sure he'll do everything he can to find our son."

"Jupiter Thunderer, I pray Rufus finds them. If he doesn't, when I'm released, I'll find the bastards and kill them myself." He slammed the side of his fist against the table and winced.

"I'm sure Helena's husband is doing everything he can," Macha answered.

Titus paced the tiny room. He clamped his lips together and shook his head. "I know Rufus is doing his best, but will it be enough? I feel like a caged lion, helpless to do a damn thing."

He snatched the wooden stool and was about to throw it against the wall. Apparently, he changed his mind. His shoulders drooped as the tension drained from his face. Exhaling, he returned it to the floor and stepped to the cell door. Titus leaned his back against it, facing Macha.

She thanked Mother Goddess Anu that her husband managed to bring his outburst under control.

"I'm sorry," he said. "Here I'm acting sorry for myself, and I've failed to ask about your feelings."

"I'm frightened, darling. The fear of what might be happening to Young Titus keeps roiling in my mind. I can hardly think about anything else. He must be found and soon. Senator Bassus has ordered the Watch to search the city just in case he's been brought here. Bassus is making his own queries, too."

"Thank the gods Senator Bassus is on our side," Titus answered. "The Watch wouldn't lift a finger to help without orders from him."

Macha described the arrest of Crixus and their use of him as a spy.

Titus returned to Macha and sat next to her his arm around her waist. "Bassus is no fool, but why did he offer Crixus immunity? He'll betray us the first time he receives a better offer."

"He believes he is our best hope to learn who is involved in the plot."

Titus pulled his arm from around Macha. He moved a short distance, turned and placed a powerful hand on her shoulder. His dark eyes like a stormy sea studied her. "Do you honestly believe anyone would confide in a man of Crixus' reputation?"

"Bassus doesn't think the nobility will—he's just not on their level." She sighed and turned her head for a few seconds. "But Crixus can listen at doors and talk to servants and learn useful information, especially, at the baths and docks. He probably wouldn't betray us because he's receiving the monopoly on all courier horses between Rome and Mediolanum."

"It must be a ploy," Titus said. He dropped his hands to his lap. For a few seconds he sat in silence as if pondering his next words. "There has to be another reason why Bassus made the offer to Crixus. The Senator has his own network of spies. They're watching Crixus for signs of betrayal."

"He denied knowing about little Titus' kidnapping. Perhaps Bassus thinks he lied."

Titus snorted. "I know he lied. Bassus wants Crixus to lead him to something else, but the question remains, what?"

"We have no choice but to wait and see."

"Pray Minerva not for long because soon I go on trial. Unless he or someone else proves my innocence, I'll be condemned as a traitor."

Macha grabbed his hands and held them tightly in hers. "That won't happen," she reassured him. "There are other people working on your behalf." She didn't have the heart to say it was only Bassus, herself and perhaps, Pomponius Appius if what Bassus said was true, that he could be trusted. And Antonia, if Macha could persuade her.

Titus stared at the cold stone wall on the opposite side of the cell. "They'll clear me," he said none too convincingly. "I don't have much choice but to put my trust in them and the gods—if they exist." For a few seconds Titus closed his eyes. Opening them once again, he said, "I don't know why I didn't think about it sooner."

"What, darling?"

He gazed at Macha. "When did the Watch's search for our son begin?"

"Last night." She explained the details of Bassus' request to the Commander of the Watch.

"Thank the gods," Titus said. "But we must be certain the search continues after Bassus leaves for Misenum."

"Why shouldn't it?"

"It's only because Bassus is a Legate that the Watch agreed to the search. They have no interest in looking for the son of an accused traitor."

"Then I shall see Pomponius Appius," Macha said interrupting Titus' thoughts. "Perhaps he'll help us. He has doubts about your arrest." She shuddered. It was unthinkable no one wanted to find her son.

Titus nodded. "Good. We need every ally we can muster. If the Watch hasn't already done so, suggest to

Appius to search the Subura District, one of the worst cess-pits in Rome." He rubbed his eyes and glanced to the gray-stone ceiling, stained from years of lamp lighted smoke. A cockroach scurried across and disappeared into a crack at the far corner. Titus shook his head and continued, "If they don't find him there, he can try the caves beneath the city around the *Cloaca Maxima*. That great sewer is an ideal place to hide a captive, stink and all."

"Darling, I'll do anything to convince him."

"That's all I ask—for our son's sake."

She hugged and kissed Titus, gave him a last smile and left his cell.

* * * * *

After Macha returned to Bassus' house, she sent a message to Pomponius Appius requesting a meeting with him. She explained Titus' concern and his suggestion where to search next for their son.

While Macha waited for his reply, she wrote a letter to her brother-in-law, Rufus. She detailed her suspicions regarding her slave, Jason, and asked him to further investigate the matter. Ever since she had left Mediolanum, the possibility of Jason being involved in the conspiracy had nagged her. Only now did she find time to contact Helena's husband. Macha hoped Appius would allow the letter to be included with the army dispatches which were sent to Mediolanum on a daily basis.

To Macha's surprise, Tribune Appius arrived at Bassus home within an hour of her sending the letter. After the usual salutations, she and Appius proceeded to the *tablinum.* They sat across from each other at a citrus wood desk, surrounded by canisters full of parchment scrolls, where she explained in greater detail Titus' request to search for their son.

For a split second, he crinkled his nose and stared through her as if seeing right into her soul. Macha shivered. "Earlier I expressed to you there may be a possibility your husband was not guilty of treason," Appius said. "And now, because of Crixus' confession and news of your son's kidnapping, I am finding it harder to believe your husband a traitor. Therefore, I will request a detachment from the Watch to continue their search."

"Thank you, I'm most grateful." Relief filled her whole being. The muscles in her legs and shoulders relaxed. The thought that Appius might have denied her request had troubled her more than she imagined.

He nodded and started to rise when Macha asked, "Tribune Appius, could you do me one more favor?"

He raised thick eyebrows and returned to his seat. "What is it?"

From where she sat, Macha reached into a fold within her stola and pulled out a sealed parchment. "Can you send this letter to Tribune Cnidius Rufus, my brother-in-law, with the other dispatches to the garrison at Mediolanum?"

"Why the army and not a private courier?"

"The letter contains my concerns about the possible involvement of my groom, Jason, in the conspiracy. My hand maiden told me what she suspected."

Appius snorted. "And based on what a slave thinks you would waste Rufus' time investigating this slave's movements? By Mars, we'll yank him off your property and torture him—he'll confess soon enough if he's involved."

"Must I remind you that anyone under torture will say anything—I saw what they did to Crixus." Her chest tightened as the memory of that night.

"It worked, didn't it?"

Macha glared. Afraid she would lose her temper she reached beneath the table and readjusted her skirt. This gave her enough time to bring her emotions under control. "It only worked because we already knew what he had done! I say it's better to place Jason under surveillance and track his movements. It may lead to the conspirators."

"Waste of manpower," he growled.

"Rufus is already searching for my son—it wouldn't take many men to keep a watch—in fact, the fewer the better." She gestured with a hand as if it were obvious. "From what my husband has told me, stealth is much better in matters like this."

For a few seconds, Appius peered at the marble bust of Emperor Vespasian on a pedestal in one corner of the library. He exhaled and turned his gaze to Macha. "All right, I'll send it. You're in luck, the next courier leaves for Mediolanum this afternoon. It's a long hard ride."

Macha was aware the rider would change horses at army way stations every twenty miles and ride well into the night before he stopped to rest. He would keep up the pace until he arrived at Mediolanum. Unless his passage was blocked by snow in the Apennines, he might reach the garrison in as little as three days. She prayed he wouldn't be delayed.

"What made you decide to allow the letter to be included?" Macha asked.

"I have my own suspicions as to why Senator Bassus was sent to Misenum. It smells like rotten mullet. Your doubts about your Greek groom might tie in somehow."

"As the playwright, Aristophanes, once said, 'Leave no stone unturned'," Macha said.

"Aye, it's worth a try. Cnidius Rufus is a good soldier. He'll see if there's any truth to your doubts. And I'm conducting my own investigation on orders from the Senator."

"What does that involve?"

"Can't say."

She was a little annoyed that Appius refused to tell her about his inquiries for Senator Bassus. "But you will assist me if I hear of anything that relates to the investigation? You can go places I can't."

"If it's something I can use, yes. But you're to stay away from any place where you can get into trouble. You've been nearly murdered twice."

Macha stood by the library entrance and watched Appius cross the atrium to the front door where he was let out by the gatekeeper. She pondered his warning and knew he was right. But again she considered the dilemma. Could she stand by and do nothing, while the Watch searched for her son, and her husband languished in prison? Mother Anu, allow Antonia to see me—and soon, Macha prayed. Something within told Macha the results of that meeting would determine her next move.

CHAPTER 24

Forbidden Trysts?

Later that afternoon Shafer returned from the Forum of Julius Caesar with a message for Macha. Fearing they might be overheard, Macha led Shafer to the middle of the garden away from any concealing shrubs before she allowed her servant to speak.

"My friend says," Shafer explained, "you are to secretly meet Sister Antonia early tomorrow morning at a deserted quarry. It's about two miles south of the city off the Ardeatina Way. She says let no one see you."

"Why the quarry?"

"It's away from the city and safer. She dare not be seen with you any longer."

"Is it because my husband has been accused of treason?"

Shafer bowed her head. "Yes, Mistress."

* * * * *

Three hours before dawn, the next morning, Macha and Shafer left Bassus' house to rendezvous with Antonia. Tiptoeing on bare feet along the dark hallway, they managed to sneak out of the home without waking anyone, including the sleeping gatekeeper.

Macha was dressed in a heavy woolen stola and mantle to protect herself from the icy air, and hidden beneath her long skirt were tartan breeches. She put woolen stockings and thick-soled sandals on after leaving the mansion. She carried a dagger tied to the waist of her trousers. Shafer wore a long homespun tunic and a cowled mantle.

Shafer quickly led the way keeping to the shadows. They trekked through the Ardeatinian Gate and down the cobbled road past one of Rome's huge smoking rubbish heaps and the dozens of mausoleums lining the highway.

In the hazy mist she saw the outline of a low-lying hill gently sloping toward the Campanian Plain. A large rocky scar carved into its side loomed out of the fog like a jagged mythological monster. The quarry. A few paces further, they encountered a thick row of thorny bushes protecting the outer perimeter, but Shafer found the hidden entrance. On the other side of the brush a wide but shallow pit yawned, leading to the base of the gouged hill. Cautiously, they made their way down a narrow rocky pathway. The women skirted a small mountain of black tailings, material from the quarry, and passed a pile of rusting chisels and shattered hammers before arriving at the bottom of the trail.

Antonia is taking a terrible chance traveling here by herself to see me, Macha thought. I know she has been forbidden to speak to me. If we are caught together, my friend will be severely punished! She closed her eyes. Please Mother Goddess Anu watch over us! I couldn't bear the thought of anything terrible happening to Antonia. Macha took a deep breath, opened her eyes again and looked about.

Gray-purple fog enshrouded everything in the pit. Danger seemed to lurk in every crevice and behind every corner. All was as quiet as the somber tombs. Even in the murkiness Shafer walked without stumbling over invisible pieces of tufa stone. Macha followed closely in Shafer's steps.

Beyond a set of rotting scaffolding at the far end, Macha strained her eyes to recognize the small figure of Antonia, shrouded in a dark mantle, hovering at the entryway to the underground vault. She was silhouetted by a lantern burning on the ground beside her.

Macha and Shafer halted by the old gantry.

"Shafer, wait here and keep a watch while I meet with Sister Antonia," Macha said and walked away from her Moorish slave.

After the usual greetings, Macha told Antonia in greater detail about young Titus' kidnapping.

"It was reading the message about your son's kidnapping that changed my mind," Antonia said. "Despite Licinia's prohibition, I won't stand by and see your son used as a pawn."

"Is it true Sister Licinia wouldn't allow you to meet with me because I'm the wife of an accused traitor?"

"Yes."

"I'm grateful you did." Macha suspected more, but decided to ask further questions later. She briefly discussed the admission of Clodia's daughter, Silvia, to the Sacred Order. Antonia promised to use her power in admitting the girl to the Vestals.

She related the news to Antonia about the murder of her slave and music teacher Nicanor and that it was witnessed by his son, Demetrios.

"The poor little boy, it must have been horrible for him to see his father die like that," Antonia said.

Macha sighed. "If that wasn't terrible enough, he was murdered at the same time my son was kidnapped."

"Oh, no! Why did they kill him?"

"I think someone knew he was in the hayloft when his father was killed. But there is more."

"Go on."

"My hand maiden, Edain, while preparing Nicanor for burial discovered a fragment of parchment on his body."

"What about it?"

"She told me that Nicanor had stolen it. He wouldn't tell her from whom. I think it was the reason why he was murdered."

"Why would they kill him for it?"

"On it was drawn a picture of an eagle, similar to the one found on legionary standards. There were parts of three names I could not decipher, and the letters, VE. I believe there may be a possible connection between the letters, VE, and the Vestal Virgins," Macha said.

Antonia's head snapped to one side as if she had been slapped in the face. A few seconds elapsed before she regained her composure. "Surely, you are mistaken, Macha. What else do you suspect?"

Macha decided she was on the right path. "Senator Bassus is investigating the matter, but yesterday the Emperor sent him to Misenum—he'll be away at least a week."

"Longer," Antonia blurted. "It's further than you think. But I hadn't heard a word of his departure."

Macha's eyebrows shot up in surprise. "What's wrong, Antonia? You look as if you've seen the Furies. It has something to do with Senator Bassus, doesn't it?" Unconsciously, she tightened the shroud around her shoulders. Something wasn't right.

At first Antonia denied any connection.

"You are retiring from the order in one month, are you not?" Macha persisted.

"Yes, you know that."

Pausing, Macha glanced in Shafer's direction and saw her tall dark outline by the scaffold, keeping guard. The silence of the quarry engulfed the women as Macha pondered her next question. "There is something more than just official business and formal greetings between you and Senator Bassus?"

"What in the name of Holy Vesta are you talking about?" For a split second Antonia's eyes seemed to focus on the ground between them.

"I may be foolish in saying this, but are you in love with Senator Bassus?"

"Now that's a silly question."

Macha narrowed her eyes. "I'm asking this as a friend of both of you. It's only a guess on my part, but I am good at keeping secrets."

"You realize, I don't have to answer your questions."

"I know, but if you are in love, it's nothing to be ashamed of. If anything, you should be happy. You have only a month before you retire. No longer will you be tied to such an unnatural commitment. You know what I mean."

Antonia sighed. "Is it so obvious?"

"Only to another woman, perhaps," Macha answered. "I saw it in your eyes when we met in the Forum. The mention of his name brought a brightness to them I hadn't seen before. You barely suppressed your smile. Has he asked to marry you?"

"No, he hasn't."

"Bassus is an honorable man. I'm sure he will."

"With a man, you can never be certain of anything."

Macha shrugged. "I know what you mean. But still why the sad face?"

"I fear for Bassus."

179

"Senator Bassus can take care of himself."

"I'm afraid of bringing disgrace upon him," Antonia said in a voice barely above a whisper.

"You? Impossible!"

"Macha, you and I have not had the opportunity to see one another very often, but I consider you a good friend."

Macha smiled. "I'm flattered, Antonia, that you honor me with such a compliment."

"You may not think so after what I am about to tell you."

For a moment Macha studied Antonia in the murky dawn light. Even the darkness couldn't hide the fear she sensed lay behind those amber eyes.

"I know you're Briton by birth," Antonia continued, "and as a child you came to Rome in chains with your mother and rebel father."

"Yes," Macha answered quietly, "that horrible time will be with me until my dying day."

Antonia stepped forward, her pale hand touching Macha's shoulder. "You don't put much stock in Roman gods, do you?"

"I've noticed most Romans only give them lip service. Then again, I have doubts about my Briton gods, too."

The priestess nodded. "Then you may not be so shocked about what I'm going to say. Whatever you think, under no circumstances must you reveal a word."

"I promise." Her hand touched her heart.

Antonia cleared her throat. "It's true I love Bassus, but I allowed my desire for him to overcome my sensibilities and duties to Mother Vesta. Instead of waiting until I retired from the Order, I broke the greatest vow of a Vestal and gave myself to Bassus."

A prickling sensation rippled through Macha's body. She turned and peered in the direction of the quarry's gloomy entrance seeking what she knew not. All she observed was the graceful silhouette of Shafer. Then she said, "My gods, you'll suffer dreadfully should anyone learn about it."

Macha found the idea of being chaste so long absurd. She knew as part of a Vestal Virgin's sacred oath, Antonia had to retain her chastity. She had heard the terrible

180

stories of Vestals discovered in sexual trysts with men. They suffered public disgrace and death. A shiver raced down her arms and back when she thought about how the victims were walled in a room underground, near the Colline Gate, with little food and water to die of starvation. She wondered why Antonia was telling her this damning information. The knowledge was dangerous. More than that it was a key—a weapon—to bring them both down at will.

"That's why I fear for Bassus more than myself," Antonia continued. "It would be a ghastly end for me, but death for him as well. He would be publicly flogged and hurled off the Tarpaen Rock on Capitoline Hill as a traitor. All his property seized by the state."

"Who else knows about your affair?"

Antonia hesitated.

"Please, Antonia, this is important, my husband's life is at stake."

"I can't tell you, except that it is another woman."

Macha's heart leaped in her chest. Who could it be? She and Antonia knew many of the same people.

"Why can't you reveal the name?" She stammered a few seconds later.

The priestess shook her head. "I don't see that it's necessary for you to know. Isn't it enough that she has knowledge?"

"Antonia, that's not enough. Continue," Macha urged.

"Very well. It all began when I rejected her advances. The woman wanted me to be her lover."

"My gods, how disgusting."

"Yes, and because I scorned her, she vowed revenge. She bribed a house slave of the Vestals to spy on me. The slave saw me with Bassus—where I don't know—and told her. She threatened to inform on me if I didn't perform certain favors."

"For instance?"

"Deposit a list of names in our sacred vault, including those which you told me about."

"Why would a list be kept in the vault? Would that not jeopardize those involve in the conspiracy?"

Antonia took a deep breath and gestured as if it were obvious. "It was deposited there because the temple of Vesta is sacrosanct. No one but the Vestals are allowed access, not even the Emperor. The idea was to use the list against any members of the conspiracy who might change their minds."

"Wouldn't the list put all members in danger?"

"No. The name of each conspirator was placed on a separate sheet and sealed in a separate box. It can be detached as if there were only one name."

"But she could still inform the Emperor."

"Nothing so direct. Her plan was more sinister. She would tell Licinia, the Chief Vestal. The woman dared not risk a direct link. But the real reason to use Licinia is because the woman is her new lover."

Macha was filled with a sense of revulsion. "Why did Licinia get involved?"

"The Virgo Maxima hates the Emperor, but doesn't know about the list yet. She knows this woman is involved with the conspiracy and has given her blessing." Antonia added that Vespasian had cut back the Imperial Subsidy to The Sacred Order as part of his plan to refill the treasury. That infuriated Licinia.

"If Sister Licinia doesn't know about the list, why don't you remove it from the vault and give it to the Emperor? It proves Titus' innocence."

"I can't."

"Why not?"

"So long as the woman is alive, she can expose me and Bassus. Even if she were arrested, she would know who revealed her involvement. I'm sorry, Macha, you must find another way of incriminating her."

"But Titus and my son's lives are in danger!"

"So are Bassus' and mine. That is why I've handed you the very key to destroy Bassus and me. I want to help, and maybe later I can remove the document, but not yet. You must trust Bassus completely. If you still doubt us, doubt him, then shout what you know from the highest temple top—it won't matter. Only if we trust each other completely can we burn that witch for what she has done to us, and our loved ones."

In her heart Macha feared making a decision that could cost her husband and son their lives. Although risks were high and failure warranted death, success spelled freedom for her men.

"Then it's settled," Macha concluded. "We must seek a way to bring down that horrid female without betraying you or Bassus. But how?"

As Macha turned and strode toward Shafer, she thought, it isn't enough that my attempts to free Titus have endangered my life and that of our son, but now I must help Antonia and Senator Bassus. Will I put their lives in peril? Mother Goddess help me!

CHAPTER 25

Unexpected Visitors

By mid-morning, after returning to Bassus' home from the secret meeting with Antonia, and no longer able to keep her eyes open, Macha lay down, but awoke several times experiencing terrible nightmares. She failed to block the horrible images from her memory. Over and over she dreamed of her son being tortured and killed.

As she tossed and turned on her goose-down bed, Macha's restless mind flashed back to Antonia and her revelations. The consequence of the tryst between her Vestal friend and Bassus was nothing short of deadly. Was there anything she could do to keep the woman, who knew of the relationship, from telling the Emperor? Who was she? I must learn who it is, she thought. It could be anyone. And I need Antonia and Bassus' help to obtain Titus's release. And there is little Titus. What else can I do to find him? I must get a grip on myself. Sleep was impossible.

Macha got up and splashed water on her face. Attempting to soothe her nerves, she strolled to the atrium and picked up her harp.

She had been sitting on a cushioned bench playing for about an hour and was starting to relax when the steward, Vasili, approached. "Lady Carataca, Tribune Rubellius Falco is here to see you. Shall I admit him?"

Macha remained motionless, silently debating whether to see Falco. She hadn't expected his arrival in Rome. She shivered. Why did he come to the city, she silently questioned, and what is his reason for seeing me? Thank the gods I'm not carrying a dagger. The temptation to use it might overcome me.

"Shall I tell him you are indisposed?" Vasili asked.

"No, let him in. I'll see what he wants." She laid down her harp, smoothed the wrinkles of the yellow stola

184

THE SIGN of the EAGLE

clinging to her legs and swept back a crimson lock falling over her lightly freckled forehead.

Shafer sat on a stool a few paces away, patching a woolen tunic. She pulled a thin whalebone needle through the tattered end of the cloth, stopped and turned to Macha. "Isn't he the Roman who thinks all women are in love with him, Lady Carataca?"

"The same."

"Do you think he'll try again?"

"I wouldn't think so. He'd be a fool if he did."

The Moorish woman sniffed and tied off a thread on the seam. "Some men are too in love with themselves to give up. He needs a swift kick between the legs."

Falco, his muscular frame draped in the uniform of a tribune, swaggered into the atrium and confidently approached Macha. His silver cuirass covering a white jerkin, a purple edge tunic and knee length breeches, didn't impress Macha. Nor did the cavalry long sword, the Spatha, sheathed in a baldric, hanging from his shoulder. Titus appears much handsomer in the same clothing, she thought. Not budging from her seat, Macha glared coldly at the tribune.

Halting before her, he removed his scarlet-plumed helmet. "Good morning, Lady Carataca. I hope you are well today?" For an instant Falco eyed Shafer, then the hallway entrance.

"She stays, Tribune Falco," Macha said. "To what do I owe this visit?"

"Last night," Falco answered, "I arrived in Rome and wanted to pay my respects to the wife of my good friend, Titus." He grinned. His dark penetrating eyes made her feel almost as violated as if he were a rapist taking his pleasure. She suppressed a shudder.

He took a seat next to Macha. She refused to move, picked up her ornately-scrolled harp and plucked a few chords on the seven-stringed instrument. A mournful but melodic sound echoed through the atrium. She stopped and turned to Falco and smiled, but inwardly her stomach churned.

"You're so kind," Macha said. "What is your real reason for visiting me?"

185

"To render you my services. Is there anything I can do to help you?"

"Get Titus released." She set down the harp once again. Not offering any to Falco, Macha took a sip of white wine from a glass cup on the small table in front of the bench. She glanced to Shafer who remained seated on the stool patching the tunic's sleeve.

He gestured with a sweep of a hand, spreading his manicured fingers. "I regret that's out of the question—only the Emperor can free him. In fact, I came to Rome to testify at his court-martial."

"Why you, Tribune Falco?" Macha took another swallow of wine.

"To verify your husband's interrogation was conducted in a lawful manner."

Shocked, Macha spewed a cascade of wine onto the floor from her mouth, barely missing Falco's sandaled boots.

He jumped to his feet, scanned the atrium, and ordered a passing slave to fetch a towel.

Shafer rushed to Macha's side and dropped to her knees. "Are you all right, Lady Carataca?"

"There's nothing wrong," Macha choked a reply. "I was just a little startled and choked."

Falco edged away and stood at the far end of the seat. "I'm sorry if I said anything to upset you, Lady Carataca."

The slave returned and handed Macha a soft towel. As he cleaned the splattered wine, Macha dabbed her mouth and face, returned the cloth to the slave, and dismissed him. Shafer returned to her seat and continued sewing.

Macha said, "It's difficult for me to believe you traveled all the way to Rome just for that one purpose."

"Reason enough, isn't it?" Falco stepped closer and lowered his head to meet her eyes. He stared through hers as if she weren't there. Macha's stomach contracted like a fist.

"Unlike the Emperors Nero and Tiberius, Vespasian wants no cloud of injustice hovering over this or any future treason trials."

She recalled the two emperors had arrested and condemned hundreds of suspected traitors, most of whom belonged to the nobility, on the flimsiest of evidence and without trial.

"I'm grateful at least for the Emperor's consideration."

Falco shook his head. "Unfortunately, Titus' chances of acquittal are bleak. The implications for you should be apparent."

"If you remember, we discussed the subject at Helena's dinner party."

"Being the widow of a condemned traitor is a consequence no woman deserves to suffer," Falco said. "Where would you go, and who would take care of you?"

"I'm not a widow." Macha inhaled deeply and stared into his eyes. "In any event it wouldn't be you, Tribune Falco, if that's what you're implying."

"I've never suggested anything of the sort, Lady." He cocked an eyebrow. "I've made sacrifices to the gods for Titus' acquittal."

She smoothed her stola with sweaty hands and turned a cold eye on Falco. "How noble. I pray the gods will answer your prayers. Then I'll not have to worry about widowhood."

Falco placed his hand on the bejeweled hilt of his sword and narrowed his black eyes. "The reality remains—Titus will be found guilty and condemned, Macha. A desirable woman like you need not be left alone without so much as a *quadran* to her name."

Macha nodded in the direction of the entryway on the other side of the atrium. "Will you leave, please? I'll not hear another word about my husband's pending execution or my future widowhood. You're no longer welcomed in this home."

"You're making a grave mistake, dear lady."

As Falco stormed through the front entrance, Shafer jabbed her middle index finger in the time-honored Greek manner in his direction. "Forgive me, lady, but he's an evil man."

A sudden chill raced through Macha's body. She wrapped her arms close around her small breasts.

"You're shivering," Shafer said as she stepped to Macha's side and laid the tunic across her shoulders.

"It's Falco's words that turned me cold," Macha answered. "Titus' chances of freedom are so remote—it frightens me." Macha hadn't told Shafer about his part, yet.

"You'll prove his innocence, I'm sure."

"I appreciate your faith in me. What I don't understand is why, with all the eligible women in the Roman Empire to choose from, Falco is pursuing me?"

"Because you are unreachable. He wants to conquer you—not to mention the glamour of being married to the daughter of a king."

"So when he becomes bored, he can use and then toss me aside like a stone," Macha said ruefully, her emerald eyes narrowed. "Falco will never touch me."

Is Falco involved with the murders of Nicanor, his son, and Metrobius? Macha puzzled. Or is it just my overwrought imagination running wild? I must get a hold of myself. Is he truly here only to testify at my husband's court-martial? I don't know what to think anymore.

Macha still possessed five black splinters found on Nicanor's body in the stable. But they held no value unless the club was recovered. Even if the weapon found its way to the capital, and she confiscated it, the slivers needed to match perfectly to be used as evidence.

* * * * *

About an hour after dusk, as she left the library, Macha heard a commotion at the front door. Close as she was, rather than sending a slave, she crossed the atrium to the entry to investigate the problem.

"I demand to see Senator Bassus."

She recognized the fractured voice of Crixus and spied him at the gate wrapped in a black woolen cloak. A huge red-bearded Dacian bodyguard accompanied the Gaul.

"The Senator is not here," Vasili answered.

"You're lying, you sniveling dog," Crixus snarled. "He'll see me, it's important."

"Let them in, Vasili," Macha ordered. "I'll speak to Crixus." Still recovering from his interrogation, the Gaul limped into the vestibule. The Dacian, who came from north of the River Danubus, wore the traditional black and smelly woolen tunic and the breeches of his people,

followed. The shadows from the torches lighting the
entryway flickered eerily on Crixus' cleaved face. Macha
swallowed gall to keep eye contact with this loathsome
creature, his appearance, his devious manner.

She led them to the garden. Spring night air grazed
Macha's face and arms like a thin veil of delicate silk. They
stopped beside a whitewashed lattice fence bordering the
gravel path at the far end, near the peristyle. Beyond the
fence a long bed of daisies and pink oleanders grew next to
the house's wall. In the corner a green-striated marble
fountain gurgled, spewing water from the mouth of a blue
dolphin. The noise of produce wagons rumbling down dark
narrow streets echoed from the city below. Crickets ceased
their chirping as they approached. Macha scanned the
area—no slaves lurked about.

"You shouldn't be here, Crixus," Macha admonished.
"By calling at the Senator's house, you place yourself in
danger. It jeopardizes our efforts to bring the real
conspirators to justice."

"But I have urgent news for Senator Bassus," Crixus
insisted. He twisted his crooked face in the direction of the
entryway to the house.

"He left for Misenum yesterday."

Crixus snapped his head back to Macha. "Gone? This is
the first time I've heard of it."

"Why don't you give me the information?" Macha
gestured toward her chest. "I'll convey it to Senator Bassus
when he returns."

"I'll wait 'til he's back," Crixus said as he shook his
head. "No one sees it but him. It's a copy of the list of
conspirators."

Macha choked. "The list! That will save my husband's
life. I'm entitled to see it. My son's life and mine are at
stake, too. I won't reveal your secret, I promise."

"Can't take the chance, it's my neck, too."

"All the more reason why I must see it, now," Macha
said in an urgent voice. "We're all in this together whether
we like it or not. We have to depend on one another if we're
to survive."

Crixus snorted. "I depend on no one for my survival. I'll
be back when the Senator returns to Rome."

189

He turned on his heels, followed by his bodyguard, and left the garden. What now? a stunned Macha thought. How can Crixus be so selfish? Macha breathed deeply. Slowly, she turned and proceeded through the garden, back to the library. She bowed her head over the citrus wood desk and prayed.

Mother Goddess Anu please change the Gaul's mind. Titus, my son—and I—depend upon it.

The goddess did not answer.

CHAPTER 26

Of Thumbs and Murder

As Macha arose to eat breakfast, the sun topped the rim of the distant Sabine Hills. She had slept poorly, too shaken knowing Crixus possessed a copy of the list and refused to share it with her.

While she dined on honeyed cakes, spring melon, and olives, Vasili entered the *triclinium* and informed her that a courier with a sealed message waited in the atrium. Macha shot him a puzzled look. No document was delivered at this time of morning unless it contained ominous news. So much had occurred during the last two weeks, she dreaded the implication. Her stomach clenched.

"I'll meet him in the library," she said.

Vasili nodded and departed.

The trooper from the Watch entered the tablinum and said, "I have a dispatch from Tribune Pomponius Appius, Lady Carataca." He halted in front of her desk. Macha reached for the sealed parchment.

"Thank you. You may leave."

"Tribune Appius has instructed me to wait for your reply."

Macha summoned a slave who lead the bucketman to the kitchen for food and drink while she read the letter.

She slashed open the document's brittle waxed seal with a needle-thin silver dagger and began to read. She gasped and dropped the scroll on the desk. "No, not Crixus! Killed!" Catching her breath, she went to the door and ordered a passing slave to find Shafer and send her to the tablinum.

Waiting for the Moorish woman, Macha returned to the table, picked up, and continued reading the missive. According to the dispatch, Horse Arse and his Dacian bodyguard had just left *The Spade and Pickaxe* Tavern, and as they stepped into the lane outside, six assassins sprang from the shadows with drawn daggers. Wearing black clothing, their faces covered, the killers repeatedly slashed the two victims. Upon finishing their grisly work, the murderers had vanished into the night as suddenly as they had appeared. Crixus died, but his personal guard, although left unconscious and bleeding badly, survived

The echo of sandals preceded Shafer down the hallway. She entered to the room and stopped when she saw Macha's agonized face. "What is it, Lady? What's wrong?"

"Crixus has been murdered!" She motioned to the message.

Her slave shot a hand to her mouth. "No! When?"

"Last night outside the *Spade and Pickaxe*, a wine shop in the Subura. It's a place frequented by laborers and thieves."

"I've heard it's a most horrible place," Shafer said, her hand falling to her side.

"Unfortunately, not for the likes of Crixus," Macha answered. She returned to the message and continued reading. "It was Pomponius Appius who learned about Crixus' death," she added.

Shafer moved closer to Macha. "Who told him?"

"One of Bassus' informants," she answered in a lowered voice, motioning Shafer to sit on a stool at the side of the desk. "Appius confirmed it with the commander of the Third Cohort of the Watch, which patrols the Subura."

Macha further explained the details she had read prior to her servant's arrival. She went on to read the bodyguard had survived to tell arriving watchmen the assassins had stolen a list from Crixus. He didn't know what it contained. Crixus had screamed before he died, "Tell Lady Macha they've got the list!"

The Watch centurion in charge of the investigation had relayed the information to his cohort commander.

Macha fell silent. She knew it was a list of conspirators, the same Crixus had in his possession when he saw her last night. She read on and discovered Pomponius Appius had reached the same conclusion. The list had been within her grasp, only to be lost. The copy was now in the hands of Titus's enemies.

"This was the extra list naming all the conspirators," Macha said aloud. "It would have cleared Titus of treason."

"But Crixus is dead, and the proof is gone," Shafer said.

"I wonder who discovered Crixus' treachery? Isn't it strange he was murdered right after Tribune Falco arrived in Rome?" Macha tossed the scroll onto the table.

"Do you think the tribune had a part in the murder?"

"It would be only a guess on my part, and I have no proof." With Crixus' death, another opportunity for Titus' vindication had evaporated like steam from a cooking pot.

Summoning the messenger, Macha informed him that she requested Tribune Pomponius Appius' presence as soon as possible.

"Can you trust Tribune Appius?" Shafer asked after the messenger left.

Macha dropped her hands to her lap. She thought about her decision. "Senator Bassus says I can. The Tribune seems to have second thoughts about my husband's guilt, and I have to trust somebody, especially, with the Senator away. I have already asked him to search for my son."

"Isn't there anyone else in Rome you could ask?"

"Not anyone I trust," Macha answered. She nodded toward the library door.

Shafer stood and scooted to the entry, took half a step outside and scanned the atrium. A slave swept the mosaic floor by the *impluvium,* sounds of a scraping reed broom echoed off the surrounding walls.

"Appius is the only official I can enlist in my search for the truth," Macha whispered, when Shafer returned. "He knows there's a list. I'm sure he wants to find it as much as I. He hasn't found my son, or he would have sent word. Nothing was mentioned in this dispatch." Macha motioned for Shafer to take the stool.

"But you said you still questioned his true involvement in the affair." Shafer glided from the door and sat.

"I do," Macha replied. "Rather, I did." She shook her head. "Now, I'm not sure. Senator Bassus said he had a reason for bringing the tribune to Rome but never said why. Since he's gone to Misenum, Pomponius Appius is the only ally I can employ, and gods forbid, protector." And

193

gods forbid if the Senator is part of the conspiracy as well, Macha added silently. Mother Goddess, I pray he is not.

"We've traveled around the city before without one, why not now?" Shafer asked, interrupting Macha's thoughts.

"We'll need a male to escort us to places where we can't go alone, such as the Subura. Going about the city disguised as prostitutes nearly got us killed. And we were equally as fortunate in seeing Antonia at the quarry without being attacked. We can't risk that again." Still suspicious of Appius and his intentions, she prayed Bassus' reason for bringing him to the capital was to help clear Titus.

A sense of desperation crept through Macha. She searched her mind for other ways to help Titus. Time was running out. In less than two weeks his trial would begin. She couldn't wait for Bassus' return to clear him. Chances of his acquittal appeared grim. So far her efforts had failed. Now that Crixus was dead, another chance for Titus' release had vanished.

Macha turned to Shafer. "Leave me, I need to be alone." As soon as the slave left, Macha quietly wept.

* * * * *

The evening shadows deepened and Macha went to her sleeping cubicle after a long strenuous day. A small olive oil lamp on the table next to the bed barely illuminated the room. In the light's flickering glow, she spotted a small gold casket placed on the silk pillow. During her absence someone had sneaked it into the room. Cautiously, she opened the box. Her heart leaped to her throat. She dropped it. The tiny thumb of a child rolled onto the cold tile. A guttural sound escaped Macha, her face growing hot. A roaring sound rushed through her head. She grasped the end of the table beside her bed until the spell passed. A note lay in the bottom of the felt lined box. Trembling, she picked up the little parchment and read:

I warned you not to meddle. Next time it will be his head.

Macha crumpled the message and threw it on the tiled floor. Someone must know she had nearly obtained the list of names. Was it the same woman who threatened to expose Antonia and Bassus? Thinking of little Titus, she began to shake and swallowed a scream.

194

Gods, they cut off his thumb! What kind of monsters would do such a thing to my innocent little boy, Macha questioned herself. What was I thinking? This is all my fault. I should never have interfered. But I can't stand by and watch Titus suffer death as a traitor. Mother Goddess Anu, what am I to do? Everything I have done has turned to ashes. Macha's face tightened and tears spilled. She flopped on the goose down bed and wept, until at last she slept.

Later, she woke suddenly, further sleep was impossible. Calmer now, she strengthened her resolve to fight on. If they had cut off little Titus's thumb, then he was already dead. Or was he? The idea repelled her, but she had to examine the thumb. There was something different, but she had been too shaken to give it much thought. She puzzled over how the box was spirited into her bed chamber. Who could have brought it into the house? Had one of the household slaves been bribed by one of the plotters to be a spy?

Reluctantly, she picked the cadaverous joint off the floor and took a closer look. The soft graying flesh felt cool in her hand. Apart from the jagged edges of the thumb, the skin's surface was free of any marks. A huge sigh escaped her lips. Relieved, she slumped onto the bed.

"Thank you, Mother Goddess," she whispered aloud. "This isn't Titus' thumb."

Both of her son's thumbs had been scarred from the attack by a feral cat in their villa's stable the year before. The left one displayed four puncture wounds from its nasty bite, and the right had a long slashing scar which had required three stitches to close.

She picked up the note and re-read it. Another glimmer of hope calmed her. The letter had warned, *next time it will be his head*. He still must live!

CHAPTER 27

A Journey for Assistance

Macha sat on the bed cubicle's only chair, wood sheathed in bronze, while Shafer combed her hair. For a moment, Macha closed her eyes and recalled the box with the severed finger. What kind of vicious creatures hacked off the fingers of innocent children? My heart goes out to the mother of the poor child that lost its thumb, she thought. I wouldn't wish such a horror on any mother's child. She shook her head and opened her eyes. I dare not speculate on what manner of cruelty might be planned for my son. The thought will drive me mad. Keep him safe, she prayed.

"I have decided to see Pollia this afternoon," Macha said. "Now, that she's back in Rome, I will ask her and Pedius to use their influence to intercede with the Emperor to save Titus." She shook her head. Prior to her decision to visit Pollia, Macha and Shafer had traveled that morning to the homes of four prominent Senators and their wives to appeal for help in freeing Titus. The matrons were mutual friends of Antonia and Macha. Unfortunately, Macha had been refused entrance at all four homes on the grounds her husband was an accused traitor. It had been Macha's intention to learn if any one of them might be the woman Antonia refused to identify as the one who threaten to expose her and Senator Bassus.

Macha's plan called for Shafer to sneak into their libraries during her visit to see if she could uncover documents with handwriting matching the note left with the thumb or other incriminating records. The odds of discovering anything useful was remote, but the attempt had to be made. Shafer could read and write Latin. Because of the possibility of being discovered, Macha knew she was taking a terrible risk.

It was only with great reluctance she decided to ask Pollia for assistance. Unlike the other women, Macha didn't know whether or not Pollia was acquainted with Antonia. But Pollia was the daughter of a Senator. Although her father was dead, she and Pedius could use the memory of him to persuade the Emperor into freeing Titus.

"Is that wise, Lady Carataca?" Shafer said interrupting Macha's thoughts. She pulled the whalebone comb down through Macha's sunset locks. "From what you have told me, she sounds evil. You could be as defenseless as a dormouse in a snake's nest. Didn't you say she didn't like you because your husband refused to marry her?"

"Honestly, Shafer, she's an insufferable snob, but I don't believe she's evil."

Shafer twisted the hair into a single braid, tying it at the nape of the neck with a band of yellow ribbon. She placed an ivory hairpin bearing the image of Pudicitia, Goddess of modesty and chastity, behind the ribbon. "I still think you are being foolish."

"I have little choice. The other families refused to see me."

"I still don't trust Lady Pollia. Rich people do evil things," Shafer said. She laid the mirror on the table.

Macha turned and stared at the Moorish woman. "Does that include my husband and me and Senator Bassus?"

"No, Mistress," Shafer gestured as if it were obvious. "You and the Master are most exceptionally kind."

"Thank you, Shafer," Macha answered in a voice of relief.

"But I know from my own experiences about what they can do," Shafer said. Her eyes narrowed. "I have been raped by my former owners and abused like a dog. Then Senator Bassus rescued me from that life. But some of his men still tried to get their way with me." She raised one foot slightly and dropped it to the floor. "That is until I kicked their private parts. Now, they leave me alone."

Macha raised her hand and briefly touched Shafer's smooth ebony arm. "I'm so sorry you were subjected to such cruelty."

"You are the only one I have ever told this to." Shafer bowed her head.

"With the exception of Senator Bassus, do you still hate all men in his household?"

Shafer raised her head and crinkled her dark eyebrows together pondering the question. "There may be one I don't," she answered slowly. "Still I'm not sure about him. He has been kind to me, but I don't know if he can be trusted."

"That could be said about all men." Although curious about the man, Macha decided Shafer would tell her when she was ready.

Macha finished touching up the makeup she had applied earlier that morning. She picked up the mirror from Shafer and gazed at her image again. Her appearance had improved, but she recalled how haggard she looked when she first awoke. Her red-rimmed eyes and drawn face had betrayed a restless night, the ragged thumb of the little child still on her mind. She certainly must have looked the part of a distraught woman, but it had not made any difference to those from who she had sought help. Perhaps Pollia would be more sympathetic.

For the first time, she noticed tiny lines forming at the corner of her kohl-daubed green eyes. She sighed and examined her earrings a cluster of little gold shanks embedded with pearls, circling a stone of green plasma. At least they hadn't aged, she thought. Macha laid the mirror down.

Shafer tied a thin necklace, stamped from sheet gold formed into shapes of tiny sea shells, around Macha's neck. The cold strands sent a shiver down Macha's spine.

An emerald silk stola trimmed in gold thread clothed Macha's willowy frame. Beneath her under-tunic was smooth Indian cotton underwear. Expensive, but worth the comfort compared to scratchy wool or linen underclothing. Nothing must distract her today.

Macha and Shafer reviewed their plan again. Macha explained that once they arrived at Pollia's, she would ask her and her husband to use their influence with the Emperor to obtain Titus' release. "While we are there," Macha whispered, "I want you to sneak into Pedius' study. If the home is like most others, it should be adjacent to the atrium."

"But Mistress, I am still afraid I will be discovered before I reach it."

"No, you won't." Macha went on to explain that during her visit with Pollia, Shafer would feign illness and ask to use the privy. Once away, she would head for Pedius' library.

"Am I to search the same way as you had planned for the other homes?" Shafer asked, frowning.

"Nothing has changed. I want you to look for business records, starting with the wax tablets, and see if you can find any documents with handwriting similar to that on the note I received from the kidnappers."

"What if I don't find any writing like that?" Shafer asked.

"Then, unfortunately, we will have to look elsewhere."

"I still doubt Lady Pollia will admit us. The other families would not."

"I got the distinct impression, when she attended the dinner party in Mediolanum, that she didn't believe my husband was a traitor. I think she will see me," Macha replied. "But I hate degrading myself before her. I'm sure she'll love gloating over my helplessness."

"Then why do you?"

Macha exhaled attempting to contain her impatience with Shafer's persistent questions. "I have already said I don't have much of a choice, and I need you to get into Pedius' office. Perhaps you won't find a thing, but we have to start somewhere."

A wave of acid welled up from Macha's stomach as she realized she was placing Shafer and herself in grave danger. She sipped a cup of water sitting on the dressing table to clear the bile from her throat. If discovered in Pedius' office, Pollia would order her retainers to seize both of them. She could summon the Praetorian Guard and have Macha arrested for treason, since she was the wife of an accused traitor. Shafer would be tortured until she confessed to gods knows what. But what else could she do?

Outside her bed cubicle, the daily activities of Bassus' household were in full stride. Macha heard the house steward chastise a slave's sloppy work dusting the master's bust and ordered another to clean the green scum clinging to the sides of the garden fountain.

"I'm ready, Shafer," Macha said a moment later.

Six slaves from Mauritania and Numidia stood beside a sedan chair in the sun- drenched courtyard waiting for Macha. Inlaid with polished agates from the east and coral from the coast of Dalmatia, its woodwork gleamed in the mid-morning sun. She entered the sedan, and the bearers lifted it effortlessly from the ground. They departed from Bassus' home and pushed into the dusty crowded street without losing stride, followed by ten slave retainers and their burly Spanish leader, Viriatus.

Shafer walked beside the litter. "I know these men," she said. "They are trustworthy and loyal to the Master. If we are attacked, they won't run away."

"I'm relieved to hear that," Macha said. "You've never said anything about them before, but I assumed they would. Why do you bring this up now?"

"As I've said, Mistress, I don't trust Lady Pollia. You are nothing to her. She might try something—what I don't know."

"I pray you are wrong."

"So do I."

"You say these men won't run away, but are they good fighters?"

"They are, especially, Viriatus. He's an ex-soldier from the Third Legion in Africa and a brave man."

Macha raised her head and studied the broad shouldered, auburn-haired Spaniard at the head of the litter bearers. He continually turned his swarthy square-jawed face about, and she knew his deep-set blue eyes were scanning the street and the jostling crowd around the entourage.

"What part of Spain is he from?" Macha asked.

"The Central Highlands," Shafer answered. "He says he is a Celt-Iberian. Do you know what that means, Mistress?"

"Yes, I know of them—it explains his large size. He belongs to a tribe that intermarried with a group of Celts that migrated to Spain hundreds of years ago from Gaul and Britannia. But why is he a slave?"

"He was escorting a prisoner to the slave market, but he escaped. Viriatus was forced to take his place as a slave."

Macha slapped a hand on her thigh. "That's horrible!"

"Yes, Mistress. The Master learned of his fate and purchased him. He promised to free the Spaniard after seven years if he served him well."

"How long has he been the Senator's slave?"

"Six years."

"We may need his strength after my discovery of the thumb last night. I know it was meant to intimidate me. More than likely, spies are watching my every move."

"Then perhaps they will be waiting for us at Pollia's doorstep."

Second thoughts about confronting Pollia crept into Macha's mind. Was she placing herself in a dangerous position after all? But she had already been to four other homes. Why was she having second thoughts now? Who else could she turn to? Her façade of the distraught and helpless wife was all too real. Macha considered returning to Bassus' house and rethinking her situation. But that would waste precious time. Perhaps I am being naïve, she thought to herself, but I can't believe Pollia would refuse to aid me. Pollia lost two children at birth, and I have heard she still grieves over their deaths. Surely her maternal instincts would be appalled by the killing of any child.

Deciding to continue as planned, Macha would stay alert for the slightest hint of trouble. May the gods forgive me if little Titus suffers because of my actions, she prayed silently. I can never forgive myself.

Several blocks down the *Vicus Sobrius* Avenue, skirting the Subura, Macha and Shafer crossed a little plaza graced with a public fountain. A stream of fresh water gushed from the sculptured head of Medusa into the broad rust-colored stone basin. Surplus water overflowed from the lower end, trickling away in a streamlet down the middle of the street and mixed with rubbish dumped by shopkeepers along the way. Older matrons and neighborhood women, younger ones with whining little children clinging to their skirts, laughed as they stopped to gossip and fetch drinking water in drab pottery jugs.

201

At one end of the square, a wizened old woman, supporting herself on a battered cane, hobbled to a little shrine of the crossroads set in a niche against the wall of the pottery shop. She pulled a crust of bread from her ragged stola and set it upon the altar before youthful male and female deities.

Despite the clattering noise of the street, Macha heard the old woman say in a loud voice, "Here you are, my good and trusty friends. I haven't forgotten you." She turned and for a few seconds glared at the women around the fountain. She snorted, "Can't say the same for the unbelievers. Nobody respects the gods anymore." She limped away, disappearing down a narrow side street.

On one side of the plaza a bakery radiated heat. Little more than a tiny ground-floor room, it faced the street and contained two ovens constructed of bricks. Charcoal fires burned on the floor beneath it. Even from the litter Macha felt the warmth and caught the smell of freshly baked bread drifting from the shop. She had eaten little at breakfast and her stomach churned and growled.

Three slaves, their gaunt faces covered with white flour, deftly inserted freshly-kneaded dough into the furnace, and as quickly removed baked loaves from the hot coals on long handled flat shovels. Their young master, who like his workers, was prematurely stooped, quietly gave orders and assisted in the chores. Macha pitied the baker and slaves alike. They plied a back-breaking unhealthy trade and would die at an early age.

On the other side of the court Macha and Shafer passed a dilapidated tavern. Painted on the wall next to the curtain opening read a message, *Please Fight Outside*. Indoor, near the open bar, Macha observed eight or nine seedy characters congregated on crowded benches, swilling wine. One appeared familiar, but she couldn't place him. A head taller than the rest, a thick jaw dominated his heavily-scarred face. The bridge of his crooked nose was divided by deeply recessed eyes.

"I don't like the looks of that place," Shafer said.

"Neither do I," Macha answered, "and for good reason. See that sign?" She pointed to the faded painted images on the stucco tavern wall. "That's the *Spade and Pickaxe*, the place where Crixus was murdered. Hurry on!" she ordered the litter bearers.

For the next three or four blocks, Macha and Shafer looked over their shoulders. Macha watched the Spaniard as he dropped back behind the entourage and kept a wary eye on the jostling crowd. No one followed and soon he returned to the head of the retinue. Macha sighed and leaned against the back of her cushioned sedan chair. Shafer stepped forward from a watchful position behind the litter and strolled beside Macha.

Macha stiffened, her hands clenched against her heart.

"What's wrong, Lady Carataca?"

From the direction of Esquiline Hill, a tribune rode a bay gelding. "Over there!" Macha motioned. "It's Falco, coming from Pollia's house."

"Turn left, down this way, hurry!" she commanded the litter bearers. They hid in the dark recesses of an alley, smelling of dung and urine and waited until Falco passed by. Why was Falco at Pollia's house? Was this part of the ongoing romantic tryst that Nicanor had observed the night of the dinner party in Mediolanum? Perhaps their intentions for one another are more serious than I first believed. Or was there something else?

Shafer stayed in the shadows of the tenement building, then edged her way back to the entrance. She peered around the corner. "He's gone," she said a few seconds later.

"Thank Mother Goddess, he didn't see us." Macha sighed in relief.

"Lady Carataca, how did you know the tribune came from Lady Pollia's home?" Shafer asked.

"He was riding from that direction. He must have been at Pollia's."

"Do you think he is bedding her?"

"Perhaps. I know Nicanor saw them together the night before he was murdered."

They arrived at Pollia's palatial mansion, framed by high walls bordered with cypress and poplars. Situated in Rome's most prestigious residential area, the imposing two-story house sprawled along the crest of Esquiline Hill.

Macha informed the gatekeeper she requested a visitation with Pollia. "Tell your mistress that I, Macha Carataca, need her help at once!"

CHAPTER 28

A Snob by Any Other Name

Waiting in the atrium for Pollia to receive her, Macha sat on an uncomfortable marble bench for nearly an hour. She's doing this deliberately, Macha thought. She heard the scraping sounds of Shafer's sandals behind her. No doubt she was getting tired of standing on the marble floor in one spot for so long.

Pollia glided into the reception area. Coiffed into a multi-set of ringlets above the forehead, the center of Pollia's hair was pulled back and rolled into a bun at the nape of her neck and tied together by a gilded leather thong. She wore a sleeveless stola of indigo silk and a pair of bejeweled doeskin sandals. Two snake-headed gold bracelets loosely encircled her wrists. Clustered like grapes, pearl earrings hung from thin ear lobes.

She extended her fingertips to Macha. "What an unexpected pleasure," she said in a honeyed voice.

"It's kind of you to see me, Pollia," Macha replied.

Pollia smiled demurely. "My, what a novel hairdo. Is that what the ladies of Mediolanum are wearing, or is it one of your quaint barbarian styles?"

Macha answered as if the insult were a compliment. "No, Pollia, it's a little something my slave dreamed up."

"Well, now that you're in Rome, you must try the latest style, like the one I'm wearing. It will do wonders for your appearance and take years off your age. Come along to the garden, where we can chat without interruption," Pollia said.

Macha followed Pollia across the mosaic floor. Shafer kept a discreet distance behind the two women. Glancing about the atrium, Macha noticed near the entryway a full-length wall portrait of a dignified Pollia and Pedius. Standing together in their finest clothing, the couple displayed the Roman symbols of importance and prosperity. Pollia held a twin-leafed wax tablet and stylus, and Pedius clenched a papyrus scroll.

A great pattern of tiny stones, laid out in spirals of black, white, and red, ran from the green striated pillars at the entryway from the atrium across to the vast garden beyond. Pink, red, and yellow roses clustered in dozens of vases and sweetened the stifling late morning heat.

"You've never been here before, have you, Macha?" Pollia asked.

"No, this is my first visit; your home is very impressive."

A patronizing smile radiated from Pollia's full lips. "Of course, it is. I personally supervised its design and decorations."

They strolled through the hallway past numerous marble busts and statues of Pedius' dour ancestors and assorted gods and goddesses lining the colonnaded hall. One caught Macha's attention near the opening to the garden—a graceful life-like statue of Venus preparing for the bath. She had seen copies of the famous work before. Priapus, the god of fertility, and her son, Cupid, assisted the nude goddess. Upon closer observation, Macha noticed a distinct difference in this model—the face resembled a youthful Pollia.

The huge terraced garden contained a forest of clipped evergreens and tree-lined walkways with ivy garlands strung from trunk to trunk. Birds rustled among the branches and shrubs chirping and squawking.

"Sit down," Pollia gestured Macha to a pink-veined marble bench facing her. Shafer stood behind Macha a few feet distant. Pollia ordered a slave to bring wine and sweetmeats. They sat amidst the blooming roses, crown daisies, and oleanders. Their mild fragrance drifting on a light breeze.

"Now tell me, what is this about wanting my help?" Pollia inquired.

"I'm desperate, Pollia. You and Pedius are the only people who can help me."

For a split second Pollia's forehead creased. She examined her long fingernails, painted with the sediment of red wine. Her gaze returned to Macha. "That depends on what you want from us."

A slave arrived with refreshments. The women said nothing further until the wine was poured and the server had departed for the kitchen. Another stood behind Pollia.

Macha barely tasted the cool Albanian wine served in a plain bronze cup. "You have influence with the Emperor. You can persuade him to free Titus," she finally said.

"You must be joking. We don't have any real influence with the Emperor." Pollia sipped her drink from a bejeweled silver goblet and smirked.

"That's not what I've heard," Macha countered. "The Emperor desperately needs your husband's loans to finance the rebuilding of the Empire. Pedius can use his resources as leverage. Surely the two of you can do something for me."

Pollia sniffed. "Why should we? My husband is an honest businessman. He wouldn't abuse his privileges to persuade Vespasian to release a traitor."

Macha thought, It's enough that Pollia insults me, but I'm certain she's lying. Macha pressed the cup to her lips pretending to sip. It was the only way she could hold her tongue. Pollia's husband has a notorious reputation for bribing Imperial officials to obtain lucrative government contracts.

Quietly, Shafer approached Macha. "Forgive my intrusion, Lady Carataca." She whispered into Macha's ear.

"Of course, Shafer," Macha said as she set the drink on the adjacent bench. "I'm sorry to bother you, Pollia, but would you be kind enough to allow one of your slaves to show mine to the privy? She has stomach problems."

Pollia crinkled her nose, turned, and nodded sharply to a slave woman standing behind her. Shafer followed.

"Contrary to what you have heard," Macha continued, "Titus is innocent. I would do anything to gain his freedom. Now that my son has been kidnapped, I need him more than ever."

"Your son? Why, Macha, that's dreadful—I had no idea." Briefly, Pollia reached over and touched Macha's wrist with an icicle-cold hand. "I'm sorry to hear about your son."

"I thought you knew. I'm nearly at my wits end." No doubt Pollia knows, Macha thought, but I need to stall her as long as possible if Shafer is to succeed. She proceeded to tell Pollia the details of the kidnapping. As Macha described the tall broken-nose bandit who had snatched her son, Pollia clenched her goblet for the space of a heartbeat. Otherwise she displayed no emotion.

"And that's about all I know right now," Macha said as she finished her story. "So far there has been no news as to where he might be."

"But the authorities are searching, are they not?"

"Yes, they are. I pray they find little Titus soon, and arrest the kidnappers."

"I'm sure they will," Pollia said. She pursed her lips for a few seconds and studied Macha. "In the meantime, wouldn't it be better if you returned home?"

Macha lowered her eyes. "I should, but I can't leave my husband." She looked up and returned Pollia's gaze without blinking. "That's why I came to you. I know you and your husband can help me. I thought you had heard about my son's abduction and might know something—you have the ear of Rome."

Pollia shook her head. "I'm afraid you're gravely mistaken, dear. I didn't have the faintest notion. And as for my husband's influence, you give him more credit than he deserves."

Macha looked about for Shafer who hadn't returned. She must think of something else to hold Pollia's attention.

"By the way, where is your husband, Pollia?" Macha inquired. "Couldn't I at least ask him?"

"He's away on business. Even if he were here, I seriously doubt he would spare any time for you." Pollia paused as if remembering something. Her cold gray eyes gazed beyond Macha to the garden entrance. "I notice your slave isn't back."

"As I said, she's has stomach problems."

Pollia eyed the slave who had led Shafer to the latrine. "Where is Lady Carataca's slave?"

"Still in the water closet, Mistress. She wasn't feeling well."

"You fool," Pollia snapped. "Why didn't you stay with her? Return at once, and see if she's still there."

Macha steeled herself not to betray her concern. But her mouth turned dry and the palm of her hands grew clammy.

"Shafer may be returning even as we speak," Macha said evenly. "I assume she went to the slave's privy."

"We shall see."

Macha struggled to breathe normally. The tension within her body grew with each passing second. Would Pollia's slave find Shafer still in the water closet? "She could have gotten lost in this mansion."

For the space of a couple of breaths, Macha hesitated. Second thoughts about seeing Pollia flooded her mind. Wasn't it obvious that Pollia was not going to aid her in getting Titus' release? If Shafer is caught in the library, Macha thought uneasily, I could be accused of using Shafer to spy on them. As the wife of an accused traitor, I might be arrested for treason. Pollia could say I attempted to plant evidence implicating that she and her husband were taking part in the conspiracy against the Emperor. Shafer would be tortured until she confessed to such a lie. Mother Goddess, I must keep a hold of myself and hope Shafer returns quickly. Macha had half expected her beating heart would burst through her chest. How much longer she could hold Pollia's attention?

"As I mentioned before," Macha continued, "Cutthroats snatched my son and who knows, they may have even murdered him. As a mother, is it not my right to seek justice?" She wanted to add that whoever they were, they had underestimated her, but she kept the thoughts to herself.

"Of course it is, but why are you telling me all this?" Pollia asked.

Macha chose her words carefully. "Because I don't want to see my husband wrongfully tried for a crime he didn't commit. I want my son found and released before he suffers real harm. That's why I'm seeking your help and influence with the Emperor to release my husband and seek my son's kidnappers."

"I'm afraid that's impossible," Pollia said in a flat voice. She seemed about to add something further when the slaves returned together.

Shafer hurried to Macha's side and knelt before her. She bowed her head, her eyes on the floor. "I'm most sorry to be away so long, my lady, but I feel much better now."

"I'm pleased you are, Shafer," Macha said, genuinely relieved by her safe return. Shafer stood and took a place at a discreet distance behind Macha.

"I found her still there, Mistress," the other slave whispered to Pollia.

"Consider yourself fortunate." Pollia said. "Otherwise, I would have flogged you until no skin was left on your back."

Pollia turned to Macha. "And now you must leave. I assure you I don't have the faintest knowledge of what you are talking about. I feel no obligation to assist the wife of a traitor."

She raised an eyebrow in the direction of a slave, which to Macha's relief escorted her and Shafer to the front gate.

Macha hoped Shafer's search had not been in vain.

As they approached the palanquin, Shafer stepped close to Macha and whispered, "Mistress, I didn't find what you wanted."

CHAPTER 29

Ambush

Beneath a glaring mid-afternoon sun, Macha and Shafer left Pollia's home. She commanded the litter bearers to head for Watch headquarters of the Fourth Cohort on *Vicus Piscinae* Road. Although slaves were prohibited by law from riding in a palanquin, Macha considered Shafer her friend and invited her to sit with her in the shaded refuge of her sedan. Viriatus and a couple of slave carriers eyed the women.

Macha nodded to the Spaniard, "Proceed." To the swaying rhythm of the litter, the two women were borne down a narrow lane from Esquiline Hill.

"It's time Pomponius Appius knows about the finger," Macha said to Shafer, "and what I suspect about Pollia."

Macha turned her head and checked to see if they were being followed. She saw nothing suspicious through the sedan's open curtains. "Now, tell me what you did after going to the privy?"

"Mother Fortuna smiled upon me," Shafer whispered. "I did all the things you told me to do. From the latrine, I kept groaning loudly so the slave outside would think I was most sick. A few minutes later I looked through the door and she was gone, so I sneaked out.

"I darted from room to room, making sure no one saw me, until I reached the library. As you guessed, it was near the atrium. Just like you instructed, I looked for any scroll or wax tablet with the same handwriting found in the accursed box with the little child's finger."

"Go on," Macha urged.

"I rummaged through all the pigeon-holed cupboards looking for scrolls and waxed tablets. At the same time I kept an ear open for footsteps coming from the hallway outside the door"

"Any luck?" Macha asked.

211

"I didn't find any writing resembling your note," Shafer answered. "I started on a bin marked accounts due and pulled five waxed-tablets from a slot. But they slipped through my fingers and clattered onto the floor."

Macha sucked in her breath. "What! Did they break? Did anyone hear you?"

"Thank gods, no," Shafer answered. "I picked them up quickly and returned them to the cupboard. Just then I saw another lying open. But I did not get close enough to examine it before I heard footsteps hurrying down the corridor towards the tablinum. I left it where I found it and barely escaped through the back door," Shafer replied. "I ran into a dark room and hid beneath the bed and squeezed myself under a bug-infested mattress."

Macha's hand shot to her mouth. "Disgusting!"

"Then I heard voices," Shafer said. "Someone said everything appeared to be in order, but I stayed where I was a little longer. It's a good thing I did. A few minutes later, I heard footsteps come into the bedroom. A man's voice mumbled nothing was there, probably a slave had dropped something in the hallway and then gone."

"What happened next?"

"As soon as I felt he wouldn't return, I left the *cubiculum* and dashed for the privy. When I got inside, I heard Lady Pollia's slave's footsteps, so I gave a loud sigh of relief. I was sitting on the latrine when she opened the door. She asked if I was feeling better, and I said, 'Gracious, yes.' After I tidied myself, she escorted me back to the garden."

"Thank Mother Goddess you safely returned to the privy," Macha said. She squeezed Shafer's hand. "Did you recognize the voices in the library?"

"I think it was the house steward and another slave."

Macha exhaled. Although disappointed that Shafer failed to find anything resembling the note left with the finger, she was relieved to escape from Pollia's home, even if she was wrong about the woman. She realized she had made a serious mistake by visiting her. Macha closed her eyes and silently asked herself why she had acted so rashly. If Pollia was involved, Macha had no proof and she should have found another way of getting into her sprawling mansion. She should have bribed one of the household slaves to spy on her. Feeling as if a cold fist was closing over her heart, Macha took several deep breaths to calm her nerves and clear her mind.

The entourage turned off the Avenue *Vicus Sobrius* and headed down a quiet lane lined with shuttered stalls. A half-dozen people wandered by Macha's palanquin, carrying towels and changes of clothing, as they headed in the opposite direction for the nearby Baths of Memnon.

Macha noticed that the siesta hour approached, street traffic dropped to a trickle. Most shops and offices were closed—except for brothels and taverns. She supposed most people were either in public baths or taking naps.

"Once I've seen Appius, I'll be happy to go home—I need a bath," Macha said to Shafer. She dabbed the perspiration from her face with a silk handkerchief. "This heat is unbearable for early April."

A half-block ahead, Macha spotted several knots of grimy-looking men wearing hoods, milling in front of a wine shop. Within seconds at least twenty banded together and approached in their direction.

"Assassins!" Viriatus cried.

He and his retainers turned about searching for an escape route. Macha scanned the area as well but found none.

"Turn around and head for the Baths of Memnon," she commanded the litter bearers and retainers. "Hurry!"

"It's the only place where we'll be safe from these devils," Shafer said. Macha saw the frightened look in her dark eyes.

Viriatus raised his arm in front of the retainers and motioned in the opposite direction. "You heard the Mistress. Move it!"

In one fluid motion, the slaves picked up their stride from a gentle swinging walk into a dead run. The women grabbed the wooden railing of the palanquin as they jolted from side to side. Despite her firm grip, Macha slid toward the edge of the silk-cushioned seat, almost falling out.

Shafer lunged over and grabbed her by the shoulder, pulling her to the middle of the sedan.

Hardly breathing, Macha turned to see the assassins gaining. She prayed she and Shafer would reach the baths in time, where the bandits wouldn't dare harm them before so many witnesses, because the Watch closely patrolled all baths. But she couldn't hold back growing terror, her knuckles growing white as she held on for her life.

The attackers broke into a dead run. Seconds later they caught up to Macha's little band. Daggers flashed in the sunlight as the assassins yanked weapons from their tunics.

Viriatus and the other nine retainers, dropped back to the rear of Macha's litter and formed a defensive line. In unison they pulled from beneath their clothing short black truncheons. A violent struggle ensued as Viriatus and his retainers withstood the onslaught of slashing blades. Swinging their clubs, they parried and blocked the killers' assaults with the skill of soldiers. The defenders smashed faces and fractured collar bones as they sent the assailants flying onto the grimy street. But a number of attackers broke through their ranks and raced after Macha and the unarmed litter bearers.

Macha grabbed a knife from a hidden fold inside her stola. My litter bearers are defenseless, she exclaimed to herself. Surely, they'll die! We'll all die!

Shafer shouted something to the litter bearers in the Moorish dialect. Lurching to a halt, they lost control and dropped the sedan chair, throwing Macha under the seat. Her head banged against one corner of the palanquin and a stinging pain shot through her skull. Darkness clouded her vision. Groaning, she shook her head, attempting to clear it. Her elbows and knees ached.

Macha pulled the red covering from the chair door off her body. Using only bare hands and fists to deflect the murderous blows, the litter bearers, yelling tribal war cries, battled the attackers. Despite Macha and Shafer's screams, no passersby or anyone from the adjacent apartments came to their assistance.

Pushing herself up on her hands and knees, Macha saw Shafer kick and gouge one villain, barely keeping out of reach of his slashing dagger. Macha spotted a bystander gazing at the death-struggle. He popped a date into his mouth and leaned against an apartment wall. Appalled, she thought, why doesn't he help us?

An assassin lunged at Shafer. Macha grabbed his ankle, throwing him off balance. He toppled to the street, shouting a stream of obscenities, sprang to his feet, knife in hand, and dived in Macha's direction.

She hurled her dagger and struck him in the chest.

A shocked look crossed his pocked face. He spat blood, spraying her cheeks, eyes and stola, before tumbling to the ground, dead.

Quickly, she wiped the hot sticky fluid from her face, smearing it on her hands. She reached out and pulled the weapon from his body and prepared to meet the next assassin—looking death in the eye.

"Mistress!" Shafer shouted. "A chariot! Heading this way!"

CHAPTER 30

An Intercession by Mother Vesta

The scar-faced bandit catapulted toward her. In the same instant someone shouted.

"Over there! In the name of Vesta, help her!" Antonia's voice.

Two burly men leaped from behind Macha and jerked the assassin away. He wrestled free and glared at her, eyes full of venom. A prickling sensation shot up Macha's spine as he turned and fled down the street.

More orders followed from Antonia. A group of passersbys and the Vestal's retainers, ran to the aid of Shafer and the litter bearers.

"Great Mother Vesta," Antonia said. "Macha, you're injured!" She stepped from her chariot and rushed to Macha's side where Macha sank to the cobbled street.

"I'm all right, Antonia. It's his blood." Macha motioned to the corpse lying at her feet, blood smeared across his chest.

"Then why did you cry out?" the priestess asked.

"I did? I had no idea. I suppose...because they almost killed me. Reason enough?"

Antonia nodded and touched Macha's shoulder with her fingers. "Who killed him?"

"I did," Macha answered, barely above a whisper. Her head was spinning. She pressed her quivering fingers to her temples. "That's the second time I've killed someone." She steadied her shaking hands, tightly clasping them together. Blood oozed between her fingers before she pulled them apart.

"You poor dear, I'm so sorry." Antonia hugged her. "You had no choice—he deserved his fate."

Macha held Antonia tightly, like a child not wanting to let go. She wanted to weep but couldn't. She wasn't sure. Gradually the dizziness subsided. She pushed herself from

216

Antonia's warm motherly hold, leaving the imprints of bloodstains on the Vestal's white stola. Antonia didn't seem to notice.

"What about Shafer and my people?" Macha asked. "Are they safe?"

"We shall see to them now," Antonia replied. The Vestal helped Macha to her feet.

"Thank you, Antonia," Macha said. "I can walk on my own."

Antonia nodded.

Twisting her head, Macha surveyed the carnage. Odors of salty blood mixed with discharged feces and urine of the dead assaulted her nostrils. She gagged. Crumpled on the roadway near the sedan chair lay the bloodied corpses of two slaves. A bandit's crushed body protruded from beneath the heavy frame of the litter which had toppled onto him during the attack. A few paces away a blood-smeared Shafer stooped and examined four wounded bearers lying against the curb.

Viriatus at a short distance, knelt next to the eight lifeless retainers. Sitting next to him was the other surviving defender, a hand to his bleeding head as he stared unseeing at the gutter. Nearby, lay twelve assassins bludgeoned to death. Blood ran down the side of the Viriatus cheek and forehead, dripping onto his tunic. As he examined the slashing wounds that killed his men, a guttural curse sprang from his lips. For a moment he cupped his face in his hands.

Shafer turned her head as Macha and Antonia approached.

"They were good men," Shafer said, motioning to the dead bearers. "They didn't deserve to die like this, Lady Carataca. They were warriors in their own tribes. They would have been honored as heroes."

"I understand, Shafer—they saved my life," Macha said. She placed her hand on Shafer's ebony shoulder. "And so did you, my friend, I won't forget this."

"But you saved mine, too."

"Both of you were very brave," Antonia said.

Macha thanked her, and Shafer bowed.

Antonia moved away and summoned her retainers to attend to the wounded and prepare the dead slaves for transport back to Senator Bassus' home.

Macha glanced at the bodies and back to Shafer. "I shall ask Senator Bassus to give their ashes a place of honor in his family tomb and reward the survivors, including you. Will you tell Viriatus to come over here?"

The Spaniard approached Macha, wiping away the blood from his face. "Yes, my lady?" he said with a bow.

Macha asked him about his wounds. He waved away the question as if to say they were minor.

"You are a brave man, Viriatus," Macha said. "From now on, you are to be my bodyguard until I return to Mediolanum."

"An honor, my lady."

"I know about your past, and I will do everything in my power to obtain your freedom when the time comes."

Shafer raised her dark eyebrows, but then a quick smile crossed her full lips. Macha wondered, despite Shafer's reputed dislike for men, whether she might have an interest in the Spaniard. Was he the only man she didn't hate?

Viriatus stepped away from Macha only to halt and turn back. "Lady, may I ask a favor?"

"If I can grant it, I will."

"I want revenge for the men who fought next to me. They were good soldiers."

"You shall have it—I promise."

Two squads totaling twenty watchmen arrived a few minutes later. Because of Antonia's position as Vestal Virgin and representative of the Emperor, the sergeant in charge obeyed her command to send part of the men to escort Macha's wounded litter bearers and surviving retainer to Bassus' home. Shafer and Viriatus went along to be treated by the Senator's household physician. The dead slaves were carried in a cart commandeered by the Watch from a nearby shop.

Before they were hauled away in another wagon to one of the garbage pits outside of Rome used for dumping the bodies of criminals, the poor, and slaves, the Watch sergeant identified the dead bandits as known street thugs.

Macha accompanied Antonia in her chariot. The remaining troops went on ahead of her to Watch headquarters to notify Tribune Pomponius Appius of the attack and say Macha and the priestess would meet him there shortly.

Noisily, the chariot bounced along the tufa-stone lane, jarring Macha. Her head ached and she touched the back of her skull, feeling a knot forming beneath her hair.

"I thank Mother Vesta the Emperor asked me to call upon a senator for him," Antonia said as they approached Watch headquarters near the *Porta Rudusculana* Gate.

"Is that where you came from when you saw us in trouble?" Macha asked, attempting to divert her mind from the dull throbbing pain.

Speaking above the noise of the chariot wheels grinding on the pavement, Antonia explained she was returning from Caelian Hill, on behalf of Emperor Vespasian. She had gone to thank a senator who anonymously donated a million sesterces to the treasury. She spoke more loudly, "Fortunately, I was returning home when I saw your perilous situation."

"How can I ever repay you, Antonia?"

"Just keep doing what you can for your husband and child."

Macha forced a smile and touched Antonia's forearm. "I thank Mother Vesta for our friendship."

At the precinct station, Macha and Antonia were met by Pomponius Appius. Upon his first look at Macha, he winced. "Jupiter Thunderer, what happened to you?"

"Assassins," Macha replied. "They attempted to murder me and my people."

"Come along," the Tribune said. "You can explain the details in my office." He barked to a passing slave to bring a towel for Macha.

He led them to a small cubicle, where the women took seats. They faced the Tribune who sat across from them at a cheap wooden table. He explained he had received the news of the attack from the returning bucketmen. The Watch Commander was unavailable, and just as well because Appius was taking charge of the investigation.

"I'm positive the tallest assassin was the same brute I saw earlier when we traveled by the *Spade and Pickaxe*," Macha said, adjusting herself in the hardback chair facing the Tribune. "His clothing couldn't mask his height and build. He would have murdered me if Priestess Antonia hadn't arrived when she did."

Before Macha continued, she wiped her face and hands of the coagulating blood with the damp towel brought by a slave. After she finished and returned the soiled cloth to him, the servant handed her a cape to wrap around her shoulders. Her stola, bloodstained was ruined beyond all cleaning. She took it off, gave it to the slave, and told him to throw it away.

Antonia glanced to Appius and shook her head. He shrugged.

Macha wanted to go home, take a hot bath, and something for her headache. She didn't believe she was suffering from any further injuries, but would ask Bassus' Alexandrian physician to examine her to make sure.

"I thank you for your assistance, Priestess Antonia," Appius said. He wiped sweat running down the side of his balding head with a linen cloth.

Antonia nodded. "It was my duty as a Priestess of Mother Vesta and Rome."

"Is there anything else about him that you can recall, Lady Macha Carataca?" Appius inquired.

Macha paused as she attempted to organize her thoughts. "Perhaps. Even when I first saw him, he looked familiar. Maybe I'm mad, but he closely matches the description of the one who kidnapped my son."

Appius raised his hand as if it were obvious. "There are lots of tall men with scarred faces and broken noses in Rome."

"I know it sounds foolish, but my instinct tells me he's the same."

For a few minutes Macha sat quietly. Appius opened his mouth to speak, but Antonia raised her eyebrows. He stopped. Macha massaged both sides of her head, hoping to ease the pain.

"I'm all right now," she said, and turned to Appius. "Since I hadn't heard anything about your search for my son, I take it you haven't found any trace of him."

"Not so far, but the Watch will keep searching."

Macha shook her head. What have I done to anger the gods? she thought. Can you not help me and the Watch find him, Mother Goddess? "I had hoped, but I'm not surprised," Macha finally said. "There are thousands of places in Rome where he could be hidden. But I have more information to add. Maybe it will help." She revealed the details about receiving the note and thumb, the visit to Pollia, and the futile library search.

The Tribune snorted and leaned forward. "You took a foolish risk going to Pollia's, especially, if your son is still alive."

Her heart lurched. *If.* Macha turned away, staring at the mural on the wall. "I thought Pollia and her husband could use their influence with the Emperor to help me. Since I was in her home, I saw no harm in having Shafer search the library for any document with handwriting matching that of the note found with the thumb."

"But she did not," Appius said.

"No."

"It was a foolish act. You had no right allowing your slave to snoop about."

Macha lowered her head. "I know, but still the attack came so soon after we left her place." She raised her head and looked into the Tribune's eyes. "It seems that was hardly coincidental and still needs to be investigated."

"We will, but you were very naïve to visit Pollia," Appius chided.

Macha bit her lip. Every muscle in her body tightened. She had acted stupidly. "I had to start some place, especially, after being turned away by four other families. Pollia has never forgiven Titus for marrying me."

"That's no proof she would conspire to have Titus accused of treason."

"No, it isn't." She took several deep breaths. It must be nerves, she thought, the aftermath of the attack. I must get myself under control.

Antonia and the Tribune watched in silence, patiently waiting for her to continue.

"If Shafter had found a tablet that matched hers or someone else's writing in the household," Macha continued, "it would prove her involvement in my son's kidnapping."

"You know better than that," Appius said. "It could have easily been someone else's."

Macha wringed her hands. "Perhaps if Shafer had seized a bill of lading or a bank draft in Pedius' handwriting from one of his businesses, a comparison could have been made to confirm or deny involvement in the kidnapping and plot."

"Most of the agreements and orders are written by his clerks," Appius advised. He rubbed his forehead.

"Right now, I can't prove anything," Macha said.

"You are to stay away from her house. If there is an outside chance she is involved, then you are putting your son's life at risk. In the meantime, I will order an immediate search for the assassins and a twenty-four-hour patrol placed around Senator Bassus' home."

Macha went on to inform Appius about seeing Falco leaving Pollia's residence.

"We'll deal with him when Senator Bassus returns," Appius said.

Macha and Antonia agreed.

"When I investigated Horse Arse's murder," Pomponius Appius continued, "no one at the tavern admitted knowing anything. But attempting to kill the wife of a Roman officer is another matter."

"I would certainly hope so," Macha said.

"You've given me the excuse I needed to round up every piece of vermin frequenting that rat's nest, that much I can do for you. I'll put the squeeze on the owner, and threaten to permanently close his pest hole unless he gives me names."

"If they tried to kill me," Macha said, "they must be the same ones who killed Crixus."

"Aye, we'll make them tell us who paid them to murder the thieving horse trader and kidnap your son."

CHAPTER 31

Uncertainty and Waiting

Pomponius Appius arrived at Bassus' home midmorning the following day and Macha led him into the atrium. They sat on cushioned benches next to the tiled basin used to catch rain water, the impluvium.

The Tribune informed her that his interrogations gained little information from the prisoners arrested at the *Spade and Pickaxe*. "So far, the assassins have eluded arrest," Appius said.

"Then you've learned nothing?" Macha frowned.

"Oh, I did," the tribune answered. He passed his helmet from hand to hand. "My threat to close the tavern assured the owner's full cooperation. One character you described, the one with the broken nose, appeared familiar to the barkeep, but he couldn't place him. The villain reminded the owner of a gladiator he once saw fighting in the arena but couldn't be positive. The proprietor guessed from the assassin's accents and clothing they were from Northern Italy."

"Could they be Gauls?" Macha asked.

"That's what he suspected," Appius replied. "They wore striped breeches and tunics, and ordered beer instead of wine, like most Gauls, and were taller and paler than his usual customers."

"Why didn't he ask them directly where they came from?"

Appius grinned. "In his trade it isn't wise to ask too many questions. He'd get his throat cut. So long as they paid for their drinks and food that's all he cares about. In places like that, you get more *answers* by watching than asking, and it's safer."

"Has he seen them since they tried murdering me and the slaves?"

He shook his head. "They haven't returned."

She glanced about to see if any servants lurked in the area. None. "Where else are you going to search?"

"The Trans-Tiber District across the river," Appius replied.

"Where the foreigners live?"

"Aye, it's another cesspit of scum and assassins—just the place to hide your son."

Her heart thumped. "When are you going there?"

"I'm sending out spies first, loaned to me by Senator Bassus."

"Why are you doing that?"

"Word is out about our raids in the Subura and *Cloaca Maxima*. Secrecy might prove more profitable in this case."

"I'll let Titus know when I see him today. He'll be pleased you are searching."

* * * * *

At the Praetorian Barracks, Macha entered Titus' little cell. After embracing, Titus took his wife's hand and led her past the plain wooden table and stool to the cot in a corner. For several minutes, sitting on the edge they looked at each other without saying a word, holding hands.

"Any news about our son?" Titus asked.

"So far Pomponius Appius and the Watch haven't found a trace," Macha replied. "He promises to search the Trans-Tiber District next."

Titus nodded. "At least he hasn't given up. Maybe he'll have better luck there."

"That isn't all," Macha said.

Titus eyed her suspiciously. "What else? What are you holding back?"

Macha related the details of her visit to Pollia and the assassination attempt on her life after she had departed Pollia's home. In addition to searching for Young Titus, Appius men were looking for the killers.

A dark smoldering look crossed his face as she described the attack on her. When she finished, he exhaled. Standing, he paced the room and kicked the three-legged stool against the wall; the crash echoed through the room.

He raised his voice. "How could you endanger your and our son's life? You could have died. For all we know young Titus is dead."

"I don't believe he is." She said in a soothing voice. "Because they sent another poor child's finger tells me he's alive."

Titus leaned against the wall and crossed his arms and hands in front of his chest. He stared at the ceiling. "It doesn't matter, Macha. Somebody knows that you know; isn't it obvious?" He glanced at Macha. "I almost wish you hadn't told me anything."

She recoiled as if being slapped in the face. "I had to, darling. I'm not about to deceive you. If I waited until later, you wouldn't have forgiven me."

Titus dropped his arms and shot Macha a menacing look, a coldness in his eyes she had never seen before. She shivered.

"The damage is done. See that you do no more." Titus had never used that tone with her before.

"I must do what I can for you and Young Titus."

"I don't care about myself; it's my son that concerns me."

"You're both important to *me*," Macha countered.

"The waiting is taking its toll on me, too."

"I know it must be dreadful, Titus. You sit in this grim cell all day staring at the walls, and hear little news. Sometimes idleness plays tricks on the mind."

Titus jutted his chin forward. For a second his frigid eyes pierced Macha, as if reaching to the depths of her soul, then turned away. Never before had he acted as though he did not love her.

Doubts about her confrontation with Pollia flooded Macha's mind. A decent mother wouldn't have acted so rashly. Macha had been warned to act responsibly. Yet she had plunged ahead anyway. She prayed to Mother Goddess Anu to forgive her for risking her son's life, and hoped she wouldn't live to regret it.

Through the upper window near the ceiling drifted the clanking sounds of arms as Praetorian troops drilled on the parade field. A centurion barked a set of commands followed by a string of obscenities.

225

For a moment, Macha closed her eyes and recalled when she and Titus were first betrothed more than nine years ago. He had just received his appointment as junior tribune in the army. Of course, she had no choice in the arrangements made by her parents, but soon Macha realized she really liked Titus. Early on he showed he was a man of honor and not self-centered like others his age. And although he was rather terse, Macha found herself drawn to his engaging smile and dry sense of humor. Because of Titus' off-handed quips, especially, when made at the expense of the nobility, she caught herself laughing on many occasions.

What happened to him? she wondered. Now, he seldom smiles or makes his comical wry comments. It's as if his life in the army and years on campaign has dried up the wonderful parts of his personality. This is not the time to bring it up, but once he is released, I must bring it to his attention. I love him too much to see him turn sour on my son and me.

"I'm not going mad if that's what you're thinking," Titus said, drawing Macha out of her thoughts.

She opened her eyes. "Of course, not, darling. I'm saying it's difficult to stand idly by and leave your fate in the hands of others. The investigation isn't over yet."

Titus stepped to the cot and sat down beside her again. Gently he took Macha by the shoulders and peered into her eyes. "I would take my life," he said evenly, "before further endangering our son's or leaving you impoverished without so much as a copper to your name."

She sat straighter. "Don't talk nonsense, Titus. Your life is more precious to me than all your wealth combined. I *love* you. Don't you understand?" A lump rose in Macha's throat which she quickly swallowed. This wasn't the Titus she knew.

Titus let out a breath, loosened his grip, and slumped forward. "I know. That's why I thought so hard on the matter. You and our son are everything to me. I refuse to see you go wanting."

Macha threw her arms around Titus, holding him close. Despite languishing in confinement, the muscles in Titus' arms and shoulders remained firm. Even in the heat, his body radiated a distinctive masculine smell.

Quill bumps ran up her arms and down her back.

"They can't take you from me, Titus." For a second, she couldn't speak. Her heart pounded and she trembled, and breathed deeply. "If anything happens, Bassus promised to become my patron."

He grimaced. "Then he knows I'm doomed."

"Not at all, my love." Macha pushed herself a few inches away and stared him in the eye. "Senator Bassus is a prudent man. He thinks of us as family. When he gives his word, he doesn't change his mind. Taking your life may be an honorable death, but young Titus would have to live with your notoriety."

"If I'm executed he'll bear the shackles anyway." Titus pushed Macha away, casting his eyes downward to the stone floor.

Macha didn't want to guess what Titus was thinking. She had never seen him so depressed and prayed he wouldn't attempt anything foolish.

Titus swung about and grabbed Macha's hands. He pressed them to his chapped lips and released them seconds later. "I'm sorry, Macha, perhaps you're right. It isn't my nature to give up, and I won't now, I promise. Gods, how I love you." He hugged her again.

"I love you, too," Macha answered with a kiss. She lingered in his arms wishing she could stay there forever, knowing she could not.

Titus exhaled and straightened his shoulders. A hint of smile crossed his lips. "Since Appius will be searching the Trans-Tiber District next, he might have better luck. That stinking hive is full of surprises."

"I pray Mother Fortuna is with his troops."

"Aye, but remember, it is he and his men who are to conduct the search," Titus added. "Do nothing further to endanger our son's life."

She clinched her jaw to hold her tongue. For the first time in their marriage, Macha knew she would disobey her husband's request.

* * * * *

Early that afternoon, Macha arrived home and found a courier waiting for her in the atrium with a message from Pomponius Appius. Once the messenger had handed her the parchment and departed, she opened and read it. Pomponius Appius wrote that his spies had found the hiding place of the assassin leader and he planned a raid late that afternoon. Spies had informed the Tribune the leader was an ex-gladiator called Pugnax the Thracian.

"The same day after the attack on you," the message continued, "he and his gang bathed at the Baths of Memnon. Pugnax is obsessed with cleanliness. No matter what the risk, he spends every afternoon bathing at the *thermae*. With any luck we will corner him and his thugs and place them under arrest."

I must be with the Watch when they find Pugnax, Macha thought. If they can capture him alive, they can force him to tell where he has hidden my son.

Macha sent a message to Appius asking to accompany him on the raid. Senator Bassus might have allowed her to go along, but she doubted the tribune would consent. Yet she had to try.

She had no sooner finished Appius' letter when the Senator Bassus entered the atrium. Eight days had passed since he departed. Light dust coated his face and military uniform, and he smelled of the road.

"Senator Bassus, you're home," Macha said in a surprised voice. "I didn't expect you back so quickly."

"No one did," he answered. "Please don't get up, Macha, I'll join you. My intention was to return as quietly as possible."

Macha had many questions to ask him about his trip but instead recounted the attempt on her life, the kidnapping of her son and Pomponius Appius subsequent investigation. Then she showed him the message from Tribune Appius in which he planned to raid the assassin's home.

"That explains the Watch patrols around the mansion," Bassus said. "They stopped me outside the gate, and even though I wore the uniform of a Legate. They knew who I was, but their orders required that I identify myself. I asked the sergeant in charge why the heavy patrol. All he could tell me was his orders came through the Watch commander and I was in danger."

"The order was issued on the advice of Tribune Appius, Senator Bassus. I agree—there is a danger to all of us."

"I'll meet with Appius immediately after conferring with the Emperor and supervise the raid."

Bassus covered his mouth with a hand to squelch a sudden yawn. For a heartbeat he closed his drooping eyes then stood and stretched, shaking the dust from his uniform, before sitting down again. "Forgive my rudeness, Macha, but I'm more tired than I realized. This has been a hard journey."

Despite her concern about the impending raid, Macha forced herself to ask the Senator about his trip south. She was almost certain what his answer would be. "Since you returned so quickly from Misenum did the audit proceed better than expected?" Macha asked.

"It was as I suspected," Bassus answered. He briefly explained that the so-called embezzlement against Admiral Apollinaris was an absolute lie. The account books were in perfect order. "I have no doubt someone was trying to get me out of Rome," he added.

"There is no question in my mind that was the reason."

Bassus stood. "I'm going to see the Emperor now. I'll see Appius when I'm finished."

"May I go along on the raid? Viriatus will be my bodyguard. With your permission, of course," Macha added hastily.

Bassus studied her for a moment. "The Thracian is an ex-gladiator and a dangerous man. Arresting him will mean a fight to the death."

Macha's heart sunk. "I know. He almost killed me. I had hoped he would be captured alive and tell us where my son is hidden."

Bassus' features hardened, and a cold look glazed his eyes. "Not him, he'd rather die first. The Spaniard can escort you, but you will do exactly as I say. I will not tolerate your headstrong ways, do you understand?"

"Yes, Senator Bassus, I do."

"It's the only way I can keep you out of further trouble, short of putting you under guard." Bassus turned to leave but stopped. He looked back at Macha. "Arm yourself. Be ready when I return from the Palace."

CHAPTER 32

Splinters Don't Lie

Macha traveled with Senator Bassus and Pomponius Appius at the head of an escort of three centuries from the Watch, one hundred men each. The clattering of troop's hobnailed sandals echoed along the narrow lane as they approached the Baths of Memnon. How they expected to surprise and capture Pugnax and his thugs in this noise was beyond Macha.

"Senator Bassus, won't this racket warn Pugnax of our approach?" she asked in spite of her skepticism.

"Doubtful. The baths are so big, he and his cronies won't hear a thing," he answered, tramping along side of her.

Another question caused Macha to ask, "Tribune Appius, I don't attend the games at the arena. As a Celt I find them barbaric, but if Pugnax is a Gaul, why is he called Thracian?"

"It's like this," Appius explained marching next to Macha. "Pugnax is a Gaul, but when he fought as a gladiator he was known as the Thracian."

"I still don't follow," Macha said.

In the afternoon heat, Macha wiped perspiration with a handkerchief. Out of the corner of her eye, she caught Viriatus, who was just behind Bassus, nod as if he knew what the Tribune meant. But *she* didn't.

"Because he fought with a curved dagger and small shield," Appius replied. "That's what Thracians of old used before we conquered them." He seemed to take delight in that knowledge.

Enslaved like the Britons, Macha thought.

Appius continued. "Spies told me. Pugnax likes to brag about his abilities to elude any trap."

Macha sniffed. "Considering how big the baths are, it must be a leaking sieve of escape routes."

231

"Aye, that's why we brought along three hundred troops."

Stepping along the cobblestone street, Macha was grateful she had decided to wear clothing that was comfortable and practical, a short-sleeved long tunic, the color of her eyes, which clung to her body in the heat. A gilt-edge white sash girdled her waist, a silver dagger hidden within. Leather sandals enclosed her feet, laced around her legs and tied above the knees. Pulled back into a single braid, Celtic style, Macha's hair fell between her shoulder blades. An eight-strand wired gold torc, symbol of Celtic nobility, surrounded her long neck.

During the hike along the narrow lane, Macha heard a bucketman in the squad behind her grumbling about dragging along a woman. She twisted her head in his direction to listen.

"You mean you haven't heard about Lady Carataca?" another trooper asked. "She's killed two assassins. Got nerves of iron, I hear. It's a good omen that she's on our side."

The bull-face bucketman glanced at Macha and silently turned his head.

If they only knew, she thought. Considering all she had experienced during the last three weeks, it was a wonder she hadn't gone mad.

Arriving late in the afternoon during the peak bathing hour, the troops quickly surrounded Memnon's complex. A huge edifice, its roof topped with dozens of painted statues and crowd-filled shops within, lined its colonnaded porticos. A riot of smells, including cooking food, steam, sweat, rancid bath oil, and wood smoke from the heating furnaces, wafted through the set of buildings. Storming the front entrance beneath a high gabled roof, the bucketmen fanned out and began searching the interior gardens, art gallery, library and multiple bathing rooms.

Macha and the Spaniard, Viriatus, followed a detachment crossing the large sandy field of the *gymnasia*. Sweaty patrons playing ball games and naked men and women coated in sand engaging in wrestling matches and foot races abruptly halted their activities. Surprised by the intrusion, pandemonium erupted among the screaming women and cursing men who ran to clothe themselves. Using shields and spears, troops blocked and herded everyone to one corner of the court. None of the men fit the description of Pugnax or his assassins, and all were released.

The bucketmen continued to the cold room where the customers took their first dip in the chilly waters of a giant pool before continuing to both the warm and hot rooms.

Macha and Bassus trailed down the noisy corridor behind the bucketmen. She raised her voice above the racket and said, "I've never been inside a mixed bathing area before."

"You haven't?" Bassus questioned.

"The times I have used the public baths, I stayed in rooms reserved for women only," she answered. "I wouldn't dream of going there like a cheap actress or prostitute. They may not care about their reputations, but I do. The women using the gymnasia are no better."

"You are a woman of principal," Bassus said. "Had you said differently, you would have lost my respect. Regardless of class, the mixed baths are no place for proper women."

Macha didn't mention that occasionally she and Titus bathed together in the privacy of their villa and made love. Then again, that wasn't the same as a public bath. She wondered if Bassus would think her so proper if he knew her thoughts. Macha tried not to let her eyes wonder, but she couldn't help noticing that these men would never measure up to her husband.

As they entered the pillared bath hall, a rush of cold air blanketed Macha's face and bare arms. Streaming through the center opening of the star-covered blue ceiling, rays of sunlight beamed on the ripples of water from the huge plunge and reflected off the armor of the watchman. Troops rumbled past the tall flesh-colored marble statues of Julius Caesar, Romulus, and other historical and mythical figures lining the walls. Clanking armor and hobnailed boots clattered on the slippery tiled floors and echoed through the cavernous room. Amidst cries and protests, giggling bathers, dived into the pool, splashing water on everyone, including Macha, drenching one side of both outer and under tunics from the waist to her sandals.

"Everyone out of the pool. Now!" Pomponius Appius barked. When a few resisted, Appius sent a detail of armed men into the water and prodded the naked citizens with spear points.

Women screamed, men cursed.

Still in the pool, a dark haired Greek in his forties protested. "This is an outrage! I am the Emperor's secretary. He will hear of this!"

A watchman, wading up from behind, jabbed a club into the Greek's ribs. He yelped and jerked away.

"Get out of the pool," the bucketman snarled, "or you'll see the Emperor with a club jammed up your arse!" He shoved the secretary forward. Dripping like a wet dog, the Greek stumbled up the steps to where the bathers were detained.

After finding no one matching the assassins' descriptions and briefly questioning the detainees, the bucketmen searched the remaining men's bathing rooms. They found nothing. Runners from other detachments reported to Bassus that so far they had discovered no sign of the killers.

"That leaves only the women's baths," Bassus said. "I'm sorry, Macha, but they must be searched."

"They're in for a rude shock," Macha said, not surprised by Bassus' decision. More than likely Pugnax and his thugs had escaped, but Bassus had to be certain by including the woman's area in the search. "I hope your men have the decency to inspect their rooms as quickly as possible and leave," she added.

"They will," Bassus said. "I'm no more fond of treating them to the indignity than you are in witnessing it. But there are clothing and storage rooms where Pugnax and his vermin could hide, and there is the women's separate entryway, another escape route, but guarded outside."

Instead of finding women relaxing naked on the warm tiles by the pool's edge, Macha and the guards were surprised to see them clothed in towels or tunics. Those still in the pool were submerged to their necks, their backs quickly turned to the men.

"One of the slaves must have warned them about the raid," Macha said. "It's the only explanation, but it won't keep them from complaining."

"They might as well protest to the statues of Diana, Minerva, and the other goddesses lining the walls for all the good it'll do them," Bassus said. "We won't leave until the search is complete."

A number of women protested to Bassus and Macha about the intrusion of armed soldiers. They had appeared as ghosts through the fine steam drifting from the tiny sitting pools at each corner of the cold plunge.

Macha attempted to reassure the indignant matrons the Vigiles were only doing their duty and would finish as quickly as possible.

"Duty indeed," a plump old dowager grumbled. "Just an excuse to feast their lusting eyes on our bodies." Two slaves attempted to keep her lumpy body covered with woolen towels as she sat on a stool beneath the marble statue of Juno. "This is the only place we can get away from obnoxious men. Is nothing sacred anymore? What's worse, it's the second intrusion by men today."

Macha, only half listening while she squeezed water out of the soaked portion of her tunic, suddenly shot a look to Bassus. He raised his bushy eyebrows. Macha turned back to the woman.

"What did they look like?" she asked.

"A disgusting bunch, especially the big one—must be a gladiator by the looks of his scarred face and ugly nose."

That sounds like Pugnax the Thracian, Macha thought. "When were they here?" she snapped.

"Couldn't be more than five minutes ago." The woman nodded toward a service exit used by the slaves.

"That leads to the furnace room," Pomponius Appius said. Through the rising steam, he approached from one end of the pool. Rivulets dripped from his hawk face, and his armor was coated with beads of water. He motioned to a centurion. "Regroup the men."

Departing the women's quarters, Macha stayed with Viriatus and Bassus as they followed behind Appius and the bucketmen. At the military quick step, they headed to the middle of the complex.

Situated on the lower level between the men's and women's hot baths, the large grated wood fire room heated both baths at one time. As they filed through the stoking area's narrow entrance, a blast of hot humid air struck Macha's face like a volcanic eruption. For a moment she thought she would bake in the same manner as if a loaf of bread. Her clothing grew hotter with each passing second. A thin cloud of smoke swirled along the cement ceiling of the poorly ventilated room, lighted only by the huge banked fire burning in the open brick furnace.

"There they are!" a trooper shouted.

In the shadowy light at the far end, Macha spotted Pugnax and his followers sneaking around a gigantic iron water tank.

"That's him!" Macha exclaimed to Bassus. She pointed to the big thick-jawed Gaul, clad in a brown and white striped tunic and breeches. "He's the one who tried to kill Shafer and me."

Viriatus grimly nodded, muttering an oath under his breath.

Grabbing burning sticks from the furnace, Pugnax and his men hurled them at the invading troops who deflected them with swords and shields. Macha stayed near the entryway guarded by the Spaniard as the bucketmen, led by Bassus and Appius, charged the assassins, shouting battle cries.

Pugnax and his bandits whipped out swords hidden beneath their tunics. To Macha's eyes, the bloody clash appeared as mass confusion. In a ringing clash of iron swords, spears and booming thuds of cloth-covered wooden shields, cornered and outnumbered, the thugs savagely fought the troops.

In an instant, Pugnax flashed his sword above a watchman's protective shield, slicing off his head. Blood splattered on the ex-gladiator's face. He turned as another bucketman jabbed his short-sword toward his side. Pugnax parried away the thrust, swinging back his weapon and sliced the trooper through the abdomen, spilling his guts.

Macha saw Appius sneaking up to Pugnax from one side as the Thracian quickly dispatched another watchman. He turned about and before he could react,

236

Appius jammed his short sword into his gullet, giving it a hard twist. Blood gushed from Pugnax's mouth. He dropped to the floor with a thud, dead.

Besides several wounded, five assassins lay dead. The rest threw down their weapons and surrendered.

"I want them alive!" Bassus shouted to the troops as they started putting the survivors to the sword.

Grumbling about not being able to finish off the assassins as they deserved, the bucketmen roughly shackled the prisoners. Macha heard Viriatus growling in accord. "Aye, they killed my men and nearly the Mistress."

Her eyes stinging from the smoke, Macha, followed by her bodyguard, edged her way between the mangled corpses lying on the tiled floor, reeking of feces and urine. Bypassing the huge pile of cordwood, Macha reached Pugnax's bloodied body where Appius stooped over the corpse. Blood oozed from a small laceration on the Tribune's cheek. He pulled up the ex-gladiator's tunic and partially pulled down his breeches. Branded into the left thigh were the letters, IVL XXX.

"What do they mean, Tribune Appius?" she asked, eyes fixed on the markings.

"He trained at the Julian School of Gladiators and killed thirty men before gaining his freedom," the tribune answered. "It's Pugnax all right."

"I didn't know they branded gladiators when they were freed."

"They don't," Appius said. "The letters, IVL, the abbreviation for Julius, were burnt into his flesh when the school purchased him as a slave. Pugnax later added the number thirty."

She understood. Pugnax was one of the fortunate ones. Few gladiators survived long enough to obtain their freedom.

"He probably showed off his victory scars in the baths," Macha said. She crinkled her lips in disgust.

"No doubt in the mixed area," Bassus added.

Macha had found the torture of Crixus repugnant and didn't argue when Bassus advised her against witnessing the prisoners' interrogations.

She was escorted home by Viriatus and a squad of watchmen. Later, when Bassus returned from Latumiae Prison, he informed Macha that although the prisoners confessed to being hired by intermediaries to assassinate her, they swore ignorance of young Titus' kidnapping.

"Now that you have finished interrogating the prisoners, what are you going to do with them?" Macha asked.

"I will send Viriatus and the surviving litter bearers to the prison to see if they can identify any of them as those who tried to kill you after you left Pollia's home."

Macha firmed her lips and frowned. "If they do identify them as assassins, what will become of them?"

"Those identified will be executed, and the rest will be released after a flogging."

* * * * *

The following morning Pomponius Appius led a detail of watchmen to a tenement, the Claudia Victoria in the Subura, to search the assassins' apartment. Curious to see if they would discover any incriminating evidence, Macha received permission from Bassus to accompany the squad of ten.

As they approached the *insula*, Macha noticed wide cracks running down the wooden wall, facing the noisy crowded street. Heavy timbers propped up its rickety side and dingy first-floor shops flanked the entrance. When Appius shoved the apartment porter out of the way, the bucketmen followed him through the dimly-lighted central portal. Greeted by the pungent odors of cooking fish and stale urine, they tramped across the middle of the courtyard passing a blackened slime-coated fountain. Despite the lattice screens hanging across the width of each of the apartment's six levels, garbage and filth still leaked onto the plaza floor. Macha covered her mouth and nose with a silk handkerchief. Even Viriatus snorted in disgust.

Heading up the flimsy wooden stairway, the bucketmen brushed aside the army of noisy grimy-faced children, playing on the steps, wearing dirt-stained ragged tunics. Peering out their doors upon hearing the commotion, tenants quickly slammed them shut when they spotted approaching troops.

Upon reaching the uppermost story, the sixth floor where the poorest lived, the detail discovered the assassin's room at the end of a gloomy graffiti-ridden hallway. A centurion kicked open the flimsy door and the men barged after him into the cramped flea-infested quarters. The apartment's only illumination streamed through a tiny window and from an open door leading to a little balcony above the street. After adjusting her eyes to the poor light, Macha noticed a fissure rippling along the ceiling's length. An army of vermin ran in and out of its gaping crevice. It was a miracle the roof tiles hadn't caved through.

Her eye fell upon a sleeping mat resting on the dirt-encrusted floor in one corner. It appeared too small even for a dwarf. Nearby on a marble slab sat three foul-smelling jars of pickled fish and four cracked wine jugs. At the foot of the bed sat an old leather-strapped chest. Slicing apart the bindings, a trooper opened and found a stack of gnawed water-stained books. Macha picked up one of the scaly parchments and unrolled the fragmented scroll. A section crumbled in her hands, but she spotted the remaining segments were written in Greek, a copy of Homer's *Iliad*. Could anyone in this foul apartment read Greek, wondered Macha.

"A feast for the unlettered mice," Macha said. Viriatus looked at her quizzically as he hovered nearby.

She dropped the book's jumbled remnants back into the trunk and wiped the gritty pieces from her hands.

As the men scoured other rooms, Macha encountered a pile of filthy clothing in another corner between the three-legged bed and the rusty brazier. Above the rags hung a wooden shelf holding a moldy chunk of cheese and a couple of stale onions. Unconsciously, she stepped back from the putrid smelling mess, and was about to skip it all together, then stopped and pondered the situation for a moment. This might be the ideal spot to hide a vital piece of evidence. She could be wrong, but it was worth a look.

"Would you please pull those rags apart with your sword?" she asked the watchman as he ripped apart the bed. It was the same one who had earlier made the snide comments about her presence.

The trooper's lips curled into a sneer and turned to her bodyguard. "Why not him?"

Viriatus nodded to Macha. "I'll take care of it, Lady."

"No you won't, Viriatus," Appius growled from where he stood in the doorway of the balcony. "He *will* do it. You heard Lady Carataca, trooper, do as she asks!"

The frowning bucketman stabbed his weapon into the middle of the rotting mound and dragged it apart. Laying on the floor beneath a wine-stained tunic, Macha spotted a black hardwood stick with splinters missing along one side. One end was filed and tapered as if for holding an axe or mallet head. The murder weapon used against her slave, Nicanor! She dropped to the floor and pulled a cloth from inside her stola. Holding her breath, Macha wrapped it around one end of the pole and dragged it free from the rags. Lifting it, she carried it across the room to the tiny window for a better look and a breath of fresh air. Her eyes searched the room. She saw Pomponius Appius conversing with the squad sergeant. "Tribune Appius, will you come here, please?" Macha asked.

"Find something, Lady Carataca?"

"This stick."

Appius glanced and shrugged. "What about it?"

"You may think I'm silly, but this appears to be the weapon used to murder my slave, Nicanor."

"I see nothing to distinguish it from any other stick."

Macha pointed to the pole. "There are splinters missing."

"Most are splintered if they've been used at all."

"I know, Tribune," Macha said, with an edge of impatience.

"Why would anyone bring it to Rome?"

"That was my thought." Macha nodded at the stick. "At one time this weapon may have had a legitimate use. You notice one end is roughened. Maybe it once held the head of a mallet or sledge hammer?"

"Possible."

"It reminds me of the kind used by officials in the gladiatorial games."

"You mean those who dress as Charon?"

"The same," she answered. Although she never attended the games, she had heard of the brutes costumed as the Etruscan God of the Underworld. They used iron mallets to club badly wounded and crippled gladiators to death in the arena.

Macha slowly turned the rough stick in her hands, carefully checking it from top to bottom. She stopped and blinked her eyes a couple of times and peered closer.

"Great Mother Goddess! Look, Tribune Appius, this belonged to Pugnax." She pointed a forefinger to the carved letters on the side of the weapon, IVL XXX, the same branded on Pugnax's thigh.

"A memento from his days as a gladiator," Appius said.

"That's why I'm taking it with me to Senator Bassus' home," Macha answered. "I have a set of splinters. I'm nearly certain they'll match the missing spots on this club. This must be the weapon used to murder Nicanor."

CHAPTER 33

Flower Shop Walls Have Ears

Macha returned to Bassus' house carrying Pugnax's club under her cloak. In the study, as Senator Bassus watched, she removed the four black slivers kept in her cosmetic box. She placed them into the crevices on the club where the splinters had been torn away.

"They match," she said. "The fit is perfect."

"Now we have conclusive evidence Pugnax murdered your slave," Bassus said, triumph in his voice. "Too bad we couldn't capture him alive. He might have answered a lot of questions."

Downhearted, Macha reluctantly agreed. "For instance, if Pugnax lived in Rome, how was he recruited so quickly to murder Nicanor and kidnap young Titus clear up in Mediolanum? It's over three-hundred miles away!"

"Last year Pugnax received his freedom and moved to Verona."

She took the splinters from the club and handed them to Bassus. "Where did you learn that?"

"From the owner of the Julian School of Gladiators," Bassus answered. He examined the slivers held in his leathery hand. "Pugnax was hired as a trainer for the new Flavian School of Gladiators, forming up north. It's my guess he was recruited in Verona by someone who lived in Northern Italy or who had traveled there, probably from Rome. Verona is on the way to Mediolanum. He could have secretly arrived there and murdered Nicanor before kidnapping your son."

"You're probably right, Senator." Macha hissed, "What a vile creature!"

Bassus placed the splinters within a fold inside his tunic. "I will see these are put in a safe place."

* * * * *

About midmorning, Macha, escorted by Viriatus, Shafer, and a new set of eight retainers and six slaves carrying the litter, went to Clodia's shop to buy flowers for Antonia and take them to the House of Vesta. She planned them as a gift in gratitude for the Vestal's rescue of her and her entourage from the assassins. Macha felt pangs of guilt because she had not done this sooner. The raid at the Baths of Memnon, and discovery of the murder weapon used on Nicanor, had occurred so soon after the assassination attempt she had completely forgotten about the matter until now. She was certain Antonia would forgive her.

Macha arrived at Clodia and Lepidus' little business after her escort had battled its way through the narrow crowded streets. Viriatus set up a screen of retainers around the outside of the store front and Macha stepped from the car. Carefully, she skirted the broken crockery and rotten vegetables scattered along the edge of the cobblestoned curb. The acidic smell of urine drifted from the fuller's shop across the street, while excited voices of shopkeepers and customers haggling over goods echoed from shabby stalls up and down the lane.

Approaching the flower stand, Macha saw no sign of Clodia. She turned to Shafer, who shrugged. They entered for a closer look at the flowers. While Clodia's husband, Lepidus, bartered with a customer, Macha stopped and inhaled deeply the fresh odor of newly-cut yellow roses.

"Aren't they lovely?" she said to Shafer, who agreed.

Clodia tapped Macha's shoulder and said quietly, "Lady Carataca."

Startled, Macha spun around.

"Please come with me. Hurry!" Clodia motioned with her head over her bony shoulder to the back wall, hidden in the darkness. Macha nodded to Shafer to come along. Pulling up the hem of her stola, Macha followed, stepping carefully along the wet planks strewn with wilted flower cuttings and vegetable scraps. Shimmying between rows of narrow tables, filled with an array of colorful flowers and fresh vegetables, the women stepped to the side of a canvas door flap facing the dingy alley. Clodia turned toward

Macha and Shafer and placed a calloused finger to her thin
pursed lips.

Staying in the shadows, Macha peered through a
corner of the narrow opening in the direction of two
echoing voices. Flies buzzed noisily on a pile of garbage. Its
reeking odor drifted through the slivered opening
cloistering the three women. She recognized Falco at once.
Disguised in a homespun worker's tunic and faded brown
cape, he stood conversing with a short curly-haired Greek
cloaked in a long white tunic. Instantly, Macha recognized
him as the Greek from the Baths of Memnon, who claimed
to be the Emperor's secretary. Was this Phidias, the one
who sent Bassus to Misenum? The pale little man carried a
leather sack filled with vegetables in one hand. The images
of the quill and wax tablet, symbols reserved exclusively for
Imperial secretaries, were embroidered in purple on his
sleeve.

"You should not have stopped me here," The Greek was
saying. "It's too dangerous; we could be seen together."

Macha leaned forward to hear.

"In a back alley, not likely, Phidias," Falco answered.

"Don't use my name! Someone may overhear us."
Phidias looked down the narrow trash-filled lane in both
directions and returned his gaze to Falco. "The danger is
real enough; I think I am being watched."

"That's why I haven't gone to your apartment. If
anyplace, the Emperor's spies are watching you there. And
I can't go to the palace; that would be too obvious."

Phidias nodded.

"Perhaps we should meet somewhere this evening,"
Falco said, "a scummy bar where everyone minds his own
business."

The secretary shook his head. "Out of the question. I
don't venture from home after dark. The city is too
dangerous."

"You'll be in greater danger if you don't. Can't you get
an escort?" Falco asked in a voice of growing impatience.

"I only have one slave, and he is useless for protection.
If I hired more, than I would draw too much attention, even
in a tavern."

"Then where can we talk?"

244

Phidias exhaled and again his eyes searched the alley. "Since you are here, you might as well speak and be done with it."

"What news of Pollia and the list?" Falco asked as he looked over his shoulder.

Macha jolted. Her hand flew to her mouth, she placed fingers between her teeth, and clamped down. So Pollia was involved in the plot after all. What does she know about Young Titus' kidnapping?

The Greek said with a long sweeping gesture to Falco, "Pollia keeps a copy of the list on her person."

"She's mad! We're damn lucky Pugnax was killed at the baths," Falco replied in a lower voice. "If he had been captured, the Watch would have tortured him, sure. He would have told them everything."

"Senator Bassus and that barbarian witch are getting too close. Either Pollia hides the list or we must get it from her," Phidias said.

"Should anyone discover Pollia's involved, she'll be arrested and the list found. Then they'll know Titus had no part in getting rid of Vespasian."

For a split second, Macha glanced at Clodia and Shafter. The emaciated shop woman touched Macha on the shoulder and nodded. A big white-toothed grin erupted across Shafer's dark face. Titus is innocent! I knew it! Macha thought to herself. She strained to hear more. Clodia and Shafer leaned slightly forward.

"Are you aware the original list is deposited in the Temple of Vesta?" the Greek asked.

"What!" For a split second, Falco violently shook his head. "No, I wasn't aware."

"It is, and only Antonia knows about it," Phidias said, his hand gesticulating again.

"How did she learn about the list? Her knowledge could destroy us."

"Pollia wouldn't say why. She says Antonia doesn't pose a threat, but I disagree. Regardless, Pollia sent me a message demanding the group act at once."

Falco turned from side to side. "That's impossible. Not everything and everybody is in place."

Macha suspicions were confirmed. Vespasian's secretary was involved in the conspiracy. And Pollia? Was she the woman Antonia refused to identify the night they met at the quarry? The one who could expose the Vestal and Bassus to public disgrace? It had to be Pollia. She glanced to the other women, who shook their heads.

Phidias narrowed his deep-set little eyes. "Don't those fools realize they must act soon? If they are discovered, Vespasian will hunt them down like dogs. Persia's the only country that will grant asylum—if they're fortunate enough to escape."

"I know only too well," Falco said through clenched teeth. "They'll have to beg the king on their hands and knees."

"See if you can get them to move at once," Phidias urged. "You have to try."

"All right," Falco said. "We don't have much of a choice. I'll contact the members and see if we have enough support now to mount an attempt."

"You must act at once before the Emperor learns."

"What about the boy?" Falco asked. "Has Pollia decided what she's going to do with him?"

Macha gasped. Fear shot down her spine like a freezing wind off the Apennines. Clodia shot a warning look in her direction. Shafer's almond eyes widened. For a second Macha feared she had been heard.

They ceased speaking—and then Phidias went on. "She sent a message to the one caring for the boy."

"Has she told you who's keeping him or where he's hidden?"

"She refuses to tell anyone anything. She has a perverse obsession about the whole affair. It won't help her. The un-named woman who is caring for the boy said it was one matter to kidnap a child, but murder was out of the question."

"Pollia must be furious."

Like dawn after a dark night, a sense of relief filled Macha. Young Titus was still alive! She continued listening to Falco and Phidias.

"Indeed, Pollia better not attempt anything foolish," Phidias said.

"How can she?" Falco asked.

"The woman has her methods."

Glancing back to where Lepidus her husband stood, Clodia saw customers filling the shop.

"Clodia!" Lepidus shouted. "Get over here; I need you to wait on customers."

Distracted by Lepidus' order, Macha and Shafer turned from the flap door. An instant later, Macha turned back to the alley. Falco and Phidias were gone. She hugged Shafer.

"Titus is still alive. Thank Mother Goddess!"

"Oh, Mistress, that's wonderful news. Now what will you do?"

"I must tell Bassus immediately. The Emperor has to be warned. Once he knows about the conversation, Pollia is certain to be taken to the palace for questioning. Falco and Phidias are sure to be arrested."

Macha and Shafer returned to the front of the stall where Clodia was bartering with a customer. They waited until she finished.

When the buyer paid for his cabbages and departed, Clodia and Macha stepped away from the counter. Clodia asked little Silvia, who had returned from an errand, to deal with the next patron.

"How did you know I would be interested in their conversation?" Macha asked.

"I overheard them mentioning your husband's name," Clodia explained. "I was about to spit in the alley when I saw them talking—it was unnerving. I stepped inside before they spotted me. But I was curious, why should they talk about *your* husband? If so, why out there where others might see them? That was strange to me. But I decided to hear the rest. First I turned to see if Lepidus needed help and saw you." She smiled.

"Did you know who they were?" Macha inquired.

"I recognized Phidias right away. He's a regular customer, one of the Emperor's secretaries. I remembered you said he sent Senator Bassus to Misenum for no good reason."

"That's right," Macha confirmed.

"Who was the other man?" Clodia asked.

"His name is Falco," Macha answered, her face growing hot.

"By the looks on your face and sound of your voice, he's someone you don't like," Clodia said.

"Falco is a tribune in the army—and a traitor," Shafer said.

"Then they're up to no good, are they?" Clodia asked.

"No good at all," Macha answered. "Why was Phidias here at this time of day?"

"He always shops at this hour," Clodia answered. "Phidias lives nearby. He says Lepidus and I are honest folk and sell the best produce in the marketplace." She smiled. "He doesn't know you and I are friends."

"Neither does Falco," Macha said. "You don't know what a great help you've been, Clodia. This will save my husband's life and maybe my son's." She embraced Clodia and smiled.

"I'm happy for you, too, Lady Carataca. I'm glad to help."

"Shafer," Macha said, "we must find Senator Bassus, quickly!"

CHAPTER 34

Incident at the House of Vesta

As shopkeepers slammed shutters over their shops and stalls for the night, Macha and Shafer hurried homeward. Long shadows crept down the dingy streets and alleys, stealthily blackening the narrow lanes. People, rich and poor, hurried to the precarious safety of their dwellings before Rome's criminal element surfaced from the caverns beneath the city. Macha pitied those unfortunate souls caught on the streets after dark. A shudder roiled through her body when she thought of how they risked the chance of being robbed and murdered. At least she had the security of Viriatus, eight new retainers, and her six litter bearers for protection. She ordered the latter to quicken the pace.

The sun dipped below the distant hills, and the evening grew cooler with each passing minute. Macha wrapped her fine woolen mantle about her shoulders and covered her head. Tucking her hands inside the garment she warmed her cold fingers.

From the passing tenements and cook houses drifted odors of baking bread, lentil soup, and broiling fish, reminding Macha she hadn't eaten since breakfast, too busy to think about it. Now she was famished.

Arriving at the torch-lit mansion, Macha stepped from the sedan. Once she told Bassus the news about Falco, she was certain he would be arrested and Titus cleared. Brushing the gatekeeper aside, she hurried into the Senator's house. Glimmering light from smoky olive oil lamps cast shadows on the muraled walls and polished mosaic floor. She entered Bassus' study, expecting to find him working on household accounts, but discovered the room empty. Disappointed, Macha wondered if he still was in his private bath. No, the hour was too late. As she started down the hallway, Vasili, the chief steward, approached her from a side entrance.

Macha stopped, placed her hands on narrow hips, and leaned forward in his direction. The gaunt servant, a head shorter than Macha, scraped his sandaled feet to a halt. "Where is Lord Bassus?" She asked.

"He went to the palace, Lady Carataca."

She stared at Vasili in disbelief. "At this hour?"

The Greek looked about as if he wanted to escape Macha's scrutiny. "The Emperor sent a messenger about an hour ago, summoning him at once."

"Whatever for?" she asked. The matter must be urgent.

Vasili swallowed and lowered his squinty eyes. "The Chief Vestal Virgin, Licinia, is dead."

Both hands shot to her face. "What did you say?" Macha choked on the words.

"She is dead, my lady—a tragic loss to Rome. According to the courier, she committed suicide."

Slowly, Macha dropped her hands. "Did you hear more?"

"Nothing, except the Emperor commanded my master to investigate the incident once he was briefed by the Praetorian Prefect."

"I wonder why he chose Senator Bassus, and not the Commander of the Praetorian Guard?"

"I'm sorry, I do not know, Lady Carataca. Lord Bassus said the Emperor wanted a thorough investigation to make certain Mother Licinia wasn't murdered."

Shock enshrouded Macha like a heavy woolen blanket. Why would the Chief Vestal take her own life? Why was Bassus chosen to investigate Licinia's death? Macha still feared once Pollia was arrested she would divulge Antonia's and Bassus' affair to the Emperor.

The word of a Vestal Virgin carried greater weight than a traitor's, but Macha was still concerned for her two dear friends and her son.

While Vasili waited to be dismissed, Macha stood on cold tiles pondering what to do next. Did Licinia commit suicide, or was this a sinister cover-up for murder? Or was there something else at stake?

"I'm going to the Palace of Augustus, Vasili," The Palace of Augustus was one of many porticoed structures making up the Imperial residence, covering Palatine Hill and rising above the Forum. The palatial compound had a commanding view of the Circus Maximus and Rome's six other hills.

Macha said a few seconds later, "I'll wait there for Bassus' return from Priestess Licinia's investigation. Let Lord Bassus know where I am. Send for my litter at once."

* * * * *

Macha arrived at the palace, and to her relief learned Bassus had returned from the House of Vesta and was conferring with the Emperor. Across the gaping audience hall, where Macha waited with Shafer and Viriatus, Bassus' footfalls echoed on the polished marble floor. According to the water clock, which sat in a gloomy niche of the hallway, two hours had dripped away since her arrival. She had grown numb waiting on the hard wooden bench for Bassus' arrival. Stiffly, she rose to her feet at his approach. The long day and investigation had taken its toll on him. In the flickering smoky light of oil lamps lining the frescoed walls, Macha noticed dark rings surrounded his bloodshot eyes and heavy gray stubble covered his face.

"This is an unexpected surprise," Bassus said in a weary voice. He ignored her hand maiden and retainer. "What are you doing here at this hour?"

"I have important news, Senator Bassus. It couldn't wait, especially, when I heard about Licinia's death, I had to see you right away."

Bassus motioned to Shafer and Viriatus and pointed to the far end of the reception room. "Wait there."

Once the two had departed, he asked, "What is it?"

Macha informed Bassus that earlier that day she, Clodia, and Shafer observed Falco and Phidias in the alley behind the shop and overheard their conversation. She gave him the details.

"This news is too serious to wait," Bassus said when Macha finished.

He summoned the court chamberlain and requested another audience with the Emperor. "Tell him it's urgent; his life is in peril."

As they waited for the Emperor's summons, Macha mulled over Licinia's death, curious about the circumstances. The muscles in her neck tightened and her stomach churned. "Senator Bassus, can you tell me what you learned about Licinia's death?"

Bassus nodded. He sat on the bench next to Macha. "Licinia committed suicide. I found no evidence of foul play."

The tension drained from Macha's body as she quietly exhaled.

"By rights the investigation of Licinia's death was the jurisdiction of the Praetorian Guard," Bassus said, "because the Vestals are answerable only to the Emperor."

"Then why were you chosen to investigate and not the Praetorian Prefect?"

He leaned closer. "Vespasian knows there are traitors among the ranks of the Praetorians and doesn't trust the Praetorian Prefect. I immediately went to the Vestals house at the head of a contingent of hand-picked Praetorian Guards. Pomponius Appius came along as my aide."

"What happened at the House of Vesta?"

Bassus shook his head. "When I arrived, I found a large noisy crowd congregating in front of the porticoed courtyard, dangerously close to the Sacred House. Word had spread like a firestorm about the high priestess' death. I ordered the troops to use their shields and javelins to shove the mob back to the lane between the Temples of Castor and Pollux and the deified Julius Caesar. That's a respectful distance from the residence."

Macha knew the home sat across from the Forum, opposite Palatine Hill where the Emperor lived. The sprawling porticoed fifty-room building surrounded a spacious courtyard, containing three large ponds and flesh-colored statues of honored Vestals. A little circular tiled-roof temple sat behind the house, protected by a high wall. Here was sheltered the Sacred Flame, symbolic of Rome's eternal power.

"Pomponius Appius and I conducted a quick but thorough investigation at the scene of the death," Bassus said, stirring Macha from her thoughts. "All household slaves and surviving priestesses were interviewed. Since we were investigating a suicide, it was one of the few times we, as men, were permitted in a house at night reserved for women only."

"What was Antonia's role in the investigation?" Macha asked.

"Antonia is now the acting Virgo Maxima."

Macha was pleased but not surprised by the revelation. Now that Licinia was dead, Antonia was senior priestess. She saw Shafer and Viriatus lingering in the shadows of the reception room and wondered if they could hear the conversation.

Bassus continued. "Antonia maintained her dignity and command of the situation. She displayed an official concern about Licinia's death and acknowledged me only as a Senator conducting an inquiry on behalf of the Emperor."

Macha twisted her fingers. "Who discovered the body and where?"

"A household slave found her in the temple," Bassus answered tersely. He rubbed his puffy eyes and glanced to the abysmal black of the audience room. "The woman attends the chief priestess in prayer. When she found the body, she fled the temple and summoned Antonia."

"What did you find when you went there, Senator?"

"Licinia's body was lying in a pool of thickening blood before a small copy of the statue of Mother Vesta."

Macha winced.

"The dagger was still wedged in her body, just as the slave described," Bassus said. "Then I watched as Tribune Appius kneeled and closely examined the body in the cubicle. He discovered bloodstains on Licinia's hands."

Macha nodded; she wasn't surprised by the revelation.

"There were no defensive wounds on her arms or hands and no residue under her finger nails to indicate an attempt to fight off any assailant," Bassus continued. "Given the evidence at the scene, the odds of her being murdered are very remote. Appius discovered a deep laceration through her stomach, and a couple of shallow slashes in the same area. They appeared to be test wounds."

For a moment Macha stared at Bassus. She had never heard of anything so bizarre. "Why would she do a thing like that before killing herself?"

"It may sound strange to you," he answered with a shrug, "but suicide victims sometimes are curious about how painful taking their life will be. For many it's too much to endure. It wasn't enough to stop Licinia."

"Did you discover anything else?"

"Her ceremonial tunic had been pulled above the wound for a clean stabbing." Bassus shook his head. "Still, it was a grisly affair. She managed to slash herself nearly straight across the torso before slicing upward."

Macha shuddered. "How horrible!"

"Indeed, whatever we might think of Licinia, it took a great deal of courage to end her life so painfully."

"What happened next?" Macha asked.

"Appius had intended to subject the household slaves to torture to ensure they weren't hiding the truth about Licinia's death," Bassus said. "But Antonia told the tribune no slaves had knowledge of Licinia's death until after her body had been discovered by the first slave."

"I'm sure that wouldn't have stopped Appius from taking the slaves to prison," Macha said.

"But she did," Bassus said. "As the acting Virgo Maxima, Antonia holds the authority to overrule his decision regarding her slaves and counter his order. She identified the bloody dagger as belonging to Pollia after it had been removed from the body.

"Do you know why Licinia committed suicide?"

"Antonia said she believed the Virgo Maxima killed herself," Bassus answered, "because her involvement in the conspiracy had been discovered."

"What? The Supreme Vestal involved in the plot against the Emperor?"

"Yes, I'm certain she was."

Macha shook her head. "Why? I don't understand."

"She and Pollia were lovers. The dagger had been a gift from her in appreciation for a sacrifice on an earlier occasion."

"Oh, Mother Goddess, what next?" Macha exhaled.

Bassus crinkled his forehead and looked about. He lowered his voice. "Didn't Antonia tell you?"

"No, what?"

"It was Pollia who was threatening Antonia and me with exposure." Bassus grabbed Macha's shoulder. "What's wrong? I thought you were going to faint."

"Nothing is wrong, Senator," Macha answered in little more than a whisper. She inhaled deeply. "I had my suspicions but until now, I wasn't sure that Pollia was the woman Antonia refused to name."

"Antonia told me she had confided in you about us, Macha."

"That's true but she didn't tell me that it was Pollia—I wished she had. Anyway, I'm grateful Antonia stopped Appius from torturing the slaves."

"It wasn't necessary at any rate. Appius examined each slave's hands and clothing. He found no bloodstains or telltale signs of struggle indicated by punctures or slashes."

Macha nodded.

"I took it upon myself," Bassus continued, "and the Emperor later concurred, to inform the public that Sister Licinia's death by suicide was the result of learning she had an incurable disease. Otherwise, she would have suffered a lingering illness ending her life in great pain."

"Why did you give out that information?"

"I don't want our enemies to learn that we know the real truth behind Licinia's death."

The court chamberlain approached the Senator and Macha. "The Emperor will see the both of you now."

CHAPTER 35

A Promise by the Emperor

Seated in his candlelit sparsely-furnished private audience chamber, the peasant-faced Emperor listened as Macha recited the details of the conversation between Falco and Phidias.

When finished, Vespasian nodded his approval to Bassus and then Macha as they stood before him. "Lady Carataca, you have done us a great service."

Before she could respond, the balding monarch raised a hand. He flicked an eyebrow in the direction of the Praetorian Prefect, hovering near the black basalt bust of Augustus. Vespasian scribbled a message on a waxed tablet resting on a bronze-framed table inlaid with ebony wood. He handed the ivory-leafed document to the Prefect.

"See that the traitors Tribune Falco and the Imperial Secretary, Phidias, are arrested at once," Vespasian commanded. "Dispatch another detail to the house of Julius Pedius and escort Lady Pollia to the palace immediately. She deserves to rot in Tullianum dungeon but she'll stay here until we have finished questioning her." Bassus added he would send a detachment of Praetorians to return Pollia's husband, Julius Pedius, in chains from their estates in Sicily where he had traveled to on business. He turned to Macha, his alert eyes studying her willowy frame for the length of a few heartbeats.

"If you speak the truth, Lady Carataca, we will release your husband before dawn."

"Thank you, Caesar, I'm eternally grateful." Titus released tomorrow morning! A surge of excitement and relief engulfed Macha. Once again she would be in his arms. Gods, she could almost feel his firm body against hers. It had been such a long time since he had held her as a free man. But what about Young Titus? Except for the awful message containing the thumb of a poor child, there had been no word about their son. Are his captors treating him well? she wondered. He must have been terribly frightened. Was he getting enough to eat? She had heard tales of kidnapped victims being starved or worse.

A concerned expression on Vespasian's face emphasized the beginnings of a double chin. His barrel-chested body showed only the faintest signs it was starting to sag. His fatherly voice jolted Macha from her thoughts. "Are you all right, my dear?" The Emperor asked.

"Yes, Caesar, I'm perfectly well," Macha answered.

"Good, for a moment you turned pale."

Macha's hand shot to her cheek. The tips of her fingers burned. She had to bring her thoughts about her son and the excitement about Titus's release under control. "It's that I am very concerned about my son. You are aware that he was kidnapped?"

"Indeed, and we'll do everything in our power to find him."

"I appreciate it, Caesar. It's just I am so afraid he has been harmed, and I keep praying that he has not."

The Emperor scowled. "For your sake, I hope you are right. Either way, they'll pay with their lives."

"I know my husband will want to be involved in his search once he is released. I say this because I am telling the truth about Pollia's involvement."

"If that is the case, he'll be allowed to take part in the search for his son," Vespasian said.

He motioned to Bassus. "When Lady Pollia arrives, you'll conduct the questioning, Senator."

"Yes, Caesar."

"In the meantime, make yourselves comfortable. Right now, I have another pressing matter requiring my attention. I'm briefing Senator Cornelius Florus, the new governor of Egypt."

Puzzled by the abrupt end to the audience, Macha looked toward Bassus. He raised an eyebrow and barely shook his head.

The Emperor summoned the chamberlain and directed him to escort Macha and Bassus to the triclinium. Shafer followed at a discreet distance behind Macha. Viriatus and the litter bearers were led to the slave's kitchen to eat.

Afterward, they would be sent to a waiting room set aside for slaves whose masters were visiting the palace.

In the dining area, Bassus ate a light meal of cold chicken and salad and sipped a light Umbrian wine, but Macha barely touched the food or drink.

"I felt uneasy about imposing on the Emperor," Macha said a few minutes later, "but I have to ask Pollia a few questions after she's brought here."

Bassus set his cup of wine on the lip of his couch and stared at Macha across the dining table. "You will not speak to her."

She raised up on her elbow. "Why not?"

"This is an Imperial matter. Civilians are forbidden to meddle in the investigation."

"I've been *meddling* in this matter since arriving in Rome. Please, Senator, don't hide behind that guise, now."

"I'm concealing nothing," he replied. "We know Titus is innocent. But until Pollia confesses and Titus is actually released, he still stands as an accused traitor. As the wife of an accused traitor, you cannot ask questions, especially, of another traitor. It's tantamount to obstruction of justice."

Macha wanted to say, Where is Titus' justice? Where is my son's justice?

"We'll ask those questions once she has been arrested. Don't worry, she'll confess."

"Yes, under torture, Pollia will say anything. If you want the real truth, let me speak to her."

"Why would she tell you anything different from the interrogators?" Bassus furrowed his eyebrows and studied her.

Clinching her fingers, Macha answered, "Don't you see? Like most patricians, she's proud of everything she's done whether it's good or evil."

"I don't see your point."

Macha sighed. "Pollia will know she's lost the game. Even when punished, she'll bear the consequences with dignity, as a patrician woman should. But she has to tell someone about her deeds—someone she hates—like me. If I confronted her, she'd take great pleasure in telling me,

258

out of spite, how she had my son kidnapped and Titus arrested for treason. Please, Senator, give me a chance."

In the soft light of the dining room, Macha watched as Bassus silently considered the suggestion.

"Perhaps you could persuade the Emperor to overhear the conversation," Macha suggested, "If he thinks I've gone too far he can stop it."

Bassus looked straight through her. "Macha, you can't be serious. The Emperor would never allow a civilian to question a traitor. The answer is still no."

"Doesn't Vespasian realize you and I are friends?" She placed her feet on the floor and sat on the couch as straight as a sword blade, stood, and paced back and forth in front of Bassus.

"Doesn't he consider it a conflict of interest that you're interviewing Pollia?" she asked.

"Not the Emperor." Bassus remained on the couch while his eyes followed Macha's movements. "He doesn't trust anyone within the ranks of the Praetorians to properly conduct the interrogation."

Macha stopped and searched Bassus' dark eyes for signs of deception. None. "Why not appoint Pomponius Appius? There was a time I would have never considered him impartial, but he has been very helpful, especially while you were at Misenum."

"I expected him to fully cooperate."

"He believes Titus is innocent?"

"Indeed, Appius has believed it nearly from the outset."

"Mother Goddess!" Stepping to Bassus' couch, Macha kneeled before him. "Honestly? Why didn't you tell me this before?"

Bassus lowered his voice. "I couldn't until now. There are too many ears in Rome."

She shook her head. Why doesn't the Senator trust me? Macha thought. I wouldn't have told a soul. At least now I know the truth. Straightening up, she returned to her couch.

"Unfortunately, Appius couldn't say it or act as if he did," Bassus said. "I'll tell you something, but you must keep it a secret until your husband and son are released."

"I promise as Mother Goddess is my witness."

"Appius is an Imperial spy in my pay."

She sniffed. "Somehow that doesn't surprise me. Why else did he journey with us to Rome when he was needed by the First Legion? But does he actually hate Titus or was that an act?"

The Senator took a long swill of Umbrian wine from his golden cup. When he finished, he wiped his mouth with a linen napkin and set the cup on the table. "He had no love for your husband and was jealous of Titus' promotion over him."

"Then why did he become your spy?"

"He knew Titus' allegiance to Vespasian was as strong as his. He became my man when I promised him a command of his own before leaving for my inspection in the East. At the time I had heard rumors about a conspiracy against the Emperor."

"So, you knew?"

"I had no proof, and my informants had learned nothing further. So, I told Appius to keep his eyes open, and send me weekly reports. I never doubted Titus' loyalty, but the initial evidence appeared overwhelming, and I've had to tread carefully, not showing favoritism."

"But why couldn't you tell me?"

"I had to be certain that he was not a traitor. And there were persons, such as Pedius, with more influence that I, who had caught the Emperor's ear. I had to obtain solid information before Titus could be cleared of all charges; now I think I have it."

"Do you mean the conversation we overheard this afternoon?"

Bassus nodded. "Since three of you overheard it, that is damning enough to keep Titus from being the public strangler's next victim."

"Are you sure? I am the wife of an accused traitor. Clodia is a Plebian, and Shafer is a slave."

"It is enough. You and Clodia are the wives of Roman Citizens, and I see no need to torture Shafer to give evidence."

"Praise Mother Goddess, but aren't you afraid Pollia will threaten to expose you and Antonia?"

He snorted. "If she does, I will advise her that no one will heed the word of a traitor. I will also say that I have forewarned the Emperor of her lies."

"What if she doesn't believe you?"

"I'll tell her Vespasian doesn't believe slanderous tales about his sacred Vestal Virgins. And I will make certain she never gets the chance to see him," he added in a menacing voice.

"I pray you are convincing." Macha frowned. She wasn't as confident as Bassus, but kept the opinion to herself.

"Regardless, once Pollia has been arrested you will stay away from her."

Knowing it would be futile, Macha didn't argue with Bassus any further. "Very well, Senator, I shall comply."

"Yes, you will," he said in a sinister growl.

The Senator's answer placed Macha on alert. She didn't like his tone of voice. "What do you mean? I said I would."

"To guarantee that you won't interfere, I'm sending you back to my house under Praetorian escort."

Macha gasped. "What? How dare you! I thought you trusted me."

"I'm sorry, Macha, I won't take further chances. You've broken promises before. You will stay at my home until I summon you."

The detail of twenty Praetorians escorted Macha and her retinue from the palace. *I'll find a way to return and confront Pollia in spite of him,* Macha thought furiously.

CHAPTER 36

Escape

Macha arrived at Bassus' home, still angry that he had ordered her confined to his house. As she stepped out of the litter, the Centurion in charge approached her. "You're to stay in Senator Bassus' house until he sends for you," he said, as though she didn't know.

"And when will that be?" Macha asked.

"My orders are to make sure you don't leave," the broken nose officer answered.

She noticed the detail of Praetorians still encircled the sedan. "What does that mean?"

"You'll see." He motioned to the troops to follow him and left Macha standing in the street. Appalled and disgusted, she watched as the troops surrounded the outside of the Senator's home.

What now? she wondered. Followed by Shafer and Viriatus, Macha went indoors and proceeded to the impluvium where she sat down in a wicker chair. Bending slightly at the waist, she placed a hand to her forehead and closed her eyes. What now? Although the hour was late, she wasn't sleepy. She pondered her dilemma in silence, staring at the square-shaped pond in the center of the room. Flames ebbed and flared from the light of oil lamps illuminating the room. Thin strands of smoke wafted toward the ceiling opening, through which rain, in stormy weather, fell to the pool below.

Opening her eyes, she straightened and motioned to Shafer and Viriatus, who hovered nearby, to take a seat on the marble bench across from her.

"I must return to the palace to question Pollia," Macha said, "She knows where my son is held captive, but with the Praetorians patrolling outside, escape is impossible." She sighed from the depth of her being. "And I have no idea if that wretched woman has even been arrested."

The slaves eyed one another. Shafer nodded.

"Mistress Carataca," Viriatus said in a low voice, "there's a secret passage leading out of the Senator's home."

Jolted by the revelation, Macha stared wide-eyed at the Spaniard. "Are you certain? I've heard of no such passage."

"It's true, Mistress," Viriatus replied.

Macha stood, walked around the impluvium and stopped at the entry leading to the atrium. She moved to the exit and scanned the hallway. No one in sight. She stepped to the edge of the basin and motioned for Shafer and Viriatus to join her. "Tell me more," Macha whispered. "Keep your voices down."

"It's behind the clothing cabinet in the Master's bed cubicle," Shafer said.

"Who told you about it?" Macha asked.

"I discovered it one day when cleaning the Master's room." Shafer glanced to the *Impluvium's* exit, the direction of the Senator's bed cubicle. "I saw a rat scoot out from beneath the bed and it ran behind his clothing cabinet. He hates rats, so I had to find a way of getting rid of it."

"But that's a large cabinet," Macha said, "I've walked by his room and could see it through the door. How did you move it?"

"I helped her," Viriatus said.

"Viriatus is very strong." A smiling Shafer turned and nearly touched his muscular shoulder with her finger. "I knew he could move it, and I had to find where the rat came from. If there was a hole, it had to be blocked."

Macha studied the two slaves, puzzled by Shafer's move. Again she wondered if there was something romantic going on between the two of them. This was not the time to ask questions.

"Did you move it?" Macha asked the Spaniard.

"Yes, Mistress."

A sense of relief filled Macha's being. Thank Mother Goddess, there is a way out of here. "I must go to the palace, at once," she said.

"But Mistress, you said yourself you don't know when they will bring Lady Pollia to the Emperor's home," Shafer said.

"I'll take care of that," Viriatus said.

"How?" Macha raised her hand.

"I'll send retainers I trust to watch the palace." The auburn-haired Spaniard gestured as if it were obvious. "They'll keep an eye on all the gates."

Macha lowered her hand and scowled. "How do they know the way?"

"We explored it after the discovery," Viriatus replied.

She glanced to Shafer and back to Viriatus. "You could have been caught."

"Aye, that's true," Viriatus answered with a shrug. "But we had to learn the way out if we were to help the Master escape in an emergency. I don't know if he's been down there, but I couldn't take the chance and tell him of our discovery--he wouldn't like it."

"If your men see Pollia, then what?" Macha asked.

"Once she's arrived, my men will return. Then we'll leave by the secret passage."

Grateful as Macha was for the assistance of Shafer and Viriatus, she was still puzzled. "Why are you doing this for me?" she asked. "You're putting your own lives at risk."

"We believe in you and in your husband's innocence," Viriatus replied.

"But you are risking the Master's wrath," Macha said.

"We've been through much with you, Mistress," Shafer said. "You are a brave woman, and you've been very kind to us."

"You've treated us fairly," Viriatus said. "I respect you for risking your life to find your son and free your husband. I hear he is a good soldier."

Macha shook her head. What had she done to earn such gratitude and loyalty from these two? They deserved to be rewarded. "When this is all over," she said, "I swear I will do everything in my power to see that both of you receive your freedom. If necessary, I will purchase you from the Senator and set you free."

Shafer and Viriatus bowed their heads in silence.

"After we escape from here," Macha said, "you'll escort me only as far as the palace. I will enter by myself."

"But Mistress," Shafer protested.

Macha shook her head. "No, I don't want any of you getting into trouble for disobeying your Master."

"But he did not actually forbid us," Shafer said, "only you did."

"Nevertheless, as slaves assigned to me, it constitutes the same thing. I'm responsible for your actions and you would be punished. You will return home once I'm inside the palace. After that my personal safety will be in my hands and in those of the gods."

Viriatus cleared his throat. "Mistress, I suggest you change your clothes while we are waiting."

"Why?"

"The cave is cold, dank, and dirty. It opens into a sewer that we'll follow to the river—you'll get filthy."

"Very well, but I'm taking these along," she motioned to her stola and palla, "in a small bundle. I'll change once we're out of the cave."

* * * * *

Macha and Shafer worried through three hours in the library until Viriatus' men returned and met with him, Macha, and Shafer. They reported Pollia had arrived at the palace under escort by way of the prisoner's entrance.

"Mistress," Viriatus said to Macha. "Before we enter the cave you should know, if you haven't already guessed, this place is very dangerous."

"I expected as much, but let's go."

"We must stay together. There are many side passages and deep pits. You'd never be found. These caves are full of thieves and murderers. They live down there by day and raid the city by night."

"I'll stay close." Mother Goddess, Macha thought, Titus had warned me the caves were hiding places for bandits. I pray our son is not held in one of the caverns.

Macha, Shafer, Viriatus, and three retainers, an African and two big Germans, quietly trekked down the hallway to Bassus' room. Macha wore a vivid blue, green, and yellow plaid tartan tunic and breeches. Leather sandals, tied with straps, fit snugly about her calves. She carried a small leather bag containing her other garments. The group entered Bassus' bed cubicle.

Viriatus motioned to the African and one of the Germans to move the clothing cabinet away from the wall. As the slaves turned the portable closet, its squat metal legs scraped along the tiled floor and emitted a loud rasping sound. The slaves froze. The Spaniard glared at them and quickly stepped to the door. His eyes searched both directions of the hallway before he returned to the group. "Nothing. Let's get out of here."

Crawling through the small opening at the base of the wall Viriatus and the African led Macha, Shafer, and the two Germans. Once inside, Macha spotted a small circular pit in the floor, illuminated by Viriatus' lantern.

"Down there," the Spaniard said.

Grappling the swaying rope ladder, Macha descended into a cavern, large enough to allow her and the others to stand upright. She and the slaves carried enclosed olive oil lanterns as they followed the cold cramped passageway. The pulsating amber lights revealed naturally hollowed out walls of hard rock and moldy earth.

Macha and her escort broke through a wall of choking cobwebs, while snaking their way through the shadowy underworld. They startled a cluster of hanging bats that took wing and flew past their faces. Later, an army of frightened, squealing, plague-infested rats scurried before them into the cave's recesses.

Perspiration poured from Macha's body. Her mouth dried from breathing stale air, making her thirsty. She took a gulp of water from the army canteen tied to the belt on her tunic.

The little entourage passed a side passage through which a howling wind swirled, startling Macha and the slaves. Reminding her of the god of wind, Aeolius, it screamed at them as if they had foolishly invaded its domain, a land of Stygian darkness. The wind seemed to laugh at their folly, sighing that they may never escape from the reaches of darkness. A shiver rippled along Macha's back and arms. The group hurried onward.

When Viriatus led the party around the next bend, he nearly tripped over a sprawled rag-covered skeleton. In the lamplight Macha saw a rusty dagger sticking between its ribs. The Spaniard and the African retainer shoved the

266

remains out of the pathway. The bones fell apart, crumpling into a jumbled pile. Bandits must have done this, Macha thought. Please Mother Goddess Anu, protect us—and my son!

Further on a fetid smell reminded Macha of a combination of sulfur and sour grapes. The sickening odor became all consuming. She gagged and covered her nose with her hand. As she moved further, a great underground sewer filled with a stream of reeking filth and garbage surged out of the darkness. The flowing sound echoed quietly through the vast cavern.

Across the turgid waterway dozens of blue flames peaked and ebbed, escaping from lignite and igneous rocks. Fires hissed and roared, lighting up both sides to reveal the enormity of the drainage pit. Macha had heard stories of escaping gases erupting from beneath the earth and the caves that riddled Rome's underground, but this was her first encounter with the phenomenon.

The little group halted at its edge. "This is the great cistern of Rome, the Cloaca Maxima," Viriatus explained.

"It smells like the world's dung has been dumped here," Shafer said.

"It has," Viriatus said. "Along with many bodies, animal and human."

"Good gods," Macha said, "It's so big you could sail a trireme down this disgusting place."

"Someone did," Viriatus replied. "You've probably heard the story. Marcus Agrippa, Caesar Augustus' son-in-law, sailed a three-banked trireme down to the Tiber when he inspected this stink hole."

Macha turned and noticed at the edge of the slimy water's darkened recesses three or four small boats huddled next to the embankment. Their circular shapes reminded her of the cowhided coracles used by the people of her native Britannia. She pointed them out to Viriatus. "Those boats, what are they doing here?"

Viriatus turned to the African. "Did you and the others use these boats to return from the river?"

The African shook his head.

"Bandits!" Viriatus warned. "They're close—get in!" he ordered with a motion of his head. Macha and the slaves ran along the bank and boarded, two to a boat. Macha and Shafer rode in the middle coracle and the two Germans followed behind. Using the small enclosed oars they moved into the middle of the slow-moving stream of sludge. Viriatus and the African led the way.

"They've got our boats!" A cry echoed from the shore. A rain of stones flew from the darkness and pummeled the little band as they paddled through the watery mess, pulling strongly. A searing pain went through Macha's skull. Something struck the side of her head. More rocks pounded Macha and Shafer about the shoulders and back. For a second she nearly lapsed into unconsciousness. Quickly, she recovered, feeling a ringing sensation within her head. Mother Goddess, she prayed, get us out of here alive. She and Shafer slashed their oars through the water as they attempted to outrun the predators.

Three or four torches flew past the boats; one so close Macha felt the heat on her face.

Hearing a loud splash near her boat, Macha looked over the side. She spotted the bobbing head of one of the attackers swimming toward them in the filth. Aghast, she wondered how can anyone could be mad enough to immerse themselves in these scummy waters? She didn't hesitate to grab the dagger from within her tunic. The bandit grabbed the edge and rocked the boat. Macha nearly fell out, her face inches from his scarred countenance, a mask of ooze and slime. She snagged the boat's side with one hand and thrust the weapon deep into his eye and twisted until she heard a snap. He screamed and fell away, sinking beneath the putrid effluvium. The coracle rocked when he released his grip.

The boat rocked again and Shafer screamed. Macha turned as another assassin reached over and pulled on her slave's side of the little craft. Instantly, Shafer reared back with her wooden oar. Holding it by the long thin handle, she lunged forward, smashed the narrow edge of the paddle's wide section into the outlaw's nose and shoved it back into his skull. He bellowed and dropped into the stygian water.

Macha turned her head toward Viriatus boat and saw him pound the face of another villain with his truncheon and shove him into the stream.

Behind her the Germans struggled with two other denizens. Their little vessel capsized and all fell into the waters still fighting. The four sank below and never surfaced.

What now? Macha wandered, appalled by the loss of these two brave slaves. Her eyes searched about expecting the onslaught to continue, but the attack ended as quickly as it had begun. How much longer must this go on? Macha wondered. How many more times will I be assaulted all because I want to free my husband and son? Gods, I hate doing this. She exhaled, knowing she had no choice.

The party made their escape. Macha's clothing stank of the sewer. The stones that had missed her and Shafer had dropped into the stream but splashed its' disgusting contents on and ruined their clothing. Because she would have to get rid of her outfit anyway, Macha wiped her bloodied knife on her breeches.

The little group followed the great cistern to its outlet on the River Tiber near the Forum Boarium. Stopping at a darkened quay, Macha and Shafer stepped from the boat. Macha rinsed her hands, arms and face in a nearby fountain. In the recesses of a covered portico while Shafer stood guard, Macha changed into her stola and palla and put on a gold necklace and earrings. Try as she might, Macha could not rid herself of the smell of the Cloaca Maxima. She stuffed the smelly tartans into her carrying bag, returned to the edge of the wharf and tossed it into the river.

Cautiously, staying in the shadows, Macha and the slaves left the river front and made their way between the outer wall of the Circus Maximus and the forested gardens along the foot of Palatine Hill.

"The best way to get in without being seen is to go through the Temple of Cybele," Macha whispered to Viriatus. "In the past it was the least guarded of all areas of the Palatine. There is a hidden passage in the back that goes into the House of Livia, the late Emperor Augustus' wife."

"Are you sure, Mistress?" the Spaniard asked.

"Yes, I've been through it before. Except for a few rooms used for storage, and office space for the Emperor's clerical staff, the old Empress' home hasn't been used since her death."

They arrived at the stairway at the foot of the incline leading up to the temple. Macha and Shafer hid in the nearby bushes, planted along the steps, while Viriatus and the African checked the area for guards. Within minutes he and the retainer returned. "No one about," he said.

"Very well, I shall go alone from here. You, Shafer, and the African are to return to Bassus' home."

"Is that wise, Mistress?" the Spaniard asked. "You'll be in grave danger. If you're spotted by the Praetorians, they'll arrest you for sure or worse."

"I know, but now I must depend on myself and the gods to get pass the guards and confront Pollia. There is no other way." Macha turned and went up the concrete stairs leading to the Temple of Cybele.

Would she reach Pollia without being arrested?

CHAPTER 37

A Delicious Traitor?

Macha's heart pounded as she entered the ancient Temple of Cybele, the *Magna Mater.* Although she had second thoughts about confronting Pollia, it had to be done. Taking a few deep breaths she steeled herself and resolved to continue. The interior of the little temple was so dark, cold, and musty it was impossible to see without the use of her covered lantern. Guided only by the shadowy lamplight, Macha quietly stepped to the back of the temple. She shivered and pulled the shroud tighter about her shoulders, sweeping a hand across her nose to erase the reek of the Great Cistern.

Hidden in the recesses, behind the statue of Cybele, was a steep stair-lined passageway leading to the House of Livia. Water seeped from the ceiling and trickled onto the slimy surface of the worn steps. Cautiously, Macha treaded the slippery way with only the flickering illumination from the lamp to guide her into the old empress' home. Macha prayed no guards were on patrol as she moved through the vast labyrinth. Now she wished she had brought along Viriatus for protection.

Fatigue played havoc with Macha's imagination, more apprehensive than she had realized, as she concentrated to stay alert. The sound of her shoes scraping on the tiled mosaic floor echoed off the cavernous walls and ceilings. She placed her feet more quietly. The light from the lantern bounced from pillar to wall in a macabre sort of dance. Statues and murals, illuminated in grotesque fashion, appeared as distorted images from the afterlife. Only *Hel,* the sinister German Goddess of the Underworld, was needed to complete the picture and lead the dead into the bowels of the earth.

Passing bed-cubicles converted to offices, Macha hurried along a maze of vaulted rooms. A staircase at the far end, bordered by a set of statues from mythology, led below. Taking the stair well, she passed the marble-lined latrine at its base.

Macha and Titus had used this passageway on an earlier visit to the palace. Stepping between the pillars of a colonnaded peristyle, Macha walked beside the impluvium, a low platform pool surrounded by semi-circular niches and channels. She entered another dark passage, the opening to the *Crypto Porticus*. Built by the mad Emperor, Caligula, to connect with the other parts of the palace complex, the twisting underground gallery was composed of many rooms. People of nobility, who were suspected of treason, had been incarcerated there in the past. Macha was certain Pollia would be detained in one of its apartments. She scanned the cavernous corridor in both directions, empty and silent. A few hanging oil lamps provided shadow-encased light.

Removing her shoes, Macha crept bare-footed along the cold inlaid marble floor. Each step felt like icy daggers shooting down her spine. Every few moments she stopped to listen before moving on. She hadn't gone far when she saw two torches set in casemates, one on each side of a door. Light emanated from the room. Pollia is confined there, Macha thought, and must be still awake. She hoped Pollia was searched for weapons. She wiped her sweaty hands on her gown.

The shadowy light illuminated a pair of Praetorians standing guard, clad in crimson tunics and cloaks and armed with polished javelins, who eyed her suspiciously, their nostrils flared at her stench as she approached.

Desperate to question Pollia before Bassus returned to start his own interrogation, she must first remove the Praetorians, who would be guarding Pollia's room. Because they might be honest, Macha had no choice but to cut to the quick. She had come too far to turn back.

"Who are you? What do you want?" The taller of the two guards asked gruffly.

"I've come to visit Lady Pollia. She's my friend," Macha answered.

"At this time of night? No visitors are allowed to see the prisoner." He scowled and shoved his javelin across her pathway. "You stink."

Macha eyes darted from him to the shorter sentry and back. "I know you're under orders, but it's important that I see her."

"That's your problem," the short one snarled.

Despite the rebuff, Macha gave the soldiers her brightest smile. "Look, I'm sure you could find it in your hearts to let me in. Even if you searched me, you'll find no weapons." She lied and prayed the bluff worked.

The tall guard's eyes scanned Macha's body as if she wore no clothes. She stiffened her spine to prevent a shudder.

"I wouldn't mind searching you anyway, even if you do smell. I might find something better," he said.

"I'm not asking you to leave your posts," Macha replied ignoring his remark. "All you have to do is step into the next room. From there you can see everything."

"I already like what I see." He took a step forward but as quickly backed away. He grunted, "What shithole did you crawl out of?"

"I slipped and fell into the gutter," she answered, the first thing that came to her mind.

"With more than a dozen customers, I'll bet." The sentry grinned. "Then again, a little stench never stopped me, and you're a good looker." He raised a hand toward her shoulder.

Horrified, Macha backed away, her knees quaking. How could I have been so foolish to have tried this approach? Macha thought. I should have known.

"Leave her alone, Taurus!" growled the other guard. "Centurion Macro warned you about toying with women while on duty."

Taurus halted and fixed his cold eyes on the shorter sentry. "At least I like women, Priscus, not young boys."

"Aye, but I wait till I'm off duty. Maybe you want to run the gauntlet, but a head bashing isn't my idea of a good time."

Taurus snorted but seemed to change his mind and stepped back.

She almost decided to flee, but keeping her fear under control, she smiled demurely but persisted. "I must see Lady Pollia alone. All I ask is your silence. I won't tell a soul. Maybe this would help you decide." She unhooked the gold necklace studded with sapphires from around her neck, hoping they were open to bribery. They locked their eyes on the sparkling ornament and drew closer.

"Here," she said and offered it to Taurus.

Taurus examined the jewelry closely and a grin rippled across his scarred mouth. "Ha! See this, Priscus? The women always pay me!" He snatched it out of her hand. "For this I'll go blind."

Macha resisted the urge to slap him, but instead turned to Priscus. "I haven't forgotten you." She gave gold earrings embossed with tiny red rubies to the shorter guard.

"What about Senator Bassus and the Emperor?" Priscus asked Taurus as he grabbed the earrings from Macha's hand. "The Senator's bound to question the prisoner."

"Not tonight," Taurus answered. "Senator Bassus left the palace. The Emperor won't do anything till he returns."

Caught by surprise, Macha choked back a response. She hadn't expected this revelation. *I hope Bassus hasn't learned of my escape,* she thought.

"Seems I've got a speck of dirt in my eyes," Priscus said as he turned away.

"What if your centurion returns?" Macha asked.

Taurus grinned and motioned to the jewelry. "We'll share this stuff with him. This is different."

"Then it's all set," Macha said. "I won't need more than a half-hour."

When Macha entered the room, she found Pollia sitting on a cushioned stool, in front of a small table, at the far end of the large cubiculum, studying herself in a hand-held silver mirror. Four olive oil lanterns illuminated the area, and in one corner a smoky fire burned in a small brazier.

"You've wasted your time bringing food, guard," Pollia said. "I told the centurion I wasn't hungry." A second passed before she turned and recognized Macha. Her face darkened as she slammed the mirror to the table and sprang to her feet.

"What are you doing here, Macha Carataca?"

"You know why, Pollia," Macha replied as she approached her.

"I don't have the slightest idea what you're talking about." Pollia crinkled her nose. "You smell of the gutter. Then again, that's where you belong."

"At least I don't stink of treason!"

"If you don't leave this instant, I'll summon the guard." Pollia nodded toward the door.

"Don't bother. They let me in." Macha glided to a stop before Pollia.

Pollia's face paled. "The dirty scum, how dare they? The Emperor shall hear of this."

A mocking smile of contempt formed on Macha's bowed lips.

"You don't have to gloat," Pollia hissed.

"I'm not. I'm here to ask questions—critical questions—about my husband and son."

"I have nothing to say."

"I overheard a conversation between Tribune Falco and Phidias."

"What's that to me?" Pollia moved away from Macha, who followed. The Roman woman stopped by a wall and leaned her shoulder against the mural depicting Venus preparing for a bath. "I don't know them."

"Have you forgotten the dinner party we attended at Helena and Rufus' home?" Macha questioned.

Pollia turned slant eyes on Macha. "What does that have to do with me?"

"Tribune Falco was there, and you know him," Macha retorted. "Ask Phidias, he certainly knows you. They discussed your part in the kidnapping of my little boy."

"That's an outrageous lie! You're making this all up!"

"No, Pollia," Macha answered, shaking her head. "I have other sources confirming what they said."

Pollia moved back to the table, where she toyed with the small glass vials of perfume. Macha followed, watching her closely.

"I know you didn't cut off my son's thumb because *his* hands are scarred," she said. "Instead, you tortured some other innocent child."

Pollia turned away from the table and faced her. "I've never harmed any child, not even those nasty urchins roaming the streets of the Subura."

"So, it was one of them, wasn't it?"

"No!"

Macha paused and looked to the door, then back at Pollia. She said slowly, enunciating each word, "I know about the list."

Pollia's eyes avoided Macha's fixed gaze. "What in Sybil's name are you talking about?"

"You know perfectly well, and there's more."

She gave Macha a scathing look. "As far as I'm concern it's enough."

"Each piece of evidence alone may not be damaging," Macha said, "but tie them together, the proof is overwhelming. The master list with all the conspirators' names sits in the vault at the Temple of Vesta. The Emperor knows about it." She raised a hand and pointed a finger at Pollia. "A drawing of an eagle was found, and there is the matter of Sister Licinia's death by your weapon." A smirk and a look of triumph crossed Macha's face.

Pollia choked. She caught her breath. "I didn't kill her!"

"Why should I believe a woman who had a love affair with the chief Vestal Virgin? After committing that sacrilege, an act of murder would be nothing to you."

"You're mad. Do you think I would endanger my own life?"

Macha refrained from laughing at Pollia's last remark and placed a hand to her own chest. "Obviously, the thought never bothered you. After Antonia scorned your advances, you threatened her with extortion, but you found Licinia to be a willing lover. Tell me, what persuaded her to conspire with you against the Emperor? Was it a huge personal gift?"

Pollia hesitated, the muscles around her jaw tightened. "Licinia hated Vespasian because he ignored the Vestals, unlike General Valens."

Macha sucked in her breath and dropped her hand. "Titus's legionary commander?"

"Why not?" Pollia smiled in defiance, thrusting her chin forward. "Compared to that son-of-a tax collector, Vespasian, he'll make a far superior Emperor. What do you think the eagle represented?" Her eyes smoldered, full of venom.

Macha parted her lips about to respond but paused.

"It was the standard of the First Italica Legion," Pollia added.

Macha's eyes widened. "So, it's true. The legion is involved."

"Of course, headed by the General Valens himself." Pollia took a few deep breaths and seemed to stand taller before Macha with all the dignity she could muster. "You must understand, Macha, as a Patrician I am neither afraid nor am I ashamed to tell you what I have done. Patricians should stand up for what they believe, no matter the circumstances. We are the rightful rulers of Rome, not that peasant, Vespasian."

"He's the best Emperor since Augustus," Macha said, "peasant or not." This woman is insufferable.

"Rubbish! But that's not all. It was I, who ordered the deaths of your stupid music teacher and your house steward."

Macha choked and for a split second closed her eyes. Oh, Mother Goddess, I should have guessed. My poor servants. But this is not the time to mourn. Regaining her composure, she said, "I'm not surprised, but why?"

"Metrobius was in my pay as a spy in your house."

"My loyal steward?"

Pollia picked up a silk handkerchief at the end of the table. She wiped her hands, tossed the cloth on the backless chair, her eyes blazed with disdain as she turned to Macha. "Why should I say anything more?"

Macha nodded and crinkled her forehead. "Consider this Pollia, if you refuse to tell me or Senator Bassus, you will be placed on the wheel and tortured like a common slave."

"They wouldn't dare! I am the wife of a Roman citizen and daughter of a Senator!"

"Oh, no? All the legal niceties of Roman Law are tossed to the Aeolian Winds when it comes to treason. Believe me, I have seen it first-hand. Torture is very painful and ugly."

Pollia's face flushed with indignation, her eyes raked the room and the front door.

"Just a moment ago, you said you weren't—"

"I know what I said!" Pollia snapped. "All right," she continued, her voice dripping with bile, "Metrobius had a copy of the list I had given him for the Gauls. The fool lost it."

That must be the list that Nicanor had stolen, Macha thought. No wonder he was murdered. But I need to hear the words from Pollia's lips. "What happened to it? Does this have something to do with Nicanor's death?"

Pollia gestured to Macha. "Everything. Metrobius had hidden the copy in a space behind your *Larium*."

"My niche for the household gods? The little shrine in the wall inset just off the atrium."

"Where else? He stuck the list behind the miniature temple, the last place anyone would look." Then in a voice close to a growl, she continued, "Unfortunately, the fool was seen by your Greek hiding it, and he in turn stole it."

"And you had him murdered?"

Pollia gave Macha a scorching look but did not answer.

"What happened to brave Patrician Pollia? You don't want to be stretched on the wheel. You would never survive the first pull of your legs and arms and would scream for a quick death."

Pollia rolled her eyes. "Yes," she said in a bitter voice, "Metrobius discovered the list missing, but a cleaning slave reported to him that he had seen Nicanor taking something from behind the shrine."

"And he told you?"

"Naturally. Metrobius came to the home where Pedius and I were staying to inform me. I sent word to Falco."

"Falco?"

"Indeed. He hired the thugs that killed the Greek."

"Poor Nicanor!" Loathing welled like acid within Macha's belly. Had she kept her dagger instead of leaving it with Viriatus at the river, she might have killed Pollia. How could Pollia be a part of such a horrible act?

Pollia grinned evilly. "When Metrobius was arrested, it was Falco who poisoned his food."

"Why Falco?" But Macha had already guessed the answer.

Pollia shook her head. "Isn't it obvious? Under torture Metrobius would have revealed everything. As an officer, Falco had access to the kitchen. He put spoiled *garum* on the food. Nobody knew the difference because the fish sauce is used on everything. That's why everyone thought he died of accidental food poisoning."

"I still don't understand why Metrobius betrayed me?"

"You were showing too much favoritism to your assistant steward, Zeno, and Metrobius was jealous. He also wanted his freedom and the gold I promised him for his cooperation sealed the bargain." She crinkled her small straight nose. "Then there was your dear husband."

"What about Titus?" Mother Goddess, what has this awful woman planned?

A crooked smile crossed Pollia's full lips. "It was I who planned Titus' doom. He and his parents scorned me. I swore one day to revenge the insult to my family. And I'll have it yet. Even as I speak, Falco is killing your husband!"

"My husband. Now! Why?" Anger shot through Macha's voice, her face grew hot.

"I see I've caught your attention." Pollia smirked. "What a delicious thought. Your husband assassinated by a good friend."

Titus killed? No! Not now, not after all she had gone through to free him? "The Praetorians and the Watch know he's wanted for treason," Macha stammered. She prayed Pollia was lying in an effort to throw her off guard.

"Falco has friends among the Praetorians who are part of the plot," Pollia said, interrupting Macha's thoughts. "They'll clear the way; it's too late to stop his death!"

"Gods forbid!"

"Our plan would have worked if you and Senator Bassus hadn't interfered. But I'll deal with you, now!"

Her back to the entryway, Pollia whipped out a dagger from within her gown and lunged at Macha. She sidestepped the jab.

"Drop your weapon!" Thundered like a voice of doom from behind Pollia.

CHAPTER 38

Surprise and Revelation

"Drop it!" The Emperor Vespasian barked from the room's entrance. "You heard me, Lady Pollia!"

For a second Pollia hesitated. Then she screamed, "You filthy peasant! I'm proud of what I've done!"

In the flickering lamplight, Macha saw shadowy silhouettes of others behind the ruler. Bassus stepped out of the darkness, and to Macha's delight, Titus. She resisted the urge to run to him. Pollia was in the way.

Vespasian motioned to the Praetorian guards following behind Titus. "Seize her!"

Instantly, as if snapping out of a trance, Pollia rushed toward Vespasian with her knife drawn with no one between her and the old warrior, Titus darted past the Emperor along with Bassus and couple of Praetorians who had drawn swords. Standing behind Pollia, Macha grabbed a mirror from the dressing table and hurled it at the woman, striking her between the shoulder blades. Pollia yelped and staggered. Macha raced to Pollia's side and grabbed the arm that held the weapon. Violently, Pollia attempted to free herself, but Macha held fast, pulling the hilt of the dagger back toward herself. Instead of resisting, Pollia suddenly slumped, and turning in Macha's direction, pushed her body against the blade. It stabbed deep between her ribs. Blood spurted from Pollia's mouth followed by a rasping gurgle.

Macha caught Pollia's falling body. Blood gushed onto her stola, she shoved the corpse backwards. It thudded against the tiled floor.

Bassus raised his eyebrows as if surprised by Macha's violent response.

"Lady Pollia deserved death," the Emperor growled.

Macha leaned over and glared at the corpse as if Pollia were still alive. She refused to hold her anger any longer.

Macha rasped at Pollia, her eyes like the dagger that killed her.

"You ruined my husband's reputation with the Emperor. You kidnapped my little Titus, murdered my music teacher, his son, and my steward. How dare you say I had the nerve to meddle in your affairs? How dare you die without telling me where you hid my son? Where is he!" She brushed her hands across her face, leaving bloody hand prints and recovered her wits.

One of the Guardsmen with Bassus stepped to the body. The Senator stayed behind and motioned to other guard to stand down. He halted and sheathed his sword, the metallic sound echoing through the room. The first Praetorian went down on one knee, examined Pollia's face and closed her eyes. He nodded to Bassus and then to Macha.

Titus sprinted to Macha's side. She fell into his arms. "Macha, it's all right. She can never hurt us again."

"But she still is, Titus...even in death. Our son is still missing," Macha whispered.

"I will find him. I promise," Titus answered softly.

Upon hearing Titus' reassuring voice, the tension drained from Macha's body. She reveled in the touch of his hands. Leaning against the firmness of his body, she ignored the strong prison smell knowing she could never get enough of him.

Seconds later, Macha blushed and realized everyone was staring at them. She slipped from Titus' loving embrace. Bassus and the Emperor chuckled.

"Remind me never to make an enemy of you, my dear," Vespasian said in a fatherly voice. He stepped closer. "Your action saved my life."

"I couldn't let her harm you, Caesar," Macha answered, embarrassed. Was that the reason, she thought, or my hatred of Pollia? She stared at the dead woman for a moment.

The Emperor's coarse warm hand touched hers. "My old soldier's instinct got the best of me. I've never been one to back away from a fight. You did well, Lady Carataca and you too, Tribune Titus, for going to your wife's aid. I'll have to be more cautious, I'm getting too old for this sort of work."

"But how did you know I would be here?" Macha asked.

"Senator Bassus can answer that," Vespasian said.

Bassus approached Macha. "I received news of your escape from home. Vasili was making late night rounds when he noticed you were missing." He shook his head. "I knew you left by the secret passage. You were already through the Cloaca Maxima by the time I received the message. That was after I had returned from freeing your husband."

"Freeing Titus?" She looked to her husband.

"More than my freedom was at stake," Titus said.

Bassus raised his hand. "The details will keep for later."

Macha was about to protest, but when Titus shook his head she thought better of it.

"The Emperor came with me out of curiosity," Bassus continued. "He wanted to learn why you were so determined to see Pollia. To be honest, he was annoyed with your disobedience of my orders. He was going to place you under arrest."

Macha blanched and stared at Vespasian.

"Fortunately," Bassus continued, "when we arrived, he saw the confrontation between you and Pollia. I was about to break it up when our Emperor whispered, 'Wait', and only interceded when Pollia pulled her knife."

Vespasian nodded to Titus. "Tribune," he said gently. "You're a lucky man; she's a very brave, persistent woman."

"What about Falco?" Macha inquired, suddenly remembering he was sent to murder her husband. "Pollia said he was about to kill you."

"He almost did," Titus said.

"Thank the gods he didn't. She laughed in my face when she spat out the words."

Macha glanced at Pollia's body and her eyes caught sight of a section of parchment protruding from her bloody stola. "What's that?"

Titus viewed Macha quizzically.

"There." Macha stepped to the corpse and pulled the item free. As she examined the bloodstained document, her

283

hand suddenly flew to her mouth. A cold prickling sensation ran down her back . "Great Mother Goddess, do you know what this is?" she asked, turning to Bassus and Titus.

"I can guess," Bassus answered.

"It's a copy listing the conspirators. It must be the one stolen from Crixus." She read aloud a few of the conspirators' names.

The Emperor, who had turned to converse with the centurion in charge of the guards, came forward. He snatched the list from Macha's hands and studied the names. Shaking his head, he stepped to the brazier a few paces away and held the list to the burning coals. The red-orange flames consumed the parchment in a hungry blaze.

Macha stared in disbelief as she watched the most incriminating of evidence disintegrate into ashes. "I don't understand, Caesar," she said a few seconds later. "Without the list it's impossible to prove they plotted against you. And my son is still in great danger! He may be killed, if he hasn't been already." She pressed her lips together to keep back the tears.

Vespasian shook his head and grunted, "We are making every effort to find your son, Lady Carataca. To arrest the people on the list would bring down the government. Too many powerful families are involved. Most of them are honorable and support me. I'm certain they have been misguided."

Macha thought the Emperor was being too merciful. Then she remembered. This was the man who as general wouldn't hesitate to execute his soldiers for disobeying orders, but was reputed to be so merciful with civilians that he openly wept at the execution of common criminals.

"However," the Emperor continued, interrupting Macha's thoughts, "I will speak to the most powerful and warn them that I know of their intentions. I will protect myself and deal with any future treasonous acts with a vengeance. My spies will watch their every move. There is your justice, and here is mine," He faced Macha and Titus. "I have dropped all charges against you, Tribune Titus Antonius. The properties of Julius Pedius and his deceased wife Pollia are hereby confiscated. For your troubles, I award you and your wife, Macha Carataca, as compensation their home here in Rome. The rest of their assets and holdings in the city and throughout the Empire will go to the state."

"Thank you, Caesar," Titus said, saluting, apparently astounded by the pronouncement. Pollia's house was among the largest in Rome and worth a fortune.

"You are more than generous, Caesar," Macha said.

"That's not all," he continued, "I am disbanding the First Italica Legion. Its men are to be scattered throughout the army. Those officers considered most dangerous are in the process of being arrested. Others under suspicion will be sent to the furthest outposts of the Empire where they can do no harm. We shall confiscate the list in the Temple of Vesta. This is my final word on the matter."

Knowing it would be foolish to argue with Vespasian and that at least his men were still searching for their son, Macha turned to a subject close to her heart. "But Caesar, if Falco was on his way to kill Titus, how did you rescue him?"

"Your husband can answer that."

After parting salutations, the Emperor left with his guards in tow, their hob-nailed sandled boots clattering on the mosaic floor. A detail of slaves followed behind and carried Pollia's body from the room.

Bassus remained behind, approached the couple and halted a couple of steps from them.

For the lapse of a few heartbeats, Macha stared past the Senator in the direction of the door and sighed. Is this nightmare truly over? she wondered. No, not yet. Turning back to Titus she asked, "Honestly, how did Falco die?"

"It's very simple; I killed him," Titus answered.

Bassus nodded.

"But how? You didn't have any weapon."

Titus grinned. "I had a stool."

"What! A stool?"

"Aye, but there is more. As soon as he came into my room, I accused Falco of being in league with the conspirators."

"How did he get by the guards?"

"Pollia was right. They were in sympathy with the plot. Once he opened my door, they disappeared from their posts. I told Falco to get out. Instead he drew his sword."

Macha touched his arm. "But, darling, what did you do?"

"I threw a stool, but he deflected it with his sword. We circled one another. I hurled a lamp followed by a straw mattress. Falco ducked the lamp and easily moved out of the mattress's way. He turned his head long enough for me to sneak a handful of salt from a bowl on the table," Titus continued. "I shoved the little table towards him as a diversion, and threw salt into his eyes, blinding him. He dropped his sword. I grabbed the weapon, and shoved it to the base of his throat. He begged for mercy."

"You believed him?" Macha asked, shaking her head.

He exhaled. "That was stupidity on my part. I backed away and lowered the sword. Falco sprang to his feet and pulled a knife from inside his waistband. But he wasn't quick enough. I jammed the sword through his ribs up into his heart."

Macha trembled. Using long fingernails, she curled her hands and gouged her palms to stop the shaking.

"About that time," Titus continued, "Senator Bassus, Appius, and the Praetorians barged into the room. They saw me standing over Falco's body. I was sure they were going to kill me."

"I shouted, 'Stand down,'" Bassus said, "'Titus, the Emperor knows the truth. You're free.'" Bassus suppressed a yawned. He motioned for them to sit on stools near the dressing table. "This has been a long night."

Once Macha and Titus sat, Bassus stood before them and continued, "When Titus and I returned to the palace. I received the message you had escaped from my house. That's when Titus and I hurried to Pollia's room. On the way, we encountered the Emperor. I explained the situation, and what I suspected about you, Macha. He followed with a guard detail.

"We heard your voices as we approached the room, the Emperor told us to wait. He whispered he wanted to listen before entering in case Pollia said something incriminating."

"We heard everything," Titus said glancing to Macha.

"Thank Mother Goddess you arrived when you did," Macha added. She touched her heart. "Why didn't the Praetorians search Pollia before confining her to the room?"

"That puzzled Vespasian, too," Bassus said. "It turns out the commanding tribune of their cohort was in league with the conspirators, and allowed Pollia to retain her dagger. He ordered she was not to be searched."

"Has he been arrested?" Macha asked.

"Yes, along with a dozen other officers. We received the information from Phidias who confessed after he was arrested. He named General Valens, officers from Legion First Italica and the Praetorian Guard involved in the plot and admitted his own part. A detachment loyal to Vespasian has been dispatched to arrest General Valens." Bassus paced about the room for a few moments before rejoining Macha and Titus. "Sorry, trying to stay awake."

"My brother-in-law, Cnidius Rufus, is not involved, is he?" Macha asked, concerned about his fate and that of Helena.

"No, like your husband, he is one of the few officers in the legion known to be loyal to the Emperor."

"Thank the gods," Macha said.

Bassus exhaled. "Remember when the Emperor said he was leaving to confer with the new governor of Egypt, and I went along?"

Macha nodded.

"That was a ruse. He and I conferred with officers loyal to the Emperor, those who had campaigned with him in Judea. We implemented plans to arrest the traitors. Then Pomponius Appius, a squad of loyal Praetorians and I hurried to the Barracks to rescue Titus. You know the rest. In any event, the Emperor is now guarded by officers and men whose true mettle is known to him."

"Yes." Relieved, Macha turned and looked deeply into Titus' eyes and then back to the Senator. "But not everything is settled. We must still find our son."

CHAPTER 39

Betrayal at Home

For the first time since his arrest, Macha and Titus slept together. Sighing, a smile framed her lips at the memory of his vigorous yet tender lovemaking, as she awoke just before dawn. Although still tired from the grueling events of the night before, she could no longer sleep. Pushing off the blanket, she sat up and placed her feet on the cold floor, rubbing her eyes, thinking about last night.

Macha groggily remembered being awakened as Titus stirred from bed. In the room's darkness, she barely perceived the outline of her husband's muscular body as he hurriedly threw on a tunic. He buckled a belt, holding a sword, around his waist. Or was she dreaming?

"You're leaving?" she asked.

"You were sleeping so soundly, I didn't want to disturb you," he answered. "A slave brought an important message."

"At this hour?"

"Aye. One of Bassus' informants reported a boy, kidnapped from Mediolanum, has been hidden somewhere in the Trans-Tiber District across the river. It has to be our son."

"Are you sure?"

"I'll learn soon enough. I'm going there with a detachment of Praetorians. Don't fret, darling. We'll scour that festering area of tenements until he's found."

"Oh, gods, I hope you're right."

Titus stooped and kissed her on the cheek. "Go back to sleep," he said softly. "You're exhausted." He quietly left the room.

My poor son, Macha thought, her mind in a slumbering daze. Mother Goddess, I must do something.

* * * * *

288

At breakfast Macha thought over what Titus had said. I'm so thankful for his release, but I hope he does find our little boy, Macha thought. How much longer must I wait? She rose from the chair and prepared to send a letter to Helena.

Macha sat at a desk in the tablinum dictating a letter to Bassus' household scribe. The message detailed the arrangements to bring her household from Mediolanum to Rome. They would journey south once Macha and Titus took possession of the home confiscated from Pollia and Pedius. The surprise of receiving Pollia's sprawling *domus* from the Emperor was finally sinking in.

Macha was about to continue dictation when she heard footsteps. Senator Bassus, draped in his official toga, entered the room. Deep lines furrowed his forehead.

Has the worst happened to young Titus? Why has he returned from the Palatine at this early hour?

"I've just come from a meeting with the Emperor." Bassus raised an eyebrow, signaling the scribe to leave. The Senator dropped onto the bench across from Macha. After the secretary had departed, Bassus said, "Your groom, Jason, has been arrested."

Fear shot through Macha's body like an earthquake. A couple of seconds passed before she calmed herself. "But why? What has he done?" Her mind had been so focused on getting Titus released and finding her kidnapped son that she had forgotten about the womanizing slave and his possible aiding of the conspirators.

"He confessed to taking part in the plot against the Emperor."

For a couple of heartbeats, Macha sat speechless, her jaw clenched, remembering her suspicions of Jason's involvement. "When did you learn about this?"

"I received the dispatch from your brother-in-law, Cnidius Rufus, this morning describing Jason's treachery."

"Who denounced him?"

"Your own handmaiden, Edain," Bassus answered, frowning.

Thank Mother Goddess that Edain followed my instructions, Macha thought. She told had Edain to notify Helena if she saw any activities out of the ordinary.

"Can you give me the details?" Macha asked.

Bassus explained that Jason had been arrested along with two Gallic merchants known to be involved in the conspiracy. He confessed under torture he had plotted with tribune Falco, the Gauls, and a half-dozen officers from the First Legion to frame Titus. The slave knew about the murders of Nicanor, Metrobius, and little Demetrios. Jason joined the others when Falco promised his freedom once Titus had been executed. He had heard that Nicanor had stolen a copy of the conspirator's list from Metrobius.

"When did this happen?" Macha studied Bassus' deep-set chestnut eyes.

"Within a few days after you arrived in Rome. Because of time and distance, we had no way of knowing until now."

"It seems so ironic to receive this on the morning after Pollia's death, and Titus' release." Macha shook her head.

"Under the circumstances, you were very brave and wise in taking steps to free Titus. If you hadn't, he might have been dead before this arrived."

Faithful Edain, Macha thought. I'm pleased she obeyed me.

"What else can you tell me?"

Bassus explained Edain had seen Falco in the courtyard at Macha's home speaking to Jason. He passed a small pouch to Jason, later discovered to have contained gold. Unfortunately, Edain had to wait a few hours before she could leave the home without arousing suspicion and report to Helena what she had seen. Helena immediately told her husband Cnidius Rufus who had suspected Falco's involvement in the plot from the beginning. By this time, Falco was on his way to Rome, and Macha's son had been kidnapped.

"How could Jason do this, Senator?" Macha asked in a voice full of disgust. "I did my best to treat all my slaves fairly."

He snorted. "Unfortunately, it happens all too often."

"Thank Mother Goddess for Edain's loyalty and friends like you and Helena," Macha said. "So when did Rufus arrest Jason?"

"Tribune Rufus placed Jason under surveillance. He believed the young Greek knew where the Gauls were hiding. With a select group of loyal troopers, Rufus followed him to the shores of a small deserted lake where he ambushed and arrested Jason while he was conferring with the two Gauls. Before taking the prisoners to the garrison, where General Valens would have interfered with the interrogation, Rufus forced the three to confess to their participation in the conspiracy. The information corroborated with what he knew, and only what a conspirator would have known about the plot. They revealed General Valens involvement and his plans to assassinate Vespasian and become the next Emperor."

Bassus paused. "What do you think, Macha?"

"This is so bizarre," she answered. "To blame this all on Titus! How could they think it would work?"

The Senator continued, "Your slave, Jason, knew Metrobius had received a copy of the list but did not where it came from. He heard that Falco had poisoned him when he was held at the stockade to make sure he would not confess."

Macha leaned her head back until it touched the high back of the chair. She closed her eyes and groaned. "Why did Metrobius have to betray me?" She wrapped her hands around both her elbows and rocked her slender body back and forth for a couple of minutes.

Bassus sat quietly, no doubt sympathetic to her plight.

"Metrobius and Jason's treachery has defiled my household," Macha rasped as she opened her eyes. "To viciously betray my husband and me out of petty jealousy and for money is unthinkable. But I'm grateful that both were exposed and arrested. Edain must be rewarded for her loyalty. Perhaps, even freedom. She has done as much as anyone else to save my husband's life and that of the Emperor."

Macha reached across the table and briefly touched Bassus forearm. "Thank you, Senator, for letting me know. I'm not completely surprised by these revelations, but it's still a shock. It's so awful what Metrobius and Jason did. I need time to absorb this—to think this through. Do you mind leaving me alone for awhile?"

"I understand, my dear." Bassus nodded and left the library.

She doubled over, putting her palms to her face and wept, shaking uncontrollably.

Later, when Macha had calmed herself, she reflected on what had occurred within the last twenty-four hours. Titus had been released and Pollia was dead. Jason had confessed to his and Metrobius' part in the plot. The conspirators were known, but Young Titus was still missing.

CHAPTER 40

A Present from Mother Vesta

At noon the following day, acting Virgo Maxima Antonia sent a message to Bassus' house. She would arrive soon to see Macha and Titus on an urgent matter.

They and Bassus waited for her in the atrium, its tiled roof open to the sunlit sky. Small paintings of theatrical scenes decorated large blue panels on surrounding walls. Near the edge of the *impluvium,* in the middle of the room, Macha sat on a cushioned wicker chair. Runoff from the previous night's rain filled the shallow blue-veined marble pool.

She closed her eyes. Drifting down from the roof's skylight, a cool breeze caressed her face, carrying the scent of roses. Why had Antonia called for this meeting today rather than yesterday? What matter was bringing her to Bassus' house so soon after being elevated to her new rank as Supreme Vestal Virgin? Could she have news of young Titus? The ache in her heart tightened. Please, let it be so.

Macha smiled as she recalled the evening meal the night before. Bassus had informed her and Titus that Antonia and he planned to marry once she retired the following month. This pleased Macha. It wasn't the only revelation. To Macha's delight, Bassus also announced he was freeing Shafer and Viriatus. The Spaniard would be reinstated as a soldier in the army and become the Senator's chief retainer. To everyone's surprise, including Shafer's, Viriatus had immediately asked for her hand in marriage. Speechless, Shafer nevertheless nodded an enthusiastic yes.

This solves the problems of all those I hold dear, Macha thought, except little Titus. And nothing really mattered except finding him.

"What's so important about Antonia's message that I have to waste my time waiting here?" Titus asked, bringing

Macha out of her thoughts. She opened her eyes. "I should be searching for our son." Dressed in his uniform as a military tribune, he paced back and forth along the little pool, the sound of his hob-nail boots echoing through the atrium.

Macha straightened her back and spoke hoping to comfort him. "I feel the same way, darling. Now that Pollia and Falco are dead, I'm praying for the best."

Titus halted, his sword and dagger slapped against his thigh. "All the more reason I ought to be out." He motioned to the front entrance. "We made a good start this morning, before I received a message to return to Bassus' home. A detachment of Praetorian Guards and I were in the process of conducting a door-to-door search in the slum-ridden Trans-Tiber district."

"We will know soon enough," Senator Bassus said. He sat down on a cedarwood chair next to a black-striated marble table, running his fingers along one of its elaborate arms carved into images of lion legs. "Antonia wouldn't call us together here if it wasn't important."

A loud clatter of footsteps echoed from the entryway. The steward, Vasili, rushed into the atrium and announced Antonia's arrival. He disappeared just as quickly.

A pocked-faced lictor, carrying a long slim bundle of tied birch rods on his shoulder, the *fasces,* entered first. He tramped into the greeting room at the head of Antonia's escort. Twenty African and German female slaves crowded the reception room behind the minor magistrate.

"In the Emperor's name, I command all to rise in the Virgo Maxima's presence!" the lictor ordered.

Antonia glided into the room, dressed in a long snow-white stola. A mantle covering the pleated white band, the holy *infula,* crowned her head. Macha, Titus, and Bassus bowed and greeted her with salutations. She received them with the formality appropriate to her new position.

With a wave of her hand, Antonia commanded the lictor and escorts to leave the room. Once they were gone, a smile graced her refined features. She stepped to Macha and gave her a warm hug. They took seats next to one another on cushions along the edge of the impluvium.

Titus and Bassus sat across from the women. Bassus ordered a slave, standing at one end of the room, to bring a good Messanian wine.

Macha spoke, clasping her hands in her lap. "Please don't keep us in suspense, Antonia. What is your news?"

The Vestal nodded to the atrium entrance where one of her slaves hovered by the *Lares*, the little household shrine. The woman drew back but reappeared a few seconds later. She moved aside, as young Titus stepped from behind her and raced straight to Macha.

"Mama!" he shouted. "Papa!"

Macha leaped up and ran toward Young Titus, his father close behind. "Titus!" she gasped. For the space of a few seconds, Macha's surroundings fell away. Was she in a daze? She didn't see or hear anyone except her beloved little boy running silently toward her. Thank you, Mother Goddess, for returning him!

"Son!" her husband boomed.

Titus's voice snapped Macha out of her reverie. She scooped Young Titus into her arms and held him tightly. "My son! My little Titus!" she cried. Tears welled in her eyes and she wept unashamedly. Rubbing the back of the boy's shoulder, her husband fought back tears.

Young Titus beamed. "I've been with Sister Antonia. She was real nice to me."

Macha's eyes widened. "What! Antonia?"

"Yes."

Macha said no more. She needed to question Antonia about this. Where did she find him? In the meantime, she was grateful her son was alive. And he seemed to be taller. At least the kidnappers had fed him. He wore a neat long-sleeved tunic and new pair of sandals. Only his red hair needed trimming.

"Why are you crying, Mama?" her son asked, "I'm all right."

"I'm so happy you're safe—look at you, you've grown!" She released little Titus from her grip and wiped the tears staining her face. His father lifted him up to his shoulder and swung him around. Young Titus laughed gleefully before his father lowered him to the floor.

295

Macha returned to her seat, and young Titus jumped onto her lap. His weight caught her by surprise. She pulled him close and held him silently as he nestled against her chest.

She eyed her friend, puzzled. Why was her son with Antonia? Gods forbid she was involved in his kidnapping? Even as she held Young Titus, one of her hands balled into a fist. "Where did you find Young Titus, Antonia?"

"He has been safely tucked away all this time in the House of Vesta," Antonia replied.

"No!" Macha's un-balled her fist. She pulled the boy tighter the fingers of both hands gouging his sides. Bassus and Titus, who had returned to their seats, glanced to one another and glared at Antonia.

Young Titus squirmed. "Mama, you're hurting me!"

Startled, Macha released her grip. "Why did you hide my boy from me?" She demanded. "Why didn't you tell me?"

"I had no choice, and he was quite safe, Macha," Antonia said evenly. "The priestesses doted on him."

"The ladies liked me," Young Titus said.

"How can that be, Antonia?" Macha questioned. "I received threats that his life was in danger. I received the thumb of some poor child who was murdered."

Young Titus glanced at his thumb, his face troubled. "I have my thumb."

Macha forced a smile. "Yes, darling, and I'm so happy you do."

"I assure you, Macha," Antonia said, "he was never in any real danger—not even from Licinia. However, we dared not say a word. Licinia threatened to kill us." She turned to Bassus and added in a pleading voice. "You must believe me, Marcus."

Bassus face darkened. Quickly, he recovered and an impassive expression blanked his face. "I do, but I had no idea you were hiding the boy."

A rush of heat flushed Macha's cheeks. She shook her head. "I can't believe you did this, Antonia. You knew how worried I was. You, my best friend, should have told me in spite of Licinia's threats. We're talking about my son!" No explanation could erase the pain she had endured.

Macha stirred from her seat, took her son by the hand, and approached Titus. Taking her husband by the other hand, she faced Bassus. "I wish to speak to Antonia, alone."

Before Titus could protest Bassus interceded. "It's all right, Titus. Leave them be. I'll speak with Antonia when you're finished, Macha."

"Titus, go to Papa. I will see you soon, I promise." Macha stooped and hugged her son, letting go of his hand.

Titus hefted the boy onto his shoulder, who squealed and laughed. "We'll see Mama in a while, Little Wolf." He kissed Macha on her lips, then jogged from the room like a frisky mount followed by Bassus.

Antonia motioned to her female servant, who departed the atrium as well.

Macha stood over Antonia and looked into her pleading eyes. "Now, I want the real reason why you kept my son from me."

Antonia's finely chiseled alabaster face tightened. "Do you have so little regard for me that you believe I would lie?"

"I don't know what to expect from you, Antonia."

The Vestal sighed and shook her head. "I'm sorry you're angry with me. I suppose that's what I deserve. Truly, I *wanted* to tell you about little Titus."

"What stopped you?"

"Had I told you that it was Pollia who had threatened to expose Bassus and me, I was afraid you wouldn't have waited for Pollia's arrest. I envisioned you demanding his immediate release at the jeopardy of everyone's safety."

Macha stared icily at her friend. Now Antonia questioned her integrity.

"You must hate me for not telling you, but I had to remain alive to help your son." Antonia touched Macha's hand who instantly pulled hers away. "Can you ever forgive me? I'm asking you for the sake of our friendship—something I hold very dear."

"I've longed treasured it," Macha answered softly. "It...," she shook her head, "it just did not occur to me that you would know where my son was hidden. You deceived me."

"That was never what I wanted, Macha, but it was the only choice I had."

"So you say."

Silence.

"Why didn't Licinia kill my son?" Macha finally asked.

Antonia studied Macha as if looking into her soul. "That's where Licinia took a stand. Pollia intended to murder him. When she demanded Licinia hand over little Titus, Licinia refused. Kidnapping was one matter, but murdering a child was out of the question."

"Thank Mother Goddess for that." Macha turned from Antonia and stepped to the opposite side of the impluvium. She sat down and gazed into the aqua pool across from Antonia. A small ripple fanned across its peaceful waters.

"Yes," the Vestal said softly. She shifted her body, her eyes watching Macha. "Fortunately, the arrest of the conspirators and deaths of Licinia, Pollia, and Falco changed everything. As acting Virgo Maxima, I immediately ordered your son's release."

Macha stared back at Antonia. "But who kidnapped little Titus? When was he brought to the temple?"

"The ex-gladiator, Pugnax, and his thugs snatched him from your sister-in-law's home. They arrived in Rome several days behind you. It was late in the evening. One of the brutes banged loudly at the front door of the sacred house waking everyone. Licinia opened the door and admitted the lot at once, including your son."

Macha took a deep breath. She glanced to the opening in the roof above the *impluvium* and back to Antonia. "What about my son? Was he all right?"

The Vestal smiled. "Oh, he was dirty, frightened, and definitely hungry, but otherwise not hurt. We fed and bathed him right away. The young novices took him under their wings and treated him like a little brother. He lost any fear he might have had of us."

For a split second Macha covered her face with the palm of her hand. "Praise Great Mother Vesta," she said in a voice little more than a whisper.

"Your son came to the Sacred House after an agreement was reached between Pollia and Licinia," Antonia said. "The

298

boy would be safe and no one would think of looking for him there."

"Did all the priestesses know?"

"Yes, but we were sworn to secrecy, and the slaves were threatened with death." Antonia exhaled. "I am so sorry. Believe me I couldn't tell anyone about your boy without exposing myself." She shook her head. "I swear I would never have allowed any harm to fall upon him even if it meant killing Pollia or Licinia myself."

Macha strode back toward Antonia and sank down heavily in the chair. She searched the priestess' face for signs of deceit. Her answers had been direct and sincere. Macha found no deception in the Vestal's eyes and had heard none in her voice. Had not Antonia been a victim as much as her son? This was a time for joy and forgiveness. She took a few deep breaths, the last of the tension drained from her body. Gods, it felt so good.

Antonia stared at the mosaic-tiled floor for a few seconds. Then she met Macha's eyes again. "I'm very sorry, Macha," she repeated. "Please forgive me."

Macha inhaled deeply, shook her head, and reached over to take Antonia's hands and squeeze them in hers. "Yes, Antonia, my dear friend, I do forgive you."

Together they wept.

* * * * *

Late in the afternoon, Titus returned from the Praetorian Barracks to Bassus' house where he and Macha were still living. Since his release the week before, Emperor Vespasian had promoted him commander of one of the Guard's cohorts. Once he had pulled off his helmet, Macha greeted him with a hug and a kiss in the atrium. She lightly fingered the old scar that ran diagonally down his forehead and across his nose. "Dinner is nearly ready," she said. "Why don't you meet me in the *triclinium* after you have cleaned up and changed your clothing?" Titus wore the scarlet and white uniform of the Emperor's household troops.

"I will, but I have news to tell you that can't wait," he grumbled.

This doesn't sound good, Macha thought. "And what is your news?" she asked cautiously.

"The Emperor is sending me on special assignment to Britannia."

"Britannia! Home of my people?" Macha stiffened. "But why? We haven't yet moved into our new home?"

"Vespasian says I have proven my loyalty to him and will trust no one else." Titus cleared his throat and huffed. "Rumor has it, one of the local governors, an ex-chieftain, has embezzled large amounts of money from the local treasury. Supposedly, his henchmen murdered several lesser officials to cover his tracks. However, there is no proof, and he wants me to investigate." He looked away, frowning.

Faded images of Macha's childhood from that distant island flooded her mind. She remembered fleeing a huge hillfort during a battle fought by her father, Caratacus. Clouded pictures of the forest and ocean surfaced but little else. Only the capture of her family and coming to Rome in chains remained vividly in her mind.

"When do we leave?" Macha asked, swallowing first to keep her voice steady.

"*I* leave next week," Titus answered. He tilted his head downward looking upon Macha's lightly freckled face. "You'll stay here with our son and get the new house in order. I shouldn't be gone more than six to twelve months."

Macha reached up and placed both hands on her husband's broad shoulders. She gazed candidly into his deep-blue eyes. "No, darling. I nearly lost you once, but I'll not lose you again. If you're leaving, I'm going with you."

"What makes you believe you and Young Titus are fit to accompany me on this assignment?" Titus asked.

"After all the danger I have been through, to set you free, I'm surprised you have to ask," Macha replied evenly. "Over the past weeks, haven't I proved that I am capable of defending myself and others with a weapon? Didn't I question witnesses, travel long distances in harsh weather, and develop a logical plan under a time constraint?" She ticked her reasons pressing each point into his shoulder with a finger. "Surely I'm a fine asset. Plus, I won't take 'no' for an answer."

Titus stepped away from his wife, crossed his arms, and for a time remained silent. Macha was certain this meant he'd refuse her request. Nevertheless, she held his gaze with a level stare. Finally, Titus let his arms drop to his side in defeat.

"I suppose two more companions wouldn't be that much of a burden," he admitted. With that, Macha and Titus embraced, and Macha smiled. Her eyes twinkled with just a touch of subtlety.

The Sign of the Eagle

Jess Steven Hughes is a retired police detective sergeant with twenty-five years experience in criminal investigation and a former U.S. Marine. He holds a Masters Degree in Public Administration and a minor in Ancient Mediterranean Civilizations from the University of Southern California. He has traveled and studied extensively in the areas forming the background of this novel, which brings vivid authenticity to the unique setting in *The Sign of the Eagle*. He currently lives with his wife, Liz, and their four horses in Eastern Washington. He is currently working on another historical novel from the First Century A.D.

CPSIA information can be obtained
at www.ICGtesting.com
Printed in the USA
LVHW091334020120
642338LV00001B/58/P

9 781620 060377